Frank Wakeley Gunsaulus

William Ewart Gladstone

A biographical study

Frank Wakeley Gunsaulus

William Ewart Gladstone
A biographical study

ISBN/EAN: 9783337011994

Printed in Europe, USA, Canada, Australia, Japan

Cover: Foto ©Raphael Reischuk / pixelio.de

More available books at **www.hansebooks.com**

WILLIAM EWART GLADSTONE.

A BIOGRAPHICAL STUDY.

BY

FRANK WAKELEY GUNSAULUS, D. D.,

PRESIDENT OF THE ARMOUR INSTITUTE OF TECHNOLOGY.

Author of "Phidias," "Monk and Knight," "The Transfiguration of Christ," "Songs of Night and Day," Etc.

"You can not fight against the future.   Time is on our side."
                                                            —Gladstone.

DEDICATED

" It is better to write one word upon the rock, than a thousand on the water or the sand: better to remove a single stray stone out of the path that mounts the hills of true culture, than to hew out miles of devious tracks, which mislead and bewilder us when we travel them, and make us more than content if we are fortunate enough to find, when we emerge out of their windings, that we have simply returned to the point in our age, from which, in sanguine youth, we set out."— Gladstone.

" *The greatest triumph of our time, a triumph in a region loftier than that of electricity and steam, will be the enthronement of this idea of Public Right, as the governing idea of European policy; as the common and precious inheritance of all lands, but superior to the passing opinion of any. The foremost among the nations will be that one, which by its conduct shall gradually engender in the minds of the others a fixed belief that it is just. In the competition for this prize, the bounty of Providence has given us a place of vantage; and nothing save our own fault or folly can wrest it from our grasp."—Gladstone.*

PREFACE.

Several years ago I began thinking that no career in modern political life abroad contained so many inspiring and excellent lessons for the youth and hope of America as that of William Ewart Gladstone. A series of lectures at the Armour Institute of Technology proved that a large number of people of every age and place in life were glad to hear the story of his life conceived and treated from an American point of view. These lectures have now been rewritten and many additions have been made to them from the large mass of material obtained during a visit to England which gave me an extraordinary opportunity for studying the great statesman and scholar. It has been a delightful task and I can hope for no richer reward for my labor and care than this, that Americans everywhere may find in reading this volume any smallest portion of such pleasure and interest as I have enjoyed in writing it.

While my point of view has been different, I have not hesitated to consult the previously composed accounts of this wonderful life. To the biographies of Mr. George W. E. Russell, Mr. G. Barnet Smith and Mr. Justin McCarthy, I have been especially grateful for many things whose value I cordially acknowledge. Besides these and an ever-present copy of Hansard, I have to mention in the same spirit of thankfulness, Mr. McCarthy's "History of Our Own Times," Mr. Molesworth's "History of England," and the "Nineteenth Century," as well as the "Edinburgh," "Contemporary" and "Fortnightly Review." I have expressed my obligations to other notable publications in the main body of the work.

The great soul has passed on; his genius, learning, eloquence, scholarship, humanity and piety are among the most splendid and indubitable treasures of the race.

F. W. G.

CONTENTS.

CONTENTS.

ILLUSTRATIONS.

ILLUSTRATIONS.

ETON COLLEGE

CHRIST CHURCH COLLEGE – OXFORD

William Ewart Gladstone:

A BIOGRAPHICAL STUDY.

CHAPTER I.

PARENTAGE AND YOUTH.

Ours has been called the century of achievements. But the nine-teenth century has produced nothing so great as its men and women. Personalities as unforgetable as time have appeared in the domain of art, philanthropy, religion, science, reform, literature, invention and commerce. It will not, however, be called a literary, a religious, or an artistic century, and even above its product of reformers, philanthro-pists and inventors, on the level of its contribution of scientists and princes of commerce, it will be memorable as having given to history four shining examples of constructive statesmanship. Into these men have entered its spirit and its qualities. They have incarnated especially its scientific method, its genius for resource, its commercial instinct, its faith in human brotherhood. Each of these men,—Cavour, Lincoln, Bismarck and Gladstone,—has been influenced after his own manner, either by art, religion, literature, or what we call business; and he, in turn, has influenced the realm which has touched his life most closely. But the more distinctively characteristic forces of the age which have been already enumerated have been the dominant energies in the soul and in the achievement of these men as statesmen. Each of them comes up out of a soil so vitalizing, and each has such intimate rela-tionship with the time and the place in which his career roots itself, that it is impossible to study the Italy of the nineteenth century successfully without finding its most complete and accurate presentation in the personality of Cavour, as Germany of the same period offers Bismarck, America Lincoln, and England Gladstone.

17

The task of duly portraying his personality and making a worthy review of his career, must be presented in the somewhat trying light which he himself has flung upon such fascinating employment. Writing in 1876 he said: "Biographies, like painted portraits, range over an immense scale of value; the highest stand at a very elevated point indeed; and the lowest, in which this age has been beyond all others fertile, descend far below zero. Human nature is in itself a thing so wonderful, so greatly paramount among all the objects offered to our knowledge, that there are few pieces or specimens of it which do not deserve and reward observation. But then they must be true, and must breathe the breath of life; they must give us, not the mere clothes, or graveclothes, of the man, but the man himself. For this reason it is that autobiographies (unless when a distinguished man is unfortunately tempted, as appears to have been the case with Lord Brougham, to write his own life from old newspapers) are commonly of real interest; for every man does his best to make his own portrait a likeness."

Now, the fact is that Mr. Gladstone has written his autobiography in the changed condition of human life in England, in a multitude of excellent essays and in some of the most brilliant and statesmanlike orations in the English language, all of which give to the duty of the biographer a peculiar tendency. The living figure abides. Any description of our time finds him a present force, and his eloquence flows forth, resistless and splendid as in other days. He was statesman, orator, and man of letters, expositor of Homer, polemic and theologian, connoisseur of art, critic of poets and philosophers, fast and genial friend, noble husband, wise and tender father, and, above all, "the grand old man" of Anglo-Saxon civilization. But a man's vitality for any length of time depends upon his spiritual attitude and the vision in which he has seen things. Gladstone was and is all these men in one, because of the perennial quality of his ideals.

He is the more interesting to Americans because he comes from the central heart, the genetic current of modern political life. The origins of his career lie and move with the great mass of people known in England as the "middle class." Much has been said about this portion of the body politic in explanation of the fact that Gladstone began his career as a

Tory and ended it as a Liberal. If it is meant by this that the middle class, having no titles to protect or venerable symbols to maintain, finds itself allied with a sort of Toryism easily transformed into Liberalism, an entirely wrong impression is conveyed, for this is not the truth about the Toryism of such people as Sir John Gladstone. When you get a Tory who finds himself born, where, with one hand he touches the aristocracy with his genius, and with the other hand, he touches the plebeian elements of society with his common clay, his Toryism is almost sure to be as fantastic and bumptious as it is uncertain of its respectability. The very circumstances of Mr. Gladstone's birth, uniting him to an element which has had so much to do with the progress of England in commerce, literature, art, and morals, would have furnished a less virile and clear-headed man with a reason for courting, throughout his whole life, aristocracies and royal families. It is usually the man who having been born in circumstances where the common things of life touch him most closely, lifted by genius into the neighborhood of the uncommon things, finds himself forgetful of any duties which he owes to those who still remain in the ordinary walks of life. True, the greatest defenders of individual and national freedom, the souls least vanquished by pretentious nobility and bejeweled royalty, as well as the wise defenders of England's constitution against a noisy lawlessness which calls itself by the sacred name of democracy, have sprung from this class. But, given such wealth and culture and associations as came to Gladstone, it must be regarded as the triumph of a truth-seeking nature over circumstances and prejudices, rather than force of prejudice and sovereignty of circumstances which lifted him into such a position in the statesmanship of our time as makes him worthy of association with the great masters of statecraft in all time.

Sir John Gladstone was simply an industrious, level-headed, clear-eyed man of affairs. He set his very life-current in the blood of his son William. Whenever in his future life William Ewart Gladstone stood in the House of Commons and made a financial Budget more interesting than the novel of his great rival, Disraeli, there was allied in him, with the scholar and the orator, the old dealer in grain at Leith, near Edinburgh, who had conveyed from generation to generation his superlative energy, as well as his clear and comprehensive philosophy as to how property is to be obtained and how property is to be kept after it is obtained. One of Sir John Gladstone's friends once heard Gladstone the younger talk for a half hour on Homer, and then drop into a discourse upon the tax on annuities. "There," said he, "I hear the Lancashire grain merchant, even if he has learned Greek poetry."

Sir John furnished his son with a passion for work and a grave conviction that life has few topics upon which the liveliest and most truly equipped intellect may not wisely spend all its powers. A purpose, tenacious as his mind was practical and intense, served to gather to itself all that this home furnished of delightful intercourse, high ideals and quick intelligence and consolidate it in this son for future service to the theories dear to the father. Mercantile pursuits did not overcloud the sky of the young book-lover; but the youth dreamed in the atmosphere of trade. That the son was manfully proud of so worthy, if commercial, an origin, is evidenced by a speech delivered in Liverpool, in 1872, in which he said: "I know not why commerce in England should not have its old families, rejoicing to be connected with commerce from generation to generation. It has been so in other countries; I trust it will be so in this country. I think it is a subject of sorrow, almost of scandal, when those families who have either acquired or recovered station and wealth through commerce, turn their backs upon it, and seem to be ashamed of it. It certainly is not so with my brothers or with me."

It is scarcely necessary for us to dwell upon the fact that the Gladstone family is of great antiquity, and that they were once called Gledstanes,—a lowland Scotch word "gled," which signifies hawk, and another word, "stane," meaning rock, uniting and forming a name long borne by a family, which, thanks to the immense services of its late representative, need care little whether or not Herbert de Gledstane, who seems to have been one of the Lairds who made oath of his loyalty to Edward the First, was really the ancestor of the orator and statesman whom we are now studying. Certain it seems that early in the sixteenth century a branch of the family settled in Clydesdale, and from it the subject of this biographical study sprang.

Gladstone's mother has scarcely figured in the accounts of his life, and, indeed, such a man as Sir John Gladstone was not likely to permit her to occupy any too dominant place in his own biography or in the customary chronicle of his son's career. The truth is, however, that Annie Robertson, who was Sir John Gladstone's second wife, imparted to her son William the very rare and delicate quality which expressed itself throughout his career in his love of art, his appreciation of the finest forms in which the literary spirit enshrines itself, and his musical sense, which is apparent in him not only as the young tenor singer in the Liverpool home, but also in that sonorous rhythm which abounds throughout his speeches. Gladstone's mother came from the ancient Donachie clan, and, besides the contributions mentioned above, there is little doubt that she contributed also to her boy a certain speculative tendency of mind which has helped him, oftentimes, to poise in the atmosphere above a subject so long as to enable him to know where truth and conscience should bid him to light.

In the home of these two,—John Gladstone and Annie Robertson—William Ewart Gladstone, the fourth son, was born December 29th, 1809.

Mr. Gladstone has been described as a man who was quite unable to keep his seat in the House of Commons or elsewhere when any subject was up for debate, upon which he knew more than anyone else speaking on the topic. Punch has contained many a lively picture of "the grand old man" vainly seeking to repress what one of the liveliest of our essayists calls his "passion for argumentation." The home of Gladstone's childhood was a school of controversy, in which he was trained as if he were to spend his whole life, and its destinies were to be decided, in a hall of debate. The House of Commons does not ordinarily furnish a man opportunity for constant contention. Human nature is commonly granted too brief a career, and the human body has usually too fragile a constitution to permit of incessant argumentation for any length of time. But Sir John Gladstone's house was a veritable gymnasium for William, and his health and length of life were such that he never needed to get over the habits of his childhood. It was a Scotch home in England,—and it must always be remembered that Gladstone is a Scotchman, with the ardor and habit of controversy which belongs to the Scotchman, supplemented by true Scotch "canniness," and Scotch love of truth. This home, with its continuous disputation, gave Gladstone's inherited Toryism,—for his father made Toryism a part of his religion,—glorious and sympathetic opportunity to literally attain its highest possible growth, or—and it is sometimes suspected that this was the case—to wear itself out in talk and discussion, so that soon he should prove that Toryism is not as essential to a Scotch mind broadening through England toward a cosmopolitan spirit as is either truth, liberty, or that which is still more important to a Scotchman,—religion. One of Gladstone's earlier biographers tells us that—

"Nothing was ever taken for granted between the father and his sons. A succession of arguments on great topics and small topics alike—arguments conducted with perfect good humor, but also with the most implacable logic—formed the staple of the family conversations. The children and their parents argued upon everything. * * * They would debate as to whether the trout should be boiled or broiled, whether a window should be opened, and whether it was like to be fine or not the next day. It was all perfectly good humored, but curious to a stranger because of the evident care which all the disputants took to advance no proposition, even as to the prospect of rain, rashly."

This state of things in his childhood will account for the gravity of Mr. Gladstone's behavior when he dealt with subjects small in proportion to other themes occupying the attention of his eager spirit. Gladstone's sense of humor has never furnished him with that perspective in which alone small things are seen in their proper relationship to great things. John Bright's humor would have saved him oftentimes from furnishing to the world a picture like that in which a steel-clad man-of-war is seen opening it batteries against an argosy of dories. Even in his childhood home, the humor of the situation did not always impress him.

As he advanced in life, William E. Gladstone grew younger with each year, and not only allowed the circumstances of his own career to be illumined by the gayeties of wit and humor, but he took an almost marvelous interest—if any interest may be called marvelous in his wonderful life—in irradiating the paths of steady thinkers and the ways pursued by overworked enthusiasts with a delicate humor and sparkling wit unknown to his friends in youth or even middle age. The fountains of humor which lay concealed in this profound and serious spirit often-times bubbled forth in unexpected places in his argument. There is always a certain intensity of conviction shining through the brilliant sayings, but the humor is so true and fresh and pure that the prismatic colors of his many-sided nature appear nowhere at better advantage.

Toryism in the home of Sir John Gladstone was what it often is,— a habit of mind. Von Bülow has spoken of the tenor voice as a disease, and to a progressive spirit such Toryism as that in which William Gladstone found himself growing from youth to manhood, and for which the whole family ran in races of argument, each unconsciously training William Gladstone in fluency of utterance and dialectical skill, must ever appear well-nigh a disease. This study of Gladstone seeks so to present his career that we may see how nobly the young Scotchman, even though oftentimes the victim of his Scotch "canniness," yet always the servitor and apostle of his Scotch religiousness, possessing the Scotch passion for controversy and the Scotch subtlety and ardor of speculation, got over this disease, as one may say. He got so well over it, that his immense industry, the splendor and richness of his oratorical gifts, the unyielding devotion of his mind to truth, his scholarship and research, his sincere attachment to all large conceptions of liberty and law, were at length converged and embodied in a forceful figure offering vast encouragement to that Americanism which is so vitally related to the English constitution whose expositor he was. Even more, Gladstone gives to all men a deeper confidence in the value and supremacy of the ideas whose champion and defender he became.

It is ennobling to believe that the human mind is open to truth, and it is an inspiring confidence that truth has a power in itself to mold and to lead the human mind. The cynic in politics, the pessimist in social reform can never have faith in these propositions. The ideas for which America exists as an experiment in human government have proved their native power to rule, in the fact that upon such a man as Gladstone, born and trained, as we have seen, in the very atmosphere of Toryism, they at last gained a supremacy and lifted him into a leader-

ship of the forces of human progress which no Toryism can ever afford
to any finest intellect.

No doubt the mind of Mr. Gladstone was so responsive to every
influence from without and to every conviction from within, that he
has furnished a good deal of evidence that human nature at its highest
and best is likely to miss what our wisdom—superior because it comes
afterward—calls the straight course.   He affords to a cursory view
the testimony, that in politics, the shortest distance between two points
is not invariably a straight line.   Burke was often quoted by his successor to this effect: "All government is founded upon compromise
and barter.   But in all fair dealing the thing bought must bear some
proportion to the purchase paid.   None will barter away the immediate
jewel of the soul."   There Gladstone has taken his stand.   Knowing
when the jewel of the soul was asked for, he has been quick to turn
about and refuse its transfer.   He has dared to be inconsistent.

Mr. Gladstone's superiority of intelligence and masterful learning
have made him all the more eminent as an example of the ease with
which an imaginative mind finds that logic is something else than a
necessity of the soul, or the bread of life.   It is a long journey from
Toryism to Liberalism in anything,—for Toryism is not so much a set
of views taken and easily looked at, as it is a point of view from which
only certain views may be taken.   A good deal might be said with reference to Mr. Gladstone and the quality of his mind and the sincerity of
his life, by comparison of Gladstone the statesman with Gladstone the
theologian.   Mr. Gladstone has always wished to be a Conservative of
the best sort,—that is to be a preserver of the good, to hold to the truth
and the institutions in whose forms truth binds the past to the future.
But he was inconvenienced by possessing a daring intellect, or rather
it possessed him.   He has seemed to speculate in statesmanship, and
at the very hour when he had gone short in the market on Conservatism
in one direction, he has hedged, so to speak, in the other, and freed himself of all Liberalism in theology.   Within a week after he made England feel that in politics, to use a word of Emerson's, "all things are
at a risk," he issued a pamphlet in championship of some venerable view of Scripture interpretation, over which the good-natured

Englishman, weary of the peril of thinking, approvingly shrugged his shoulders while he drained his glass of port and caressed his copy of Butler's Analogy, saying to himself meanwhile: "Well, everything in the Church at least is secure, and it will be, just as it was in the time of the Bishop of Durham, if Gladstone only has his way."

This is not the place, even if there be any in this volume, to treat of Gladstone's theological and ecclesiastical excursions, but any study of the subject in comparison with his career as a politician, would simply throw into relief the ideas already expressed. The distance between Toryism and Liberalism in any realm of life,—having consented to the fact that Toryism is a habit of mind, rather than a set of opinions—is so great, and the rocks and shoals and currents are so numerous, the vacant spaces where motion seems to fail and where the ship is sure to be becalmed, are also so many, there is such necessity for taking advantage of this breath of air or the fringe of that gale or the edge of this tempest, that any worthy sailor, especially when he has a crew on board, all of whom have the liberty to give orders, granted by a constitutional government, and all of whom have to be at least consulted whenever their opinions are of the least possible value, must be allowed to tack ship. Mr. Gladstone has often tacked ship, to the everlasting embarrassment of his friends and to the horror of his foes, but his life and its achievements prove that, in spite of all these difficulties hitherto mentioned, and, indeed, while supremely conquering them, he has always known where he was going, and he has signally triumphed in arriving there.

Mr. Gladstone's journey from Toryism to Liberalism pulled every heartstring which united him to his home, and yet it is astonishing that he drew after him, by might of his own convictions and the influence of his progressive eloquence, many who seemed hopelessly involved with the antiquities and prejudices of the Tory position. Disraeli, at a later time, with that sneer which traversed often across the delicate and sensitive nerves which bound Gladstone to his past, taunted him with regard to his departure from parental dogmas, and Gladstone swiftly and honorably acknowledged the nature of his former position in these words: "I was bred under the shadow of the great

name of Canning; every influence connected with that great name gov·-
erned the politics of my childhood and of my youth."

The school-boy days passed in the genial and lovely environment
of the Vicarage of Seaforth. Here the boy sported and dreamed and
became acquainted with the literatures of the leading nations of the
world.

In the "Life and Letters of Dean Stanley" (Charles Scribner's Sons,
N. Y.), we are told some things about Seaforth, which is described as:
"then a quiet seaside hamlet at the mouth of the Mersey, now transformed into a populous suburb of Liverpool." The school was cared for
by the incumbent of the church near Seaforth.

In a note, we are informed that "the name Seaforth, as denoting
a locality in the neighborhood of Liverpool, demands a word of explanation. It was borrowed, early in the present century, for his house, and
the surrounding land, at that time entirely uninhabited, by the elder
Mr. Gladstone, from the title of Lord Seaforth, the head of the Macken-
zies, the family to which his mother belonged."

The biography further says: "Among the very first letters is one
of November, 1824, to his mother, recounting a visit to Mr. Gladstone's,
describing fully the stuffed animals which he saw there, and, after telling her that he 'has quite finished As in Præsenti,' adding, 'there is an
Illiad (sic) here which I like very much, for it is all about the gods and
the Grecians and Trojans.' From that time the current flows home-
ward unceasingly, though he often deprecates his sister Mary's reproaches. 'You know I am always a shocking letter-writer. Sometimes
I am in a humor for writing, and sometimes not.' 'No such things happen at school as at home.' A day's visit to Liverpool is welcomed because it 'gives him something to write about,' but in the main the facile
pen of the future is already there in germ.

" 'He is grown,' his mother writes in December, 1824, on his first
return home, 'and his hands feel more substantial. The report of him
is that he is as rough as the other boys when with them, but of this there
is no symptom. The shyness, coloring, reserve and susceptibility seem
to be rather increased.' But his lips were clearly unlocked towards his
schoolfellows. Southey had been, and still was, his favorite poet. 'We

have great fun,' he writes to Mrs. Stanley in February, 1825, 'playing at "Thalaba and Kehama." I am Khawla and Handfield is Mo-
hareb, and I tell them stories at night.' Canon Rawstorne, his school-
fellow at Seaforth, and afterwards his fag at Rugby, remembers 'his
remarkable gift as a raconteur, and his relating to a group of boys in
a corner of the sand hills a great part of the story of "Kenilworth,"
especially that part about Wayland Smith. I think all his stories were
recollections from books, for he was never very great at invention.'

"He has been taken to Liverpool, and writes, in a letter to his sister,
that he has 'seen a giant, who said he had been in Bonaparte's army;'
and again, 'I have seen "Waverly" acted, and liked it very much;' and
there is a graphic account on November 12, which assumes larger proportions in each successive year, of the bonfire and fireworks on the 5th
of November. 'One of the boys had bought a very tall Pope for the
bonfire, and a Guy Fawkes, . . . Mr. Gladstone gave the wood,
and we had tar barrels, and it was great fun.' But his heart was more
in his books than in his play, and with each half-year the literary instinct becomes more developed. 'How do you like "Madoc"?' he asks
his sister; 'not so much as "Roderic," I am sure.' "

So much is reprinted as showing Gladstone's early environment, for
he was Stanley's fellow pupil under Mr. Rawson.

From a letter of Stanley's, June 26, we reproduce the following:
"How delightful—how enchanting—how charming! How much better
than Rouen is this, so far away, so nice to have Auntie and Lucy, so
romantic to ride over the mountains on mules, through verdant valleys
and snow-capped hills! And the Spaniards, too, and the Cagots—I
must get benighted and go to a 'Cagot's' hut. . . . William Gladstone is at home now, and last Tuesday I and one of the other boys
were invited to breakfast with him; so we went, had breakfast in grand
style, went into the garden and devoured strawberries, which were
there in great abundance, unchained the great Newfoundland, and
swam him in the pond; we walked about the garden, went into the
house and saw beautiful pictures of Shakespeare's plays, and came
away at twelve o'clock. It was very good fun, and I don't think I was
very shy, for I talked to William Gladstone almost all the time about

all sorts of things. He was so very good-natured, and I like him very much. He talked a great deal about Eton, and said it was a very good place for those who liked boating and Latin verses. I think from what he said, I might get to like it. . . . He was very good-natured to us all the time, and lent me books to read when we went away, 'The Etonian,' etc. . . . Oh! how soon—next Tuesday week, and then the sea, the Pyrenees!"

Gladstone did not look back upon his Eton days as days in which his religious sensibilities had their best environment. In his famous "Chapter of Autobiography" he referred to the churches of that time: "That time was a time such as comes after sickness, to a man in the flower of life, with an unimpaired and buoyant constitution; the time in which, though health is as yet incomplete, the sense and the joy of health are keener, as the fresh and living current first flows in, than are conveyed by its even and undisturbed possession.

"The Church of England had been passing through a long period of deep and chronic religious lethargy. For many years, perhaps for some generations, Christendom might have been challenged to show, either then or from any former age, a clergy (with exception) so secular and lax, or congregations so cold, irreverent, and indevout. The process of awakening had, indeed, begun many years before; but a very long time is required to stir up effectually a torpid body, whose dimensions overspread a great country. Active piety and zeal among the clergy, and yet more among the laity, had been in a great degree confined within the narrow limits of a party, which, however meritorious in its work, presented in the main phenomena of transition, and laid but little hold on the higher intellect and cultivation of the country.

"Our churches and our worship bore in general too conclusive testimony to a frozen indifference. No effort had been made either to overtake the religious destitution of the multitudes at home, or to follow the numerous children of the church, migrating into distant lands, with any due provision for their spiritual wants. The richer benefices were very commonly regarded as a suitable provision for such members of the higher families, as were least fit to push their way in any profession requiring thought or labor. The abuses of plurality and non-residence were at a height, which, if not proved by statistical returns, it would now be scarcely possible to believe. At Eton, the greatest public school of the country (and I presume it may be taken as a sample of the rest), the actual teaching of Christianity was all but dead, though happily none of its forms had been surrendered. It is a retrospect full of gloom; and with all our Romanizing, and all our Rationalizing, what man of sense would wish to go back upon those dreary times:

" 'Domos Ditis vacuas, et inania regna?' "

Later in life he said he would think better of Eton if Homer had been studied there.

As an old man, in March, 1891, he gave another picture of Eton, or one from another point of view. He said to the Eton students:

"When I was a boy I cared nothing at all about the Homeric gods. I did not enter into the subject until thirty or forty years afterwards, when, in a conversation with Dr. Pusey, who, like me, had been an Eton boy, he told me, having more sense and brains than I had, that he took the deepest interest and had the greatest curiosity about these Homeric gods. They are of the greatest interest, and you cannot really study the text of Homer without gathering fruits; and the more you study him the more you will be astonished at the multitude of lessons and the completeness of the picture which he gives you. There is a perfect encyclopædia of human character and human experience in the poems of Homer, more complete in every detail than is elsewhere furnished to us of Achaian life."

CHAPTER II.

SCHOOL DAYS AT ETON.

Mr. Gladstone has always appeared with such attractions and graces adding their charm to his figure and the influence diffusing from his physical presence, that one can readily believe what Sir Francis Murchison says, that "he was the prettiest boy that ever went to Eton." He was eleven years of age at this time. No one at Eton, except that embodiment of "spiritual splendor" known as Arthur Henry Hallam, furnished such a fascinating picture of childhood, docile, happy, innocent, graceful and promising, opening its treasure-house of possibility to the influences of culture and yielding to the forces of literature and science and the guidance of such teachers as then made Eton the most desirable place for such a youth. Gladstone's spirit was even then lofty and sovereign over his companions. Bishop Hamilton of Salisbury is not the only prelate, statesman, or man of letters who has left a statement of his gratitude that Providence gave to his young life the pure and uplifting influence of William Ewart Gladstone. Arthur Henry Hallam, whom Tennyson's poetry has enshrined with scarcely more of richness than the less musical prose of Mr. Gladstone, writes of his companion and friend: " . . . Whatever may be our lot, I am convinced that he is a bud that will bloom with a richer fragrance than almost any other whose early promise I have witnessed." This statement must be taken, however, in full view of the fact that there were other men, either students or teachers, at Eton, who were attracted by Hallam's genius, who also believed that he, and not Gladstone, would be the great man of England.

The almost unmatched laboriousness of later days was prophesied in the scholarly habits and zeal of the Eton pupil at this time. In the holidays he studied mathematics and read poetry. He wandered into the regions which history makes easy of access, and he put behind his

active career the vast and illuminative background of the countless years
and processes along which man had come to the problems which he was
to confront as an English statesman. No wonder that in 1860, as the
officer of the University of Edinburgh, he could address the multitude
of expectant and ardent students in these sentences:

"The mountain-tops of Scotland behold on every side of them the witness, and many a one, of what were once her morasses and her moorlands,
now blossoming as the rose, carries on its face the proof of how truly it is
in man and not in his circumstances that the secret of his destiny resides.
For most of you that destiny will take its final bent towards evil or towards
good, not from the information you imbibe, but from the habits of thought,
mind and life that you shall acquire, during your academical career. Could
you with the bodily eye watch the moments of it as they fly, you would see
them all pass you, as the bee that has rifled the heather bears its honey
through the air, charged with the promise, or it may be the menace, of the
future. In many things it is wise to believe before experience; to believe,
until you may know; and believe me when I tell you that the thrift of time
will repay you in after life with an usury of profit beyond your most sanguine dreams, and that the waste of it will make you dwindle alike in intellectual and in moral stature, beneath your darkest reckoning."

Yet Gladstone was no saint, or ascetic, or scholarly recluse wasting
fiber and blood in unwise pursuit even of the truths of science and mathematics. He was always a great walker, easily able to tire out three or
four other men in the course of a day, while he talked incessantly either
of poetry, art, old china, religion, or politics. This habit began with
him at Eton, where he constantly exercised his body by rowing, and
prepared his physical nature to endure the terrible strain of the stormful
years to come. His contentiousness was easily excited, and there can
be little doubt that Gladstone was willing to take care of himself in
an affair involving the use of his fists rather than the exercise of his
powers of thought. His manly courage expressed itself in his moderation, and at one time he made stern refusal to drink the customary toast
at an anniversary dinner. He challenged a bully with the same eagerness, and handled him with the same skill and strength as many another
youth has done who had nothing of Gladstone's hope of future greatness. But the literary and eloquent man is so often a physical coward

that it is fair to state here that Mr. Gladstone has never failed when it was necessary or advisable to enter any kind of conflict. As a boy at Eton or at Oxford he was in the habit of obeying Sir Philip Sidney's word, and if he heard of a good fight, he went to it and did his part.

There were no prizes for Gladstone at Eton. He read a great deal outside of the prescribed books, and made himself familiar with those pages of English poetry from which he quoted all his life. It was natural that this should stir a verse-writing tendency in his own rhythmic nature, and he produced verses of such excellence that he was "visited with honor. A literary career seemed to be most attractive to him at this time. It is his mind which most of all guides and enriches the "Eton Miscellany." The calmness and literary poise of his work here are equaled only by its brilliant promise. Somewhat too majestic are his early utterances, but the fact is that a man who is not very lofty or very florid in his youth, is not likely to be either high or even interesting in his old age. The closing passage of his introduction has humor:

"I was surprised to see some works with the names of Shakespeare and Milton on them sharing the common destiny; but on examination I found that those of the latter were some political rhapsodies which richly deserved their fate; and that the former consisted of some editions of his works which had been burdened with notes and mangled with emendations by his merciless commentators. In other places I perceived authors worked up into a frenzy by seeing their own compositions descending like the rest. Often did the infuriated scribes extend their hands, and make a plunge to endeavor to save their beloved offspring, but in vain. I pitied the anguish of their disappointment, but with feelings of the same commiseration as that which one feels for a malefactor on beholding his death, being at the same time fully conscious how well he deserved it."

He rendered a chorus of the "Hecuba of Euripides," and it is instinct with the spirit of the original. The sense of humor which came to be a redeeming feature in many of the stormful times of his later life, which was never as large and spontaneous as it might have been, expressed itself in his "Views of Lethe," which was one of his many contributions to the "Eton Miscellany:"

DINING HALL—CHRIST COLLEGE, OXFORD

COURT OF ORIEL COLLEGE—OXFORD

"In my present undertaking there is one gulf in which I fear to sink, and that gulf is Lethe. There is one stream which I dread my inability to stem; it is the tide of Popular Opinion. . . . At present it is hope alone that buoys me up; for more substantial support I must be indebted to my own exertions, well knowing that in this land of literature merit never wants its reward. That such merit is mine I dare not presume to think; but still there is something within me that bids me hope that I may be able to glide prosperously down the stream of public estimation; or, in the words of Virgil:

"—Celerare viam rumore secundo."
("To take my way amid the world's acclaim.")

Gladstone could hardly be called a very precocious youth. Indeed, so solid were his attainments that they scarcely demand remark, save in this, that they were such attainments as in the after life of this scholar and statesman have been of the utmost value.

No suggestion of future greatness was unfulfilled in Gladstone, largely because at a time when others have fanned the flame of genius, his mind was directed to acquire for himself habits of mind and wealth of information such as would strengthen him for the conflict with ignorance and prejudice and wrong. Beautiful indeed has been the picture of this boy romping about Windsor, filling his spirit with that flood of historic intelligence which comes through every such place and appeals strongly to every such spirit, learning to do his duty and to revere the institutions which had come out of the sacred past, and thrilled now and then with the vision of the future which made his blood run more swiftly in pure and healthy veins, and his mind attach itself through warm affections to the young men who furnished him with the rarest companionship in thought and in hope, and to his teachers, who, from the first, saw rising before them a personality whose contribution, either to literature, politics, art, or religion, was worthy to be guarded and preserved.

Capacity for friendship has been one of Gladstone's most notable qualities, and it is doubtful if more of his genius has not been invested in his personal friendships than in aught else in his life. When one considers the number and kinds of letters which have been written out of his heart and have found their way into the biographies published in the last fifty years, and especially when one looks upon these letters as the personal bonds along which traveled from mind to mind the best life of the writer and the reader, one has some conception of how intense and comprehensive and true was the soul whose outpourings they are. They evince an incisive intellect; they prove a tender heart. Many of his friendships began in early life. At Eton he was warmly attached to Alexander Kinglake, who afterwards differed from him with that severity and outspokenness which have left their mark in historical literature, and Frederick Tennyson,—far too little read and appreciated as a student of classical life and as a poet bringing back to us the light and atmosphere of Greece—spent many a long evening with young Gladstone over subjects which the latter was to master and illuminate. He knew well the two boys who were to become, the one Earl of Elgin, the other Earl Canning. The friendship of Gladstone and Kinglake was never broken, though the former was likely to write of Gladstone in the manner which the following extract will indicate:

"If Mr. Gladstone was famous among us for the splendor of his eloquence, his unaffected piety, and for his blameless life he was also celebrated far and wide for a more than common liveliness of conscience. He had once imagined it to be his duty to quit a government, and to burst through strong ties of friendship and gratitude, by reason of a thin shade of difference on the subject of white or brown sugar. . . . His friends lived in dread of his virtues, as tending to make him whimsical and unstable; and the practical politicians, perceiving he was not to be depended on for party purposes, and was bent upon none but lofty objects, used to look upon him as dangerous, used to call him behind his back a good man, in the worst sense of the term."

This was written in 1865, after Oxford had been represented by him in the House of Commons and Gladstone had grown beyond the confines of its Conservative sympathies. It was also after the great Chancellor of the Exchequer had opposed the Crimean War, whose historian Kinglake became.

Most intimate among Gladstone's friends was the beautiful and promising youth already referred to, whose personality Tennyson has

memorialized in the largest and sweetest threnody in any language—
Arthur Henry Hallam. Gladstone and Hallam were breakfasting together, walking together, rowing together, reading poetry together,
discussing historical characters and marking out courses each for the
other, during school time, and in the short vacations they entered into
lively correspondence, some of which is as tender and beautiful as the
lines of the late Poet Laureate, whose love for Hallam was equalled only
by Gladstone's. Gladstone seems never to have passed from under
the subtle and glowing influence of Hallam. He saw him at the dawn,
and all the tremulous colors of that era of his life drifted into the soul
and memory of the great political leader who then shared his friendship
so profoundly.

Hallam persisted that Gladstone could write better things than even
his early verses on Canning:

> Yet while I mourn with low and feeble strain,
>   The dearth of children of the lofty lyre,
> And while I weep for that Parnassian plain,
>   Where wont to gleam the Poet's noble fire;
> Where old Mæonides sublimer sings,
> Than e'er on earth, of heroes, sages, kings;
> Where Virgil quaffs the waters of the blest—
> The sacred bands in seats of gladness rest—
> Yet let my Muse her humble tribute pay
> To Canning's eloquence, to Canning's lay.
> Say not the flow'rs of poesy are dead,
> While the Nine wreathe with laurels Canning's head:
> Say not the fount of eloquence is dry,
> It springs from Canning's lip, and sparkles in his eye!
> Yet, ah! the bright but evanescent fire
> Burn'd but to die, and gleam'd but to expire!
> The buds of Poesy the Muses gave,
> Neglected lie, and wither in the grave.
> Far other tasks his patriot care demand,
>   Far other thoughts his ardent soul employ;
> The helm of England needs his guiding hand,
>   A nation's wonder, and a nation's joy.
> He is the pilot that our God hath sent
> To guide the vessel that was tost and rent!

Exalt thine head, Etona, and rejoice,
Glad in a nation's loud acclaiming voice;
And 'mid the tumult and the clamor wild,
Exult in Canning—say, he was thy child.

It is at this time that Gladstone first appeared before his contemporaries as a promising orator. It required not a stroke of genius to discover soon that the literary attainments and dialectical skill of this youth would probably be swept into the stream of eloquence which his lips alone might bring forth. Gladstone became less interested in games as he went on toward manhood, and perhaps a little less popular, even, avoiding the usual course of such a man in declining to enter the debates of the Literati, which society dominated at Eton in the very way in which Gladstone himself was to dominate elsewhere. Young men at this time of life are not likely to avoid themes of the largest importance, and Gladstone soon was toiling with questions of literature, politics, history, and philosophy, giving to each theme a laboriousness and skill, a courage and earnestness truly audacious except in a stripling certain to be one of the most forceful debaters of all time.

It was very evident that Gladstone had breathed and assimilated Toryism when he debated on the fate of Thomas Wentworth, Earl of Strafford. He afterwards had a good deal of difficulty in reconciling the progress of his mind with either Strafford or Charles the First, but on this occasion he dignifiedly patronizes the House of Commons, "which," he says, "we ought to be able to revere as our glory and confide in as our protection."

In one of the most interesting of the earlier biographies of Gladstone we are told that, in closing a speech on the question whether Queen Anne's ministers, in the last four years of her reign, deserved well of their country, his already growing powers, as well as his earlier political faith, are strikingly illustrated:

"Thus much, sir, I have said as conceiving myself bound in fairness not to regard the names under which men have hidden their designs so much as the designs themselves. I am well aware that my prejudices have long been enlisted on the side of Toryism (cheers) and that in a case like this I am not likely to be influenced unfairly against men having that name and professing to act on the principles which I have always been accustomed to revere. But the good of my country must stand on a higher ground than distinctions like these. In common fairness and in common candor, I feel myself compelled to give my decisive verdict against the conduct of men whose measures I firmly believe to have been hostile to British interests, destructive of British glory, and subversive of the splendid, and, I trust, lasting fabric of the British Constitution."

This suggestion of Gladstone's youthful and self-satisfying Toryism leads us to remember that this school was the hot-bed of just such Toryism as was most satisfactory to Sir John Gladstone. Cromwell could not have found at Cambridge in the early part of the seventeenth century a Puritanism more radical than was the Toryism which young Gladstone found here. The young orator's leanings in this direction are further exemplified in the following anecdote of Sir Francis Doyle, who says: "One day I was steadily computing the odds for the Derby, as they stood in a morning newspaper. Mr. Gladstone leaned on my shoulder to look at the lot of horses named. Now it happened that the Duke of Grafton owned a colt named Hampden, who figured in the aforesaid lot. 'Well,' cried Mr. Gladstone, reading off the odds, 'Hampden, at any rate, I see, is in his proper place, between Zeal and Lunacy,' for such, in truth, was the position occupied by the four-footed namesake of that illustrious rebel."

One of Gladstone's ardent schoolmates urged his wish to accompany his friend to Oxford, giving as a reason for his choice the prospect of their continued intimacy, and adding: "Gladstone is no ordinary individual,—and perhaps, if I were called on to select the individual I am most intimate with to whom I should first turn in an emergency, and whom I thought in every way pre-eminently distinguished for high excellence, I think I should turn to Gladstone. . . . If you finally decide in favor of Cambridge, my separation from Gladstone will be a source of great sorrow to me."

Having left Eton at Christmas, 1827, the young man was favored by a short time of study with the best private tutors Sir John Gladstone could obtain. The boy occupied himself in study and in the development of his bodily functions, and his artistic nature found its fullest expression in some excellent wood-carving. He now entered

Christchurch College, Oxford.   Here the young Tory found himself at home, and the very air and spirit of the place matched the hopes and proclivities of his own abounding nature.   His mother wished him to go to Cambridge; but Oxford was his place.   Years after this, the statesman and scholar spoke thus of both seats of learning:

"The enormous efforts which they have made for self-renovation and extension prove that, after so many ages, they are still young; and afford the brightest promise for their future.   But it cannot be, as it was in the last century, a future of somnolent predominance.   Youthful and active companions have come into the field, to extend the range of culture, and to insure its adaptation to modern wants; perhaps also to forbid relapses into lethargy, and to provide a fresh access of material for the finishing hand to work on.   To secure their position, as well as to attain their proper ends, the nation will ask from her ancient and still paramount Universities a constant increase of energetic exertion. Doubtless they may learn one from the other; but neither, I trust, will ever be ashamed of its distinctive character, which has been main- tained through the vicissitudes of so long a time.   We have each, whether individuals or institutions, to recognize the determining lines of our own several formations, which are in truth conditions essential for turning those formations to the best account.   The chief dangers before them are probably two: one that in research, considered as apart from their teaching office, they should relax and consequently dwindle; the other that, under pressure from without, they should lean, if ever so little, to that theory of education which would have it to construct machines of so many horse-power, rather than to form character, and to rear into true excellence the marvelous creature we call man; which gloats upon success in life, instead of studying to secure that the man shall ever be greater than his work and never bounded by it, but that his eye shall boldly run (in the language of Wordsworth)—

"Along the line of limitless desires."

CHAPTER III.

CHRISTCHURCH COLLEGE, OXFORD.

At one time in his career it was strongly suspected that Father Newman had so influenced Gladstone that he was likely to become a Roman Catholic. Vast as were the differences of constitution, the mighty and beautiful spirit of Newman was sure to find a most sympathetic echo for many of his utterances in Gladstone. This much is said because it is of great importance in the estimate of Gladstone that we should remember how much and how little Christchurch College did for him, and also how much and how little the subtle and charming personality of another Oxford College did for him through Newman. Gladstone's nature was churchly, and he might have sung with Emerson:

> I like a monk; I like a cowl;
> I love a prophet of the soul;
> And on my heart monastic aisles
> Fall like sweet strains or pensive smiles.

Christchurch College, Oxford, was created in the hour when mediæval Catholicism found itself compelled to express its spirit in such a foundation. Cardinal Wolsey's princely benefactions came from his magnificence and ambition at the time when he was master of England and desirous of the papal tiara. Goldwin Smith says of Christchurch College: "Here we stand on the point of transition between Catholic and Protestant England." There have been times in Gladstone's life when the same might have been said, and was said, of him. Not only did Oxford influence him by its scholasticism, but Christchurch College, Oxford, influenced him by a peculiarity all its own. Here, before the august façade and in the spacious hall, this sensitive and religious youth was sympathetic with the phases of churchmanship persistent in his mind and affection to the very last. The reformation which swept over Christchurch College has never taken from it or from that gallery of

39

portraits which enriched the walls, a certain monastic quality and tendency of piety to which Gladstone has been easily reconciled.   The associations here were as fine as could be desired.   The two Chairs of Greek and Latin which Fox had established "to extirpate barbarism," gathered around themselves classical scholars like Liddell and Tait which latter was to be the future Archbishop of Canterbury.   Here were Sidney Herbert and Sir Francis Doyle, whose reminiscences of Gladstone and of those times are so entertaining and just; here was Robert Lowe, whose influence upon Gladstone at that time has been too little appreciated and whose force as an orator and skill as a debater Gladstone later on acknowledged in a most charming manner.   Writing in 1877 on the County Franchise, he says:

"Mr. Lowe and I are, in some respects, not ill fitted for a friendly duel on the subject of the representation of the people in Parliament.   He did not confer, and I did not inflict, a speech on the House of Commons, when the subject was recently under discussion.   We are agreed, as I believe, on most questions of politics, indeed rather closely agreed on some important matters, such as public thrift, in which few agree with either of us; and we are united, as I hope, in mutual regard.   Moreover, we have already, many years ago, exhibited opposite leanings upon the question whether the general idea of extension of the suffrage is one which ought to be viewed with favor, or the reverse."

He seems to understand Lowe's value and his limitations, and to have felt something of the good humor of those early times in the conclusion of his argument, when he says:

"Let me not then be too sanguine, and let Mr. Lowe abate his alarms.   His 'excellent principle,' especially when mounted upon such a charger as himself, will yet do service in the field.   It is a veteran that has stood, and will stand, much battering.   It may be long before the country is able to reckon with it, and the reckoning, when it does come, will be but mild.   Do not then let it exasperate the nation, by an obstinate withholding of the County Franchise from that moiety of our householders which is not the least qualified to use it innocently and well.   This in the meantime, with good measure for the cheapening of elections, will be a great and signal boon.   And we shall lie at the foot of the precipice, as we now stand at the top, in perfect comfort. And our Constitution, 'which has been the admiration of the world for five hundred years.' Much, when all these matters are settled, will have been done to invigorate the institutions of the land, to strengthen the national cohesion, to increase the sum total of the public energies, to establish confidence between class and class, to train the people for the habitual, hereditary discharge of public duty. But I am sorry that my harp, like the harp 'in Tara's hall,' must yet, amidst all this prospective joy, be again 'tuned to notes of sadness.' We shall not have landed in Utopia. Some new leaks will open where old ones have been stopped. That ancient trio, the world, the flesh, and the devil, will be too strong for even an approach to the abstract standard of a polity. The public, a fine animal, is strong but sleepy. When he gets active, he gets tired; they tell him he has been excited, and it has been bad for his health; he lays his head upon his pillow; but the interests, ever so anxious lest he should hurt himself by over-exertion, ever wakeful, ever nimble, ever 'redeeming the time,' that is to say, selling it in the best market—they settle to while he is asleep, and make a night of it. There will always be scandals to make us humble, and faults and wants crying aloud to make us diligent; but political progress, if intermittent and qualified, has on the whole been practical and real, and such, in this land of ours, may it ever be."

But we will come in closer proximity to Lowe by awaiting a greater day for Gladstone. Here also he knew Robert Scott, Lord Elgin, Lord Douglas; but the two men who most influenced him then and in after life, with whom he came into sharp controversy, yet to whose friendship he always paid affectionate devotion, were Henry Edward Manning, afterwards Cardinal Archbishop of Westminster, and George Cornewall Lewis, who was Gladstone's successor as Chancellor of the Exchequer.

In the "Life of Cardinal Manning," by Mr. Purcell, we get several sights of Mr. Gladstone which tenderly and powerfully relate themselves to these early days. Manning was in the habit of saying: "Mr. Gladstone's geese are all swans," and thus he paid a tribute to that opulent imagination and extreme generosity which in Gladstone's early youth enabled him to see much more in some boys than one less highly gifted might discover. Mr. Gladstone says of Manning:

"On our leaving Oxford we naturally lost sight of each other; Manning went down into the country in charge of a small parish and I lived in London following political pursuits and finishing my education—at least as regards foreign languages and literature. It was only several

years later that I met Manning by accident. It was on the occasion
of a great meeting in 1835 or 1836, I think, called by Archbishop Howley—a revered man—in connection with the Christian Knowledge Society. The extreme section of the Evangelicals had been getting too
much the upper hand, and the object of the meeting was to put restraint
on their action. I was walking with the Lord Cholmondeley, a leading
man among the Evangelicals but not a factionist, on our way to the
meeting with the view of supporting the Archbishop, when, in turning
out of Queen Street into Lincoln's Inn Fields, we rubbed shoulders with
Manning. After a friendly interchange of greetings and questionings,
I asked Manning what had brought him, a country clergyman, up to
town. 'To defend,' was his answer, 'the Evangelical cause against the
attempts of the Archbishop.' That shows," added Mr. Gladstone,
"that Manning belonged at that time to the section of the extreme
Evangelicals."—(Purcell's Biography I, 372.)

The biographer himself adds, on page 97 of the first volume of this
excellent work:

"In Manning's letter to his brother or to his father and mother,
perhaps very naturally, not the remotest hint is given that the sight
of an apron and shovel hat provoked him to laughter, or that the little
'Father in God' moved him to anger. But it is more strange that not
a trace of this contemptuous aversion to the outward honors and dignity of an Anglican bishop is to be found in contemporary evidence.
Far from exhibiting such aversion, Mr. Gladstone says:—'Manning was
always most loyal to the Church, and spoke of its bishops with great
reverence. I remember on the occasion of an address of sympathy
being presented to Archbishop Howley, Manning spoke of the Archbishop of Canterbury as being the head of the Church.' Some de-
murred to the use of the term 'Head.' 'But,' added Mr. Gladstone,
laughing, 'head is a very elastic word.' Then he suggested as an explanation, 'that Manning, who was always very ascetic, might have objected to bishops on account of their wealth and pomp."

Surely one of these remarks is quite Gladstonian, and indicates
the agility of Gladstone's mind quite as much as the force and clearness
of the great Cardinal's mind are indicated by the statement which the

latter laid down to Mr. Gladstone in a private letter which recalls these very Oxford days. The Cardinal said "The last act of Reason is the first act of Faith."

A noted biographer aptly remarks that there was an absolute necessity, for the sake of historical fitness, that the youth Gladstone should have been sent to Oxford. "The entire atmosphere of the place, steeped in its peculiar traditions and its mediævalism, seemed exactly suited to the whole temperament and genius of the youthful Gladstone." In this judgment we may well coincide with, and pay our gratitude to, Mr. Justin McCarthy for many of the truest and most interesting things said of the statesman whose career has swept his own into the more powerful stream.

Mr. Walter Bagehot, from whom much else might be quoted, wrote with his usual acuteness, concerning the extraordinary and peculiar influence which Oxford had upon Mr. Gladstone's career. Bagehot says, speaking of a later date:

"During the discussion on the Budget, an old Whig who did not approve of it, but who had to vote for it, muttered of its author, 'Ah, Oxford on the surface, but Liverpool below.' And there is truth in the observation, though not in the splenetic sense in which it was uttered. Mr. Gladstone does combine, in a very curious way, many of the characteristics which we generally associate with the place of his education and many of those which we usually connect with the place of his birth. No one can question the first part of the observation. No man has through life been more markedly an Oxford man than Mr. Gladstone. His 'Church and State,' published after he had been several years in public life, was instinct with the very spirit of the Oxford of that time. His 'Homer,' published the other day, bears nearly equal traces of the school in which he was educated. Even in his ordinary style there is a tinge of half theological, half classical, which recalls the studies of his youth. Many Oxford men much object to the opinions of their distinguished representative, but none of them would deny that he remarkably embodies the result of the peculiar teaching of the place."

Mr. Augustine Birrell, in his vigorous essay on Truth Hunting,

gives another light, as if by contrast, in which we may view Mr. Gladstone. As he compares him with that other Oxonian who so charmed
and attracted all young men of genius in his time, John Henry Newman, Mr. Birrell says:

"Where is the actuary who can appraise the value of a man's opinions? 'When we speak of a man's opinions,' says Dr. Newman, 'what
do we mean but the collection of notions he happens to have?' Happens to have! How did he come by them? It is the knowledge we all
possess of the sorts of ways in which men get their opinions that makes
us so little affected in our own minds by those of men for whose characters and intellects we may have great admiration. A sturdy Non-
conformist minister, who thinks Mr. Gladstone the ablest and most
honest man, as well as the ripest scholar within the three kingdoms, is
no whit shaken in his Nonconformity by knowing that his idol has
written in defense of the Apostolical Succession, and believes in special
sacramental graces. Mr. Gladstone may have been a great student
of church history, whilst Nonconformist reading under that head
usually begins with Luther's Theses—but what of that? Is it not all
explained by the fact that Mr. Gladstone was at Oxford in 1831? So
at least the Nonconformist minister will think."

These are interesting bits of criticism, and may help us to some
clearer understanding of the really great man with whom we have to
deal. Mr. Bagehot used to say: "England must comprehend Mr.
Gladstone," for every bright man saw, many years ago, how forceful was
the intellect, and how valuable might be the services of such a man. It
is scarcely to be doubted that such a youth as George Cornewall Lewis,
standing side by side with Gladstone in the Oxford days, accentuated
likeness and unlikeness, as in their later careers it was almost impossible
to feel that there could be a more interesting biographical and psycho-
logical study than the attitude and manner of thought with reference
to the age and its problems, furnished by these two men. If Lewis'
memory was called dry, Gladstone's memory was dewy and as full of
lively sap as a beechen tree on a spring morning. If Lewis had not the
power to exaggerate which belongs to public opinion, Gladstone could
meet popular opinion and tell it on Monday night how much more ex-

aggerated it would be next morning. Both men could flood a subject with unsuspected streams of light, but Gladstone's light has never been dry light; Sir George Lewis' information was often so dry as to be in peril of spontaneous combustion; Gladstone's vast stores of knowledge had been vitalized by omnipresent imagination. Oxford may have made Lewis less enthusiastic, and added a touch of sadness to his native indifference; but Gladstone's interest in everything worthy of a man,— indeed, his interest in a good many things unworthy of so great a man, —has never flagged, and it did not feel a shock of opposition at the Oxford which has made so many promising men apathetic. There has been nothing cynical in Mr. Gladstone, and his almost imperial serious- ness is never sad. If such a man as Lewis was strongest in judgment, his young friend Gladstone was sure to be strongest in impulse for great statesmanship. Gladstone was sure never to be puzzled by the passions of mankind. Within his own soul these forces, unknown in their might and majesty to other men, have swept and stormed and been subdued into calm. Oxford may have taught Mr. Gladstone a scholastic method and filled him with a speculative audacity such as have been balanced only by his intense zeal, his practical human brotherliness, and his merchant-like demand for results; but all these have been suffused and irradiated, and, indeed, led to triumphant achievements, oftentimes re- luctantly, but nevertheless steadily, by an imagination which Oxford could not entirely devote or pledge to ecclesiasticism, and which, like the imagination of a great scientist, has always been ardent with the genius of discovery. Only a youth such as he who afterwards became Sir George Lewis was likely to influence strongly a man who, possessing the courage which afterwards would withstand public opinion, as did Lewis, also might lead and utter the deepest sentiments of the public, as Lewis never could, and as Gladstone has done.

The flexibility of this youth, whose character we are now to study more at length, which was sure to give him the problems and prizes which come to a great orator, was matched by devotion to the solid qualities of scholarship, earnest thinking, and careful research. Glad- stone became master of that high logic which does not down before two aspects of one truth. Oxford and its associations could not harm this. Lewis might not be able to "take a test without qualification," but Gladstone would be able to approve the consistency of two apparently opposing principles. In their youth it was the fortune or fate of Oxford to emphasize in each of these men his most evident weakness, as well as to nurture his most valuable powers.

Speaking of his Oxford days, Gladstone's own account furnishes the best account of the state of atmosphere religiously and politically. He says, writing in 1848:

"Of this great renovating movement, a large part centered in Oxford. At the time, indeed, when I resided there, from 1828 to 1831, no sign of it had yet appeared. A steady, clear, but dry Anglican orthodoxy bore sway; and frowned, this way or that, on the first indication of any tendency to diverge from the beaten path. Dr. Pusey was, at that time, revered, indeed, for his piety and charity, no less than admired for his learning and talents, but suspected (I believe) of sympathy with the German theology, in which he was known to be profoundly versed. Dr. Newman was thought to have about him the flavor of what, he has now told the world, were the opinions he had derived in youth from the works of Thomas Scott. Mr. Keble, the 'sweet singer of Israel,' and a true saint, if this generation has seen one, did not reside in Oxford. The chief Chair of Theology had been occupied by Bishop Lloyd, the old tutor, and the attached and intimate friend, of Peel; a man of powerful talents, and of a character both winning and decided, who, had his life been spared, might have modified essentially for good the fortunes of the Church of England, by guiding the energetic influences which his teaching had done much to form. But he had been hurried away in 1829 by early death; and Dr. Whately, who was also in his own way, a known power in the University, was in 1830 induced to accept the Archbishopric of Dublin. There was nothing, at that time, in the theology, or in the religious life, of the University to indicate what was soon to come.

"But when, shortly afterwards, the great heart of England began to beat with the quickened pulsations of a more energetic religious life, it was in Oxford that the stroke was most distinct and loud. An extraordinary change appeared to pass upon the spirit of the place. I believe it would be a moderate estimate to say that much beyond one half of the very flower of its youth chose the profession of Holy Orders; while an impression, scarcely less deep, seemed to be stamped upon a large portion of its lay pupils.   I doubt whether at any period of its existence, either since the Reformation, or perhaps before it, the Church of England had reaped from either University, in so short a time, so rich a harvest.   At Cambridge a similar lifting up of heart and mind seems to have been going on;   and numbers of persons of my own generation, who at their public schools had been careless and thoughtless like the rest, appeared in their early manhood as soldiers of Christ, and ministers to the wants of His people, worthy, I believe, as far as man can be worthy, through their zeal, devotion, powers of mind, and attainments, of their high vocation.

"It was not then foreseen what storms were about to rise.   Not only in Oxford, but in England, during the years to which I refer, party spirit within the Church was reduced to a low ebb.   Indiscretions there might be, but authority did not take alarm; it smiled rather, on the contrary, on what was thought to be in the main a recurrence both to first principles and to forgotten obligations.   Purity, unity, and energy seemed, as three fair sisters hand in hand, to advance together. Such a state of things was eminently suited to act on impressible and sanguine minds.   I, for one, formed a completely false estimate of what was about to happen, and believed that the Church of England, through the medium of a regenerated clergy and an intelligent and attached laity, would not only hold her ground, but would even in great part probably revive the love and the allegiance both of the masses who were wholly falling away from religious observances, and of those large and powerful nonconforming bodies, the existence of which was supposed to have no other cause than the neglect of its duties by the National Church, which had long left the people as sheep without a shepherd.

"And surely it would have required either a deeply saturnine or a marvelously prophetic mind to foretell that, in ten or twelve more years, that powerful and distinguished generation of clergy would be broken up; that at least a moiety of the most gifted sons, whom Oxford

had reared for the service of the Church of England, would be hurling
at her head the hottest bolts of the Vatican: that, with their deviation
on the one side, there would arise a not less convulsive rationalistic
movement on the other; and that the natural consequences would be
developed in endless contention and estrangement, and in suspicions
worse than either, because even less accessible, and even more intract-
able. Since that time, the Church of England may be said to have bled
at every pore; and at this hour it seems occasionally to quiver to its
very base. And yet, all the while, the religious life throbs more and
more powerfully within her. Shorn of what may be called the romance
and poetry of her revival, she abates nothing of her toil; and in the
midst of every sort of partial indiscretion and extravagance, her great
office in the care of souls is, from year to year, less and less imperfectly
discharged. But the idea of asserting on her part those exclusive
claims, which become positively unjust in a divided country governed
on popular principles, has been abandoned by all parties in the State."

DANIEL O'CONNELL

CHAPTER IV.

THE OXFORD STUDENT.

Gladstone's career at Oxford was worthy of his name and the fame of his after life. He was an enthusiastic and painstaking student, and his reading embraced almost every realm of literature into which he afterwards went with graceful ease and distinguished power. Perhaps this was the time when he dwelt most joyously with the poets, and realized for himself, in short vacations, something of the Arcadian existence of which they sang. His conduct was above reproach, and, indeed, his influence at Oxford was exalting and regenerating in the highest degree. Lord Houghton, who visited Oxford in 1829, afterwards wrote:

"The man that took me was the youngest Gladstone of Liverpool— I am sure a very superior person." He was inalterably opposed to the riotous conduct of certain undergraduates whose wanton excesses and brutality caused the death of one of their number in 1831; and that portion of American youth whose proper sphere is in the shambles rather than in the company of college gentlemen, may derive a salutary lesson from Gladstone's decorous and sensible university career.

Whatever we may think of modern systems of education, and of the policy of relegating the classics to the rear, in order that what are called "practical studies" may come to the front, Gladstone's career furnishes indubitable evidence that such a mind as his can scarcely be expected to perform its work in the world without the exacting and stimulating culture which these studies offered. He was deeply interested in the life of Greece and Rome as they were expressed in their literatures. Even then he was a book-lover in the best sense, and began to form his collection of the finest editions of the classics. First editions of modern authors, "with the author's compliments," were to cover his tables in due time. Every subject allied itself with every other subject, so that his reading took him beyond the established courses of study, and it was soon understood that Gladstone possessed an amount of information of which no other student could boast. To have heard him when he presented a Budget before the House of Commons, dealing with statistics and figures with unsurpassed art and charm, made one readily believe that he enjoyed the contest in which he engaged as a student at Oxford for a "double first," exacting from himself the incessant labors required to secure the prize in classics and the honors in mathematics.

Perhaps to the cursory view Gladstone would have seemed over-religious and slightly feminine in the cast of his mind. Certain it is that a friend and companion, writing in 1829, regrets that "Gladstone has mixed himself up so much as he has done with the St. Mary's Hall and Oriel set, who are really, for the most part, only fit to live with maiden aunts and keep tame rabbits." These were the men soon to be bound by the spell of John Henry Newman. His masculine quality of mind saved him, and he even then looked at life with full-hearted and muscular faith. Speaking many years later, he appears as that same young man grown none the less believing because of years. He says:

"Life is still as full of deep, of varied, of ecstatic, of harrowing interests as it ever was. The heart of man still beats and bounds, exults and suffers, from causes which are only less salient and conspicuous, because they are more mixed and diversified. It still undergoes every phase of emotion, and even, as seems probable, with a susceptibility which has increased and is increasing, and which has its index and outer form in the growing delicacy and complexities of the nervous system. Does any one believe that ever at any time there was a greater number of deaths referable to that comprehensive cause, a broken heart? Let none fear that this age, or any coming one, will extirpate the material of poetry. The more reasonable apprehension might be lest it should sap the vital force necessary to handle that material, and mould it into appropriate forms."

Mr. Gladstone has indeed never disdained the proper enjoyment of life's full stream of pleasure. He posed not as a pale ascetic. He could afterwards fully appreciate Lord Macaulay's love of innocent festivities, for he did not then refuse to sip from a glass of wine or divide a well-cooked bird with his friends. He appears to be talking of himself, when, nearly half a century after this date, he writes of the essayist and historian:

"Macaulay was singularly free of vices, and not in the sense in which, according to Swift's note on Burnet, William III. held such a freedom; that is to say, 'as a man is free of a corporation.' One point only we reverse—an occasional tinge of at least literary vindictiveness. Was he envious? Never. Was he servile? No. Was he insolent? No. Was he selfish? No. Was he prodigal? No. Was he avaricious? No. Was he idle? The question is ridiculous. Was he false? No; but true as steel, and transparent as crystal. Was he vain? We hold that he was not. At every point in the ugly list he stands the trial; and though in his history he judges mildly some sins of appetite or passion, there is no sign in his life, or his remembered character, that he was compounding for what he was inclined to.

"The most disputable of the negatives we have pronounced is that which relates to vanity; a defect rather than a vice; never admitted into the septenary catalogue of the mortal sins of Dante and the Church; often lodged by the side of high and strict virtue, often allied with an amiable and playful innocence; a token of perfection, a deduction from greatness; and no more. For this imputation on Macaulay there are apparent, but, as we think, only apparent, grounds.

"His moderation in luxuries and pleasures is the more notable and praiseworthy because he was a man who, with extreme healthiness of faculty, enjoyed keenly what he enjoyed at all. Take in proof the following hearty notice of a dinner *a quattr' occhi* to his friend: 'Ellis came to dinner at seven. I gave him a lobster-curry, woodcock, and macaroni. I think that I will note dinners, as honest Pepys did.'"

Such also was the young and full-blooded son of Sir John Gladstone.

An essay-society was constituted, called the W. E. G., and the young man now presented one of his first studies upon the literature and philosophy of Greece, namely, a disquisition on Socrates' belief in immortality. The Oxford Union at length took most of his time for these exercises, and he thus united himself with an historical society which, as much as any institution in Oxford, has stimulated literary productiveness and enthusiasm in England. Within its walls, bishops, prime-ministers, historians, essayists, poets, and orators have been trained, as in almost no other similar society's meeting-place in the educational world. On the 30th of February, he delivered his maiden speech there, at which time the young orator established a reputation which led his friends, from that moment on, to anticipate for him a remarkable career as an orator. It is interesting in this speech to note his rather stern opposition to the removal of Jewish Disabilities. Years after, his chief antagonist, whom Gladstone always held in high admiration, and to whom he showed every personal kindness, was the Jew, Benjamin Disraeli, and Gladstone himself ably defended the policy of admitting Jews to Parliament. Perhaps his greatest success as a young orator, namely, the speech against the Whig Reform Bill, was even better than his pious fulminations against the removal of Jewish Disabilities, and it will show the point of view then held by this promising youth, and the glorious journey which lay before him ere he should reach the hour when Disraeli's Ministry should be compelled to adopt Household Suffrage, and when he would see the electoral power of the English people safely confided to populations whose every existence, at that time, he could scarce contemplate without a tremor. Gladstone was at this time, as he afterwards acknowledged, under the spell of his father's great friend, George Canning. Years afterward he wrote of Canning:

"It is for those who revered him in the plenitude of his meridian glory to mourn over him in the darkness of his premature extinction; to mourn over the hopes that are buried in his grave, and the evils that arise from his withdrawing from the scene of life. Surely if eloquence never excelled and seldom equalled—if an expanded mind and judgment whose vigor was paralleled only by its soundness—if brilliant wit —if a glowing imagination—if a warm heart, and an unbending firmness—could have strengthened the frail tenure, and prolonged the momentary duration of human existence, that man had been immortal! But nature could endure no longer. Thus has Providence ordained that inasmuch as the intellect is more brilliant, it shall be more short-lived; as its sphere is more expanded, more swiftly is it summoned away. Lest we should give the man honor due to God—lest we should exalt the object of our admiration into a divinity for our worship—He who calls the weary and the mourner to eternal rest hath been pleased to remove him from our eyes."

One thing that Canning said, Gladstone did not forget and the advice served him often: "Give plenty of time to your verses. Every good copy you do will set in your memory some poetical thought or some well turned form of speech which you will find useful when you speak in public."

Young Gladstone's addresses were so powerful and prophetic that such men as Bishop Wordsworth anticipated that Gladstone would one day become Premier of the realm, and Arthur Henry Hallam, rejoicing in the richness of his friendship, predicted that there was no place in the Government of Great Britain which he might not some day adorn. He could hardly breathe any other air at Oxford than that of Toryism, for Toryism was in the buildings, overgrown with ivy, and it dictated attitude and behavior in cloister and market-place.

Sir John Gladstone might easily content himself, as he reflected that his young son would hear nothing there which would lead him to trust the masses, or make him willing to teach them anything but obedience to their masters. But Sir John had not calculated upon the fact that his son had been blessed by a mother whose more plastic and eager nature belonged to him, and that the world into which his boy was to go was full of ideas to which Sir John's mind was a stranger. He doubtless went along with others in the feeling that Sir Robert Peel had been rightly deprived of his seat in Oxford University, because he had made a slight concession in the name of justice to the Catholics, but it is certain that there lay before him in the utterances and person of John Henry Newman a series of arguments which should deeply stir his nature, and command his reverence, even though he could not go with Newman to the Roman Catholic church.

Another rare personality soon exercised a beneficent influence upon

him and upon Arthur Henry Hallam. The former defended Frederic
Denison Maurice, while in disagreement with his churchmanship.

But the responsiveness of Gladstone's mind to the sincere thinking
of differently constituted intellects, the ability he has shown to appreciate even an antagonist's point of view and the unique capacity he
has shown for hospitably entertaining the spirit of such men as Maurice, without fixing himself to their opinions, have often made proof
of themselves, greatly to the sweetening of otherwise hopelessly bitter
waters of controversy. He might have said of Maurice what Maurice
said of him: He "has disappointed me more than I like to confess, but
he seems to be 'an excellent and really wise man." After all, it is difficult for such high spirits to avoid the glory of character which is in-
tenser than that of creed.

The present writer cannot forget the lively sentiments of gratitude
which Mr. Gladstone indicated, when once, at eventide, he talked at
length of the Broad-Church movement in England, its strength and
weakness, and stopped to pay a warm tribute to Frederic Denison
Maurice. There was no poem of Tennyson's, among the latter's slighter
productions, to which Gladstone turned for biographical interest, with
more of that delicate enthusiasm which expressed itself in his reading
of it on that evening, than the following:

> Come, when no graver cares employ,
> Godfather, come and see your boy:
>   Your presence will be sun in winter,
> Making the little one leap for joy.
>
> For, being of that honest few,
> Who give the Fiend himself his due,
>   Should eight-thousand college-councils
> Thunder "Anathema," friend at you;
>
> Should all our churchmen foam in spite
> At you, so careful of the right,
>   Yet one lay-hearth would give you welcome
> (Take it and come) to the Isle of Wight;
>
> Where, far from noise and smoke of town,
> I watch the twilight falling brown
>   All round a careless-order'd garden
> Close to the ridge of a noble down.

You'll have no scandal while you dine,
But honest talk and wholesome wine,
    And only hear the magpie gossip
Garrulous under a roof of pine:

For groves of pine on either hand,
To break the blast of winter, stand;
    And further on, the hoary Channel
Tumbles a billow on chalk and sand;

Where, if below the milky steep
Some ship of battle slowly creep,
    And on thro' zones of light and shadow
Glimmer away to the lonely deep,

We might discuss the Northern sin
Which made a selfish war begin;
    Dispute the claims, arrange the chances;
Emperor, Ottoman, which shall win:

Or whether war's avenging rod
Shall lash all Europe into blood;
    Till you should turn to dearer matters,
Dear to the man that is dear to God;

How best to help the slender store;
How mend the dwellings, of the poor;
    How gain in life, as life advances,
Valor and charity more and more.

This was written in January, 1854, and, by this time, Tennyson and Gladstone had discovered the value of that bond uniting them in deep friendship. Tennyson has happily touched upon the qualities in Maurice and the interests of his life and thought which afterwards did much to attach Gladstone to the valorous man and teacher, and to liberalize as well as humanize his spirit.

In 1875, in the controversy which drew from him the famous article, "Is the Church of England Worth Preserving?" Mr. Gladstone said, speaking of the folly of attempting to adjust ecclesiastical difficulties in courts of law:

"Unhappily they came upon a country little conversant with theological, historical, or ecclesiastical science, and a country which had not been used, for three hundred years, with the rarest exceptions, to raise these questions before the tribunals. The only one of them in which

I have taken a part was the summary proceeding of the Council of King's College against Mr. Maurice. I made an ineffectual endeavor, with the support of Judge Patteson and Sir B. Brodie, and the approval of Bishop Blomfield, to check what seemed to me the unwise and ruthless vehemence of the majority which dismissed that gentleman from his office."

Speaking in 1878 of Oxford, Mr. Gladstone said:

"I trace in the education of Oxford of my own time one great defect. Perhaps it was my own fault; but I must admit that I did not learn, when at Oxford, that which I have learned since, viz., to set a due value on the imperishable and the inestimable principles of human liberty."

Surely it was a long journey, but one nobly accomplished, from his point of view, as a churchman, when he left his University, to that point of view occupied by him when he wrote the following:

"The Gospel gave to the life of civilized man a real resurrection, and its second birth was followed by its second youth. This rejuvenescence was allotted to those wonderful centuries which popular ignorance confounded with the Dark Ages properly so called—an identification about as rational as if we were to compare our own life within the womb to the same life in intelligent though early childhood. Awakened to aspirations at once fresh and ancient, the mind of man took hold of the venerable ideas bequeathed to us by the Greeks as a precious part of its inheritance, and gave them again to the light, appropriated but also renewed. The old materials came forth, but not alone; for the types which human genius had formerly conceived were now submitted to the transfiguring action of a law from on high. Nature herself prompted the effort to bring the old patterns of worldly excellence and greatness—or rather the copies of those patterns still legible, though depraved, and still rich with living suggestion—into harmony with that higher Pattern, once seen by the eyes and handled by the hands of men, and faithfully delineated in the Gospels for the profit of all generations. The life of our Savior, in its external aspect, was that of a teacher. It was, in principle, a model for all; but it left space and scope for adaptations to the lay life of Christians in general, such as those by whom the every-day business of the world is to be carried on. It remained for man to make his best endeavor to exhibit the great model on its terrestrial side, in its contact with the world. Here is the true source of that new and noble Cycle which the Middle Ages have handed down to us in duality of form, but with a closely related substance, under the royal scepters of Arthur in England and of Charlemagne in France."

At this time began many of the studies to which Gladstone gave much of labor, thought and passionate devotion in later years. His love of Dante and the completeness of the statesman's understanding of the far-away poet had their roots in the soil of these days, and much that Gladstone afterwards said in exposition of the Italian poet came to him in those years when he looked upon Dante as a great theologian, such as Homer was to Greece. Years after he expressed an opinion which he wrote out in other form, in 1832:

"Dante might, far better than Milton, be compared with Homer; for while he is in the Purgatoria and Paradiso far more heavenly than Milton, he is also throughout the Divina Commedia truly and profoundly human. He is incessantly conversant with the nature and the life of man; and though for the most part he draws us, as Flaxman has drawn him, in outline only, yet by the strength and depth of his touch he has produced figures, for example Francesca and Ugolino, that have as largely become the common property of mankind, if not as Achilles and Ulysses, yet as Lear and Hamlet. Still the theological basis, and the extra-terrene theater of Dante's poem remove him to a great distance from Homer, from whom he seems to have derived little, and with whom we may therefore feel assured he could have been but little acquainted."

It was fortunate for him now that he was permitted to visit Italy. He there entered with renewed vigor on the study of Dante, meanwhile writing some accounts, such as the following, of what he saw:

"After Etna, the temples are certainly the great charm and attraction of Sicily. I do not know whether there is any one among them which, taken alone, exceeds in interest and beauty that of Neptune at Paestum; but they have the advantage of number and variety,

as well as of highly interesting positions. At Segesta the temple is
enthroned in a perfect mountain solitude, and it is like a beautiful
touch of its religion, so stately, so entire; while around, but for one
solitary house of the keeper, there is nothing, absolutely nothing, to
disturb the apparent reign of silence and of death. At Selinus, the
huge fragments on the plain seem to make an eminence themselves,
and they listen to the ever young and unwearied waves which almost
wash their base, and mock their desolation by the image of perpetual
life and motion they present, while the tone of their heavy fall upon the
beach well accords with the solemnity of the scene. At Girgenti the
ridge visible to the mariner from afar is still crowned by a long line of
fabrics, presenting to the eye a considerable mass and regularity of
structure, and the town is near and visible; yet that town is so entirely
the mere phantom of its former glory within its now shrunken limits,
that instead of disturbing the effect, it rather seems to add a new image
and enhance it. The temples enshrine a most pure and salutary principle of art, that which connects grandeur of effect with simplicity
of detail; and retaining their beauty and their dignity in their decay,
they represent the great man when fallen, as types of that almost
highest of human qualities—silent, yet not sullen, endurance."

Here also he found some of the most interesting and deeply potent
associations of his life. Together with friends from whom he was not
to part he began the study of Virgil, and it was to one of these friends,
many years after, that he read one of his famous essays for the first
time—the essay in which occurs the following interesting passage:

"With rare exceptions, the reader of Virgil finds himself utterly at
a loss to see at any point the soul of the poet reflected in his work.
We cannot tell, amidst the splendid phantasmagoria, where is his heart,
where lie his sympathies. In Homer a genial spirit, breathed from
the poet himself, is translucent through the whole; in the Æneid we
look in vain almost for a single ray of it. Again, Virgil lived at a time
when the prevailing religion had lost whatever elements of real influence
that of Homer's era either possessed in its own right, or inherited from
pristine traditions. It was undermined at once by philosophy and by
licentiousness; and it subsisted only as a machinery, a machinery too,

already terribly discredited, for civil ends. Thus he lost one great element of truth and nature, as well as of sublimity and pathos. The extinction of liberty utterly deprived him of another. Homer saw before him both a religion and a polity young, fresh, and vigorous; for Virgil both were practically dead: and whatever this world has of true greatness is so closely dependent upon them, that it was not his fault if his poem felt and bears cogent witness to the loss. Even the sphere of personal morality was not open to him; for what principle of truth or righteousness could he worthily have glorified, without passing severe condemnation on some capital act of the man whom it was his chief obligation to exalt?

"And once more. Homer sang to his own people of the glorious deeds of their sires, to whom they were united by fond recollection, and by near and historic ties. This was at once a stimulus and a check; it cheered his labor, and at the same time it absolutely required him to study moral harmony and consistency. Virgil sang to the Romans of the deeds of those who were not Romans, and whom only a most hollow fiction connected with his hearers, through the dim vista of a thousand years, and under circumstances which made the pretense to historical continuity little better than ridiculous. It appears, however, as if this great and splendid poet, being thrown out of his true bearings in regard to all the deeper sources of interest on which an epic writer must depend, such as religion, patriotism, and liberty, became consequently reckless, alike in major and in minor matters, as to all the inner harmonies of his work, and contented himself with the most unwearied and fastidious labors in its outward elaboration, where he could give scope to his extraordinary powers of versification and of diction without fear of stumbling upon anything unfit for the artificial atmosphere of the Roman court. The consequence is, that a vein of untruthfulness runs throughout the whole Æneid, as strong and as remarkable as is the genuineness of thought and feeling in the Homeric poems. Homer walks in the open day, Virgil by lamplight. Homer gives us figures that breathe and move. Virgil usually treats us to waxwork. Homer has the full force and play of the drama, Virgil is essentially operatic. From Virgil back to Homer is a greater distance than from Homer back to life."

CHAPTER V.

COMING TO HIS OPPORTUNITY.

As Napoleon was swept into power by the last wave of a revolution destructive and ominous, so Gladstone came to his own opportunity as a statesman by a wave of reform constructive and full of brightest promise for England. If it is proper to call Queen Victoria "the first of the constitutional rulers of England," it must be said that William the Fourth, powerless with the tide of modern life, totally unable to see anything in the development of republican and democratic sentiment save peril to all institutions, was the last sullen and determined unconstitutional ruler of England. He serves as a sort of memorial of that vanished day when the gentlemen and lords of England gathered pathetically around such a royal phantom as was he, and condoled with him upon what they thought was to be the ruin of England and the abolition of all rights of property. The truth is that at the close of 1832 England was full of that excitement and expectancy which the trees of the forest and the grasses of the earth know when Spring first strolls through the world. The landed classes and the haughty courtiers saw something frightful in the melting of the ancient privileges and icy prejudices, and Lord Kenyon cried out: "This Reform, so-called, will be the destruction of the monarchy!" Though the king refused to assent in royal person to the Reform Bill, which was really a great act of legislation, the thing was done, the waves of agitation rolled back, and even the most cordial supporters of the measure of reform, which transformed the whole electoral scheme of England, found their hearts anxious and looked to the future with assurance touched with something of fear. This tremor of doubt was, for the most part, almost wholly controlled by abounding faith in the principles which had been asserted. It was indeed April in English politics, and everything was in bud.

60

What could be more to the liking of Sir John Gladstone, the Tory, and less apparently helpful to the development of the nascent Liberalism of his son, than that just now the Duke of Newcastle should send for the young man and ask him to seek the seat in Parliament representing Newark? The Duke had no idea that anyone else doubted his right to arrange the representation, first of all for himself, and, incidentally, for the benefit of the other inhabitants of this borough. But the Duke of Newcastle overdid it. His Toryism furnished Gladstone's mobile and free spirit with a kind of chain for his wearing which was certain speedily to make him care very little for that kind of a constituency and that sort of lordly supervision.

Of course Sir John Gladstone was pleased when the young man came back from the Continent and began to canvass for votes. No one thought of the young orator save as one of the chosen bulwarks able to defend the ruling classes against the aggression of popular reform, and none suspected that probably in the course of that connection with the Duke of Newcastle as a sort of feudal lord assuming to own the votes of his tenantry, Gladstone would get some notions of the elective franchise which later on would refuse the accepted theory of such as the Duke of Newcastle, namely, that the pyramid of government in England ought to stand on its sharpest height instead of on its broadest base.

Gladstone brought to this canvass of the Newark borough the same supple and pure muscular fiber which, in a campaign nearly sixty years after, was to endure more than even then, when, at twenty-three years of age, it was possible for it to stand amazing labors. The intense and luminous eyes which for fifty years were to glow and dart and illuminate and burn amidst the storm of debate, or in quiet hours of friendship to shine out with all the tremulous messages of a loving heart, then exercised their sovereign influence, as this attractive and really eloquent young man poured forth his theories and propositions in remarkably full and ready speech. These and other striking features of his body he brought to the service of a mind intent on defending that Toryism which he was predestined to despise. He was opposing those measures of reform which were certain to be but prophetic of the larger changes he would inaugurate in English government.

Perhaps even at this time there was enough of the method of current theology in him to account for the mixture of dogmatism and indirection which these speeches indicate. One could easily understand at that time how naturally he had desired to take holy orders in preference to his seat in the House of Commons. There was a pious and churchly air about him as a speaker. All of the critics of Gladstone fail not to tell us that Gladstone was "so much more dangerous as a demagogue" because he at least appeared to be religious. A grandly earnest spirit, full of faith, is likely to offend those who are never to be suspected of religious conviction. No doubt Gladstone perplexed the orthodox in politics. A skillful critic indicates that at this moment Gladstone was able to give the Duke of Newcastle a good deal of concern as to the future from the flashes of day-time which came in now and then upon the almost hopeless night of his Conservatism. This critic says:

"He was bound by the opinions of no man and no party (Liberal), but felt it a duty to watch and resist that growing desire for change which threatened to produce, 'along with partial good, a melancholy preponderance of mischief' (Conservative). The first principle to which he looked for national salvation was that 'the duties of governors are strictly and peculiarly religious, and that legislatures, like individuals, are bound to carry throughout their acts the spirit of the high truths they have acknowledged.' (Conservative-Oxford.) The condition of the poor demanded special attention; labor should receive adequate remuneration, and he thought favorably of the 'allotment of cottage grounds.' (Liberal.) He regarded slavery as sanctioned by Holy Scriptures (Conservative-Oxford), but the slaves were to be educated, and gradually emancipated. (Liberal.)"

Surely there is a good opportunity here to remark concerning Gladstone's being on both sides of the fence at the same time, but we think a closer view will indicate that he was then only in a teachable frame of mind and was learning something.

The contest was very acrimonious and prolonged, but Gladstone won, his name coming in at the head of the poll.

When the Reform Parliament of 1833 met, there began the career of Gladstone as a debater and master of dialectics in the region of political thought. The Liberal side was represented by brains and numerical strength, and that contingent was surveyed by eyes no less shrewd and penetrating than those of Sir Robert Peel. The moderate and timid began to find safe places for themselves, for it became certain that, with O'Connell leading the large body of Irish members in his antagonism to the ministry, and the fresh and powerful wave of Liberalism mounting in opposition to Sir Robert Peel, even he whose skill and formidable talents had been able to mould, if not to conquer, opposition, could not prevent stormful times. The Tory missed the disenfranchised rotten boroughs upon which he had been accustomed to rely, and though in many cases property was represented by some Conservative proprietor, the nobility and the large landed interests were evidently in a situation where a lesson of lasting influence must be learned. The King's speech was an echo of a vanishing past. Ireland's disorder continued, perpetuating a theme which was to grow more interesting for the young member from Newark. With Earl Grey and Lord Brougham regretting some of the methods of progress, with the Earl of Ripon, and Stanley, and Sir James Graham vehement in their opposition, with O'Connell standing up for order in the mind of England as a promise of order in the behavior of Ireland, Gladstone saw the Government majority at first overwhelming all antagonism, and yet, although the Ministry had conceded much, he was sure of the strong opposition awaiting it in the House of Lords. Here he studied the qualifications for Parliament, and he afterwards made the following remarks upon the subject:

"The qualifications which attract the favor of a constituency are very various; birth, station, talent, character, former service, landed possessions, commercial and manufacturing connection, and lastly money. The two circumstances which strike me most forcibly, and most painfully, are, first, the rapid and constant advance of the money power; secondly, the reduction almost to zero, of the chances of entrance into Parliament for men who have nothing to rely upon but their talent and their character; nothing that is to say, but the two qualities, which certainly stand before all others in the capacity of rendering service to the country. These again, are chiefly the young; for such men have usually, by the time they reach middle life, attained, with great difficulty, to wealth or to competence. But they have then passed the proper period for beginning an effective Parliamentary education. There have been honorable and distinguished exceptions, but, as a rule, it would be as rational to begin training for the ballot at forty-five or fifty, as for the real, testing work of the Cabinet. That union of suppleness and strength which is absolutely requisite for the higher labors of the administrator and the statesman is a gift the development of which, unless it be commenced betimes, nature soon places beyond reach. There is indeed scope and function in Parliament for the middle-aged man, and even for men like myself, no longer middle-aged; but nothing can compensate for a falling off in the stock of the young men whom we need for the coming time, and we need the choicest in the country. The only education for the highest work in the House of Commons is, as a rule, given in the House of Commons."

These conceptions he never lost sight of through the discussion of the question of the Disestablishment of the Church in Ireland, and Ireland's social condition, with which themes he has had so much to do. These subjects were before the House of Commons at that time, and also the condition of the poor in England, and the fact of slavery in the British colonies attracted anxious thought. On the subject of slavery Gladstone spoke on May 17th and on June 3d, and in his speech he was compelled to reply to the charges against his father who had used slavery for the ends of business in his Demera estates. Gladstone repeated the provisions which he had indicated in his address before the people—that "emancipation should be effected gradually, and after due preparation; that the slaves should be educated and stimulated to spontaneous industry; and that the masters should be liberally compensated." He said: "I do not view property as an abstract thing; it is the creature of civil society. By the Legislature it is granted, and by the Legislature it is destroyed."

Gladstone does not seem to have stormed the House, or to have

THE RIGHT HONORABLE WILLLIAM EWART GLADSTONE, M.P.

HAWARDEN CASTLE—THE HOME OF GLADSTONE

failed, as did his great rival; and, unlike Disraeli, he left no announcement that some day England would listen and hear him. His fluency and vigorous delivery lost nothing by the "Lancashire burr" which, it is said, was on his tongue from the first to the last; and his success as an orator was steadily increasing while the House was abolishing slavery and Gladstone was helping to see that the slave-owners received twenty million pounds sterling as their remuneration. His friendship with Bishop Wilberforce at this time was a delight and honor to both, and the Bishop expressed himself as certain that the young politician had even larger work than this laid out before him in the providence of heaven.

Gladstone added to his fame as a speaker and man of affairs by his terrible denunciation of bribery and corruption with which the Liverpool elections had been conducted. It was impossible for him to avoid Church matters, and he entered into the discussion consequent upon the introduction of the Church Temporalities Bill. He spoke with all the ardor of a polemic. He desired the support and prestige of the Protestant Bishops in Ireland and the other clergy to be increased rather than diminished. Indeed, Gladstone strangely turned to Ireland from the beginning of his career to the end, as that distressed and oftentimes outraged people, adding so often to their own distresses and multiplying outrage by outrage, commended itself to this man of faith and action. Belief in the improvability of the human species always saves a man from cynicism in all crises, and rescues him from the habit of Toryism which is hopeless in the presence of an abuse, unto that Liberalism of spirit which will not admit of a defeat for righteousness in advance of every effort for its victory. Meantime, O'Connell's speeches and the manner of their reception in the House of Commons will give some idea of the attitude of England toward the Irish question. Here is one of the liberator's addresses in the House:

"Shall Ireland (he asked) be governed by a section? (Vehement shouts from the opposition.) I thank you—(noise renewed)—for that shriek. Many a shout of insolent domination—(noise)—despicable and contemptible as it is—(noise)—have I heard against my country. (Uproar continued, during which Mr. O'Connell, with uplifted fist and great violence of manner, uttered several sentences which were inaudible in the gallery. The speaker was at last obliged to interfere and call the House to order.) Let them shout. It is a senseless yell. It is the spirit of the party that has placed you there. Ireland will hear your shrieks. (Continued uproar.) Yes, you may want us again. (Roars of laughter.) What would Waterloo have been if we had not been there? (Ministerial cheers and Opposition laughter.)"

In 1889 Mr. Gladstone spoke on O'Connell, and the "Spectator" thus commented upon it:

"O'Connell, if he can now see what Mr. Gladstone is doing to exalt the Irish agitator's fame in the first place, and in the second and more important place, to effect that virtual separation between Ireland and England at far greater sacrifice and in far more signal contrast to the significance of his early career, which O'Connell vainly sought to bring within the limits of serious Parliamentary consideration, must experience the curious feeling that he has at last made, as a living writer once generously expressed it, a most magnificent 'posthumous convert in tardy compensation for contemporaneous obloquy.'   And certainly whatever Mr. Gladstone may have lately done to emulate the big, passionate, careless, and almost slovenly genius of the mighty agitator, no one who remembers his earlier career could hope to find a more remarkable contrast to O'Connell than that earlier career exhibited. Young, refined, subtle, accurate, delighting in distinctions of all kinds, almost academic in his cast of mind, an orator who loved to find unexpected reasons for what the majority of his party wished to think or do, a careful student, and most painstaking in establishing the premises on which he proposed to build his inferences, but with all his care and subtlety, one who had at command the subdued passion which fills abstract reasoning with life and persuasiveness, Mr. Gladstone in 1834 must have presented as extraordinary a contrast as it would be possible to find under the sun to the wily, unscrupulous agitator, with his glowing rhetoric, with his 'broad brush and dirty colors,' and, finally, with those liberal and reiterated promises of immediate repeal which Mr. Gladstone to a sanguine temperament, but which we should rather attribute to a somewhat scornful indifference to minutiæ in all cases where O'Connell's wish to persuade was strong."

It is not necessary to describe the condition of things in the Protestant portions of Ireland at this time, further than to say that 9,000 crimes in the districts which were naturally rebellious against the sort of thing as has been called government in Ireland, added to more than 300 bloody assaults, in the course of one short year, might justify the notion of the best equipped historians and publicists that, perhaps, under no flag claiming to be a flag of civilization, was there such a state of poverty, ignorance, wretchedness, rebellion, and such a general disposition to fight somebody, in the hope of righting affairs.

Of course the only respectably orthodox and English remedy for this state of things for a long time had been coercion, and such an indomitable Englishman as Earl Grey had an immense following of men who could think of nothing else at this period, though O'Connell was alert and obstructive and eloquent with a noble opposition. Soon the plastic mind of Gladstone was taught as to coercion in the results obtained; and we are bound to say that coercion then was apparently a more successful way of persuading people into order in Ireland than it has ever been since. Measures of constructive statesmanship looking toward healing the causes of discontent were determined upon, and Gladstone was not a little interested, even in 1833, in the fact that Irishmen complained most seriously of having to pay the expenses of a church in which they did not worship and for which they did not care. It was subjection of the most serious and annoying kind, for it touched their religious sensibilities, and Gladstone always understood these elements of human nature and their sensitiveness, as he understood nothing else. It had seemed pretty good statesmanship to count upon the fact that no set of people are likely to be very loyal to a government which outrages them at this point. Gladstone knew his own soul and he knew this. The Disestablishment of the Irish Church already moved vaguely before the eye of the young thinker. Even the Radicals at that time were able to get his ear as they argued that all ecclesiastical property ought to be secularized, but he instantly saw that this probably touched not only the Irish, but the English Church establishment, and of course the Oxonian, who was then seeking to find in Protestantism some sort of churchmanship which he could defend against Father Newman's position, revolted at so revolutionary a measure. Father Newman was simply a High Tory in Church affairs, and it led him to Rome. Logic was with him, his premises being granted, as it never was with Gladstone.

Another very sensitive point was concealed in the fact that Nonconformists who did not believe in all the thirty-nine articles at the tender age in which such a soul as Shelley is most likely to be exhibiting its crude protests, were unable to enter the Universities unless they subscribed to these statements at the time of matriculation. The whole scheme produced dogmatism or dishonesty. Here Gladstone found himself in difficulties, but he met them with the skill of a trained dialectician. He said that the Bill proposed to give remedy could not effect much, if anything, at the Universities, because of the fact that "both in study and in discipline they aimed at the formation of a moral character, and that aim could not be attained if every student were at liberty to exclude himself from the religious training of the place." Gladstone guarded and modified his position on this matter with so much of tolerance and with so shrewd an appreciation of the larger ideals of education and justice coming into the mind of England that the speech itself held a certain promise of a deeper philosophy and a more radical statesmanship in years to come. A large majority passed the bill.

Gladstone was already recognized as the man for an emergency, and Sir Robert Peel did not need to draw the attention of the party leaders to the new member from Newark. Indeed Sir Robert Peel at this time had already felt the influence upon himself exercised by the depth and sobriety, matched with the ardor and wide range of this young man's political thought. It is useless to deny that Gladstone, young as he was, genuinely served the great Tory leader in the development of his political philosophy. As both of them had taken a "double first" in their college examinations, so now they were about to take a "double first," if such a thing were possible, in their progress toward liberal opinions.

CHAPTER VI.

JUNIOR LORD OF THE TREASURY AND AUTHOR.

Lord Grey resigned in 1834, and the King summoned the Duke of Wellington to constitute a Government to his liking. Wellington was sensible enough to know that the will which had conquered at Waterloo might be stiff enough, but scarcely mobile enough, to serve the purpose of England at this time. The Iron Duke unwittingly urged a man whose temper of mind would enable him to lead the Conservative party further, if such a thing were possible, as he had already led the party far in the direction of something quite as important as the repeal of the Corn Laws. A middle-class man was Robert Peel, yet he held the heart of the aristocracy of England in his hand. The Duke strongly urged Peel as the leader of the new Administration, and it was not long before he accepted the task and formed a Ministry. He immediately called Gladstone to the office of Junior Lord of the Treasury. The young man had already given intimation of that genius for finance which made him at last the most skillful and philosophic expositor of a Budget the Anglo-Saxon world has ever known.

Gladstone was then twenty-five years of age, and he had been lifted, in his first Parliament, to a position to which his natural taste fitted him, and in February, 1835, after having made it clear that he had the capacity and training to fill almost any position in English political life, he became Under Secretary of the Colonies. Here his great business ability demonstrated itself for a better regulation of the carriage of passengers in merchant vessels. Prose was made to yield to poetry, for he touched every topic with the light of imagination. But more than intellect and fancy were here. In this very Bill which he proposed humanity and justice to the oppressed gave evidence of their sway over his mind. Gladstone was learning much from O'Connell as the latter watched and labored for the interests of his beloved Ireland;

and he also learned another kind of lesson from Sir Robert Peel, who had O'Connell and his party to handle. This latter lesson had to do with the weakness of any policy of intimidation, and the probable outcome of a policy of justice with regard to that distressed Ireland.

But Gladstone was a long while journeying toward Home Rule, though, like every other Briton, at this time he was greatly taken with the idea of O'Connell's, that "no revolution is worth the shedding of a drop of blood;"—especially English blood by Irish malcontents. He held this along with the other idea that people ought, on general principles, to obey the English Government.

Lord John Russell soon precipitated the question as to the efficiency of the Irish State Church, and such was the feeling in Parliament and England that Sir Robert Peel, with Gladstone and Lord Aberdeen, with whom the latter was to be pleasantly associated after a while, left their offices. This leisure gave him opportunity for study, and in the course of a few months he began to work along lines of investigation which yielded him the largest results in the form of information which he kept always in large quantities for questions in Parliament and in the form of essays and reviews of ecclesiastical and literary questions whose treatment he made so thorough and attractive that these studies have passed into literature.

Before he left the office, he had measurably enlarged the sphere of his influence as a political orator and thinker.

Among the oratorical efforts of this period should be cited Gladstone's impassioned opposition to a rearrangement of Church rates, involving an abridgment of ecclesiastical prerogative. True to his cardinal conviction that religion is the basis of the greatness of a State, he drew a powerful comparison between Rome and England. "It was not," said he, "by the active strength and resistless prowess of her legions, the bold independence of her citizens, or the well-maintained equilibrium of her constitution, or by the judicious adaptation of various measures to the various circumstances of her subject States, that the Roman power was upheld. Its foundation lay in the prevailing feeling of religion. This was the superior power which curbed the license of individual rule, and engendered in the people a lofty disinterestedness and disregard of personal motives, and devotion to the glory of the republic."

The brilliant achievements which had already marked his entrance into political life augured in every way favorably for his sure and steady advancement. His friend, Bishop Wilberforce, wrote prophetically: "There is no height to which you might not fairly rise. If it please God to spare us violent convulsions and the loss of our liberties, you may at a future day wield the whole government of this land. . . Act now with a view to then."

His intellectual life also found expression in the publication of his first book, "The State in its Relations with the Church." The Catholic revival, so-called, had swept Oxford, and the spell of John Henry Newman, to whom the highest High Churchism was soon to prove too low, reached every spirit such as young Gladstone's with almost determining force. This book was the rather overwrought plea of Toryism in ecclesiastics. Now Macaulay, who had met and admired Gladstone in Rome, was the sworn opponent of Tory churchmanship. He said, on reading the book: "The Lord hath delivered him into our hands."

Gladstone might well have anticipated Mr. William Watson and prayed:

"I do not ask to have my fill
    Of wine, or love, or fame.
I do not, for a little ill,
    Against the gods exclaim.

One boon of fortune I implore,
    With one petition kneel:
At least caress me not, before
    Thou break me on thy wheel."

Macaulay's first paragraph was indeed pleasing, even if it contained something of apparent patronage. The reviewer said:

"The author of this volume is a young man of unblemished character, and of distinguished parliamentary talents, the rising hope of those stern and unbending Tories who follow, reluctantly and mutinously, a leader whose experience and eloquence are indispensable to them, but whose cautious temper and moderate opinions they abhor. It would not be at all strange if Mr. Gladstone was one of the most unpopular men in England. But we believe that we do him no more than justice when we say that his abilities and his demeanor have obtained for him the respect and good will of all parties. His first appearance in the character of an author is therefore an interesting event; and it is natural that the gentle wishes of the public should go with him to his trial."

He proceeded to congratulate the world that there was a young man in England, and especially one in public life, who would set himself to such a serious task. He said:

"We are much pleased, without any reference to the soundness or unsoundness of Mr. Gladstone's theories, to see a grave and elaborate treatise on an important part of the Philosophy of Government proceed from the pen of a young man who is rising to eminence in the House of Commons. There is little danger that people engaged in the conflicts of active life will be too much addicted to general speculation. The opposite vice is that which most easily besets them. The times and tides of business and debate tarry for no man. A politician must often talk and act before he has thought and read."

It is very doubtful if young Gladstone's friends could have asked more than this from the richly endowed Macaulay. But Gladstone's difficulty in after life was not that he went to any subjects, except, perhaps, those of modern science, unequipped and willing to talk before he had thought and read. Macaulay spoke most pleasantly, too, of Gladstone's qualifications for a work involving much philosophic and careful thinking. He said:

"Mr. Gladstone seems to us to be, in many respects, exceedingly well qualified for philosophical investigation. His mind is of large grasp; nor is he deficient in dialectical skill. But he does not give his intellect fair play. There is no want of light, but a great want of what Bacon would have called dry light. Whatever Mr. Gladstone sees is refracted and distorted by a false medium of passions and prejudices. His style bears a remarkable analogy to his mode of thinking. His rhetoric, though often good of its kind, darkens and perplexes the logic which it should illustrate. Half his acuteness and diligence, with a barren imagination and a scanty vocabulary, would have saved him

from almost all his mistakes.   He has one gift most dangerous to a
speculator, a vast command of a kind of language, grave and majestic,
but of vague and uncertain import; of a kind of language which affects
us much in the same way in which the lofty diction of the Chorus of
Clouds affected the simple-hearted Athenian.

"When propositions have been established, and nothing remains but
to amplify and decorate them, this dim magnificence may be in place.
But if it is admitted into a demonstration, it is very much worse than
absolute nonsense; just as that transparent haze, through which the
sailor sees capes and mountains of false sizes and in false bearings, is
more dangerous than utter darkness.   Now, Mr. Gladstone is fond of
employing the phraseology of which we speak in those parts of his
work which require the utmost perspicuity and precision of which
human language is capable; and in this way he deludes first himself
and his readers.   The foundations of his theory, which ought to be
buttresses of adamant, are made out of the flimsy materials which are
fit only for perorations.   This fault is one which no subsequent care
or industry can correct.   The more strictly Mr. Gladstone reasons on
his premises, the more absurd are the conclusions which he brings out;
and, when at last his good sense and good nature recoil from the horrible practical inferences to which his theory leads, he is reduced sometimes to take refuge in arguments inconsistent with his fundamental
doctrines, and sometimes to escape from the legitimate consequences
of his false principles, under cover of equally false history."

All this was introductory to the carrying out of Macaulay's plan,
namely, to crush the young Tory's theory of Church and State, which
had such admirable statement at his hands.   Macaulay disclaims any
intention of attacking the Church.   He said:

"It is possible that some persons that have read Mr. Gladstone's
book carelessly, and others who have merely heard in conversation,
or seen in a newspaper, that the member for Newark has written in
defense of the Church of England against the supporters of the voluntary system, may imagine that we are writing in defense of the
voluntary system, and that we desire the abolition of the Established
Church.   This is not the case.   It would be as unjust to accuse us

of attacking the Church, because we attack Mr. Gladstone's doctrines, as it would be to accuse Locke of wishing for anarchy, because he refuted Filmer's patriarchal theory of government, or to accuse Blackstone of recommending the confiscation of ecclesiastical property, because he denied that the right of the rector to tithe was derived from the Levitical law. It is to be observed, that Mr. Gladstone rests his case on entirely new grounds, and does not differ more widely from us than from some of those who have hitherto been considered as the most illustrious champions of the Church. He is not content with the Ecclesiastical Polity, and rejoices that the latter part of that celebrated work 'does not carry with it the weight of Hooker's authority.' He is not content with Bishop Warburton's Alliance of Church and State. 'The propositions of that work generally,' he says, 'are to be received with qualification;' and he agrees with Bolingbroke in thinking that Warburton's whole theory rests on fiction. He is still less satisfied with Paley's defense of the Church, which he pronounces to be 'tainted by the original vice of false ethical principles,' and 'full of the seeds of evil.' He conceives that Dr. Chalmers has taken a partial view of the subject, and 'put forth much questionable matter.' In truth, on almost every point on which we are opposed to Mr. Gladstone, we have on our side the authority of some divine, eminent as a defender of existing establishments.

"Mr. Gladstone's whole theory rests on this great fundamental proposition, that the propagation of religious truth is one of the principal ends of government, as government. If Mr. Gladstone has not proved this proposition, his system vanishes at once."

He had now stated the fundamental principle upon which Gladstone's theory rested. In Macaulay's handling of the subject he was not unfair enough to give Gladstone slender opportunity to speak for himself. Indeed, he says:

"The following paragraph is a specimen of the arguments by which Mr. Gladstone has, as he conceives, established his great fundamental proposition:

" 'We may state the same proposition in a more general form, in which it surely must command universal assent. Wherever there is power in the universe, that power is the property of God, the King of that universe—his property of right, however for a time withholden or abused. Now this property is, as it were, realized, is used according to the will of the owner, when it is used for the purposes he has ordained, and in the temper of mercy, justice, truth, and faith which he has taught us. But those principles can never be truly, never can be permanently, entertained in the human breast, except by a continual reference to their source and the supply of the Divine grace. The powers, therefore, that dwell in individuals acting as a government, as well as those that dwell in individuals acting for themselves, can only be secured for right uses by applying to them a religion.'

"Here are propositions of vast and indefinite extent, conveyed in language which has a certain obscure dignity and sanctity, attractive, we doubt not, to many minds. But the moment that we examine these propositions closely, the moment that we bring them to the test by running over but a very few of the particulars which are included in them, we find them to be false and extravagant. The doctrine which 'must surely command universal assent' in this, that every association of human beings which exercises any power whatever, that is to say, every association of human beings, is bound, as such association, to profess a religion. Imagine the effect which would follow if this principle were really in force during four-and-twenty hours. Take one instance out of a million. A stage-coach company has power over its horses. This power is the property of God. It is used according to the will of God when it is used with mercy. But the principle of mercy can never be truly or permanently entertained in the human breast without continual reference to God. The powers, therefore, that dwell in individuals, acting as a stage-coach company, can only be secured for right uses by applying to them a religion. Every stage-coach company ought, therefore, in its collective capacity, to profess some one faith, to have its articles, and its public worship, and its tests. That this conclusion, and an infinite number of other conclusions equally strange, follow of necessity from Mr. Gladstone's principle, is as certain as it is that two and two make four. And, if the legitimate conclusions be so absurd, there must be something unsound in the principle."

It is a curious fact that Macaulay placed his finger at once upon the quality of Gladstone's language, insisting that it had "a certain obscure dignity and sanctity, attractive, no doubt, to many minds." Gladstone never lost his churchliness of literary style. After dealing with this passage quoted from Gladstone, Macaulay says:

"We will quote another passage of the same sort:

" 'Why, then, we now come to ask, should the governing body in a state profess a religion? First, because it is composed of individual men; and they, being appointed to act in a definite moral capacity, must sanctify their acts done in that capacity by the offices of religion; inasmuch as the acts cannot otherwise be acceptable to God, or anything but sinful and punishable in themselves. And whenever we turn our face away from God in our conduct, we are living atheistically. . . In fulfilment, then, of his obligations as an individual, the statesman must be a worshiping man. But his acts are public—the powers and instruments with which he works are public—acting under and by the authority of the law, he moves at his word ten thousand subject arms; and because such energies are thus essentially public, and wholly out of the range of mere individual agency, they must be sanctified not only by the private personal prayers and piety of those who fill public situations, but also by public acts of the men composing the public body. They must offer prayer and praise in their public and collective character—in that character wherein they constitute the organ of the nation, and wield its collective force. Wherever there is a reasoning agency, there is a moral duty and responsibility involved in it. The governors are reasoning agents for the nation, in their conjoint acts as such. And therefore there must be attached to this agency, as that without which none of our responsibilities can be met, a religion. And this religion must be that of the conscience of the governor, or none.'

"Here again we find propositions of vast sweep, and of sound so orthodox and solemn that many good people, we doubt not, have been greatly edified by it. But let us examine the words closely; and it will immediately become plain that, if these principles be once admitted, there is an end of all society. No combination can be formed for any purpose of mutual help, for trade, for public works, for the relief of the sick or the poor, for the promotion of art or science, unless the members of the combination agree in their theological opinions. Take any such combination at random, the London and Birmingham Railway Company, for example, and observe to what consequences Mr. Gladstone's arguments inevitably lead. 'Why should the directors of the Railway Company, in their collective capacity, profess a religion? First, because the direction is composed of individual men appointed to act in a definite moral capacity, bound to look carefully to the property, the limbs, and the lives of their fellow-creatures, bound to act diligently for their constituents, bound to govern their servants with humanity and justice, bound to fulfill with fidelity many important contracts. They must, therefore, sanctify their acts by the offices of religion or these acts will be sinful and punishable in themselves.

" 'In fulfillment, then, of his obligations as an individual, the Director of the London and Birmingham Railway Company must be a worshiping man. But his acts are public. He acts for a body. And because these energies are out of the range of his mere individual agency, they must be sanctified by public acts of devotion. The Railway directors must offer prayer and praise in their public and collective character, in that character wherewith they constitute the organ of the company, and wield its collected power. Wherever there is reasoning agency, there is moral responsibility. The directors are reasoning agents for the company. And therefore there must be attached to this agency, as that without which none of our responsibilities can be met, a religion. And this religion must be that of the conscience of the director himself, or none. There must be public worship and a test. No Jew, no Socinian, no Presbyterian, no Catholic, no Quaker, must be permitted to be the organ of the company, and to wield its collected force.' Would Mr. Gladstone really defend this proposition?"

It is thus that the well-informed historian, uttering the voice of England's somewhat worldly common sense, pushes his inquiry upon the churchman. No more fair treatment has any young man of first-

rate genius received from an elder essayist. Macaulay's fairness is
proved also when near the conclusion of the essay, he says:

"We have now said almost all that we think it necessary to say
respecting Mr. Gladstone's theory. And perhaps it would be safest for
us to stop here. It is much easier to pull down than to build up. Yet,
that we may give Mr. Gladstone his revenge, we will state concisely our
own views respecting the alliance of Church and State.

"We set out in company with Warburton, and remain with him
pretty sociably till we come to his contract; a contract which Mr.
Gladstone very properly designates as a fiction. We consider the primary end of government as a purely temporal end, the protection of
the persons and the property of men.

"We think that government, like every other contrivance of human
wisdom, from the highest to the lowest, is likely to answer its main end
best when it is constructed with a single view to that end. Mr. Gladstone, who loves Plato, will not quarrel with us for illustrating our
proposition, after Plato's fashion, from the most familiar objects. Take
cutlery, for example. A blade which is designed both to shave and to
carve will certainly not shave so well as a razor, or carve so well as a
carving-knife. An academy of painting, which should also be a bank,
would in all probability, exhibit very bad pictures and discount very
bad bills. A gas company, which should also be an infant school society,
would, we apprehend, light the streets ill, and teach the children ill. On
this principle, we think that government should be organized solely
with a view to its main end; and that no part of its efficiency for that
end should be sacrificed in order to promote any other end, however
excellent.

"But does it follow from hence that governments ought never to
pursue any end other than their main end? In no wise. Though it
is desirable that every institution should have a main end, and should
be so formed as to be in the highest degree efficient for that main end;
yet if, without any sacrifice of its efficiency for that end, it can pursue
any other good end, it ought to do so. Thus, the end for which a
hospital is built is the relief of the sick, not the beautifying of the street.
To sacrifice the health of the sick to splendor of architectural effect,

to place the building in a bad air only that it may present a more commanding front to a great public place, to make the wards hotter or cooler than they ought to be, in order that the columns and windows of the exterior may please the passers-by, would be monstrous. But if, without any sacrifice of the chief object, the hospital can be made an ornament to the metropolis, it would be absurd not to make it so.

"In the same manner, if a government can, without any sacrifice of its main end, promote any other good work, it ought to do so. The encouragement of the fine arts, for example, is by no means the main end of government; and it would be absurd, in constituting a government, to bestow a thought on the question, whether it would be a government likely to train Raphaels and Domenichinos. But it by no means follows that it is improper for a government to form a national gallery of pictures. The same may be said of patronage bestowed on learned men, of the publication of archives, of the collecting of libraries, menageries, plants, fossils, antiques, of journeys and voyages for purposes of geographical discovery or astronomical observation. It is not for these ends that government may have at its command resources which will enable it, without injury to its main end, to pursue these collateral ends far more effectually than any individual or any voluntary association could do. If so, government ought to pursue these collateral ends.

"It is still more evidently the duty of government to promote, always in subordination to its main end, everything which is useful as a means for the attaining of that main end. The improvement of steam navigation, for example, is by no means a primary object of government. But as steam vessels are useful for the purpose of national defense, and for the purpose of facilitating intercourse between distant provinces, and of thereby consolidating the force of the empire, it may be the bounden duty of government to encourage ingenious men to perfect an invention which so directly tends to make the State more efficient for its great primary end."

But this is not enough. He adds, after outlining the necessary failure of a church which depends upon the State:

"A statesman, judging on our principles, would pronounce without hesitation that a church, such as we have last described, never ought to have been set up. Further than this we will not venture to speak for him. He would doubtless remember that the world is full of institutions which, though they never ought to have been set up, yet, having been set up, ought not to be rudely pulled down; and that it is often wise in practice to be content with the mitigation of an abuse which, looking at it in the abstract, we might feel impatient to destroy."

He concludes by saying:

"We have done; and nothing remains but that we part from Mr. Gladstone with the courtesy of antagonists who bear no malice. We dissent from his opinions, but we admire his talents; we respect his integrity and benevolence; and we hope that he will not suffer political avocations so entirely to engross him, as to leave him no leisure for literature and philosophy."

Macaulay was abundantly pleased with Gladstone in after years.

Gladstone himself, in his famous "Chapter of Autobiography," speaks thus of Macaulay's review of his book:

"An early copy of the Review containing the powerful essay of Lord Macaulay was sent to me, and I found that to the main proposition, sufficiently startling, of the work itself, the Reviewer had added this assumption, that it contemplated not indeed persecution, but yet the retrogressive progress of disabling and disqualifying from civil office all those who did not adhere to the religion of the State. Before (I think) the number of the 'Edinburgh Review' for April, 1839, could have been in the hands of the public, I had addressed to Lord (then Mr.) Macaulay the following letter, which I shall make no apology for inserting, inasmuch as it will precede and introduce one more morsel of his writing, for which the public justly shows a keen and insatiable appetite."

"6 Carlton Gardens, April 10th, 1839.

"Dear Sir,

"I have been favored with a forthcoming number of the 'Edinburgh Review,' and I perhaps too much presume upon the bare acquaintance with you of which alone I can boast, in thus unceremoniously assuming you to be the author of the article entitled 'Church and State,' and in offering you my very warm and cordial thanks for the manner in which you have

ROBERT PEEL

BENJ. DISRAELI

treated both the work and the author on whom you deigned to bestow your attention. In whatever you write, you can hardly hope for the privilege of most anonymous productions, a real concealment; but if it had been possible not to recognize you, I should have questioned your authorship in this particular case, because the candor and single-mindedness which it exhibits are, in one who has long been connected in the most distinguished manner with political party, so rare as to be almost incredible.

"I hope to derive material benefit, at some more tranquil season, from a consideration of your argument throughout. I am painfully sensible, whenever I have occasion to reopen the book, of its shortcomings, not only of the subject, but even of my own conceptions; and I am led to suspect that, under the influence of most kindly feelings, you have omitted to criticise many things besides the argument, which might fairly have come within your animadversion.

"In the meantime I hope you will allow me to apprise you that on one material point especially I am not so far removed from you as you suppose. I am not conscious that I have said either that the Test Act should be repealed, or that it should not have been passed: and though on such subjects language has many bearings which escape the view of the writer at the moment when the pen is in his hand, yet I think that I can hardly have put forth either of these propositions, because I have never entertained the corresponding sentiments. Undoubtedly I should speak of the pure abstract idea of Church and State as implying that they are coextensive; and I should regard the present composition of the State of the United Kingdom as a deviation from that pure idea, but only in the same sense as all differences of religious opinion in the Church are a deviation from its pure idea, while I not only allow that they are permitted, but believe that (within limits) they were intended to be permitted. There are some of these deflections from abstract theory which appear to me allowable; and that of the admission of persons not holding the national creed into civil office is one which, in my view, must be determined by times and circumstances. At the same time I do not recede from any protest which I have made against the principle, that religious differences are irrelevant to the question of competency for civil office: but I would take my stand between the opposite extremes, the one that no such differences are to be taken into view, the other that all such differences are to constitute disqualifications.

"I need hardly say the question I raise is not whether you have misrepresented me, for, were I disposed to anything so weak, the whole internal evidence and clear intention of your article would confute me: indeed, I feel I ought to apologize for even supposing that you may have been mistaken in the apprehension of my meaning, and I freely admit on the other hand the possibility that, totally without my own knowledge, my language may have led to such an interpretation.

"In these lacerating times one clings to anything of personal kindness in the past, to husband it for the future, and if you will allow me I shall earnestly desire to carry with me such a recollection of your mode of dealing with the subject; inasmuch as the attainment of truth, we shall agree, so materially depends upon the temper, in which the search for it is instituted and conducted.

"I did not mean to have troubled you at so much length, and I have only to add that I am, with much respect,

"Dear Sir,

"Very truly yours,

"T. B. MACAULAY, Esq."   "W. E. GLADSTONE."

"To this letter I promptly received the following reply:

"3 Clarges Street, April 11th, 1839.

"My Dear Sir,

"I have very seldom been more gratified than by the very kind note which I have just received from you. Your book itself, and everything that I heard about you, though almost all my information came—to the honor, I must say, of our troubled times—from people very strongly opposed to you in politics, led me to regard you with respect and goodwill, and I am truly glad that I have succeeded in marking those feelings. I was half afraid when I read myself over again in print, that the button, as is too common in controversial fencing, even between friends, had once or twice come off the foil.

"I am very glad to find that we do not differ so widely as I had appre-hended about the Test Act. I can easily explain the way in which I was misled. Your general principle is that religious non-conformity ought to be a disqualification for civil office. In page 238 you say that the true and authentic mode of ascertaining conformity is the Act of Com-munion. I thought, therefore, that your theory pointed directly to a renewal of the Test Act. And I do not recollect that you have ever used any expression importing that your theory ought in practice to be modified by any considerations of civil prudence. All the exceptions that you mention are, as far as I remember, founded on positive contract—not one on expediency, even in cases where expediency is so strong and so obvious that most statesmen would call it necessity. If I had understood that you meant your rules to be followed out in practice only so far as might be consistent with the peace and good government of society, I should certainly have expressed myself very differently in several parts of my article.

"Accept my warm thanks for your kindness, and believe me, with every good wish.

"My Dear Sir,

"Very truly yours,

"T. B. MACAULAY."

"W. E. GLADSTONE, Esq., M. P."

Meantime Gladstone was learning the fallacies of Toryism by other means.   Poor Sir John Gladstone was preparing to say of William, when the time of the Corn Law agitation should come: "There stands my son, helping to ruin his country."   Another was watching. The exquisite and brilliant Disraeli was waiting for a chance to do something, and Gladstone was slowly but surely making ready to leave such room in the Tory mansion as would grant to the audacious master of words an excellent front apartment.

CHAPTER VII.

A GREAT PROBLEM IN SIGHT.

It is certain that, under the new Government, Ireland's condition was less distressing, and Thomas Drummond, whom Gladstone in many ways admired greatly, almost persuaded England that ability and courage would settle the question without much legal change. Orangemen intimidated Catholics in the North, and the Catholics often made things disorderly elsewhere. Landlords and tenants were at war, and Drummond acted upon the principle that there was one law for all. This ought not to have seemed remarkable, but it was a new view to both classes. The very landlords who afterwards were outraged at Gladstone were exasperated now with Drummond. O'Connell looked upon Drummond as "a man of the present," and in spite of Gladstone's insistence and his friends' reiteration that the latter could not be anything but a Tory believing that coercion was what the Irish·people needed, O'Connell still, as he said, "claimed the half of him for the future."

Many a time, in after years, Gladstone put his finger upon the words of Thomas Drummond, spoken in his letter to the magistrates of Tipperary: "Property has its duties as well as its rights." True, the magistrates of that time suppressed the letter for a little while, but years afterwards it seemed to be embodied in flesh and blood in Gladstone.

In 1838 the Poor Law was passed, and one of the main causes of discontent was removed, and Parliament enacted that tithes should not be levied on the tenant, but rather on the landlord.

On June 20, 1837, the King had died and the young Victoria was awakened at Kensington to meet the Archbishop of Canterbury and the Lord Chamberlain, who told her of her uncle's decease, and that she was to be crowned Queen. The fact that the Kingdom of Hanover

84

could not pass into the hands of a female sovereign delivered England of all problems which might have come had the two kingdoms continued under one head as hitherto. Queen Victoria came to power immediately after her uncle left the world, succeeding a man who at last became kind and good-natured enough, but who had been distinguished in middle life by a blunt stubbornness which oftentimes became a little contemptuous of the rights of others, and especially irritated at what we now call the progress of mankind. Victoria's Coronation-day was indeed the advent of another spirit in English life which the young Queen brought with her,—a spirit in which constitutional government, enlivened with larger sympathy for the rights of the people, and emboldened with the largest hope for better days, was sure to thrive and win its way. Her grace and beauty, her dignity and womanliness, were all able to obtain for her a popularity which grew at once more deep and secure because of the conviction which delighted England that the sovereign was a woman of intellectual power. Parliament, of course, was dissolved, and the Queen was held up as a person who now needed the support of her friends, and that body was begged to send in a Government which she would like. When the votes were counted, the House of Commons was found to be very much like the old one. The Whigs, Radicals and Conservatives, however, came up from the counties and boroughs, which had apparently changed their political complexion. The party decidedly victorious was the party of Daniel O'Connell.

The short session produced almost nothing of importance, but when Parliament reassembled, it was evident that everything must wait for the coronation of the Queen. London was crowded upon that occasion only as it was crowded sixty years later, at the Diamond Jubilee. The Duke of Wellington rode amidst a storm of applause and cheers. He was at the very height of his popularity, but the day of the Duke's policy was passing. The day of a battle for ideas more distinctly important to England than the battle of Waterloo had come. Ireland was everywhere pressing for attention, when Parliament opened for business. The Government had to resign in the face of famine and discontent, even in England. Sir Robert Peel, who had the management of her new administration, proposed a list of ministers and asked that certain ladies who had been related to the Court in the past—members of the Queen's household—should be dismissed. The Queen refused, and Sir Robert declined his task. Melbourne tried to save the hour, but all these things were pointing only in one direction,—privilege and class were being attacked, and popular sympathies were gaining the day. Lord Brougham stirred everybody by telling the ministers that they had lost the confidence of the House of Commons, that they had never had the confidence of the House of Lords, and that they only kept the faith of the Queen. The truth was that England did not want these gentlemen in office. They could not carry any measures, and that is what officials exist for. The whole realm was beholding the imbecility of a Government standing on its apex instead of on its base. Peel had no responsibility, and could stand off and wait, while the Bedchamber question was inspiring other agitations in the mind of England.

Gladstone wrote in 1875 as follows on the former subject:

"It was a question whether the ladies of the Court, who had been politically appointed, should or should not retire from office. The Queen, not yet twenty years old, but capable of contracting attachments at once quick and durable, resisted the demand. There can be no doubt that if Sir Robert Peel had been allowed at that time to proceed with his task, the Ministry he would then have formed would have been possessed of reasonable stability. But the power of the young Sovereign, applied with the skillful use of opportunity, sufficed to prolong the duration of the Liberal Government until the summer of 1841, a period of nearly two and a half years. Its exercise produced, at the time, no revulsion in the public mind. The final judgment upon the conduct of the parties to the crisis has been more favorable to the Minister than to the Monarch. Baron Stockmar himself has expressed this opinion. But the question specially involved was the claim of the woman in her early youth. It was a claim of which, confined within certain limits, equity would surely have recommended the allowance. Possibly it was suspicion, the most obstinate among the besetting sins of politicians, even in men of upright nature, which interfered on the side of rigor."

In the course of the winter of 1838-39, which he passed in Rome, he had met Miss Glynne, daughter of Sir Stephen Richard Glynne, of Flintshire. Gladstone soon sued for her heart and hand, and their married life has been a noble witness to the sacredness and sublimity of perfect affection.

Gladstone wrote these words in his review of the "Life of the Prince Consort:" "Happy marriages, it may be thankfully acknowledged, are rather the rule among us, than the exception; but even among happy marriages this marriage was exceptional, so nearly did the union of thought, heart, and action both fulfill the ideal, and bring duality near to the borders of identity. Not uncommonly, the wife is to the husband as the adjective is to the substantive." No one has entertained or defended loftier views of the marriage relation than he, and no home in England has furnished brighter or dearer pictures to our age of the operation of those forces on which governments as well as homes rest than Hawarden Castle.

In 1841 Gladstone again found himself in an official position. A reform had been inaugurated in the Postoffice, Parliament had constituted its committee on education and left the management of that subject in its hands with thirty thousand pounds sterling, the Queen had married Prince Albert and added his learning and poise to her own accomplishments. He furnished England with a royal gentleman— something Englishmen had not beheld for a long time. Palmerston had made his play with the Spaniards, and then with the Carlists, who had been defeated. The war between the Turks and Egyptians had broken out, and Palmerston had sought to strengthen the power of the Sultan. The Turk had been overpowered, the poor in England had suffered in spite of all beneficial legislation, but most important of all, the Anti-Corn Law League had been organized and was prospering, under Villiers, Richard Cobden and John Bright. The Melbourne ministry had fallen before the violence of English opposition, which never can tolerate indebtedness and expenditure unprovided for by John Bull, shopkeeper. The last effort to handle this deficit was a proposal which agitated the whole question of protection and free trade. Peel had the ear of England when he said that such a Ministry was incapable of handling such a large question. Down it went, and Sir Robert Peel brought to his help William Ewart Gladstone, whose understanding of the "dismal science" of political economy, whose grasp of the large principles of finance, and whose lucidity of statement when it was necessary to explain these principles and their application, were unmatched in all the realm. It is well to understand that Sir Robert Peel had proposed, instead of a duty of eight shillings per quarter on wheat, a sliding scale, and on this question an appeal had been made to the country. To Gladstone had been given the post of Vice-President of the Board of Trade and Master of the Mint. It is to be noted that even at this period, when finance demanded so much attention, Gladstone's interest in Ireland was pronounced, and he had wished and hoped to be sent to Dublin Castle as Chief Secretary. We have it upon the authority of Mrs. Gladstone that he was quite depressed by his new appointment, and that "from the very outset of his career he had an intense ambition to take hold of the Irish question."

The first Budget of the new Government was that of 1842, to present which involved the explanation of a revised tariff, and Mr. Gladstone had to make exposition in answer to the thousand questions of Parliament upon the effect of this tariff on more than a thousand articles of trade. The principle involved the reimposition, for a term of three years, of the income tax. There was certainly necessity for this, or for something like it, and it has been compared with the income tax which Pitt insisted upon as necessary to carry on the war with France.

Gladstone stood close to Peel and helped to carry what must have seemed a continuously recurring deficiency. The young financier insisted, in season and out of season, upon financial reforms which would enable England to get resources annually of increasing proportions. There was a large element of protection in the Budget, and it favored home manufactures and the farmers. Sternly did they both refuse to make any large reduction of the duties on corn, but the effect of Cobden's argument and the utterances of Villiers and Bright were already manifest in the fact that the sliding scale on this topic was modified. It was a distinct movement toward free trade, and yet a heroic effort to clutch at protection. It is doubful if Peel could have accomplished his act of stretching from one point to another and holding both, even with the slight satisfactoriness which the act occasioned, if it had not been for Gladstone. Fortunately for England's opinion of the commercial genius of this son of the Liverpool merchant, fortunately for Peel's administration, fortunately for those who on the one side thought free trade had obtained too little and those who on the other side thought free trade had obtained too much, prosperity came to the realm, and Gladstone's defense of the Budget appeared to be even a more brilliant prophecy than it was when he made the desert of finance blossom as the rose, by his eloquent exposition.

It was now becoming evident to sober England, that Gladstone was all that Sir Robert Peel had been, with a still livelier imagination and perhaps a greater ability to hold fast to the revered past and grasp the rather undesired future. He was a greater orator, he was a greater financier, and people said he was a greater "straddler." In Gladstone's case, this is to say that his mind was comprehensive enough to see that evolution in opinion is the law of all progress; and, to adapt a saying of Douglas Jerrold, Gladstone knew it is not profanity of the old moon to indicate one's admiration and willingness to take light from the new. The same heavens furnish both.

Together were Gladstone and Lord Aberdeen associated, as in the previous ministry, and together they dealt with the affair of the boundary between the English colonies and the United States and labored to promote cordiality, which at last Guizot and Aberdeen put in due form.

It is most interesting to find that here Gladstone's mind was devoting some of its best hours to the Irish question. In Fitzpatrick's excellent collection of the letters of Daniel O'Connell, we have interesting information with regard to the persons who embodied at that moment a spirit with which Gladstone would have much to do in later years. The Editor says:

"Old politicians will remember three prominent members—Colonel Verner, Sibthorpe, and Perceval. Two of the trio looked as if they had never need to shave, the third colonel was all beard—a most unusual display in days which knew not a full-bearded Premier, as now. All three having opposed a small grant to Maynooth College, as 'subversive of morality,' O'Connell called them 'the Church militant of the House,' and raised a peal of laughter by concluding with a parody on Dryden's verses.

> " 'Three colonels in three different counties born
> Did Lincoln, Sligo, and Armagh adorn;
> The first in gravity of face surpassed,
> The next in bigotry—in both the last.
> The force of Nature could no further go;
> To beard the third she shaved the other two.'

"Canon O'Rorke in his 'Life of O'Connell' states on hearsay (page 249) that the above was written by Ronayne, who showed it to O'Connell merely for his opinion."

At later dates Gladstone found it necessary to keep some company which in the earlier hours of his career he might not have looked upon with delight. It is at this time that he is least sure he has found his vocation as an associate of Peel in Government. He writes to his intimate friend:

"My Dear Hope:— . . . I am very well content to look forward and pack up my things. If there were any reasons which made it desirable with reference to the future, or the paulo-post future, that I should be in office under the present Government, I think they are now satisfied and exhausted. As connected with trade, I am certainly a cause of weakness and not of strength to Sir Robert Peel in the two Houses of Parliament. It is not my opinion that on this score he will readily part with me: but it removes a cause of regret that I should have had, if the case had stood otherwise. And I do not think that another session or two would pass without my exciting more mistrust. I am strongly and painfully impressed with recent disclosures concerning the physical state of the peasantry: for whose sake mainly, as my notion has been, we have maintained the Corn Laws. Last session I had to answer a speech of Cobden's on this subject, five-sixths of which I should have been glad to have spoken. My conviction is, that our course in these matters has been generally right—but it involves progression, and it is a high probability that one bad harvest, or at all events two, would break up the Corn Law and with it the party. Hitherto, it has worked better than could have been hoped, but I cannot deny that it is a law mainly dependent on the weather. I have not in office spoken so much free trade as Sir Robert Peel. On the contrary, scarcely anything of dogma is to be gathered from my effusions, but people will naturally and properly bear from him a great deal which they will not take from a whipper-snapper.

"The purpose of Parliamentary life resolves itself with me simply and wholly into one question—Will it ever afford the means under God of rectifying the relations between the Church and the State, and give me the opportunity of setting forward such a work? There must be either such a readjustment, or a violent crisis. The present state of discipline cannot be borne for very many years; and here lies the pinch. Towards the settlement of money questions something has been done by the Church Commission and the Government, and I think they may do more.

"As to the general objects of political life, they are not my objects. Upon the whole, I do not expect from the good sense of the English people, the force of the principle of property, and the conservative influence of the Church, less than the maintenance of our present monarchical and parliamentary circumstances: And I do not flatter myself with the notion that this will be better done by my remaining to take part in it. But the real renovation of the country does not depend upon law and government: and those who desire to take part in the work, except so far as it is connected with the specific readjustments to which I have referred, must, I think, seek their province elsewhere.

"Here is a very slight and naked sketch. If I were to fill it up, I should break the back of a rickety postman who daily carries the Fettercairn letters at two miles an hour toward Montrose.

"Believe me always

"Your obliged and attached friend,

"W. E. GLADSTONE."

Other equally able men have felt that nothing is gained by overloading the postman at such times as these.

As a young man, Gladstone cordially enjoyed the privilege extended him of visiting at the house of one of the most notable of England's bibliophiles, the Right Honorable Thomas Grenville. This high-minded benefactor and friend of all who love literature has left his name forever associated with the ever-widening influence of the British Museum, for to that institution he gave the invaluable collection called The Grenville Collection. He had been, as Gladstone was later, a

Christ Church student and the younger scholar shared many of his tastes. At his table, Gladstone was made acquainted with the learning of Macaulay, the wit of Sydney Smith, the gravity of Hallam, the geniality of Samuel Rogers the poet-banker, and the multifarious information and sincere patriotism of a fascinating foreigner who was to be Librarian of the British Museum and who was to be known also as Senator of Italy, and Sir Anthony Panizzi, K. C. B.   Grenville at that time was very interesting to the young statesman.   Fox had trusted Grenville with arranging the terms of treaty between Great Britain and America, after the separation.   He had been sent by Earl Spencer in 1794 as Minister Extraordinary to the court of Vienna, and, after having been Privy Councilor and Special Ambassador to the court of Berlin, he had become Chief Justice in Eyre in 1800.   He had seen much of the great men of whom he talked as entertainingly with Gladstone as with the elder and then more illustrious members of the circle of friends he often invited to dine with him or to pass a day or an evening with him and his books.   Gladstone often referred to the delight with which this or that gem now in the Grenville collection in the British Museum was welcomed and exhibited, read and enriched with notes from the old bibliophile's hand, for, like Gladstone in after life, Grenville permitted no curiosity as to rare tomes to keep him from enjoying their treasures.   Panizzi's biographer tells us that Sydney Smith "with reverent appreciation remarked to Panizzi, apropos of the host's dignity and cheerfulness, 'There, that is a man from whom we all ought to learn how to grow old.'"   Gladstone truly learned the lesson as to the fact that a green old age is as secure as May itself in the serene companionship of books.   He enjoyed, even as a young man, the old man's delight as he gathered the twenty thousand volumes for which he had gladly paid nearly fifty thousand guineas, and, in the British Museum with Sir Anthony, he after related book-yarns in which Grenville, many years before, and he, later, figured as one who had landed a rare or valuable "find."   One can fancy the pleasure to Gladstone of such association as would invite him into all the interesting conversation consequent upon being allowed to read and discuss the following letter, for example, which Grenville the host had received from the bibliomaniac, Panizzi:

"B. M., May 2, 1845.

"My Dear Sir,

"I hope you will do me the honor of placing in your library a Latin poem, by one Thomas Prati, printed at Treviso about 1475, on the martyrdom said to have been suffered in that year by one Simon or Symeon, at the hands of the Jews of Trento. The event seems to have created a great sensation at the time, and even at a much later period its truth has been the subject of learned investigations.

"It may be true that a boy was murdered at Trento in March, 1475, but that he fell a sacrifice to the Jews' hatred of our religion, is as incredible as it is unproved. So late as about a hundred years ago, a dissertation was inserted in the 48th volume of Calagiero Raccolta d'opuscoli, page 409 (De cultu Sancti Simonis, the martyr, has been canonized and his life and miracles are chronicled in the Acta Sanctorum Pueri Tridentini et Martyris apud Venetos). That dissertation, written to prove the truth of the story, seems to me conclusive against it.

"Several poems are said to have been written on this subject. One of them in Italian stanzas, utterly worthless, by one Fra Giovanni, was printed so late as 1690, at Padua, and is in the British Museum. Federici (Tipografia Trevigiana, p. 91) mentions four tracts printed by Celerio in 1480, on the martyrdom of Simon, but none written by Prati. He moreover mentions two (p. 52) printed by Gherard de Lysa, one of which would seem to be precisely like that which I now offer to you, if we were to judge from the title only, but the particulars into which he enters show, 1st, that Federici never saw even the book which he describes; 2nd, that whatever that book be, it is a different one from this.

"As you possess the very rare edition of Dante, published by Tuppo, at Naples, in the colophon of which Tuppo alludes to the murder of Simon 'non sono molti anni,' and as the fact is said to have happened in 1475, according to all authorities, it may be of some interest to you to possess an uncommonly rare book, which may be of use in fixing at about 1480 the date of your Dante, the very year when Tuppo began to print separately from Reussinger.

"Yours, etc., etc.,

"A. PANIZZI."

A decade afterward, we find Gladstone, although apparently overwhelmed with other labors, coming up out of them all for a breath of fresh air, as was his wont, and writing to Panizzi, as though there were no other than literary questions in all the universe.

Mr. Gladstone, writing at a much later date, to the son of his old friend, Lord Aberdeen, with whom he was closely associated in Cabinet life, said:

"I may first refer to the earliest occasion on which I saw him; for it illustrates a point not unimportant in his history. On an evening in the month of January, 1835, during what is called the short Government of Sir Robert Peel, I was sent for by Sir Robert Peel, and received from him the offer, which I accepted, of the Under-Secretaryship for the Colonies. From him I went on to your father, who was then Secretary of State in that department, and who was thus to be, in official home-talk, my master. Without any apprehension of hurting you, I may confess that I went in fear and trembling. I knew Lord Aberdeen only by public rumor. Distinction of itself, naturally and properly, rather alarms the young. I had heard of his high character, but I had also heard of him as a man of cold manners, and close and even haughty reserve. It was dusk when I entered his room—the room on the first floor, with the bow-window looking to the Park—so that I saw his figure rather than his countenance. I do not recollect the matter of the conversation; but I well remember that before I had been three minutes with him, all my apprehensions had melted away as snow in the sun; and I came away from that interview conscious indeed—as who could fail to be conscious?—of his dignity, but of a dignity so tempered by a peculiar purity and gentleness, and so associated with impressions of his kindness, and even friendship, that I believe I thought more about the wonder of his being at that time so misunderstood by the outer world, than about the new duties and responsibilities of my new office. I was only, I think, for about ten weeks his under-secretary. But as some men hate those whom they have injured, so others love those whom they have obliged; and his friendship continued warm and uninter-mitting for the subsequent twenty-six years of his life."

CHAPTER VIII.

GLADSTONE AND SIR ROBERT PEEL.

The year 1843 brought O'Connell forward with his proposal for the repeal of the Union. He predicted that the proposition would succeed in the course of the year. Monster meetings were gathered, and while O'Connell was urging his compatriots to avoid bloodshed, he was arrested for sedition and conspiracy. A jury of Protestants convicted him, and he was fined and imprisoned. Five lawyers in the House of Lords reversed the judgment in his favor. The spirit of O'Connell was broken, because his health was in no way able to support the drafts made upon his power and he had no impulse for a new agitation. Four years were to elapse, as he quietly went down the hill to the grave, passing out of sight in 1847. England continued to evict tenants who had taken the bad lands of Ireland owned by landlords in England, and made them rich and valuable, and of course Ireland continued to rebel and outrage and murder. A superficial statesmanship—Peel was always master of this kind of thing, while he was capable of far better achievements—passed a law forbidding Irishmen to carry arms except by special license, and, to equal this by an act of genuine statesmanship, he issued a commission to inquire into the causes of Irish discontent.

Gladstone's service to him at this point had been of the greatest importance, and now they were to separate. Peel proposed that the Government should grant to the College of Maynooth an increased amount for education. Nothing could have been more characteristic of Sir Robert Peel than this effort to conciliate Irish opinion. At this college the Roman Catholic priesthood were educated. Nine thousand pounds had been spent the year before; it was now proposed that twenty-six thousand pounds should be spent there, and, further, that the laity should have three Queen's colleges for unsectarian education.

Gladstone was placed in a perplexing situation. He could not be accused of any foolish anti-Romanism, but he was the author of a work on Church and State and he was trying to be consistent with that production. Sensitive as only the father of one literary child may be, he beheld everything from the outlook occupied by the cradle of this infant which was to give him a good deal of difficulty, as his opinions grew and his outlook widened in the years to follow. Besides, he had not fully considered the measure, as he insisted. Gladstone has often been accused of postponing the consideration of certain themes because they involved just the difficulties presented here. It was a good time for him to insist upon his own conscience, and yet it was a poor time to be what is known as a "crank," especially if the basis of it all was the fact that he had written a book from whose decisions robust common sense was sure to lead him to depart, at least in some measure, by and by. His old Eton friend, Manning, who was yet a Protestant, urged him to remain in Peel's cabinet. George Cornewall Lewis and others who admired Gladstone's financial genius, and Robert Lowe, who had no patience whatever with Gladstone's wasting his time on ecclesiastical matters, urged him to pause before he threw away his time and gifts as a financial administrator "on a mere matter of religious agitation." Gladstone, however, was as firm in his purpose as if he were Bishop of London—an office which many of his most intelligent admirers believed he would have filled as none other had ever filled it. He resigned and sought to defend the act with that turgid and indirect utterance which, we are bound to say, has betrayed him whenever he has forced himself or been forced into a position such as this. He now astonished a good many of his friends by saying that while he resigned his place in the Administration, he would not oppose the scheme of the Government as a private member. He afterwards wrote:

"My whole purpose was to place myself in a position in which I should be free to consider my course without being liable to any just suspicion on the ground of personal interest. It is not profane if I now say 'With a great price obtained I this freedom.' The political association in which I stood was to me, at the time, the alpha and omega of public life. The Government of Sir Robert Peel was be-

E. G. STANLEY

THE RIGHT HONORABLE THE EARL OF ABERDEEN, K.G.

lieved to be of immovable strength. My place, as President of the Board of Trade, was at the very kernel of its most interesting operations, for it was in progress from year to year, with continually waxing courage, toward the emancipation of industry, and therein towards the accomplishment of another great and blessed work of public justice. Giving up what I highly prized . . . . . I felt myself open to the charge of being opinionated and wanting in deference to really great authorities, and I could not but know that I should inevitably be regarded as fastidious and fanciful, fitter for a dreamer, or possibly a schoolman, than for the active purposes of public life in a busy and moving age."

Overshadowing all this is the fact that Gladstone was making a tremendous effort to be consistent with his book on Church and State. His one effort to be consistent—a state of mind and a method of action which his critics have always recommended to him, even with fierceness—offers results which indicate how much more grand and important to civilization has been his apparent inconsistency.

The Greville Memoirs furnish us with this interesting page with reference to Gladstone's resignation from Peel's Cabinet on the matter of the Maynooth grant:

"February 6th. On Tuesday night, for the first time for some years, I went to the House of Commons, principally to hear Gladstone's explanation. John Russell called on me in the morning and told me that he and Palmerston had talked over French politics, and were both of one mind, and both disposed to say nothing offensive or hostile to France or Guizot. Lord John spoke, but not at all well, in a bad spirit, taunting and raking up all subjects of bitterness, accusing the Government of inconsistency, without much reason, and not very wisely or fairly, and casting in their teeth expressions which he had culled out of old files of the Times. His speech disappointed me, but it afforded Peel an opportunity of which he availed himself remarkably well, and his retort gave him all the advantage of the night. What he said of France was perfect, excellent in tone and manner, all that Guizot could require without being at all servile or even accommodating. Gladstone's explanation was ludicrous. Everybody said

7

that he had only succeeded in showing that his resignation was quite uncalled for.

"Peel put an end to any mystery about his measures and stated in general terms all he intended to do. The Government, however, expect a good deal of opposition and excitement from the religious part of the community, Dissenters and Scotch. Ashley has put himself at the head of the Low Church party, and will make a great clatter. Sandon did not dare accept the Board of Trade and seat in the Cabinet, for fear of disgusting the Liverpool Protestants. Such is the fear that men have of avowing their real sentiments on those delicate questions. Neither Gladstone nor Sandon have really any objection to the Government measures; were they unfettered and uncompromised they would support and defend them. As it is, they do not dare do so, and thus they mislead others. They overlook the undoubted fact that inferences will be drawn by others as to their opinions the reverse of the truth, and that those inferences have a material influence upon the conduct of those who draw them. Peel told Gladstone beforehand that his explanation would be considered quite insufficient to account for his conduct. However, in his speech he lavished praise and regrets upon him in a tone quite affectionate. He was in a very laudatory vein, for he complimented the mover and seconder (Frank Charteris and Tom Baring) with unusual warmth."

His retirement from official life did not last long. He had supported the increased grant to the College of Maynooth, and had escaped dropping into ecclesiastical debates, but he had prepared himself most thoroughly to take a prominent part in the free trade struggle. Peel now saw that in order to deal successfully with Ireland or with any other territory, he must attend to the financial processes by which England's revenues were to be equal to her expenditures. This required a firm and intelligent hand. The income tax of which we have spoken poured in its last sovereign at the end of three years, in 1845. Peel persuaded Parliament to give him three more years of the same revenue. He found himself strongly intrenched with the aid of Gladstone and a surplus. Gladstone insisted that trade should be liberated by the taking off of every duty on imports where it was possible. Free

trade was coming, and Peel and he made every effort to lower other
duties, while all the duties on exports were swept away. Of course
the farmers and stockmen stood for lard and hides, and insisted that
their occupation would soon be gone if the duties on these articles were
removed. The potato crop in Ireland had failed, and famine gauntly
looked in upon the British Parliament. The Anti-Corn Law agitators
were gaining everywhere for the cause of unfettered commerce. John
Bright and Richard Cobden kept England in a healthful state of
thought on the outside of Parliament, and Villiers, within the House of
Commons, urged the Anti-Corn Laws with skill and strength. The
famine grew more severe, and foreign corn went into Ireland without
restriction, and humanity applauded. Such men as John Stuart Mill
were beginning to appreciate the situation and urge a juster view of
Irish affairs. This suddenly imposed study of affairs led Gladstone to
the Irish land legislation which more than a quarter of a century afterwards he proposed.

Peel's Government was now feeling the opposition of the country.
Even yet a majority of the middle classes—the brain and brawn of that
England to which Peel and Gladstone always lent an ear—rallied
around him. There now arose a man whose very nature and training,
whose brilliant qualities and boundless ambition, whose oratorical gifts
and genius for theatrical effect enabled him during almost all the life
of Gladstone either to organize into successful garrison of defense the
Lords and other timorous and well-intentioned conservatives on the
one side and the rabble in the streets on the other, or to unite into
a pursuing battalion the malcontents of both these classes, thus im-
peding or harassing such legislation as looked toward a broadening
of British constitutional government and the strengthening of England's position as a power in the progress of humanity. Benjamin
Disraeli knew the weak point of Sir Robert Peel, and in the presence
of Peel's somewhat slow-going qualities, Disraeli's rapidity of movement seemed genius itself. This fantastic young man was original
enough to make Peel's solid and somewhat heavy qualities appear
positively dull before the radiance which the young literateur threw
upon almost everything he touched. Disraeli saw that Peel held the

middle classes and understood their tendencies. In the middle classes Disraeli did not believe, and he abhorred their tendencies. As he entered politics, he was the same supercilious and foppish young gentleman who appeared in the drawing-rooms and in the portraits which his friends kept to show their country visitors. He saw his chance for a future; he discerned an opening in the vacancies of the Conservative household. Gladstone was sure to leave the old home in due course of time. Here was a young man able at one and the same time to gather together the leaderless and numerous Conservative malcontents, and to make a bold and strong fight against the Peel party and its leader. Peel had once declined to let him have office. That only stirred his soul for vindication. He would make his way by another means to the office he desired. His talk upon Peel's Government was singularly shrewd and powerful. Not for a moment, when he rode out, panoplied as the longed-for knight of Conservatism, did he compromise his radical convictions. He was not to fail to keep in connection with aristocracy and democracy. Indeed Disraeli never lost touch with the crowd of half-fed and half-clothed people—the tramp in politics—with whose nights on the streets and with whose ability to create a tumult at the door of Parliament Gladstone had to reckon.

Disraeli had a past to get over much more annoying than Gladstone's. For long years, it was impossible for him to get England to take him seriously; he had been only an exquisite fop possessed of genius. The recollection of his first speech in the House of Commons was abroad in the land; and as an illustration of some of the difficulties Gladstone's chief rival had to surmount, we reprint Disraeli's effort to speak—for it was little else. Surely, as Gladstone once confessed, a foe in debate who could outlive this was worthy of admiration. Disraeli said:

. "I stand here to-night, sir, not formally, but in some degree virtually, the representative of a considerable number of Members of Parliament. (Bursts of laughter.) Now, why smile? (Continued laughter.) Why envy me? (Here the laughter became long and general.) Why should not I have a tale to unfold to-night? (Roars of laughter.) Do you forget that band of 158 members—those ingenuous and inexperienced youths to whose unsophisticated minds the Chancellor of the Exchequer, in those tones of winning pathos—(Excessive laughter and loud cries of 'Question!')   Now a considerable misconception exists in the minds of many members on this side of the House as to the conduct of Her Majesty's Government with respect to these elections, and I wish to remove it.   I will not twit the noble lord opposite with opinions which are not ascribable to him or to his more immediate supporters, but which were expressed by the more popular section of his party some few months back.   About that time, sir, when the bell of our cathedral announced the death of the monarch—(laughter)—we all read then, sir—(groans and cries of 'Oh!')—we all then read—(laughter and great interruption)—"

So ended the laborious endeavor.   He then promised them that he would be heard.   He had now redeemed his promise and the gladiator was on his feet.   Disraeli made England believe for a moment that he had actually "caught the Whigs bathing and had walked away with their clothes," and that the best Peel could do in the way of making a Conservative Government was to create "an organized conspiracy."

Disraeli's tastes were not likely to lead him to foresee the power of young Gladstone, whom he heard speak in the House of Commons when the latter retired from the presidency of the Board of Trade, in February, 1845.   Disraeli writes: "Gladstone's address was involved and ineffective.   He may have an *avenir*, but I hardly think it."   Later on Mr. Disraeli attended an Academy dinner, and Mr. Gladstone sat next to him.   He writes at this time that he found him "particularly agreeable."

CHAPTER IX.

THE CORN LAW AGITATION.

The agricultural population was by this time in deep distress, and protection had made the manufacturers rich. Peel's sympathy with free trade was matched with Gladstone's, and both believed that, because there were more consumers than there were producers, and because producers were better off than consumers, who were usually poor, legislation ought to make goods cheap for the sake of the consumers rather than dear for the sake of the producers. Here was the matter of corn. It was evident that the nation would be better off by letting corn come in at a low price and having everybody fed, than to keep up the price of corn by the imposition of duties and have only the producers of corn able to eat it. Bright's warm oratory and Cobden's clear logic illuminated these propositions; but Peel and Gladstone were not yet ready to forsake their position that Parliament ought to keep up the price of corn at least as an insurance for the farmers of a future time, and not for the benefit of living Englishmen. This meant that they saw Great Britain would have to depend for her food upon foreign countries at some time. War some day might make England hungry. But here was actual hunger staring them in the face at the present time. The starving people of the present would not down before the possibly starving people of the future. There was no reason to suppose that this present starvation in England could be done away with unless corn could come in free. And now Peel's position was made for him by force of a resistless event: eight million people in Ireland had been living on potatoes, and one night the potato plants became black and corrupt. Misery brought its argument to Sir Robert and his Cabinet, and it conquered.

In October, he asked his Cabinet to support him, for he wished to remove the duty from corn. Lord John Russell opposed him with all his force. The Cabinet refused. Peel resigned, and Lord Russell was called to constitute an administration. He found it impossible. Peel returned to office, with Gladstone, upon whom he leaned as the strongest and best debater of free traders among the Tories. Gladstone was Home Secretary for the Colonies, but his marvelous financial genius gave all its learning in service to his chief, while Peel wrestled with the problem as to the repealing of the Corn Law. Lord Stanley, whom we shall know soon as Lord Derby, now resigned and led the Protectionists in opposition to Peel. But a change was imminent. Lord Russell came over to the side of Peel, bringing the Whigs with him.

January, 1846, came, and Peel proposed to bring in a bill for the abolition of the Corn Laws. By the first of July the bill had triumphed in the Commons and in the Lords, and, though it took three years to complete the abolition, the Corn Laws were repealed. The most advanced statesman on this question in the Cabinet of Sir Robert Peel, and altogether the most skillful swordsman in defense of this position was none other than Gladstone. He was great enough to serve his chief. In a later period his presence was more manifest, but there could be no doubt but that Gladstone was the right-hand man of the Prime Minister in the carrying of this measure, and out of Parliament as he was, his learning and industry wrought immeasurably toward the defeat of the ancient folly which employs artificial means to keep up the price of human food.

When Gladstone accepted the office of Secretary of State for the Colonies he sent an address to those who had elected him from the Newark borough. He said:

"By accepting the office of Secretary of State for the Colonies I have ceased to be your representative in Parliament. On several accounts I should have been peculiarly desirous at the present time of giving you an opportunity to pronounce your constitutional judgment on my public conduct by soliciting at your hands a renewal of the trust which I have already received from you on five successive occasions, and held during a period of thirteen years. But, as I have good reason to believe that a candidate recommended to your favor through local connections may ask your suffrages, it becomes my very painful duty to announce to you, on that ground alone, my retirement from a position which has afforded me so much honor and satisfaction."

This was an excellent opportunity for him to leave his old friends with the best of feelings. But Mr. Gladstone was no longer a representative of Newark. Moreover, he was finding other views developing in his mind to which he knew the Duke of Newcastle, dear old friend and ardent supporter as he had been, could not be expected to offer his agreement. It was therefore well that Gladstone sent such an address to the electors. The truth is that in the year 1845 he had given some exposition of new views on the subject of the Irish Established Church. It was very evident that Mr. Gladstone no longer stood by the fixed Toryism of the Duke of Newcastle and Sir John Gladstone on this subject. "Yes," said the proud father, "William has ability; but has he stability?" Surely not on this or any question, if stability means mental immovableness. Eighteen hundred and forty-five seems a long while ago when we contemplate what Gladstone has done for Ireland, but it was in a letter to Bishop Wilberforce at this time that he gave clearest statement as to the honest doubt out of which better faith grew. He said:

"I am sorry to express my apprehension that the Irish Church is not in a large sense efficient; the working results of the last ten years have disappointed me. It may be answered, 'Have faith in the ordinance of God;' but then I must see the seal and signature, and how can I separate these from ecclesiastical descent? The title, in short, is questioned, and vehemently, not only by the Radicalism of the day, but by the Roman Bishops, who claim to hold the succession of St. Patrick; and this claim has been alive all along from the Reformation."

It was well for those who were watching the growth of Mr. Gladstone's statesmanship to remember that while Peel's Ministry was closing, while Indian corn brought cheaply to Ireland was relieving somewhat of its distress, while public works were inaugurated to furnish a living to Irish laborers, Gladstone saw the injustice of compelling these people to support a church in which they did not believe at all, and for which they had no use, either in this world or in the next.

Meanwhile landlord and tenant were outraging one another, one with the law on his side, the other without law, and Peel was compelled to bring in a bill for the protection of human life in Ireland.   Lord Russell and his contingent opposed its stringency.   Disraeli, standing behind the dignified figure of Lord Bentinck, offered a powerful and stinging opposition; and so successful was this antagonism, that, on the very day on which the Corn Law Bill triumphed in the House of Lords, the Irish Bill was defeated in the House of Commons.   Two days afterwards Peel resigned his position.

Lord John Russell was forming a new Ministry, assured as he was of the support of Peel and Gladstone.   Just at this time Ireland was seen standing and weeping over the body of one who had been called "the big beggar-man"—the great orator and prophet of Ireland's better day—Daniel O'Connell.   It was remarkable that at that grave Ireland was quiet and orderly.   The derision of puny enemies, the noisy hate of bigoted Protestants, the blustering antagonism of respectable ignorance, all vanished away, and one eye at least, the eye of William E. Gladstone, saw in the behavior of Ireland, while the body of O'Connell was being lowered into its last resting-place, a hope that a wiser and juster statesmanship than had hitherto been applied to the Irish difficulty might win this hot-headed and rebellious people into something like loyal support to the hopes and aims of the British Empire.

Soon it was known that the potato crop in Ireland was an entire failure again, and that Peel's efforts to give a job to every Irishman who needed it had been greatly abused.   Public works had not been created save at a loss of respect for law and a regard for honesty.   The roads upon which the laborers had lounged and dug were worse than ever, and private employers had found the distraction of being unable to compete with public authorities in paying wages.   Gladstone assisted Russell with all his might to check these evils.   He was not in the House of Commons, but elsewhere he was in work up to his eyes for a better day in Ireland and England.

The autumn session of 1847 found him in the House of Commons again.   Oxford University had returned him and he had before him eighteen years in which to represent them.   Every taste of his nature was delighted with the prospect. Except for the tumult in his blood and the growing ferment of ideas, he may now prepare to grow more learnedly and happily conservative. Instantly he was compelled to consider and defend a bill for enabling the guardians of the poor to give outdoor relief. This relief had been forbidden in 1839, but now the poor-houses were surrounded with people needing food, and for every three inside, there were a hundred persons starving outside. Disraeli was developing his sneer again, which he visited upon much that was dear to the heart of human progress, while Gladstone was developing strength of conviction to deal with a problem deeper than any Poor Law could reach in Ireland. No amount of mercy can atone for delayed justice. English charity could not remedy the state of things to the helping of which America offered an eager and affectionate hand, and three millions of the Irish people perished. There was no avoiding the fact that neither peace nor prosperity would be satisfied until the legal relations between landlord and tenant were altered. The 8,000 pounds left after mortgages of 9,000 pounds had been taken from the entire rental of 17,000 pounds, could not feed the Irish poor and support and pay the debts of the landlords. The tenants were almost crushed beneath the demands of the landlords who were tempted by their debts to oppress them. Improvements in land and in property by the tenant did not often result in anything but a demand on the part of the landlord that the tenant should pay a higher rent or be evicted. Gladstone behaved as a merchant's son from Liverpool gradually shaking off Oxford, or as an Oxonian happily forgetful, oftentimes, that he had the interests of Liverpool merchandise to be looked out after. He was growing to be larger and truer than either, or both, to the higher destinies of the English people. Now, however, came the question upon which he could easily show himself a narrow bigot or a liberal statesman.

Here and now came an opportunity for the liberalizing forces in Gladstone's mind to assert their power. The city of London had returned Baron Rothschild as her representative in the House of Commons. Gladstone nobly responded to the demand of the hour and maintained "that if they admitted Jews into Parliament, prejudice might be awakened for a while, but the good sense of the people would soon allay it, and members would have the consolation of knowing that in a case of difficulty they had yielded to a sense of justice, and by so doing had not disparaged religion or lowered Christianity, but had rather elevated both in all reflecting and well-regulated minds."

A motion in favor of Jewish privileges was carried and Oxford was alarmed as to the sanity of her representative and son.

One thing at this time was becoming clear to him—the importance of England's position in Christendom. To this matter he gave much thought. He said, on this theme:

"The political power of England is great; but its religious influence is limited. The sympathies even of Nonconforming England with Continental Protestantisms are, and must be, partial; the dominant tone and direction of the two are far from identical. The Church, though in rather more free contact than our Nonconforming bodies with the learning of Protestant Germany, is of course more remote from its religious tendencies. The Latin communion forces the Church of England more and more into antagonism; and we are only beginning to sound the possibilities of an honorable, but independent, relation of friendship with the East. In matters of religion, poetry might still with some truth sing of the *penitus toto divisos orbe Britannos.* We of all nations have the greatest amount, perhaps, of religious individuality, certainly of religious self-sufficiency. A moral, as well as a natural, sea surrounds us; and at once protects and isolates us from the world. But this is, of course, in a sense which is comparative, not absolute. The electric forces which pervade the Christian atmosphere touch us largely, outer barbarians though we be; and they touch us increasingly. And a multitude of circumstances make us aware that, if we are at least open to criticism as our neighbors, yet we have like them a part to play in Christendom, and a broad field to occupy with our sympathies, under the guidance of such intelligence as we may possess."

It is interesting to take from Gladstone's own pen some account of his position in 1847. He is speaking of the emancipation which was effected from the net in which he had been bound on the subject of the Church and State, especially on the Irish Church Question. He says:

"In 1846 it was suggested to me that I should oppose a member of the newly-formed Government of Lord John Russell. In my reply, declining the proposal, I wrote thus to the late Duke of Newcastle: 'As to the Irish Church, I am not able to go to war with them on the ground that they will not pledge themselves to the maintenance of the existing appropriation of church property in Ireland.' This, however, was a private proceeding.

"But, early in 1847, Mr. Estcourt announced his resignation of the seat he held, amidst universal respect, for the University of Oxford. The partiality of friends proposed me as a candidate. The representation of the University was, I think, stated by Mr. Canning to be to him the most coveted prize of political life. I am not ashamed to own that I desired it with almost passionate fondness. For besides all the associations it maintained and revived, it was in those days an honor not only given without solicitation, but, when once given, not withdrawn. The contest was conducted with much activity and some heat. I was, naturally enough, challenged as to my opinions on the Established Church of Ireland. My friend Mr. Coleridge, then young, but already distinguished, was one of my most active and able supporters. He has borne spontaneous testimony, within the last few weeks, to the manner in which the challenge was met:

" 'Gentlemen, I must be permitted—because an attack has been made upon Mr. Gladstone, and it has been suggested that his conversion to his present principles is recent—to mention what is within my own knowledge and experience with regard to him. In 1847, when I was just leaving Oxford, I had the great honor of being secretary to his first election committee for that university and I well recollect, how, upon that occasion, some older and more moderate supporters were extremely anxious to draw from him some pledge that he should stand by the Irish Church. He distinctly refused to pledge himself to anything of the kind.' "

The year 1848 witnessed the agitation in Parliament of the demand that the expenditure of the nation should be brought down to the level of the nation's receipts. Commerce and manufacturers had suffered, and protectionists rejoiced that this was a witness to the truth of their theory as to the disaster sure to be brought about by free trade. Gladstone and Disraeli found themselves on different sides when Sir Robert Peel supported the ministers and when Gladstone defended his faith in that financial system which has the income tax as its chief feature. Disraeli pretended to be blind to the great difficulties under which England labored in the distressing condition of affairs in all the realm. Cobden outstripped Gladstone himself in his plea for direct taxation, and influenced Gladstone greatly in the effort to remove any inequalities in the income tax. France, meanwhile, was suffering the throes of a revolution. Everywhere in Europe the malcontents, and especially the Irish malcontents, who were against the government, wherever it was, and whatever it was at that time, seized upon the fancy that this might be another French Revolution where the hopes of the discontented could at least have full utterance. The acknowledgment of this feeling simply produced a series of repressive measures to which the English Government did not like to resort. There was no O'Connell now to advise caution and peace when Ireland became violent. The danger of Ireland's rising in bloody rebellion was met by the fear Ireland had at that moment that those who were doing all the talking and threatening could not possibly help Ireland, if indeed Ireland were to be separated from England. Therefore most of the Irish men acquiesced when Mr. Smith O'Brien, the leader of the malcontents, was transported. Constructive and far-sighted, Mr. Gladstone labored with Lord John Russell and the Government to bring forward measures which were conceived for the purpose of remedying affairs in Ireland. It was almost impossible to get the Irish people to hear any plan for a gradual relief of suffering, or any kind of improvement of the situation save that which could be brought about by separation. Lord John Russell said he was helpless. He insisted that the Protestants of Ireland had the right to an Established Church. He went over the obstacles in the way of establishing a Roman Catholic Church in the same territory. Lord Russell proposed a bill known as the Encumbered Estates Act, proposing to sell estates that were deeply mort-

gaged, and hoping that tenants thereby might be better treated. He
insisted that the landlords should compensate evicted tenants for improvements they had made, and the member from Oxford stood by him
in his wish to introduce a clause forbidding any landlord to evict a tenant
if that tenant had held land under certain conditions and had made
improvements. Gladstone's Tory friends admonished him that this
was not to be borne by Oxford.

It was impossible to keep the revolution of 1848, which shocked
all Europe, from creating a timidity in the mind of English statesmen-
ship which expressed itself in English legislation. Chartists had risen
in England, and the working-classes seemed ready to imitate the
laborers in the French nation, and they were crying for a people's
charter, granting them something approaching a republic in England.
Now, statesmanship had to deal with the English laborer as it had
failed to deal successfully with the Irish laborer. The influence of the
Reform Bill of years before had been to broaden the franchise and
create in the minds of Englishmen the idea of governmental responsibility. Those who opposed the reform bill had sought such representation, even in the first reformed Parliament, as would state the progress
of popular government. Some of the working classes were greatly
disappointed in the slender share of benefits which they obtained from
the reform bill. The indolent and the intelligent united; the clean and
the unclean fused, and the moral force chartists and the physical force
chartists confronted English legislation with various principles embodying the same purpose. For ten years now this agitation had voiced the
ideas which would have made England a laborer's republic, if they had
been adopted.

Mr. Gladstone was not unintelligent of these movements and lent
his great services to the Government as this scheme proceeded toward
its wreck. Meantime Lord George Bentinck died, and Gladstone's
great rival, Disraeli, was recognized as the only leader worthy of the
attention of his party.

CHAPTER X.

THE VALOROUS CHURCHMAN.

In the decade previous to this date, and especially within the three years preceding, Mr. Gladstone's ecclesiastical and literary tendencies led him to express his convictions on a variety of subjects, and there is no surer way of appreciating the growth of a great man in various ways, than by a careful study, such as the size of this volume unhappily will not permit us to make, of Mr. Gladstone's literary work in this period. Let us confine ourselves to one line of his publications—those on church affairs. They show the religious basis of his faith in constitutional government in England, and this when England's mind was confused. Writing of one of his essays thirty-five years after the date of its publication, he says: "There is something of a sanguine crudity in this essay." He adds: "It must, however, serve as a part of the material history of a critical period which will have finally to be written." The period is that of the Oxford movement which the "Edinburgh Review" sought to explain in 1838 and again in the year 1843. Gladstone made an apology for dealing with the subject, calling it "sacred ground,"—a phrase he would scarce have used in later life, and he pleaded that the "rapid growth of the question in its importance and pressure upon the minds of men and the immense moment of its issues," was reason enough why he should approach it as he did, "with the deepest impression, that in the present condition of church charity founded upon a sense of our Christian brotherhood, forbearance, and considerate, fair thought, are the very first requisites of a useful discussion of her concerns, and if we positively offend against this rule, we have thus supplied at the outset the means of judging us out of our own mouth." This somewhat too elaborate statement of a fact which no one would question is testimony of the condition of Gladstone's mind at that time, and his mental method. He has not been flippant with anything;

III

scarcely has he had a light touch for any subject; he began life seriously and he has lived seriously while thinking on all subjects with equal intensity and care. Gladstone never could think of the Oxford movement which influenced him, as "little more than a feeble, casual and desultory effort of the enthusiasm or caprice of a small knot of persons." This was the "Edinburgh Review's" estimate of it, but it is given in Gladstone's language. The latter is quite excited as he thinks that people such as read the "Edinburgh Review" may underestimate the testimony "afforded to the magnitude in which the subject now presents itself to the public eye, to its comprehensive range, and the searching nature of its influences." Gladstone gravely says: "The stone has grown into a rock, if not a mountain. In places and in publications, usually the most abhorrent of religious discussion, force of circumstances has compelled the discussion of some notice of these controversies." Here we see the Gladstone of 1843. He is delighted that,

"on several occasions during the past year, while the Factory Education clauses were before the House of Commons, the increasing prevalence of Catholic sentiments in the Church, has formed a prominent topic in the debates of that assembly; the lower organs of the press are loud, and of course extravagant, in their statements of the progress of the contagion; and even the philosophic radicalism of the 'Westminster Review' has condescended to notice the matter, with censure full of apprehension and alarm."

It is the Oxford man, unforgetful of the charm of John Henry Newman and the others, speaking, when he calls attention to the fact that some ten years before "four or five clergymen of the University of Oxford met together, alarmed at the course of Parliamentary legislation with respect to the Church, at the very menacing and formidable attitude of dissent, in its alliance with Liberalism, and at the disposition manifested in the establishment itself, to tamper with the distinctive principles of its formularies." There is a gravity almost humorous, as we look back from the point of view occupied by the Grand Old Man, who marshaled dissenters as he could no other class, upon those circumstantial events which he restores to history. Out of those events were coming the famous "Tracts for the Times." It is the churchman,

RICHARD COBDEN

THE RIGHT HONORABLE LORD MACAULAY

and the Oxford churchman, and the churchman who after fifty years did have the deepest interest in the Pope's opinion of the validity of Dean Farrar's ecclesiastical orders, who tells us that the movement had no help from "secular power," "Episcopal sentence," "courtly, aristocratic, or popular influences." He compares the secession with a like event in the history of the Scottish Revolution, and he says: "The English Church, put upon her mettle, has shaken off the conventional and secular influences which clothes her in an Erastian disguise, and has lighted up, with the rapidity of wildfire, the blazing title of Catholicity upon her brow."

Certainly this is lively writing, even for an advanced English churchman. The conclusion of it all is that the Oxford movement was "a development from within of something rooted in the mind and sense of the Church itself." It was something "not proceeding from fortuitous causes, not colored by individual caprice, nor by merely individual genius, piety, or learning, but a tribute providentially supplied to the imperious necessities of the time, whose emphatic language sounded in the ears of the English Church, bidding her either to descend from her high place or else to assert its prerogatives, discharge its duties." He adds:

"It was impossible for her any longer to stand in the public opinion upon the grounds of political utility, of national tradition, of an accommodating tone of doctrine, too long and too widely prevalent, which, instead of rousing dead consciences like a trumpet, made itself in a certain sense agreeable and popular, by humming and lulling into deeper slumbers. Administrative abuses, such as non-residents, pluralities, and the progressive reduction of sacraments and other services, had reached a most frightful height; and the progress of reforms, late begun, for some time appeared to be so slow, that it was to be feared the scythe of the destroyer might overtake them, and remove the abuse and the thing abused together. The clergy were, as a body, secular in their habits; and, unless in individual instances, had fallen altogether below the proper level of their lofty calling, although they continued to be much above that of general society."

Carlyle had called the Church a sham, and Gladstone saw hope in

8

this movement, which, in 1833, commenced to infuse new life by insisting upon faithfulness to old principles, and thus making the Church
something else besides a sham. As Gladstone, a few years later, thinks
of it all, looking back upon the efforts of such saintly men as Dr. Blomfield, he says "that something which brought great personal zeal, new
forms of association into existence alone was valuable." But the
power which was to save and bless was not the old Puritanical scheme
of the evangelicals. His friend, Mr. Scott, he believes would have
brought the Church of England closer to John Calvin theologically,
but the Church wanted something more than a new theological position, and he adds:

"The popular divinity of thirty years ago, although it had indeed
many recommendations in comparison with that which it resisted and
displaced and although it sprang from the vivid reawakening of religious instincts and desires, yet did not spring out of, nor stand in harmonious relations with those principles which belonged to the constitution of the Church, and did not avail to secure for those principles,
and that constitution, their proper place in the Christian system. And
thus the restorative process, which we rejoice to honor even in its
crude commencement, was both narrow in its extent, and, what was
worse, faulty in its quality, because it did not comprehend the elements
necessary for its own permanent immunity from the deteriorating
influences."

Mr. Gladstone could not look upon the Oxford movement but as a
"link in the great chain of causes and effects, by which the mind of this
country has now, for half a century and more, been made the subject
of so remarkable and of so general a religious progression and development." He thought that "to have the smallest share in impelling the
movement of which we speak, was indeed an honor; to have had a
greater share in directing it, a surpassing crown; to have marred it by
temerity or excess, among the heaviest of sorrows." It is no wonder
that his friends thought him about ready to go with Father Newman,
but he was too masterful of his own personality to fail here. While
the Oxford movement was, as he said, "the infallible sequel and com-
plement of the work of religious renovation," the larger movement lay

in learning its lesson, and, using all its force, perhaps, was to accomplish a wider result. It is a terrible indictment which he draws against the Church of England of that moment, yet he believes that there is a way to be churchly and Christian and thoroughly moral without leaving the Church of England and going over to Rome. He talks of the Roman Church in excellent words:

"We are in honor bound to do justice to her antiquity, to the benefits which we ourselves received at her hands, to the firmness with which she has ever contended in behalf of the Catholic Creeds, to the profound and comprehensive wisdom that pervade many of her institutions, to the high and noble degrees of saintly perfection that have been attained within her pale. And yet we are not so to speak as to incur the risk of aiding to mislead others by these glowing recitals; as it is to be feared we do aid, unless we join with them the most marked and definite notice of the frightful evils which deform her system. These, it is to be observed, are not merely evils within her pale, but evils which she seems to take to her bosom and to cherish there; which have established themselves about the very seat and organs of life, and which the better elements of her nature have not energy sufficient to eject. The practical withholding or stinting of the Divine Word; the fearful tampering with the attribute of God, by extravagant regard to creatures; the grossness of her purgatorial system, as represented in the actually prevailing tone of her authorized and ordinary pastoral teaching and discipline; the tyranny of her impositions of tenets, not revealed, upon the consciences of men; and her schismatical usurpations of the rights and claims of other Churches; all these are topics, concerning which to speak slightly, is by implication to betray the truth of God, and to expose the souls of our brethren to terrific peril."

It would seem that he had little anticipation here of ever being able to do much on any Irish question with the consent of the Roman Church. Later on he was still more fearless as he examined the Vatican decrees. He appreciated the state of confusion out of which a man could utter criticisms of either the Church of England or the Church of Rome, and he was willing to agree that something more positive than criticism ought to be offered by the critic. He says:

"It certainly indicates a state of great moral disorder in the Christian world, when individuals without authority bring charges against the most extended of Christian Churches, that she tampers with the attributes of God by the toleration and the parent encouragement of idolatrous regard to creatures. If the accusation is false, no words can express its guilt; if it be true, yet still it seems too great a weight for the private person to carry, a weapon not intended for his arm to wield. Sad is the necessity which requires such things to be said at all; sadder yet, if in such modes. He that utters them should at least join with the active utterance every sobering and chastening reflection, that may prevent it from becoming an act of self-glorification."

Dr. Newman's ninetieth tract is not passed without remark, and Gladstone could only mention the lesson which was taught to those who would believe the Church of England in her present form to be equal to the conflict with evil. He felt that unbelief had cooled the ardor of her heart, and he says:

"Those who argue for the Catholicity of the Church of England in all points which relate to her constitution and rites, to her view of the Episcopate and the sacraments, found themselves upon the tone of her authorized formularies in order to make good their case. But, undoubtedly, there are those within her, and even within the order of her priesthood, who do not scruple to assert in some cases so much as that the Episcopate, the ministry, and the visible framework of the Church, are human institutions; and even in the teeth of the Catechism appointed to be taught to all our young persons, that the new birth unto righteousness is not the proper inward part of the sacrament of Baptism, and that the Body and Blood of Christ are not really received by the faithful in the holy Eucharist."

The fact stood out bare and bold that the Catholic Church on the one side had actual charge of a large number of human beings, and the English Church, on the other side, had lost hold entirely on another great section of humanity. For these two churches to enter into communion was most desirable, but Gladstone was sure that communion with the Church of Rome was impossible. He says:

"Her whole scheme of operations is founded upon her exclusive pretensions, and upon the assertion of the illegitimacy of all Churches not under her jurisdiction. Everywhere, therefore, in their territories, she appears as an intruder and an aggressor; and the admission of her supreme control is made by her the first condition of intercourse. In fact, it is not a question of communion, but of subjection; and for any other Church to acknowledge the present claims of Rome is to disown herself, her own acts, her own children, dead as well as living, her relation to her Lord. Nor is this any mere point of earthly honor, any contest of simple dignity or precedence; in lowering to her the fasces, we should admit the practical sway of her dictatorship. We should be called on to make those additions to the Catholic and Apostolic Creed, which she has been bold enough, under Pope Pius IV., to attach to it. Or, if she, from charity or policy, would excuse our immediate adoption of them, the exemption should be one durante beneplacito alone, and revocable at her will. Nor do we see what permanent guarantee for any, even the smallest, degree of spiritual liberty she could furnish, so long as the preposterous claim of infallibility continues to be made, as we have seen it recently made in official documents, by the incumbent of the Papal See."

It is astonishing to those of us who live in the sober evening of the nineteenth century, after Gladstone's contemporaries, Huxley, Darwin and Spencer, have lived and wrought, after others have drawn away some of the millinery from apparently sacred objects, to see a man of such reasoning capacity in such a gale of excitement about the necessity of certain people understanding certain other people about the church services and the like. He says:

"It may be true, that there is at this moment a Romanizing school in the Church of England. These are men, who are not content with respecting or revering Catholicity in the Church of Rome, but who take her, such as she is, in the mass, for a standard of imitation, and would have the Church of England made like her, at least so far as might be necessary in order to re-establish communion with her. They are unable to fix their affections upon the Church of England, such as she is in the mass; but, while sincerely respecting and revering the Catholicity or vestiges of Catholicity that they find in her, nevertheless recoil from the anti-Romish elements with which that Catholicity is combined, and pay to her, as a whole, a loveless and constrained, even if a punctual and conscientious allegiance."

Surely the Oxonian could not well go further than this. He goes trotting on interestingly to the very edge of the brook, and refuses to jump. He certainly underestimated the power which other men had at that time and their willingness to take the leap. He says:

"It may be, that the teaching of this school, as it has perhaps already helped to produce, so will hereafter from time to time aid in producing, defections from the Church of England of erratic and ill-balanced minds; of minds wanting that searching truth of perception, and vigor of determination which all times, the times of confusion most especially, required. But as to bringing the millions of this Church and nation into harmony with actual Rome, in our view, the perversion of Mr. Sibthorp and a few more, does not abridge even one inch of the all but immeasurable distance at which if any where within the bounds of possibility, such an event is set. We will not allow that there is the minutest symptom, the faintest or most shadowy indication, of any impression of such a kind upon the English mind."

Newman and Manning and Hope-Scott are names amidst a multitude of nimble-footed figures, and, withal, high-minded men. Gladstone certainly longed for a spiritual revival. He says:

"That effort for spiritual revival, of which we have spoken, aims at assimilation, not to Rome, but to something quite distinct, something higher and better than Rome; to that original of which Rome is a mutilated copy, that standard which she seems with us to acknowledge, but beneath which we both, though in different degrees and modes, have sunk. May we not redeem our own shortcomings without adopting hers? The end proposed is that end which this Church acknowledges; the means employed are, walking in the path of her ordinances, and cherishing the spirit that pervades them. In pursuing such an end, by such means, we can only approximate to Rome where she approximates, or shall approximate, to truth. We must remove farther and farther from her, where she departs from it. And if it be a duty to desire and hope for such removal, with surely at least equal earnestness should we labor, yearn and pray for such approximation."

This was the burden of his heart, and no doubt the sincere desire of his spirit. At that very time the retraction of Newman from what seemed extreme positions taken against Protestantism had compelled attention, and many journals reprinted the collection of those very fierce attacks which he made upon the evils of Romanism. Gladstone insisted that his English friends had the right to desire "that he ought more exactly to define what he proposes to substitute for Protestantism thus withdrawn." The answer to all this ultimately came, and John Henry Newman became Father Newman of the Roman Catholic communion. Gladstone closed his really comprehensive, though, as he says, sanguinely crude study of the question, with these words:

"And now we have done with our mighty theme. The brain almost reels at the magnitude of the interests, and therefore of the hazards, involved in it. It has been our desire to handle it with a freedom proportioned to the necessities of the case, but not exceeding them. If towards any communion, Protestant or unreformed, towards any person of whatever station or whatever sentiments, we have entertained convictions or uttered language wanting in charity, or respect, we acknowledge the heaviness of the fault, and implore pardon. And, at least, we cannot draw the curtain upon the sad picture of Christian division and dissension, without beseeching the reader to offer up to God the fervent prayer, that the afflicting contemplation of such a scene may inspire him with the resolution to 'seek peace and ensue it' in the vineyard of the Lord on earth; and, if he cannot here enjoy his soul's desire, then, that he may be moved by the prevailing discord the more manfully to press towards the mark for the prize of entering that rest, wherein the unclouded presence of God shall enlighten His people, and His unity shall enfold them for evermore."

He had written a fierce indictment against the English Church, and a fierce indictment against the Roman Church and State, yet amidst the storm and shell against both, men like Newman and Manning were passing from one into the other. Gladstone almost alone saw that England was needing a revival of genuine religion.

CHAPTER XI.

OXFORD'S REPRESENTATIVE.

In 1849 the Government proposed the repeal of the Navigation laws. The commercial interests of England, to which the son of the Liverpool merchant was always attentive, were not the only interests involved in this discussion. Yet Gladstone's support was most effective, and it indicated how clearly he saw at that time that England is the home of a seafaring people, and London must be the exchange-place of the merchants of the world because of England's position in matters affecting shipping. Yet there was more than this in Gladstone's mind. He was bound to realize his ideas of making the sea "That great highway of nations, as free to the ships that traverse its bosom as the winds that sweep over it." In the same year he presented his argument on the question of paying indemnity to those who had lost property in the Candian riots. Here he announced his conviction that "The House of Commons has a perfect right to be heard and to be obeyed in imperial concerns." This was the statement of his faith as to the unity of the British Empire, and as to the sort of services he would render toward consolidating and exalting it.

While Oxford had returned him by an excellent majority, Mrs. Gladstone had felt it necessary for her to take a part in the canvass, and now Oxford beheld him, as he grew steadily toward the Liberalism whose champion he was to be. Across his triumphs as a debater there came a shadow, for in 1850 his little daughter died, and added to that shadow was another, which came from the fact that the godfathers of his oldest son, Henry Manning and Mr. Hope-Scott, went over to the Church of Rome. No biographer has failed to quote at least the conclusion of the letter which Gladstone wrote to his old friend. He said:

"My Dear Hope:—

" . . . Affection which is fed by intercourse, and above all, by co-operation for sacred ends, has little need of verbal expression, but such expression is deeply ennobling when active relations have changed. It is no matter of merit to me to feel strongly on the subject of that change. It may be little better than pure selfishness. I have too good reason to know what this year has cost me; and so little hope have I that the places now vacant can be filled up for me, that the marked character of these events in reference to myself rather teaches me this lesson—the work to which I aspired is reserved for other and better men. And if that be the Divine will, I so entirely recognize its fitness, that the grief would so far be such to me were I alone concerned. The pain, the wounds, and the mystery is this,—that you should have refused the higher vocation you had before you. . . . There is one word, and one only, in your letter that I do not interpret closely. Separated we are, but I hope and think not yet estranged. Were I more estranged I should bear the separation better. . . . I honor you even in what I think your error. Why, then, should my feelings to you alter in anything else? It seems to me as though in these fearful times, events were more and more growing too large for our puny grasp, and we should the more look for and trust the Divine purpose in them, when we find they have wholly passed beyond the reach and measure of our own. . . . For the present we have to endure, to trust, and to pray that each day may bring its strength with its burden, and its lamp for its gloom. Ever yours with unaltered affection,

"W. E. GLADSTONE."

Gladstone became deeply interested in the subject of the orthodoxy of the Church of England, which he thought now to be seriously attacked. He had defended his position, which favored diplomacy on the part of England with the Court at Rome, but he could not look elsewhere than to the Church of England for security in ecclesiastical and religious affairs. In the same year he wrote the famous letter to the Bishop of London, in which he took the ground that he could not support the Privy Council as the last Court of Appeal in religious matters, and that the Royal supremacy was consistent with the religious activity and hope of the English Church. Gladstone has labored, as a genuine revivalist must, for the spiritual life of the religious establishment. This letter is only an example of his profound interest in these subjects. He said in conclusion:

I find it no part of my duty, my Lord, to idolize the Bishops of England and Wales, or to place my conscience in their keeping. I do not presume or dare to speculate upon their particular decisions; but I say that, acting jointly, publicly, solemnly, responsibly, they are the best and most natural organs of the judicial office of the Church in matters of heresy, and, according to reason, history, and the Constitution, in that subject-matter the fittest and safest counsellors of the Crown.

.   .   .   .

We should, indeed, have a consolation, the greatest perhaps which times of heavy trouble and affliction can afford, in the reduction of the whole matter to a short, clear, and simple issue; because such a resolution, when once unequivocally made clear by acts, would sum up the whole case before the Church to the effect of these words: "You have our decision; take your own; choose between the mess of pottage, and the birthright of the Bride of Christ."

Those that are awake might hardly require a voice of such appalling clearness; those that sleep, it surely would awaken; of those that would not hear, it must be said, "Neither would they hear, though one rose from the dead."

But She that, a stranger and a pilgrim in this world, is wedded to the Lord, and lives only in the hope of His Coming, would know her part; and while going forth to her work with steady step and bounding heart, would look back with deep compassion upon the region she had quitted— upon the slumbering millions, no less blind to the Future, than ungrateful to the Past.

This is the year in which occurred those memorable debates in the House of Commons, "which," as Dean Stanley says, "decided the fate of the Universities." He thus writes of the scene to his Oxford friend, Jowett:

"I postponed writing till the debate of last night was over. Marshall, the Proctor, and myself represented the University in the Speakers' gallery, and Liddell below the Bar. The Ministerial speeches were very feeble, perhaps purposely so, with a view of closing the debate. Gladstone's was very powerful, and said, in a most effective manner, anything which could be said against the Commission. His allusion to Peel was very touching, and the House responded to it by profound and sympathetic silence, with the exception of two M. P.'s, who, having been for some time lying head to head in the Members' gallery, were roused from repose by the pause, and, hearing what it was, exclaimed to one another: 'Balderdash!' 'D——d balderdash!' and so to sleep again. Heywood's closing speech was happily drowned in the roar of 'Divide,' so that nothing could be heard but the name of 'Cardinal Wolsey,' thrice repeated.

"Altogether I confess that I should have been relieved had the majority been the other way. 'Put not your trust in Prime Ministers' is the chief moral I derive from the recent events."

In 1850 a person named Don Pacifico, a subject of Her Majesty living in Athens, was attacked by a mob of Greeks, who looted his house. When he appealed to the Greek Government for redress and remuneration that Government, perhaps astonished into silence by the size of his claim, refused to heed him. The sum of more than 30,000 pounds was too much for Greece to pay, especially when the belongings of Don Pacifico were proven to have been of very small value. At the same time Lord Palmerston was having another quarrel with Greece, the noble lord taking the part of an English resident in Athens, and contending that the government there would not pay him proper compensation for some land they had taken. Some of the Ionian subjects of Great Britain made a complaint that they had been illy treated. It was enough for Palmerston. He inaugurated what England has heard of as "a spirited foreign policy." The British fleet soon seized all Greek shipping found in the harbor of the Piræus. Palmerston flew into a fury at the thought that France had interfered in the affair, and the House of Commons was called on to act. To the debate Palmerston made a contribution five hours' long, in which he referred to the Roman phrase: "Civis Romanus," and he transferred all its boasting jingoism to the lips of England. Gladstone's peace-loving mind, steadily acting under the dominion of just principles, sought to change the course of things by a masterly speech, in which he said:

"Sir, great as is the influence and power of Britain, she cannot afford to follow, for any length of time, a self-isolating policy. It would be a contravention of the law of nature and of God, if it were possible for any single nation of Christendom to emancipate itself from the obligations which bind all other nations, and to arrogate, in the face of mankind, a position of peculiar privilege. And now I will grapple with the noble lord on the ground which he selected for himself, in the most triumphant portion of his speech, by his reference to those emphatic words, 'Civis Romanus sum.' He vaunted, amidst the cheers of his supporters, that under his Administration an Englishman should be, throughout the world, what the citizen of Rome had been. What, then, sir, was a Roman citizen? He was the member of a privileged caste; he belonged to a conquering race, to a nation that held all others bound down by the strong arm of power. For him there was to be an exceptional system of law; for him principles were to be asserted, and by him rights were to be enjoyed, that were denied to the rest of the world. Is such, then, the view of the noble lord as to the relation which is to subsist between England and other countries? Does he make the claim for us that we are to be uplifted upon a platform high above the standing-ground of all other nations? It is, indeed, too clear, not only from the expressions but from the whole tone of the speech of the noble viscount, that too much of this notion is lurking in his mind; that he adopts, in part, that vain conception that we, forsooth, have a mission to be the censors of vice and folly, of abuse and imperfection, among the other countries of the world; that we are to be the universal schoolmasters; and that all those who hesitate to recognize our office can be governed only by prejudice or personal animosity, and should have the blind war of diplomacy forthwith declared against them. And certainly, if the business of a Foreign Secretary properly were to carry on diplomatic wars, all must admit that the noble lord is a master in the discharge of his functions. What, sir, ought a Foreign Secretary to be? Is he to be like some gallant knight at a tournament of old, pricking forth into the lists, armed at all points, confiding in his sinews and his skill, challenging all comers for the sake of honor, and having no other duty than to lay as many as possible of his adversaries sprawling in the dust? If such is the idea of a good Foreign Secretary, I, for one, would vote to the noble lord his present appointment for his life. But, sir, I do not understand the duty of a Secretary for Foreign Affairs to be of such a character. I understand it to be his duty to conciliate peace with dignity. I think it to be the very first of all his duties studiously to observe, and to exalt in honor among mankind, that great code of principles which is termed the law of nations, which the learned and honorable member for Sheffield has found, indeed, to be very vague in their nature, and greatly dependent on the discretion of each particular country, but in which I find, on the contrary, a great and noble monument of human wisdom, founded on the combined dictates of reason and experience, a precious inheritance bequeathed to us by the generations that have gone before us, and a firm foundation on which we must take care to build whatever it may be our part to add to their acquisitions, if indeed, we wish to maintain and to consolidate the brotherhood of nations and to promote the peace and welfare of the world.

.   .   .   .

"Sir, I say the policy of the noble lord tends to encourage and confirm in us that which is our besetting fault and weakness, both as a nation and as individuals. Let an Englishman travel where he will as a private person, he is found in general to be upright, high-minded, brave, liberal and true; but, with all this, foreigners are too often sensible of something that galls them in his presence, and I apprehend it is because he has too great a tendency to self-esteem—too little disposition to regard the feelings, the habits, and the ideas of others. Sir, I find this characteristic too plainly legible in the policy of the noble lord. I doubt not that use will be made of our present debate to work upon this peculiar weakness of the English mind. The people will be told that those who oppose the motion are governed by personal motives, have no regard for public principles, no enlarged ideas of national policy. You will take your case before a favorable jury, and you think to gain your verdict, but, sir, let the House of Commons be warned— let it warn itself—against all illusions. There is in this case also a course of appeal. There is an appeal, such as the honorable and learned member for Sheffield has made, from the one House of Parliament to the other. There is a further appeal from this House of Parliament to the people of England; but lastly, there is also an appeal from the people of England to the general sentiment of the civilized world, and I, for my part, am of opinion that England will stand shorn of a chief part of her glory and pride if she shall be found to have separated herself, through the policy she pursues abroad, from the moral support which the general and fixed convictions of mankind afford—if the day shall come when she may continue to excite the wonder and the fear of other nations, but in which she shall have no part in their affection and regard.

"No, sir, let it not be so; let us recognize, and recognize with frankness, the equality of the weak with the strong, the principles of brotherhood among nations, and of their sacred independence. When we are asking for the maintenance of the rights which belong to our fellow-subjects resident in Greece, let us do as we would be done by, and let us pay all respect to a feeble State, and to the infancy of free institutions, which we should desire and should exact from others towards their maturity and their strength. Let us refrain from all gratuitous and arbitrary meddling in the internal concerns of other States, even as we should resent the same interference if it were attempted to be practiced towards ourselves. If the noble lord has indeed acted on these principles, let the Government to which he belongs have your verdict in its favor, but if he has departed from them, as I contend, and as I humbly think and urge upon you that it has been too amply proved, then the House of Commons must not shrink from the performance of its duty under whatever expectations of momentary obloquy or reproach, because we shall have done what is right; we shall enjoy the peace of our own consciences, and receive, whether a little sooner or a little later, the approval of the public voice for having entered our solemn protest against a system of policy which we believe, nay, which we know, whatever may be its first aspect, must, of necessity, in its final results be unfavorable even to the security of British subjects resident abroad, which it professes so much to study—unfavorable to the dignity of the country, which the motion of the honorable and learned member asserts it preserves—and equally unfavorable to that other great and sacred object, which also it suggests to our recollection, the maintenance of peace with the nations of the world."

But Lord Palmerston's project was carried by a majority of forty-six.

Gladstone suffered an immeasurable loss, as did England, in the death of Sir Robert Peel, who received fatal injuries in being thrown from his horse, on June 29th. Speaking in the House of Commons Gladstone said:

"I am quite sure that every heart is much too full to allow us, at a

period so early, to enter upon a consideration the amount of that
calamity with which the country has been visited in his, I must even
say, premature death; for though he has died full of years and full of
honors, yet it is a death which our human eyes will regard as premature; because we had fondly hoped that, in whatever position he was
placed, by the weight of his character, by the splendor of his talents,
by the purity of his virtues, he would still have been spared to render to
his country the most essential services.   I will only, sir, quote those
most touching and feeling lines which were applied by one of the great
poets of this country to the memory of a man great indeed, but yet not
greater than Sir Robert Peel:

> " 'Now is the stately column broke,
>   The beacon light is quenched in smoke
>   The trumpet's silver voice is still
>   The warder silent on the hill.'

"Sir, I will add no more—in saying this I have, perhaps, said too
much.   It might have been better had I simply confined myself to sec-
onding the motion.   I am sure the tribute of respect which we now offer
will be all the more valuable from the silence with which the motion
is received, and which I well know has not arisen from the want, but
from the excess, of feeling on the part of this House!"

In his letter to the Bishop of London on the Royal Supremacy,
Gladstone took the highest ground of loyalty to the King or Queen
in Church affairs.   He said:

"The trust reposed by the Constitution in the King with respect
to civil purposes was this: that he would commonly act in the spirit
of the Constitution, and would avail himself of the best assistance which
the country might afford for ascertaining, fostering, and upholding that
spirit, and for detailing according to its dictates with public exigencies
as they should arise.   And this trust was a trust not speculative only,
but accompanied with practical safeguards.   They were these in particular; that for making laws the Sovereign must act with the advice
and consent of the estates of the realm; and that, for administering
them, he would act by and through the persons who had made the laws

the study and business of their lives, and who would be best able to interpret them according to their own general spirit, and to the analogies
which the spirit supplied as well as to the mere precedents which its
history afforded. I speak of the constitutional system, which was in
course of being gradually elaborated and matured in England. Its
essential features had for many generations exercised a marked influence over the fortunes of the country, and in time they attained such a
ripeness, as to place both our legislative and judicial systems beyond
the reach of the arbitrary will, or the personal caprice, of Sovereigns.

"Now, I say, that the intention of the reformation, taken generally,
was to place our religious liberties on a footing analogous to that on
which our civil liberties had long stood. A supremacy of power in making and administering Church law as well as State law was to vest in the
Sovereign; but in making Church law he was to ratify the acts of the
Church herself, represented in Convocation, and if there were need of
the highest civil sanctions, then to have the aid of Parliament also. In
administering Church law, he was to discharge this function through
the medium of Bishops and divines, Canonists and civilians, as her own
most fully authorized, best instructed sons following in each case the
analogy of his ordinary procedure as head of the State."

Referring to the compact between Sovereign and subjects, he said
also:

"The ancient idea of compact had never been extinguished; and
upon an adequate occasion, namely, at the Revolution, it was reani-
mated, in terms indeed open to dispute, but in substance with a solemnity and weight of sanction which it has never lost. Now this great
and fundamental idea of compact, if it applies to individual subjects,
applies also yet more formally to the Estates of the realm, and involves
more than the mere personal conduct of the Sovereign. If the tenure
of the throne itself depends upon the observance of a compact, much
more does every other relation that binds together the several com-
ponent parts of the body politic, in its several orders and degrees of
men, as spirituality and temporality."

Gladstone's famous pamphlet on the Royal Supremacy was attract-
ing greatest attention. His shrewdest critics have proven to his most

PALMERSTON

QUEEN VICTORIA

loyal admirers that here is furnished perhaps the most conspicuous illustration of that habit of mind, which, in affairs of more importance than this, has operated to confuse rather than guide plain people in search of truth in its simplicity or facts in their completeness. Bagehot wrote:

"For the purpose of this case, it was of the last importance to determine the exact position of the Crown with respect to ecclesiastical affairs, and especially to the offense of heresy. The law at first seems distinct enough on the matter. The 1st of Elizabeth provides 'that such jurisdictions, privileges, superiorities and pre-eminences, spiritual and ecclesiastical, as by any spiritual or ecclesiastical power or authority hath heretofore been or may lawfully be exercised or used for the visitation of the ecclesiastical state and persons, and for reformation, order and correction of the same, and of all manner of errors, heresies, schisms, abuses, offenses, contempts and enormities, shall forever, by authority of this present parliament, be united and annexed to the imperial Crown of this realm.' These words would have seemed distinct and clear to most persons. They would have seemed to give to the Crown all the power it could wish to exercise—all that any spiritual authority had ever 'theretofore exercised'—all that any temporal authority could ever use. We should think it was clear Queen Elizabeth would have applied a rather summary method of instruction to any one who attempted to limit the jurisdiction conferred by this enactment. If Mr. Gladstone had lived in the times about which he was writing, he might have had to make a choice between being silent and being punished; but in the times of Queen Victoria he is not subject to an alternative so painful. He writes securely:

'We have now before us the terms of the great statute which from the time it was passed, has been the actual basis of the royal authority in matters ecclesiastical; and I do not load these pages by reference to declarations of the Crown, and other public documents less in authority than this, in order that we may fix our view the more closely upon the expressions of what may fairly be termed a fundamental law in relation to the subject matter before us.

'The first observation I make is this: There is no evidence in the words which have been quoted that the Sovereign is, according to the in-

9

tention of the statute, the source or fountain-head of ecclesiastical jurisdiction. They have no trace of such a meaning, in so far as it exceeds (and it does exceed) the proposition, that this jurisdiction has been by law united or annexed to the Crown.

'I do not now ask what have been the glosses of lawyers—what are the reproaches of polemical writers—or even what attributes may be ascribed to prerogative, independent of statute, and therefore applicable to the Church before as well as after the reformation. I must for the purposes of this argument assume what I shall never cease to believe until the contrary conclusion is demonstrated by fact, namely, that, in the case of the Church, justice is to be administered from the English bench upon the same principles as in all other cases—that our judges, or our judicial committees, are not to be our legislators—and that the statutes of the realm, as they are above the sacred majesty of the Queen, so are likewise above their ministerial interpreters. It was by statutes that the changes in the position of the Church at that great epoch were measured—by statute that the position itself is defined; and the statute, I say, contains no trace of such a meaning as that the Crown either originally was the source and spring of ecclesiastical jurisdiction, or was to become such in virtue of the annexation to it of the powers recited; but simply bears the meaning, that it was to be master over its administration.'

So that which seems a despotism is gradually pruned down into a vicegerency. "All the superiorities and pre-eminences spiritual and ecclesiastical," which had ever been lawfully exercised, are restricted to the single function of regulation; and by a judicious elaboration the Crown becomes scarcely the head of the Church, but only the visitor and corrector of it, as of several other corporations. We are not now concerned with the royal supremacy—we have no wish to hint or to intimate an opinion on a vast legal discussion; but we are concerned with Mr. Gladstone. And we venture to say that a subtler gloss, more scholastically expressed, never fell from lawyer in the present age, or from schoolmen in times of old."

We see in this only the necessary witness made by a man of Gladstone's temperament that, in progress of all kinds, the old bark does not fall off entirely until new bark forces it off from beneath.

CHAPTER XII.

THE NEAPOLITAN OUTRAGES.

In the course of the winter of 1850-51, Gladstone, yielding to a necessity brought about by the illness of one of his children, visited Naples, and spent nearly four months in that city. Here was a citizen of the world whose heart heard the cry of humanity as he saw seventy of the hundred and forty Deputies of the Chamber arrested or sent into exile, and more than 20,000 offenders against a base policy imprisoned under an indictment which meant their death. He hastened to the charge, and addressed an historical letter to his friend, Lord Aberdeen, in England, in which he said:

"It is not mere imperfection, not corruption in low quarters, not occasional severity, that I am about to describe; it is incessant, systematic, deliberate violation of the law by the Power appointed to watch over and maintain it. It is such violation of human and written law as this, carried on for the purpose of violating every other law, unwritten and eternal, human and divine; it is the wholesale persecution of virtue when united with intelligence, operating upon such a scale that entire classes may with truth be said to be its object, so that the Government is in bitter and cruel, as well as utterly illegal, hostility to whatever in the nation really lives and moves, and forms the mainspring of practical progress and improvement; it is the awful profanation of public religion, by its notorious alliance, in the governing powers, with the violation of every moral law under the stimulants of fear and vengeance; it is the perfect prostitution of the judicial office, which has made it, under veils only too threadbare and transparent, the degraded recipient of the vilest and clumsiest forgeries got up wilfully and deliberately, by the immediate advisers of the Crown, for the purpose of destroying the peace, the freedom, ay, and even if not by capital sentences the life, of men among the most virtuous, upright, intelligent,

131

distinguished, and refined of the whole community; it is the savage and cowardly system of moral, as well as in a lower degree of physical, torture through which the sentences extracted from the debased courts of justice are carried into effect. The effect of all this is, total inversion of all the moral and social ideas. Law, instead of being respected, is odious. Force, and not affection, is the foundation of Government. There is not association, but a violent antagonism, between the idea of freedom and that of order. The governing power, which teaches of itself that it is the image of God upon earth, is clothed, in the view of the overwhelming majority of the thinking public, with all the vices for its attributes. I have seen and heard the strong and too true expression used, 'This is the negation of God erected into a system of Government.' "

He said in his reply to the criticism of his letter from Naples:

"I express the hope that while there is time, while there is quiet, while dignity may yet be saved in showing mercy, and in the blessed work of restoring Justice to her seat, the Government of Naples may set its hand in earnest to work of real and searching, however quiet and unostentatious, reform; that it may not become unavoidable to reiterate these appeals from the hand of power to the one common heart of mankind; to produce those painful documents, those harrowing descriptions, which might be supplied in rank abundance, of which I have scarcely given the faintest idea or sketch, and which, if they were laid from time to time before the world, would bear down like a deluge every effort at apology or palliation, and would cause all that has recently been made known to be forgotten and eclipsed in deeper horrors yet; lest the strength of offended and indignant humanity should rise up as a giant refreshed with wine, and, while sweeping away these abominations from the eye of Heaven, should sweep away along with them things pure and honest, ancient, venerable, salutary to mankind, crowned with the glories of the past, and still capable of bearing future fruit."

He added: "The principle of conservation and the principle of progress are both sound in themselves; they have ever existed and must ever exist together in European society, in qualified opposition, but in vital harmony and concurrence; and for each of those principles it is a matter of deep and essential concern, that iniquities committed under the shelter of its name should be stripped of that shelter. Most of all is this the case where iniquity, towering on high, usurps the name and authority of that Heaven to which it lifts its head, and wears the double mask of Order and of Religion. Nor has it ever fallen to my lot to perform an office so truly conservative, as in the endeavor I have made to shut and mark off from the sacred cause of Government in general, a system which I believe was bringing the name and idea of Government into shame and hatred, and converting the thing from a necessity and a blessing into a sheer curse to human kind."—Reply to the Neapolitan Government, 1852.

Too little, at all events, but the most Gladstone could do, was done, and the horrible truth had been revealed in all its ghastliness. Cavour was working night and day for the unification of Italy, and the expulsion of Ferdinand II. was most desired. Lord John Russell had introduced the Ecclesiastical Titles Bill. The Roman Pontiff had issued an order creating a Roman Hierarchy in England. Protestantism revolted against what certainly appeared to be an attack upon their faith. The Pope had practically abolished the Church of England, so far as its authority and its position were concerned. Her Majesty's place as the potentate of England appeared to be a thing of no importance to His Holiness. The country was one wild scene of excitement. Lord John Russell urged his measure forbidding the Pope to constitute Roman Catholic bishops in England, according to the new map which the Vatican had invented. But Lord John Russell had gone too far. In his intemperate attack, he had denounced the High Church party as the ally of Rome. Disraeli directed his fiery scorn against the Bill, and Mr. Gladstone condemned it unsparingly. The Bill pleased nobody but the author, many good people blaming it for its concessions to Rome, others opposing it because it appeared to be an expedient violating religious liberty. When it passed finally, its agency was moribund. Twenty years after, under Gladstone, it was repealed.

CHAPTER XIII.

PALMERSTON OVERTHROWN.

The Government now was becoming unpopular. Lord Palmerston's policy had done only what a jingo policy can do for any country which adopts it. Of course, it failed to maintain the honor of England. Palmerston had become unmanageable and neglectful of his duties toward Her Majesty, while at the same time he had left on record of his willingness to connive with Louis Napoleon, who suddenly made himself Emperor of the French. When this was discovered, Palmerston had to go as Foreign Minister. The Queen called upon Lord Stanley and Lord Aberdeen, but both declined to constitute a Government. At last the Derby-Disraeli Cabinet was formed, the latter becoming Chancellor of the Exchequer and Leader of the House of Commons.

Disraeli introduced a Budget intended to bridge over the stream which was flowing rapidly and dangerously against their Government. Parliament was dissolved on July 1st, and Gladstone came back from Oxford with an increased majority. Now Disraeli introduced a Budget which he and his friends had pronounced a masterpiece. Lord Palmerston was out of the way, having had a delicious revenge when the Bill for the reorganization of the militia, as against France, was up, and he helped the Tories to defeat the Government which had dropped him. But the Government, and especially Mr. Disraeli, had a contest on hand of large proportions. Disraeli was able to meet manifold criticism of his Budget, and destroy or conceal it, for the most part, with his bursting fusilade of brilliant utterance and his steady fire of scorching sarcasm. He was simply exhibiting the sword with which he was about to enter into a lifelong duel with William E. Gladstone.

Gladstone arose at a moment when Disraeli's audacious utterance had clearly intimidated the House. His reply was perhaps the least apparently prepared speech he ever made, but, in point of fact, the

134

preparation of all his preceding years showed in the sinewy strength and resistless onset furnished by his unpremeditated sentences. In twenty minutes, the House of Commons, which had previously been cowed under the haughty demeanor of Disraeli, rose to cheer Gladstone, and the tumult of applause which broke in upon his fervid reply reached the streets outside the building. Disraeli and his government were defeated by nineteen votes. Soon the Queen received the announcement from Lord Derby, and the latter went to Osborne with his resignation. England was in a state of frenzied excitement. Gladstone's name was the one name heard everywhere, and the middle classes of England believed that the fame of William Pitt was to be eclipsed by this new finance-minister. On the other hand, Gladstone was attacked by a ruffianly crowd at the Carlton Club. Mr. Greville says of these criminals who had no other effective instrumentalities but their knuckles, "After dinner, when they got drunk, they went up stairs and finding Gladstone alone in the drawing-room, some of them proposed to throw him out of the window. This they did not quite dare do, but contented themselves with giving some insulting message or order to the waiter, and then went away."

Lord Aberdeen, who became Prime Minister, made Gladstone Chancellor of the Exchequer, and Gladstone found at his side his excellent friends, Sir James Graham and Sidney Herbert. But the Chancellor could no longer count upon the enthusiastic support of Oxford. Lord Derby had been elected Chancellor of the University, and the Oxford constituency felt that Gladstone was becoming a Liberal. He fought inch by inch during the canvass, and after the poll had been kept open for fifteen days and every effort had been made to defeat him, he was returned, with the idea in his own mind certainly that Oxford would not care for his services in some not far-away future. He presented his first Budget. Months before the Duke of Wellington had died, and his death had drawn from Gladstone a fine eulogium.

"While many of the actions of his life," said the speaker, "while many of the qualities he possessed are unattainable by others, there are lessons which we may all derive from the life and actions of that illustrious man. It may never be given to another subject of the British Crown to perform services so brilliant as he performed; it may never be given to another man to hold the sword which was to gain the independence of Europe, to rally the nations around it, and while England saved herself by her constancy, to save Europe by her example; it may never be given to another man, after having attained such eminence, after such an unexampled series of victories, to show equal moderation in peace as he has shown greatness in war, and to devote the remainder of his life to the cause of external and internal peace for that country which he has so served; it may never be given to another man to have equal authority both with the Sovereign he served, and with the Senate of which he was to the end a venerated member; it may never be given to another man, after such a career, to preserve even to the last the full possession of those great faculties with which he was endowed, and to carry on the services of one of the most important departments of the State with unexampled regularity and success, even to the latest day of his life. These are circumstances, these are qualities, which may never occur again in the history of this country. But there are qualities which the Duke of Wellington displayed, of which we may all act in humble imitation: that sincere and unceasing devotion to our country; that honest and upright determination to act for the benefit of the country on every occasion; that devoted loyalty, which, while it made him ever anxious to serve the Crown, never induced him to conceal from his Sovereign that which he believed to be the truth; that devotedness in the constant performance of duty; that temperance of his life which enabled him at all times to give his mind and his faculties to the services which he was called on to perform; that regular, consistent, and unceasing piety by which he was distinguished at all times in his life; these are qualities that are attainable by others, and should not be lost as an example."

Gladstone's Budget was offered for the consideration of the House April 18, 1853. It was a marvel of sound statesmanship, and it was witness to the fact that Gladstone's sympathy was with the classes who had hitherto found life difficult of support in England. Onerous taxes were remitted, arbitrary charges on ordinary business, on loco-

motion, on postal facilities, on things usually needed for the support
of everyday life, were removed. He proposed to meet any deficiency
by increasing the duty on spirits, extending the Income Tax, and
putting a Legacy Duty on real property. He had clearly deserted the
privileged few and gone over to the side of the toiling many. Five
million pounds of custom and excise duties were ruthlessly removed,
and the fortunate were asked to bear burdens with the unfortunate,
in all the realm. If Gladstone had ever shown genuine political power,
it was reserved for this occasion to give it its noblest exhibition.

No man has ever so charmingly elucidated the tortuous ways in
which facts hide themselves in figures as has Gladstone. For those
five hours, he illumined long fiscal statements, and a surprising mass of
dry fiscal details, having to do with all sorts of usually uninteresting
subjects, with the light of his genius. He never for a moment suffered
the attention of the House to flag, while his picturesque sentences
carried into the mind of the dullest hearer his own clear view of the
great and complex plan. No description of it is so worthy as some
extracts from the speech itself. He said this on the Income Tax:

"If the Committee have followed me, they will understand that we
stand on the principle that the Income Tax ought to be marked as a
temporary measure; that the public feeling that relief should be given
to intelligence and skill as compared with property ought to be met,
and may be met; that the Income Tax in its operation ought to be
mitigated by every rational means, compatible with its integrity; and,
above all, that it should be associated in the last term of its existence,
as it was in the first, with those remissions of indirect taxation which
have so greatly redounded to the profit of this country, and have set
so admirable an example—an example that has already in some quarters
proved contagious to other nations of the earth. These are the principles on which we stand, and the figures. I have shown you that
if you grant us the taxes which we ask, the moderate amount of £2,500,-
000 in the whole, and much less than that sum for the present year,
you, or the Parliament which may be in existence in 1860, will be in
the condition, if you so think fit, to part with the Income Tax. I am
almost afraid to look at the clock, shamefully reminding me, as it must,

how long I have trespassed on the time of the House. All I can say in apology is that I have endeavored to keep closely to the topics which I had before me—

> —immensum spatiis confecimus æquor,
> Et jam tempus equum fumantia solvere colla."

He then added in conclusion:

"These are the proposals of the Government. They may be approved or they may be condemned, but I have this full confidence that it will be admitted that we have not sought to evade the difficulties of the position; that we have not concealed those difficulties either from ourselves of from others; that we have not attempted to counteract them by narrow or flimsy expedients; that we have prepared plans, which, if you will adopt them, will go some way to close up many vexed financial questions, which, if not settled now, may be attended with public inconvenience, and even with public danger, in future years and under less favorable circumstances; that we have endeavored, in the plans that we have now submitted to you, to make the path of our successors in future years not more arduous but more easy; and I may be permitted to add that, while we sought to do justice to the great labor community of England by furthering their relief from indirect taxation, we have not been guided by any desire to put one class against another. We have felt that we should best maintain our own honor, that we should best meet the views of Parliament, and best promote the interests of the country, by declining to draw any invidious distinction between class and class, by adopting it to ourselves as a sacred aim to diffuse and distribute the burdens with equal and impartial hand; and we have the consolation of believing that by proposals such as these we contribute, as far as in us lies, not only to develop the material resources of the country, but to knit the various parts of this great nation yet more closely than ever to that Throne, and to those institutions under which it is our happiness to live."

Greville speaks of some matters of minor importance which occurred at this time, and then says, under date of April 21, 1853:

"These little battles were, however, of little moment compared with the great event of Gladstone's Budget, which came off on Monday night. He had kept his secret so well, that nobody had the least idea what it was to be, only it oozed out that the Income Tax was not to be differentiated. He spoke for five hours, and by universal consent it was one of the grandest' displays and most able financial statements that ever was heard in the House of Commons; a great scheme, boldly, skillfully, and honestly devised, disdaining popular clamor and pressure from without, and the execution of its absolute perfection. Even those who do not admire the Budget, or who are injured by it, admit the merit of the performance. It has raised Gladstone to a great political elevation, and, what is of far greater consequence than the measure itself, has given the country assurance of a man equal to great political necessities, and fit to lead parties and direct governments.

"April 22d: I met Gladstone last night, and had the pleasure of congratulating him and his wife, which I did with great sincerity, for his success is a public benefit. They have been overwhelmed with compliments and congratulations. Prince Albert and the Queen both wrote to him, and John Russell, who is spitefully reported to have been jealous, has, on the contrary, shown the warmest interest and satisfaction in his success. The only one of his colleagues who may have been mortified is Charles Wood, who must have compared Gladstone's triumph with his own failures. From all one can see at present it promises certain success, though many parts of the Budget are caviled at. It will be difficult, if not impossible, to find any common ground on which Radicals or Irish can join the Derbyites to overthrow it, and the sanguine expectations which the latter have been entertaining for some time, of putting the Government into some inexplicable fix, have given way to perplexity and despondency; and they evidently do not know what to do, nor how to give effect to their rancor and spite. Lord Derby had a great meeting not many days ago, at which he recommended union, and cheered them in opposition, of course, for form's sake, talking of moderation and principles, neither of which he cares a fig for. Mischief and confusion, vengeance against the coalition, and taking the chance of what may happen next, are all that he and Disraeli are bent upon. I met the latter worthy in

10

the street just before the Budget, a day or two previous. He asked
me what I thought of the state of affairs, and I told him I thought
it very unpleasant, and it seemed next to impossible to carry on the
Government at all, everybody running riot in the House of Commons,
and following his own fancies and crotchets; nor did I see how it
could be otherwise in the present state of parties and the country;
that since Peel's administration, which was a strong Government, there
had been and apparently there could be none. The present Government
was not strong, and they were perpetually defeated, on minor points,
indeed, but in a way that showed they had no power to work through
Parliament. I said of course they would dissolve if this continued, but
that Gladstone's Budget might make a difference one way or the other.
Disraeli scouted the idea of a dissolution, by which, he said, they would
certainly gain nothing. Why, he asked, did not the Peelites join us
again? As I don't want to quarrel with anybody, I restrained what
was on my lips, to say—'You could not possibly expect them to join
you'—but I did tell him that, even if the present Government could
not maintain itself, of all impossible things the most impossible was the
restoration of his Government *tale quale,* to which he made no reply.
To be sure, the Protectionist seceders from Peel have now drunk the
cup of mortification, disgrace, and disaster to the very dregs. They
are a factious and (as I hope) impotent Opposition, under the un-
principled guidance of men, who, clever and plausible though they be,
are totally destitute of wisdom, sincerity, and truth. They have not
only lost all the Protection for the maintenance of which they made
such struggles and sacrifices, but they have likewise brought upon
themselves the still heavier blow to the landed interest which is going
to be inflicted in the shape of the legacy duty. Had they possessed
more foresight, and been less violent and unreasonable, this could
not have happened to them; for if Peel's original Government had
held together, and they had been content to accept his guidance, no
Budget would have contained this measure."

CHAPTER XIV.

AFTER THE TRIUMPH.

Gladstone was a name gladly spoken by every lip. From the Queen and the Prince Consort came a letter of congratulation. The strongest and best men in all the realm forwarded words significant of their admiration and confidence. England felt a thrill of pride that at last her great Pitt had a successor worthy to wear his robes, and the Opposition itself took a just delight in the fact that so skillful and lucid an expositor of finance belonged to the English nation. Greville, under date of May 23, 1853, gave an account of an interview with Gladstone's friend, Sir James Graham. The former says:

"Graham seemed in excellent spirits about their political state and prospects, all owing to Gladstone and the complete success of his Budget. The long and numerous Cabinets, which were attributed by the 'Times' to disunion, were occupied in minute consideration of the Budget, which was there fully discussed; and Gladstone spoke in the Cabinet one day for three hours rehearsing his speech in the House of Commons, though not quite at such length. . . . . He talked of a future head, as Aberdeen is always ready to retire at any moment; but it is very difficult to find anyone to succeed him. I suggested Gladstone. He shook his head and said it would not do. . . . He spoke of the grand mistakes Derby had made. Gladstone's object certainly was for a long time to be at the head of the Conservative party in the House of Commons, and to join with Derby, who might, in fact, have had all the Peelites if he would have chosen to ally himself with them, instead of with Disraeli; thus the latter had been the cause of the ruin of the party. Graham thought that Derby had committed himself to Disraeli in George Bentinck's lifetime in some way which prevented his shaking him off, as it would have been his interest to do. The Peelites would have united with Derby, but would have nothing to do with Disraeli."

Nothing but the stubborn and bloody fact of war could have thwarted Gladstone in securing for the English people the benefits proposed by this Budget. But the Crimean War was already in sight.

At this time in Gladstone's life, as it would appear to most readers, there was little time for composing essays or studying Homer, but in point of fact, Gladstone was never more productive. In his letter to the Bishop of Aberdeen he had spoken on freedom and authority, and his words are of the utmost value to those who would comprehend that subject or understand Gladstone's career. He said:

"Miserable would be the prospect of the coming times, if we believed that authority and freedom were simply conflicting and contradictory elements in the constitution of a community, so that whatever is given to the one must be deducted from the other. But no Briton, who has devoted any portion of his thoughts to the history of his country, or the character of its inhabitants, can for a moment be ensnared into that, for him, false and degrading belief. It has been providentially allotted to this favored isle that it should show to all the world how freedom and authority, in their due and wise developments, not only may coexist in the same body, but may, instead of impairing, sustain and strengthen one another. Among Britons it is the extent and security of freedom which renders it safe to entrust large powers to Government, and it is the very largeness of those powers and the vigor of their exercise which constitute to each individual of the community the great practical safeguard of his liberties in return. The free expression of opinion, as our experience has taught us, is the safety-valve of passion. That noise of the rushing steam, when it escapes, alarms the timid; but it is the sign that we are safe. The concession of reasonable privilege anticipates the growth of furious appetite."

At no time in his life, however, was he more true to the England of Alfred and Hampden. This was evidenced in his letter to the Bishop of London on the Royal Supremacy, in which he says:

"The monarchy of England has been from early times a free monarchy. The idea of law was altogether paramount, in this happy constitution, to that of any personal will. Nothing could be more complete than the recognition of the Sovereign as the source both of legislative and of judicial authority for the exigencies of the passing day; but it was the felicity of this country that its people did not regard the labors of their forefathers as naught. In such manner they realized the inheritance they had received from preceding generations, that at all times what was to be done was with them secondary, and what had been done, primary; and the highest works of the actual legislator always aimed at the vindication and re-establishment of the labors and acquisitions of those who had preceded him. Here lay the grand cause of the success of our English revolutions, that the people never rent the web of history, but repaired its rents; never interposed a chasm between, never separated, the national life of the present and that of the past, but even when they seemed most violently to alter the momentary, always aimed at recovering the general, direction of their career. Thus everybody knew that there were laws superior to the Sovereign, and liberties which he could not infringe; that he was King in order to be the guardian of those laws and liberties, and to direct both the legislative and all other governing powers in the spirit which they breathed, and within the lines which they marked out for him."

In the same, he writes: "A spirit of trust and confidence almost unbounded then, was, and still is, the spirit of the British Constitution. Even now, after three centuries of progress towards democratic sway, the Crown has prerogatives, by acting upon which, within their strict and unquestioned bounds, it might at any time throw the country into confusion. And so has each House of Parliament. Why is this the case? Because it is impossible to tie down by literal enactments the sovereign power in a State, since by virtue of its sovereignty it can get rid of the limitations imposed upon it, however strict may be their letter. Yet if that sovereign power be well advised, if the different elements of the social body be duly represented and organized, there arises out of their wise adjustment a system of balance and limitation infinitely more effective than any mere statutory bonds. So it has been in the State of England; so, it might well be hoped, three hundred years ago, that it would be with the Church."

Steadily as he was traveling in the direction of Liberalism, so strongly also did he adhere to the great and fundamental principles of English constitutional Government.

But there could be no question that Gladstone saw in the progress of these events, and felt in his own experience that England needed to be told over and over again to do what we here in America see was and is characteristic of the progress of every free government. He said: •

"As we follow the course of history, we find that unwise concession has been the parent of many evils. But unwise resistance is answerable for many more; nay, is too frequently the primary source of the mischief ostensibly arising from the opposite policy, because it is commonly unwise resistance which so dams up the stream and accumulates the waters that, when the day of their bursting comes, they are absolutely ungovernable. A little modicum of time, indeed, may thus be realized by gigantic labors in repression, during which not even the slightest ripple shall be audible. And within that little time statesmen, dressed in their brief authority, may claim credit with the world for the peremptory assertion of power; and for having crushed, as the phrase goes at Naples, the hydra of revolution. But every hour of that time is not bought, it is borrowed, and borrowed at a rate of interest, with which the annals of usury itself have nothing to compare. The hydra of revolution is not really to be crushed by the attempt to crush, or even by momentary success in crushing, under the name of revolution, a mixed and heterogeneous mass of influences, feelings, and opinions, bound together absolutely by nothing except repugnance to the prevailing rigors and corruptions. Viewed as mere matter of policy, this is simply to undertake the service of enlistment for the army of the foe. It is a certain proposition that, when a Government thus treats enmity to abuse as identical with purposes of subversion, it, according to the laws of our mixed nature, partially amalgamates the two, and fulfills at length its own miserable predictions in its own more miserable ruin."

WM. E. GLADSTONE—ENGLISH STATESMAN

WINDSOR CASTLE

CHAPTER XV.

THE CRIMEAN WAR.

In spite of all that the great powers of Europe could do, the war in the Crimea assumed its fearful proportions, and the Government was committed to projects which left Gladstone's brilliant achievements a series of proposals that could not be carried out. Nevertheless the finances under Gladstone's administration improved progressively, and in spite of the dark cloud which broke forth in desolating war from the East, England was prosperous in trade, manufacture and agriculture. In the matter of the Crimean War, Mr. Gladstone offered his opposition with sober strength, and seemed willing, if not to trust, at least to approve all schemes for peace, before admitting the necessity for bloody strife. The war, of course, was opposed most strenuously by all who accepted the leadership of John Bright in the name of peace. On the 31st of March, 1854, Parliament received the Royal message, and Bright threw himself heart and soul into antagonism. Mr. Gladstone referred afterwards to this occurrence in the following language:

"We ought to be ready," said he, "as my right hon. friend, Mr. Bright, showed himself to be ready at the time of the Crimean War to lay his popularity as a sacrifice—(loud cheers)—upon the altar of his duty, I will say without a moment of regret, because I am sure that to a man of his feelings and strong sympathies it must have been a matter of regret to find himself less in harmony for a time with the sentiment of that day than he had been heretofore. Perhaps with many sentiments, many moments of regret, but without one sentiment or one moment of hesitation. (Cheers.) That, in my opinion, is the conduct which beyond all others ennobles the man that pursues it and the country that produces such men. It is not every one who has the opportunity of making such splendid offerings to duty as he did, because it is not every one that can accumulate the stock of public approbation and esteem out of which alone they can be made. But every one of us can, from early life onwards, to some extent imitate such conduct, though we may be content to labor in the dark—content to labor under suspicion, content to labor under reproach, well assured that if we keep the pole-star of duty well fixed in our vision we never shall fail to reach the end which we have in view, as far as it involves the good of the country, and to reach such mode and measure of public approval as may be good and sufficient for ourselves." (Hear, hear.)

Gladstone remained in his position, even though he had been fighting against the drift of things toward war, and he stood because he believed if he resigned a war ministry would be formed immediately.

He afterwards wrote of the war, in his review of Sir Theodore Martin's Life of the Prince Consort:

"At the outset, the quarrel was one between Russia and France in regard to ecclesiastical privileges at the Holy Places. England was but an amicus curiæ; and, in that capacity, she thought Russia in the right. As, however, the communications went on, the Czar, unfortunately, committed his case to a special envoy, Prince Menschikoff, whose demands upon the Porte appeared to the British Government to render harmony in the Turkish Empire, if they should be accepted, thenceforth impossible. In the further stages of the correspondence, which had thus shifted its ground, we found ourselves in company with France; and not with France only, but with Europe. At one particular point, it must in fairness be allowed that Russia, with her single rapier, had all her antagonists at a disadvantage. They had collectively accepted, and they proposed to her a Note, known as the Vienna Note, which she also accepted; and they afterwards receded from it, upon objection taken to it by Turkey. Russia, however, covered the miscarriage of her opponents by sustaining the Turkish interpretation of the words, and thus sheltered their retreat from the support of the document they themselves had framed. But it was not upon this miscarriage that the dispute came to a final issue. The broken threads of negotiation were pieced together; and, about the time when the year expired, a new instrument, of a moderate and

conciliatory character, was framed at Constantinople, and approved
by the Cabinets of the five Powers, still in unbroken union. It was
the rejection of this plan by the Emperor Nicholas, when it was presented to him in January, 1854, and not his refusal of the Turkish
amendments to the Vienna Note, that brought about the war in the
following March.

"That war passed through all the phases of popularity; the people,
and especially the newspapers, were so fond of it while it lasted, that
they were, as we have seen, reluctant to let it end. It is an unquestionable fact, that Mr. Cobden and Mr. Bright, who stoutly and most dis-
interestedly opposed it, and who, with the bloom of the Corn Law
triumph upon them, were before it began the most popular men in the
country, lost for the time, by their opposition to it, all hold upon the
general public. The war, however, soon and even rapidly waned in
favor. At length it came to be looked upon by many, if not by most,
as an admitted folly. The nation appeared to have come round to
the opinion of Cobden and of Bright. And yet the war had attained
its purpose; which was, to repress effectually the aggression of Russia,
and to secure to Turkey breathing-time and full scope for the reform of
its government.

"It may be said that, after all, she did not reform her government.
Most true; but it is only within a short time that this fact has become
at all generally known to our countrymen. And, moreover, this reform was not, properly speaking, the object of the war, but rather an
aim incidental to the conditions of the Peace. Why, then, did it fall
into disfavor? Because men estimated its object, not as it was drawn
out in the minds of the statesmen who made the war, but according
to their own unauthorized and exaggerated ideas of its aim, and of the
position of the several parties. Turkey, it had been too commonly
held, was a young and vigorous country, only waiting an open and
calm atmosphere to break out into the beauty and bloom of a young
civilization. Russia was to be cut into morsels, or at the least to be
crippled by the amputation of important members. The extravagance
of these anticipations led to disappointment; and the disappointment,

for which people had themselves, or perhaps their newspapers, to thank, was avenged upon the Crimean War.

"The persons who are really entitled to vaunt their foresight in this matter, as superior alike to the views of Sovereigns and of statesmen, are the few, the very few, who objected to the war from the beginning to the end, and who founded this objection not upon a philanthropic yet scarcely rational proscription of war under all circumstances and conditions, but upon a deeper insight into the nature and foundations of Mahometan power over Christian races, than had fallen to the lot either of diplomacy or of statesmanship. Of these, perhaps the most distinguished are Mr. Freeman and Dr. Newman, both of whom in 1853 proclaimed the hopeless nature, not of the Ottoman as such, but of the Ottoman ascendancy. Both have republished their works of that date, and Mr. Freeman has taken a most active and able part in all the recent controversies; in which, to the surprise of many admirers, the living voice of Dr. Newman has not once been heard."

But Mr. Gladstone had been heard. The war had come, with its desolations, its terrible blunders, its heroisms, and its attendant expense. In 1854 Mr. Gladstone offered his Budget, but the circumstances contrasted widely with those of a year previous. Yet the Finance Minister was sure footed and able. Greville writes:

"May 7th: The failure of Gladstone's Exchequer Bill scheme has been very injurious to the Government, and particularly to him. The prodigious applause and admiration with which he was greeted last year have given way to distrust and apprehension of him as a finance minister, and the repeated failures of his different schemes here in a very short time materially damaged his reputation, and destroyed the prestige of his great abilities. All practical men in the city severely blame him for having exposed himself to the defeat thus sustained. The consequences will not probably be serious, but the Government is weakened by it, and the diminution of public confidence in Gladstone is a public misfortune."

Greville adds, under date of May 7th and 10th, 1854, the following:

"May 7th: It is scarcely a year ago that I was writing enthusiastic panegyrics on Gladstone, and describing him as the great ornament and support of the Government, and as the future Prime Minister. This was after the prodigious success of his first Budget and his able speeches, but a few months seem to have overturned all his power and authority. I hear nothing but complaints of his rashness and passion for his experiments; and on all sides, from men, for example, like Tom Baring and Robarts, one a Tory, the other a Whig, that the city and the moneyed men have lost all confidence in him. To-morrow night he is to make his financial statement, and intense curiosity prevails to see how he will provide the ways and means for carrying on the war. Everybody expects that he will make an able speech; but brilliant speeches do not produce great effect, and more anxiety is felt for the measures he will propose than for the dexterity and ingenuity he may display for proposing them. Parliament is ready to vote without grumbling any money that is asked for, and as yet at the very beginning of this horrible mess, and the people are still looking with eager interest to the successes they anticipate, and have not yet begun to feel the cost.

"May 10th: Gladstone made a great speech on Monday night. He spoke for nearly four hours, occupying the first half of the time in an elaborate and not unsuccessful defense of his former measures. His speech was certainly very able, was well received, and the Budget pronounced an honorable and creditable one. If he had chosen to sacrifice his conscientious convictions to popularity, he might have gained a great amount of the latter by proposing a loan, and no more taxes than would be necessary for the interest of it. I do not yet know whether his defense of his abortive schemes has satisfied the monetary critics. It was certainly very plausible, and will be probably sufficient for the uninformed and the half-informed, who cannot detect any fallacies which may lurk within it. He attacked some of his opponents with great severity, particularly Disraeli and Monteagle, but I doubt if this was prudent. He flung about his sarcasms upon smaller fry, and this certainly was not discreet. I think this speech has been of service to his financial character, and done a good deal towards the restoration of his credit."

The Crimean War had made it impossible for him to go far in financial reform. Lord John Russell and he were both pained because their plans had been broken in upon by the strife, and taxation had been increased. He asked the House of Commons to double the income tax so long as the war lasted, in order that posterity might not have to pay the chief cost of the war. Gladstone had spoken amidst the applause of a great nation. He said, among other things:

"We have entered upon a great struggle, but we have entered upon it under favorable circumstances. We have proposed to you to make great efforts, and you have nobly and cheerfully backed our proposals. You have already by your votes added nearly 40,000 men to the establishments of the country; and taking into account changes that have actually been carried into effect with regard to the return of soldiers from the Colonies, and the arrangements which, in the present state of Ireland, might be made—but which are not made—with respect to the constabulary force, in order to render the military force disposable to the utmost possible extent, it is not too much to say that we have virtually an addition to the disposable forces of the country, by land and by sea, at the present moment, as compared with our position twelve months ago, to the extent of nearly 50,000 men. This looks like your intention to carry on your war with vigor, and the wish and hope of Her Majesty's Government is, that that may be truly said of the people of England, with regard to this war, which was, I am afraid, not so truly said of Charles II. by a courtly but great poet, Dryden—

> He without fear a dangerous war pursues,
> Which without rashness he began before.

That, we trust, will be the motto of the people of England; and you have this advantage, that the sentiment of Europe, and we trust the might of Europe, is with you. These circumstances—though we must not be sanguine, though it would be the wildest presumption for any man to say, when the ravages of European war had once begun, where and at what point it would be stayed—these circumstances justify us in cherishing the hope that possibly this may not be a long war."

He wrote years afterward in his review of "The Life of the Prince Consort," of the events of this time:

"The attachment of the Sovereign and her Consort to Sir Robert Peel, the Duke of Wellington, and Lord Aberdeen, led them to watch with interest the working of the Aberdeen Cabinet, in which the Peelites held no less than six offices, besides having four members of their small party in the most important positions outside the Cabinet. The six Cabinet Ministers were Lord Aberdeen, the Duke of Argyll,* Sir James Graham, the Duke of Newcastle, Mr. Gladstone, and Mr. Sydney Herbert. The four outside the door were Mr. Cardwell at the Board of Trade, Lord Canning at the Post Office, Lord St. Germans, Viceroy of Ireland, and Sir John Young, Chief Secretary. Another Cabinet Minister, Sir William Molesworth, was perhaps more nearly associated with them than with the Whigs. Holding this large share of official power, the Peelites did not bring more than about thirty independent votes to the support of the Ministry, in addition to which they neutralized the Opposition of perhaps as many more members who sat on the other side of the House. Mr. Martin says (p. 90), 'It was apparent to all the world that no cordial unanimity existed between the Peelite section of the Ministry and their colleagues.'

"This is an entire mistake. It must be stated, to the credit of all parties, but especially of the Whig section of that Cabinet, that although the proportions of official power were so different from those of the voting strength in Parliament, there was no sectional demarcation, nor any approach to it, within the Cabinet. In proof of this statement, it may be mentioned that when, in the recess of 1853-4, Lord Palmerston had resigned his office on account of the impending Reform Bill, and it was desired to induce him to reconsider his decision, the two persons who were chosen for the duty of communicating to him the wish of his colleagues were the Duke of Newcastle and Mr. Gladstone.

---

* The Duke of Argyll was invited at a very early age, on account of his high personal character and his talent, to enter the Cabinet of Lord Aberdeen, but he did not belong to the ex-official corps who passed by the name of Peelites, while he was in political accordance with them.

CHAPTER XVI.

A NEW GOVERNMENT.

On the 25th of January, 1855, Mr. Roebuck began his attack upon the Ministry. It was a censure on the War Department and the conduct of the war. Lord Russell wrote to Aberdeen, telling him his only course was to tender his resignation. Soon the Ministry had resigned. Lord Russell and Lord Derby each failed to form an administration, and on the 6th of February, 1855, it was announced in the House of Lords by Lord Granville that a government had been constituted. Lord Palmerston was at the head. "The inevitable man" was active at the outset. Mr. Gladstone, with his friends, Sir James Graham and Mr. Sidney Herbert, still antagonized the forces which caused Lord Aberdeen to resign. Mr. Gladstone was succeeded in office by his schoolmate of other days, Sir George Cornewall Lewis. The triumvirate which was formed by Herbert, Gladstone and Sir James Graham was described by Gladstone as "a set of roving icebergs, on which men could land with safety, but with which ships might come into perilous collision."

When the year 1856 closed, the heavens were brighter, for peace had come, and any difficulties with the United States on the Enlistment question had vanished away. England and the other European powers were satisfied with each other, and all seemed to point toward an era of prosperity for the English people. It was no doubt the desire of Gladstone at this time to pursue his task of fiscal reform. On the 3d of February, 1857, Parliament was opened. Mr. Cobden soon made his motion condemning the conduct of the Government and proposing an inquiry into the state of England's commercial relations with China. In this debate Gladstone became involved in fierce controversy with Lord Palmerston who defended the Government. The point upon which the discussion turned was very unimportant, apparently, but the debate brought Lord Palmerston within sight of a resignation. The Government, however, determined not to resign, but to dissolve. The electoral conflict was immediately on, and Mr. Gladstone was everywhere eloquent and forceful as he journeyed through the country delivering his glowing and patriotic addresses. Cobden, Bright, Milner Gibson and Fox, were rejected by their constituents, and Bright took leave of the electors of Manchester in a speech calm, dignified, yet deeply pathetic. Lord John Russell stood third on the poll for the City of London, and it was evident that the constituencies supported and approved Palmerston, whom Disraeli had called "the Tory chief of a Radical Cabinet." Any chance for Gladstone's fiscal reform seemed indefinitely removed; but in the first session of the new Parliament Gladstone found himself eagerly engaged in a contest against the passing of a divorce bill which strongly offended his ecclesiastical and highly conservative sensibilities and convictions. Many times the proposal to "facilitate the breaking of marriage bonds," as he saw it, had come to the front, and had occupied a large share of legislative attention. The Prime Minister now stood behind it, and the measure was carried, in spite of conscientious and enthusiastic opposition.

It is very easy for a less grave and strenuous soul to misunderstand the earnestness of such a man as Gladstone when he knew that such another man as Palmerston was utterly reckless of the command of great moral sentiments. While Palmerston never really believed that any man need to care a penny for ancient wrongs, which ever tend to become venerable to that class of men, Gladstone's grave and chaster spirit chafed at the very thought of their existence, and if he was fierce in his attack upon Palmerston, or "anxious to be in office," as has been so often said of him, it was because he saw crouching behind such a figure as Palmerston gigantic evils which the progress of mankind must extirpate, and he discerned in office the opportunity for such a man as Gladstone proved himself to be, to strike, and strike home, against respectable evil.

When Palmerston resigned early in 1858, he had the joy of remembering that his Chinese policy had been victorious, and Canton had surrendered to the armies of England. It was with much difficulty

that Lord Derby, under command of his Sovereign, constituted a government. He was conscious that he had on hand very serious problems. Disraeli was, however, able to announce in Parliament that the
peace between England and France, which was threatened, was more
strong and promising than ever, now that the reply had been given to
the note of Count Walewski, the minister of foreign affairs at Paris,
who had accused England of harboring such criminals as had attacked
the French Emperor. Gladstone at this time was studying profoundly
both his Homer and his schemes for financial reform. He, however,
could not allow his Government to make a slight answer to the charges
of France. Some one must explain the law of England, as it had to do
with a criminal, who, having gone from London to Paris, had attacked
the Emperor of the French. Gladstone spoke noble words in Parliament. He believed in the law of England, and he urged that that law
should be vindicated. His spirit would not for a moment permit him
or his country to "lie under a cloud of accusation," of which "the law,"
at least, was "totally innocent." He added:

These times are grave for liberty. We live in the nineteenth century;
we talk of progress; we believe that we are advancing, but can any man
of observation who has watched the events of the last few years in Europe
have failed to perceive that there is a movement indeed, but a downward
and backward movement? There are a few spots in which institutions that
claim our sympathy still exist and flourish. They are secondary places—
nay, they are almost the holes and corners of Europe so far as mere material
greatness is concerned, although their moral greatness will, I trust, ensure
them long prosperity and happiness. But in these times more than ever
does responsibility center upon the institutions of England; and if it does
center upon England, upon her principles, upon her laws, and upon her
governors, then I say that a measure passed by this House of Commons—the chief hope of freedom—which attempts to establish a moral
complicity between us and those who seek safety in repressive measures,
will be a blow and a discouragement to that sacred cause in every country
in the world.

Disraeli's India Bill did not demand Gladstone's fierce denunciation
to render it sufficiently unpopular and to give it no chance for a second
reading.   A compromise was offered in July on the aggravating sub-

ject of Jewish Disabilities, and the oath was administered in the Lower House to Baron Rothschild. Bright was arguing eloquently for a larger franchise, and Lord Derby and Disraeli were becoming conscious that reform must be made strongly and at once or there was danger of their government being overwhelmed.

In 1859, after changes in the Ministry almost unmatched in number in any generation in England, Mr. Gladstone acceded to the Ministry and confronted a contest for his seat for the University of Oxford. There was no longer any question that Gladstone was grandly inconsistent with his past. More and more clearly defined was the hitherto vague Liberalism of this man whom Macaulay had once called "the hope of those stern and unbending Tories." Oxford was becoming a little restive, but even Oxford was charmed with him and proud withal when once more he introduced a Budget, and on the 18th of July made another splendid exposition of financial principles, creating genuine enthusiasm as he spoke of penny stamps, bankers' checks, malt credits, and the like. Fortunately, prosperity revived, and the year's revenue exceeded that of any previous year by more than two million pounds. Verily Gladstone had Providence with him.

People are not usually anxious for reform when they are prosperous in the most worldly sense, and this was a time when nobody was demanding it and nobody feared it. It was therefore a good time for moderate counsels. Mr. Disraeli had agreed to yield as much as Lord John Russell desired, and the Queen's speech indicated that the Government was willing to put a broader, firmer basis under national representation. Cobden was arranging a treaty with France, and free trade had its widest victory in that commercial amity which took the form of the treaty.

In all this discussion, Mr. Gladstone never failed to recognize the excellent service of men who differed from him in temperament and oftentimes in the means employed to the end of national growth and safe constitutional development. An example of this may be found in the fact that when Mr. Gladstone introduced his Budget, which set forth the provisions of the treaty making peace, he said of Cobden:

"It is a great privilege of any man who, having fifteen years ago rendered to his country one important and signal service, now enjoys the singular good fortune of having in his power—undecorated, bearing no mark of rank or title from his sovereign, or from the people—to perform another signal service in the same cause for the benefit of, I hope, a not ungrateful country."

It was a singularly shrewd, if it had not been a perfectly just, recognition of the man who had completed commercial relations with France, and who was so intimately associated with one who was so intolerant of war as Mr. Bright. The latter had no hesitancy in creating a progressive opinion in behalf of peace and thus enabling the Chancellor of the Exchequer to deal with other problems.

"Politically," observed Mr. Bright, "I live and move and have my being only in the hope that I may advance the cause of truth and your cause, if only by a single step. (Cheers.) If I tell you that peace and peaceful industry is your path of wisdom and of greatness; if I say it is your taxes that are spent, your sweat which is pawned, your blood which is shed in war, am I the less your countryman? (Loud cheers and cries of "No.") If your Sunday prayer for peace be not a mockery and offensive in the sight of Heaven, then I am justified in denouncing, as I now heartily denounce, them who in the Parliament or in your Press are striving to involve the most potent nations of the earth in the crimes and in the calamities of war." (Loud cheers.)

Gladstone seemed to handle the finances with so sure a grasp that England gave Providence no particular praise for a state of things in which the able Finance Minister appeared positively brilliant.

April 25th, 1858, Greville tells us of the attack Gladstone made upon Palmerston, in his review article in the Quarterly on France and the Ministry:

"April 29th: Every day the position of the Government gets worse. The disposition there was to give them a fair opportunity of carrying on public affairs as well as they could has given way to disgust and contempt at their blundering and stupidity, and those who have all along resented their attempt to hold office at all are becoming more impatient and more anxious to turn them out. There is a very temperate, but very just, article in the 'Times' to-day, which contains all that is to be said on the subject, stated without bitterness or exaggeration. The Whigs, however, seem aware that it is not expedient to push such matters to extremity, and to force their resignation, until the quarrels of the Liberal party are made up, and till Palmerston and John Russell are brought together and prepared to join in taking office, and to effect this object the most tremendous effort are making. What the pacificators aim at is, that Palmerston should go as Premier to the House of Lords, and leave Lord John to lead the House of Commons. This is the most reasonable compromise, and one which ought to be satisfactory to both; but even if this leading condition were agreed to, it is not certain that there might not be other presenting great obstacles to the union, such as whether Lord John would agree to join without bringing a certain number of men with him, and whether Palmerston would consent to exclude so many of his former Cabinet to make room for them. Graham, Lord John would, I suppose, certainly insist upon; Gladstone would probably be no party to any arrangement, and he has recently evinced his extreme antipathy to Palmerston by a bitter though able review in the 'Quarterly' on France and the late Ministry, in which he attacks Palmerston with extraordinary asperity.

"Ever since he resigned, Palmerston has been very active in the House of Commons, and kept himself constantly before the public, evidently with the object of recovering his former popularity as much as possible, and he made a very clever and lively speech two nights ago, which his friends praise up to the skies.

"I met Derby yesterday, and soon after the Chancellor in Piccadilly, and had some talk with both of them. They were neither of them in a very sanguine mood, and apparently well aware of the precariousness of their position. Derby attributed the state of affairs, which he owned was very bad, to the caprice and perverseness of the House of Commons, which he said was manageable. I did not, as I might have done, tell him that he had no right to complain of this House, and that it was the mismanagement of his own colleagues which was the cause of the evil. Lyndhurst made an extraordinary speech on the Jew Bill on Tuesday night."

CHAPTER XVII.

THE IONIAN ISLANDS.

It was in 1858 that Gladstone was besought by Lord Derby to visit the Ionian Isles as Lord High Commissioner Extraordinary from England. Nothing could have been more to his liking as a student of Greece than such an opportunity as was this, to bathe his spirit in the very atmosphere of Greek freedom, and catch some of the echoes of Greek literature under the sky which had arched itself over the heads of Homer and Sappho. However great his enthusiasm over his proposed visit was from a literary point of view, the interest in his departure lay more largely in the fact that these Islands, which had been under English protection, wished to unite themselves to Greece. Of course, with a desire of that kind to deal with, the business of governing them on the part of England had become very complex and arduous.

If England had expected this plastic and sympathetic scholar to go forth with the usual panoply of John Bull, and wrest from the Islands their wish and aspiration toward Greece, England had sorely miscalculated and provided for a grievous disappointment.

Gladstone went, and on the 3d of December, the Senate of the Ionian Islands was charmed and inspired by a characteristic address delivered by the eloquent Englishman in the Italian language. It is very doubtful if ever a representative of a strong nation stood in a more happy frame of mind or conducted his task with more of genuine humanity and comprehensive wisdom, than did Gladstone on this occasion. He was invited as the official of Great Britain to meet the citizens of the Islands at levees, and from platforms erected in the most significant spots he spoke with extraordinary foresight and impassioned eloquence. Lord Aberdeen, who was usually willing to estimate properly the poetic and romantic side of Gladstone's nature, looked over seas, and beheld him arranging a scheme of government for these Islands which John Bull laughed at, and even Aberdeen called fanciful. Gladstone, as Lord High Commissioner, did not need a brilliant genius to discover that the inhabitants of the Islands wished to be connected with Greece by the closest political relationships; indeed, that they desired nothing less than union. They sent their petitioner to Her Majesty in England, and Gladstone came back to London, having performed his task to his taste and to his honor.

We have already swiftly sketched the movements which were immediately related to these events. The air was full of cries for reform, and on the 28th of February, 1859, Disraeli had introduced his Reform Bill. It was a very great disappointment for those who were expecting some relief from the intolerable burdens which everywhere were resting heavily upon the shoulders of the common people. The Reform question was not one which Disraeli had created, and there can be no question that his party was not anxious to admit reform. But it appeared to him the only course to take, and he ran off with the reform movement, bag and baggage, appropriating it for his own genius and his party's future. He had stolen the admired livery of his rivals. John Bright was never more serviceable as an orator supporting the larger conceptions of English constitutional government, than he became in his speeches delivered before vast audiences, or in his attacks upon the Bill in the House of Commons. Disraeli's cleverness at political chicanery never escaped Gladstone's eye or the crushing power of his strong hand when it was necessary for him to administer a bold and fatal rebuke. But Bright possessed a fund of humor which Gladstone never had, and Bright allowed himself to deal with Disraeli's weaknesses of character and explosive brilliancies, in the spirit of a humorist. Just at this time he invented the phrase, descriptive of the effect of Disraeli's proposed legislation—"fancy franchises." The House of Commons and the whole country took hold of the phrase, as they had taken hold of other phrases he had spoken with reference to Disraeli, and, indeed, as England always takes hold of a phrase from a bright and witty man, and the epithet prevailed everywhere. Mr. Gladstone spoke with an astonishing force of appeal, reminding Eng-

land how many great men had begun their careers by means of help
from some pocket borough, or, having already been thrown overboard
by the City, they had not appealed in vain to some pocket borough to
keep them in Parliament until they were heard. It was a curious production, even from Gladstone, but it illuminated the point of view from
which he regarded things. The old bark had not yet quite fallen from
the growing tree. However, he was to be defeated. Thirty-nine votes
registered themselves against the side upon which Gladstone voted. A
dissolution of Parliament was advised and accomplished, and Oxford
sent Gladstone back to the first session of the new Parliament early in
June. The speech from the Throne had hardly been read, when Lord
Hartington moved a vote indicating a lack of confidence in the ministers, and again Gladstone's side was defeated, for he voted with the
Government, and it was overthrown by a majority of thirteen. Granville, whom the Queen asked to form a Government, failed, and Palmerston again was placed at the head, with Gladstone in charge of Finance
and Lord John Russell in charge of Foreign Affairs. Oxford had lost
patience. Her pride and glory had evinced a startling independence of
character. Now Oxford rose in opposition to her eminent son, and one
of the most distinguished of the professors of that seat of learning addressed a manifesto to the voters in which he announced that Gladstone's acceptance of office "must now be considered as giving his
definite adhesion to the Liberal party."

THE RIGHT HONORABLE LORD JOHN RUSSELL

HOUSES OF PARLIAMENT AND WESTMINSTER ABBEY

CHAPTER XVIII.

GLADSTONE AND MACAULAY.

The year 1859 marks a date in the history of English historical writing, from the fact that Henry Hallam and Lord Macaulay had died. We have already found Macaulay dealing, in his superior wisdom and riper years, with the man who was sure, in the course of time, to produce one of the best and most carefully reasoned essays upon the brilliant historian and acute essayist. Macaulay showed how trenchant and resistless he could become while toying with a young man of brilliant attainments as a cat might play with a fat mouse, in the essay which he wrote upon Gladstone's book on Church and State. Both of these men were students of the Scriptures, and Thomas Babbington Macaulay had received from Zachary Macaulay a stream of Whiggery as certainly as had William Ewart Gladstone received from Sir John Gladstone a stream of Toryism, by the fact that each child had studied the Scriptures under the influence of his father. In later years Gladstone was to eclipse Macaulay in his studies of the Greek authors and the Christian fathers. Gladstone's career at Oxford was as brilliant as Macaulay's career at Cambridge. Both were sons of men easily able to help their children to any profession. Everybody said that Macaulay was to be a lawyer, and he turned out a literary man; everybody said Gladstone was to be a churchman, and he turned out a statesman. These same differing sets of people were very much alike and formed a great general public which the older and younger men addressed through the great reviews of England. Mr. Gladstone's ability to look upon a subject without prejudice may be inferred from the fact that he was, at the time of his life when he was most easily hurt, severely handled by the reviewer of his dearly-loved first production. The best and worst of Macaulay's literary methods,—his straightforwardness and his utter devotion to the present and its circle of judgment—appeared

in his review of Gladstone. It gives us a fine faith in human nature and
its ability to rise into an atmosphere where justice may be done both to
the great ideal to which an antagonist was untrue and to his own
signal abilities and attendant virtues, when we read such a passage as
this in Gladstone's essay on Macaulay:

"One of the very first things that must strike the observer of this
man is, that he was very unlike to any other man. And yet this unlikeness, this monopoly of the model in which he was made, did not spring
from violent or eccentric features of originality, for eccentricity he had
none whatever, but from the peculiar mode in which the ingredients
were put together to make up the composition. In one sense, beyond
doubt, such powers as his famous memory, his rare power of illustration, his command of language, separated him broadly from others; but
gifts like these do not make the man; and we now for the first time
know that he possessed, in a far larger sense, the stamp of a real and
strong individuality. The most splendid and complete assemblage of
intellectual endowments does not of itself suffice to create an interest of
the kind that is, and will be, now felt in Macaulay. It is from ethical
gifts alone that such an interest can spring. These existed in him not
only in abundance, but in forms distinct from, and even contrasted with,
the fashion of his intellectual faculties, and in conjunctions which come
near to paradox. Behind the mask of splendor lay a singular simplicity,
behind a literary severity which sometimes approached to vengeance,
an extreme tenderness; behind a rigid repudiation of the sentimental,
a sensibility at all times quick, and in the latest times almost threatening
to sap, though never sapping, his manhood."

One of the elements which pervaded Gladstone's whole personality
is that Scotch force of vision which looks at a subject so long as to
see it completely, if not interiorly, which in Macaulay was oftentimes
splendidly in evidence. The Englishman Gladstone and the Englishman Macaulay at last came nearly understanding one another through
the Scotchman in both of them. Nothing in English criticism is finer
than Gladstone's treatment of Macaulay's hobby-riding and the influence which his passion for a chase on the hobby may have exercised
upon his power for finding truth.

"Macaulay was not only accustomed, like many more of us, to go out hobby-riding, but, from the portentous vigor of the animal he mounted, was liable, more than most of us, to be run away with. His merit is, that he could keep his seat in the wildest steeplechase; but, as the object in view is arbitrarily chosen, so it is reached by cutting up the fields, spoiling the crops, and spoiling or breaking down the fences needful to secure for labor its profit, and to man at large the full enjoyment of the fruits of the earth. Such is the overpowering glow of color, such the fascination of the grouping in the first sketches which he draws, that, when he has grown hot upon his work, he seems to lose all sense of the restraints of fact, and the laws of moderation; he vents the strangest paradoxes, sets up the most violent caricatures, and handles the false weight and measure as effectively as he did it knowingly. A man so able and so upright is never indeed wholly wrong. He never for a moment consciously pursues anything but truth. But truth depends, above all, on proportion and relation. The greater human vividness with which Macaulay sees his object, absolutely casts a shadow upon what lies around; he loses his perspective; and imagination, impelled headlong by the strong consciousness of honesty in purpose, achieves the work of fraud. All things for him stand in violent contrast to one another. For the shadows, the gradations, the middle and transition touches, which make up the bulk of human life, character, and action, he has neither eye nor taste. They are not taken account of in his practice, and they at length die away from the ranges of his vision."

Still further did Gladstone appreciate most truly Macaulay's argumentative impulse, for the historian was always a debater. Gladstone was a thorough student of Macaulay's speeches and was often heard to regret that British eloquence was not enriched more largely by a career which was devoted not so much to speaking as to writing. Macaulay's industry has been more than matched by Gladstone's, but nothing commanded a man to Gladstone so truly as plenty of industry and plenty of good intentions. So, and only so, could he acquit Macaulay of some unfairness in his writings. His own statement is as follows:

"He may not have possessed that scrupulously tender sense of obligation, that nice tact of exact justice, which is among the very rarest, as well as the most precious, of human virtues. But there never was a writer less capable of intentional unfairness. This during his lifetime was the belief of his friends, but was hardly admitted by opponents. His biographer has really lifted the question out of the range of controversy. He wrote for truth; but, of course, for truth such as he saw it; and his sight was colored from within. This color, once attached, was what in manufacture is called a mordant; it was a fast color; he could not distinguish between what his mind had received, and what his mind had imparted. Hence, when he was wrong, he could not see that he was wrong; and of those calamities which are due to the intellect only, and not the heart, there can hardly be a greater. The hope of amending is, after all, our very best and brightest hope; of amending our works as well as ourselves."

So much attention has been given here to Gladstone's essay on Macaulay, because it is perhaps the very best of his efforts to appreciate a man who once urged against him the very principles to which Mr. Gladstone, later on in life, became more friendly, if not sincerely attached. Gladstone's gradual change from a proud and self-contained Toryism to a broad, teachable and progressive Liberalism, did not occur without offering serious opportunities for a mind as mobile and responsive as his own to acquire certain twists and wrenches which leave themselves in the form of chronic inability to perceive the half-truth which one has brought out of a former association and to unite it to the half-truth toward which one journeys in the course of the intellectual change. When Mr. Gladstone first read Macaulay's History, he must have felt that the principles of the Whigs were unduly idealized. No radiance of genius could keep him from seeing that there was a truth in the position which he was gradually leaving, to which Macaulay was strangely, if not wilfully, blind. Gladstone's transformation from a Conservatism gone to seed to a Liberalism full of sap and promising with buds, found nothing in Macaulay's persistent bias and ungrowing measure of mind to generate strong praise. But as a specimen of fair-mindedness and conscientious fidelity in appreciation, rather than in criticism, this passage from Gladstone's essay must be regarded as characteristic:

"The contemporary mind may in rare cases be taken by storm; but posterity never. The tribunal of the present is accessible to influence; that of the future is incorrupt. The coming generations will not give Macaulay up: but they will, probably, attach much less value than we have done to his ipse dixit. They will hardly accept from him his net solutions of literary, and still less of historic problems. Yet they will obtain from his marked and telling points of view great aid in solving them. We sometimes fancy that ere long there will be editions of his works in which his readers may be saved from pitfalls by brief, respectful, and judicious commentary, and that his great achievements may be at once commemorated and corrected by men of slower pace, of drier light, and of more tranquil, broadset, and comprehensive judgment. For his works are in many respects among the prodigies of literature; in some, they have never been surpassed. As lights that have shone through the whole universe of letters, they have made their title to a place in the solid firmament of fame. But the tree is greater and better than its fruit; and greater and better yet than the works themselves are the lofty aims and conceptions, the large heart, the independent, manful mind, the pure and noble career, which in this biography have disclosed to us the true figure of the man who wrote them."

The political friendship of Lord John Russell and Mr. Gladstone at this point was very deep and sympathetic, and they agreed one with the other in most schemes of the Government. Not for a moment did Mr. Gladstone relax his energies as a thinker on the subject of education, and in the early part of 1860, he prepared an address which he delivered, April 16th of the same year, as Lord Rector of the University of Edinburgh. In this inaugural he said:

"Subject to certain cycles of partial revolution, it is true that, as in the material so in the moral world, every generation of men is a laborer for that which is to succeed it, and makes an addition to that great sumtotal of achieved results, which may, in commercial phrase, be called the capital of the race. Of all the conditions of existence in which man differs from the brutes, there is not one of greater moment than this, that each one of them commences life as if he were the first of a species, whereas man inherits largely from those who have gone before. How largely, none of us can say; but my belief is that, as years gather more and more upon you, you will estimate more and more highly your debt to preceding ages. If, on the one hand, that debt is capable of being exaggerated or misapprehended; if arguments are sometimes strangely used which would imply that, because they have done much, we ought to do nothing more; yet, on the other hand, it is no less true that the obligation is one so vast and manifold, that it can never as a whole be adequately measured. It is not only in possessions, available for use, enjoyment, and security; it is not only in language, laws, institutions, arts, religion; it is not only in what we have; but in what we are. For, as character is formed by the action and reaction of the human being and the circumstances in which he lives, it follows that, as those circumstances vary, he alters too; and he transmits a modified—it ought to be also an expanded and expanding—nature onwards in his turn to his posterity, under that profound law which establishes, between every generation and its predecessors, a moral as well as a physical association.

"In what degree this process is marred, on the one hand, by the perversity and by the infirmity of man, or restored and extended, on the other, by the remedial provisions of the Divine mercy, this is not the place to inquire. The progress of mankind is, upon the whole, a checkered and an intercepted progress; and even where it is full formed, still, just as in the individual youth has charms, that maturity under an inexorable law must lose, so the earlier ages of the world will ever continue to delight and instruct us by beauties that are exclusively or peculiarly their own. Again, it would seem as though this progress (and here is a chastening and a humbling thought) were a progress of mankind, and not of the individual man; for it seems to be quite clear that whatever be the comparative greatness of the race now and in its infant or early stages, what may be called the normal specimens, so far as they have been made known to us either through external form or through the works of the intellect, have tended rather to dwindle, or at least to diminish, than to grow in the highest elements of greatness."

He concluded as follows:

"And, gentlemen, if you let yourselves enjoy the praise of your teachers, let me beseech you to repay their care, and to help their arduous work, by entering into it with them, and by showing that you meet their exertions neither with a churlish mistrust, nor with a passive indifference, but with free and ready gratitude. Rely upon it, they require your sympathy; and they require it more in proportion as they are worthy of their work. The faithful and able teacher, says an old adage, is 'in loco parentis.' His charge certainly resembles the mother's care in this, that, if he be devoted to his task, you can measure neither the cost to him of the efforts which he makes, nor the debt of gratitude you owe him. The great poet of Italy—the profound and lofty Dante —had had for an instructor one whom, for a miserable vice, his poem places in the regions of the damned; and yet this lord of song—this prophet of all the knowledge of his time—this master of every gift that can adorn the human mind—when in those dreary regions he sees the known image of his tutor, avows in language of a magnificence all his own, that he cannot, even now, withhold his sympathy and sorrow from his unhappy teacher, for he recollects how, in the upper world, with a father's tender care, that teacher had pointed to him the way by which man becomes immortal.

"Gentlemen, I have detained you long. Perhaps I have not had time to be brief; certainly I could have wished for much larger opportunities of maturing and verifying what I have addressed to you upon subjects which have always possessed a hold on my heart, and have long had public and palpable claims on my attention.* Such as I have, I give. And now, finally, in bidding you farewell, let me invoke every blessing upon your venerable University in its new career; upon the youth by whom its halls are gladdened, and upon the distinguished Head, and able teachers, by whom its places of authority are adorned."

---

* Many years after this, Gladstone suggestively added this footnote to the published address:

[As Representative for the University of Oxford, 1847-1865; *dum fata Deusque sinebant.*—W. E. G., 1879.]

CHAPTER XIX.

GLADSTONE'S BUDGET OF 1860.

In spite of the increasingly autocratic manner and cynical temper of Lord Palmerston, Gladstone remained as Chancellor of the Exchequer, and in 1860 he proposed a Budget which must always remain distinguished from others which he introduced, by the fact that it recognized the achievements of Richard Cobden. Cobden was an admirable man for England at a time when Bright's eloquence and Gladstone's enthusiasm were educating Liberalism. It was exceedingly fortunate that, while he was a Radical of the Radicals, he could meet such a man as the Emperor Napoleon and talk with him good-humoredly and yet profoundly, until the outcome of it all was a commercial treaty between France and England by which a complete and rational understanding was arrived at and the honor of both nations preserved.

Gladstone's Budget in 1860 contained another thing of still greater importance. The French Government had now entered into an engagement looking toward free trade in staples raised or made by British hands. Now Gladstone proposed, in the interests of the public wanting intelligence, that the duty on paper should be abolished. Nothing that he ever undertook was more to his taste as a believer in the value of "light and leading" for the people of a constitutional Government, and nothing aroused a more pronounced opposition. The tremendous amount of money invested in the newspaper business made itself felt everywhere in antagonism to Gladstone's scheme. Journals which had professed to exist for the sake of educating the public hurled caustic diatribes against the proposer of this measure and against any kind of journalism which might come to the people cheaply. Gladstone knew that the reading public was behind him, and he saw that it was impossible to have cheap news for the people so long as the imposition of this duty remained possible. His speech on the Budget of 1860 takes a large place in every journal of the times.

In this speech, he spoke as follows with reference to France and the treaty:

"I do not forget, sir, that there was once a time when close relations of amity were established between the Governments of England and France. It was in the reign of the later Stuarts; it marks a dark spot in our annals; but the spot is dark because the union was an union formed in a spirit of domineering ambition on the one side, and of base and most corrupt servility on the other. But that, sir, was not a union of the nations; it was an union of the Governments. This is not to be an union of the Governments apart from the countries; it is, as we hope, to be an union of the nations themselves; and I confidently say again, as I have already ventured to say in this House, that there never can be any union between the nations of England and France, except an union beneficial to the world, because that directly one or the other of the two begins to harbor schemes of selfish aggrandizement, that moment the jealousy of its neighbor will be aroused, and will beget a powerful reaction; and the very fact of their being in harmony will of itself at all times be the most conclusive proof that neither of them can be engaged in meditating anything which is dangerous to Europe."

Every such collection of reminiscences as the Greville Memoirs indicates how greatly Gladstone had surprised England with the result of his commission as Commissioner to the Ionian Islands: The Greville Memoirs perpetuate also the memory of Gladstone's speech:

"Bath, February 15th: When I left London a fortnight ago the world was anxiously expecting Gladstone's speech in which he was to put the Commercial Treaty and the Budget before the world. His own confidence and that of most of his colleagues in his success was unbounded, but many inveighed bitterly against the treaty, and looked forward with great alarm and aversion to the Budget. Clarendon shook his head; Overstone pronounced against the Treaty, the 'Times' thundered against it, and there is little doubt that it was popular, and becoming more so every day. Then came Gladstone's unlucky illness, which compelled him to put off his exposé, and made it doubtful whether he would not be physically disabled from doing justice to the subject. His doctor says he ought to have taken two months' rest instead of two

days'. However, at the end of two days' delay he came forth, and
consensu omnium achieved one of the greatest triumphs that the
House of Commons ever witnessed. Everybody I have heard from ad-
mits that it was a magnificent display, not to be surpassed in ability of
execution, and that he carried the House of Commons completely with
him. I can well believe it, for when I read the report of it the next day
(a report I take to have given the speech verbatim) it carried me along
with it likewise. For the moment opposition and criticism were
silenced, and nothing was heard but the second praise and admiration.
In a day or two, however, men began to disengage their minds from the
bewitching influence of this great oratorical power, to examine calmly
the different parts of the wonderful piece of machinery which Gladstone
had constructed, and to detect and expose the weak points and objec-
tionable provisions which it contained. I say it, for, as the Speaker
writes me, it must be taken as a whole or rejected as a whole, and he adds
the first will be its fate.

"Clarendon, who has all along disapproved of the Treaty, wrote to
me that Gladstone's success was complete, and public opinion in his
favor. He says, 'I expect that the London feeling will be reflected
from the country, so that there will be no danger of rejection, though I
think that the more the whole thing is considered, the less popular it
will become. The no-provision for the enormous deficit that will exist
next year will strike people as well as the fact that the Budget is made
up of expeditions for the present year. The non-payment of the Exchequer bonds is to all intents and purposes a loan; the war tax on tea
and sugar, the windfall of the Spanish payment, the making the malt-
sters and hopgrowers pay in advance, etc., are all stopgaps. If anybody
purposes it, I shall not be surprised if an additional 1d Income Tax in
place of the war duties was accepted by Gladstone. He has a fervent
imagination, which furnishes facts and arguments in support of them;
he is an audacious innovator, because he has an insatiable desire for
popularity, in his notions of government he is a far more sincere Republican than Bright, for his ungratified personal vanity makes him wish to
subvert the institutions and the classes that stand in the way of his
ambition. The two are converging from different points to the same

end, and if Gladstone remains in office long enough and is not more opposed by his colleagues than he has been hitherto, we shall see him propose a graduate Income Tax.' These are the only objections to the Budget, and speculations (curious ones) as to the character and purity of Gladstone.

"In another note he says: 'Gladstone made a fair defense of the Treaty, though there are things in it which deserve the severest criticism and will get it, such as tying ourselves down about the exportation of coal (which is a munition of war), letting in French silks free, while ours are to pay thirty per cent, and establishing a differential duty of nearly fifty per cent in favor of light French wines against the stronger wines of Spain and Portugal, for that would be the operation of the Treaty.' Since all this was written there has been a meeting of the Conservative party, and I hear this morning that Derby has decided to take the field with all his forces, with a resolution against the condition about the exportation of coal, and confining himself to that, which will very likely be carried. On the other hand, the publicans and licensed victualers appear to be in arms against that part of the Budget which more immediately interests them, and are waging a fierce war in the press by their paper, the 'Morning Advertiser,' so that in spite of his great triumph and all the admiration of his eloquence and skill elicited, it is not all sunshine and plain sailing with his measure. Delane writes to me that Gladstone will find it hard work to get his Budget through, that Peel when he brought forward his Budget had a majority of ninety, all of which he required to do it, whereas Palmerston cannot command a majority of nine."

Whatever the result, Gladstone's eloquence had achieved a new triumph. No richness of language or accuracy of scholarship, no breadth of thought or comprehensiveness of information, no fullest passion for facts or industry in research, but that seemed to yield its tribute and its results to the orator, as he proceeded with his explanation, and met the excited anticipations of the country with a speech of the deepest historical value and of profound fiscal philosophy.

Mr. Gladstone was above all else, an industrious man. His almost royal imagination gave him sovereignty over every theme, but it would

furnish only a sign of most pitiful weakness if it had not been true that
his zeal and laboriousness were driven by some fortune of nature to the
doing of those duties which oftentimes escape the attention of imaginative minds.

Here stood the man, who, in the course of those very days, was din·
ing and conversing with men who were fascinated by his discourse upon
Homer, or stimulated and educated by his utterances on theological
subjects; and now, for hours in the Parliament of England, he was
devoting the same gifts of thought, prophetic fancy and solid scholarship, to flax, hair, bark, stoneware, covenants, duties on wine, wool and
annuities; and in all his long address, the marvelous collocation of
powers shone forth and illuminated the subject itself and the minds
of those who were trying to understand the finances of England. He
concluded as follows:

"Our proposals involve a great reform in our tariff; they involve a
large remission of taxation, and last of all, though not least, they include that commercial treaty with France which, though we have to
apprehend that objections in some quarters will be taken to it, we confidently recommend, not only on moral, and social, and political, but
also, and with equal confidence, on economical and fiscal grounds.
. . . There were times, now long by, when Sovereigns made progress through the land, and when, at the proclamation of their heralds,
they caused to be scattered whole showers of coin among the people
who thronged upon their steps. That may have been a goodly spectacle; but it is also a goodly spectacle, and one adapted to the altered
spirit and circumstances of our times when our Sovereign is enabled,
through the wisdom of her great Council, assembled in Parliament
around her, again to scatter blessings among her subjects by means of
wise and prudent laws; of which laws do not sap in any respects the
foundations of duty or of manhood, but which strike away the shackles
from the arm of industry, which give new incentives and new rewards to
toil, and which win more and more for the Throne and for the institutions of the country the gratitude, the confidence and the love of an
united people. Let me say, even to those who are anxious, and justly
anxious, on the subject of our national defenses, that that which stirs the

flame of patriotism in men, that which binds them in one heart and soul, that which gives them increased confidence in their rulers, that which makes them feel and know that they are treated with justice, and that we who represent them are laboring incessantly and earnestly for their good—is in itself no small, no feeble, and no transitory part of national defense. We recommend these proposals to your impartial and searching inquiry. We do not presume, indeed, to make a claim on your acknowledgments; but neither do we desire to draw on your unrequited confidence, nor to lodge an appeal to your compassion. We ask for nothing more than your dispassionate judgment, and for nothing less; we know that our plan will receive that justice at your hands; and we confidently anticipate on its behalf the approval alike of the Parliament and the Nation."

Under date of February 26th, Greville makes the following entry with regard to Gladstone:

"February 26th: On Friday night Gladstone had another great triumph. He made a splendid speech, and obtained a majority of 116, which put an end to the contest. He is now the great man of to-day, but these recent proceedings have strikingly displayed the disorganized condition of the Conservative party and their undisguised dislike of their leader. A great many of them voted with Government on Friday night, and more expressed satisfaction at the result being a defeat of Disraeli. The Treaty and the Budget, though many parts of both are obnoxious to criticism, more or less well founded, seem on the whole not unpopular, and since their first introduction to have undoubtedly gained in public favor. This fact and the state opposition prove the impossibility of any change of Government. Gladstone, too, as he is strong, seems disposed to be merciful, and has expressed his intention of taking fairly into consideration the various objections that may be brought forward, and to consent to reasonable alterations when good cases are made out for them. There seems no doubt that his great measures were not approved by the majority of the Cabinet, but the malcontents do not seem to have been disposed to fight much of the battle against the minority, which included both Palmerston and Lord John."

It was not to be wondered at that the proprietors of newspapers and the manufacturers of paper should still resolve to continue their opposition, and that, also, Gladstone's popularity should suffer amongst the favored population they represented. His majorities were sure to be lessening. Fifty-three votes carried the second reading; only nine were given for the third. The House of Lords, of course, were delighted, and the aged Lord Lyndhurst tottered to his place and joined with Lord Derby in beseeching the House of Lords to crush this instrument of legislation which had been introduced in the interests of popular intelligence.

Mr. Gladstone was making promises that all means should be tried and no power left unexhausted of its energies to preserve the friendship between England and France, and he went further than ever before in saying that he was desirous of reducing the military and naval armament of England when other nations would give the slightest testimony of their wish for peace. Disraeli had said that no government could raise seventy millions pounds a year constantly by taxation when the nation was enjoying peace. Cobden's treaty with France, which Gladstone did much to praise, had placed England upon a firmer foundation with reference to all future pacific measures. The House of Lords was still fighting the repeal of the Paper Tax which the House of Commons had authorized. Lord Palmerston was not content with the power which the House of Lords had wielded in this matter, and he moved a Committee to ascertain and report on the attitude of each House toward such questions, hoping that some arrangement might be made whereby the House of Lords could interfere with the results of agitation and the reform spirit which grievously irritated these excellent persons.

John Bright's attack upon the House of Lords as a body willing to exceed the provisions of the English Constitution, unable, however, to reimpose a tax which had been repealed by the House of Commons, was said to have been seconded by Gladstone himself. But many who were posing as the amiable friends of a man perfectly able to take care of himself, explained that Gladstone had done it only to please Bright and the Radicals.

The hour now came for monster meetings everywhere, and the

nation uttered a protest against the House of Lords. Palmerston was obdurate and desired evidently to stifle the rising spirit of the people. Placards all over London announced the aggression of the House of Lords in bold letters, and with much display of brilliant ink. From thousands of throats came the uttered cry that the House of Lords must be abolished. Gladstone was being educated for events twenty years away. The Lords had thrown out the Paper Duty Bill and had aroused the country against themselves. Gladstone made a speech in which he scored Lord Palmerston with merciless invective, and even Lord Russell called it "magnificently mad." England was in a tumult, and opinion swayed back and forth, as it had in May, when Greville placed the following item in his journal, with reference to the reaction against Gladstone:

"May 12th: Not more than three months ago Gladstone was triumphant and jubilant; he had taken the House of Commons and the country captive by his eloquence, and nothing was heard everywhere but songs of praise and admiration at his marvelous success and prodigious genius. There never was a greater reaction in a shorter time. Everybody's voice is now against him, and his famous Treaty and his Budget are pronounced enormous and dangerous blunders. Those who were most captivated now seem to be most vexed and ashamed of their former fascination. They are provoked with themselves for having been so duped, and a feeling of resentment and bitterness against him has become widely diffused in and out of the House of Commons, on his own side as well as on the other. It was the operation of this feeling which caused the narrow majority on the Paper Duties the other night, when it seems as if a little more management and activity might have put him in a minority, and it is the same thing which is now encouraging the House of Lords, urged on by Derby, to throw out the resolution when it comes before them. Derby has announced that he shall exert himself to the utmost to procure the rejection of the Bill in the House of Lords, and if he perseveres he will probably obtain a very unwise and perilous success, which he will before long have to regret."

It was of little account now that Gladstone denounced the action of the House of Lords as "a gigantic innovation," or that Lord Palmerston did not himself like it. Things were in transition, and it looked as though Gladstone, in his journey from pole to pole in politics, was going so swiftly that, as one of his old friends said: "He could not take time to stop at the station called Whig Politics in his flight from Conservatism to Liberalism." Certain it is that the Radicals were most proud of his utterance, though he had a faith that the House of Lords might recover its reason, which Radicals did not have. Palmerston was angered by Gladstone, and Radicalism read and reread the words the latter spoke with reference to Cobden.

Meanwhile Disraeli was shrewd enough to see that though, in the year 1860, Gladstone had succeeded in carrying his Resolution for removing as much of the Customs Duty on imported paper as exceeded the Excise Duty on paper manufactured in England, and though the Government had abandoned their Reform Bill and brought in another on the first of March, his condemnation could not wisely shut out the possibility of his introducing a Reform Bill at a later date, which would dazzle, if not please, the Radicals, more truly than any which Gladstone's genius had supported. Bright and Cobden were ever faithful to Lord John Russell's scheme of Reform. Disraeli talked about it as "a measure of a mediæval character without the inspiration of a feudal system or the genius of the middle ages," and Lord Palmerston did not care what become of it. It was not long before Palmerston's supporters concluded that he would like to see it defeated. Gladstone's old friend at Christchurch, Oxford, George Cornewall Lewis, made a speech for the Bill which brought out all the characteristics of a nature strongly influential and strangely different from the nature of Gladstone. The novelist, Bulwer-Lytton, spoke of Lewis' speech as one which proved that he had "come to bury Cæsar, not to praise him." The session was rapidly drifting into a debating school in which the chief result was the consumption of time. At last the whole affair became ludicrous and Lord John Russell announced the withdrawal of the Bill on June 11th.

THE THRONE ROOM—WINDSOR CASTLE

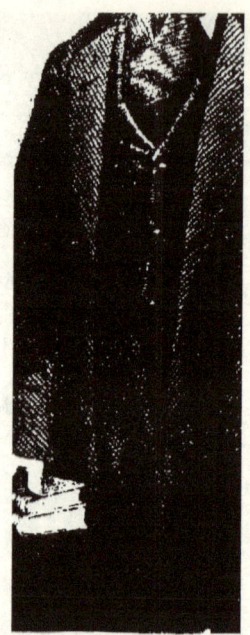

THE EARL OF DERBY

CHAPTER XX.

THE BUDGET OF 1861.

The Session of 1861 opened on the 5th of February, and all London crowded to Buckingham Palace to cheer the Queen on her way to the Houses of Parliament. Great questions were to come up, and they came close to Mr. Gladstone's heart. The existence of a national church was connected with the question of church rates, and in defense of the latter, Mr. Gladstone spoke so powerfully that the Opposition cheered loudly. In this he found himself opposed to his colleague, Lord John Russell.

April 15, the Chancellor of the Exchequer offered his annual financial statement. He had a surplus of nearly 2,000,000 pounds for their rejoicing. His propositions came, one after the other, in precise and eloquent language, but the public was not willing for another Bill to be sent up for the repeal of the paper duties, if that Bill was to be rejected in the House of Lords. Gladstone, throughout his dealing with the subject, seemed to feel behind him the majority of the English people. These are some of his utterances:

We have seen this country during the last few years without European war, but under a burden of taxation, such as, out of a European war, it was never called upon to bear; we have also seen it last year under the pressure of a season of blight, such as hardly any living man can recollect; yet, on looking abroad over the face of England, no one is sensible of any signs of decay, least of all can such an apprehension be felt with regard to those attributes which are perhaps the highest of all, and on which most of all depends our national existence—the spirit and courage of the country. It is needless to say that neither the sovereign on the throne, nor the nobles and the gentry that fill the place of the gallant chieftains of the Middle Ages, nor the citizens who represent the invincible soldiery of Cromwell, nor the peasantry who are the children of those sturdy archers that drew the crossbows of England in the fields of France—none of these betray either inclina-

12

tion or tendency to depart from the tradition of their forefathers. If there be any danger which has recently in an especial manner beset us, I confess that, though it may be owing to some peculiarity in my position, or some weakness in my vision, it has seemed to me to be, during recent years chiefly, in our proneness to constant, and apparently almost boundless, augmentations of expenditure, and in the consequences that are associated with them. * * * Sir, I do trust that the day has come when a check has begun to be put to the movement in this direction; and I think, as far as I have been able to trace the sentiments of the House, and the indications of general opinion during the present session, that the tendency to which I have adverted is at least partially on the decline. I trust it will altogether subside and disappear. The spirit of the people is excellent. There never was a nation in the whole history of the world more willing to bear the heavy burdens under which it lies—more generously disposed to overlook the errors of those who have the direction of its affairs. For my own part, I hold that, if this country can steadily and constantly remain as wise in the use of her treasure as she is unrivaled in its production, and as moderate in the exercise of her strength as she is rich in its possession, that we may well cherish the hope that there is yet reserved for England a great work to do on her own part and on the part of others, and that for many a generation yet to come she will continue to hold a foremost place among the nations of the world.

He had met a scene the like of which he had not hitherto beheld, even in the hours of his supreme mastery of public opinion in England. For long hours before the moment arrived for Gladstone's appearance, St. Stephen's had been besieged by a crowd, the hall was thronged by persons who had tickets and by those who had none, and thousands had gone without the mid-day meal with the hope that somehow there might be room for them within the sound of the Chancellor's voice. He had spoken and triumphed.

Perhaps the presentation of this Budget furnishes the student of oratory with the best specimen of Gladstone's eloquence in the direction of lucidity of statement in explanation of financial problems.

After a severe struggle, he accomplished what was a virtual defeat of the aristocracy. Mr. Gladstone was attacked most violently by Lord Robert Cecil, and his plans were nearly defeated while Daly, the priest, was attempting to force Irish Liberal members into their support of the Conservative party. The peers were defeated, and Mr. Disraeli was with them.

Gladstone was the first man, after the decease of the younger Pitt, who gave England the consciousness that she possessed the greatest Finance Minister in the world, and John Bull, shopkeeper and banker, exchanger and fiscal actuary for the most of this planet of ours, has not failed to appreciate these men whose lives present many points by which they may be compared or contrasted. Each of them was born amidst circumstances almost determining the political character of his career, Lord Chatham being scarcely more eager and confident that the son whose education in affairs, patriotism and eloquence he himself had directed, should rise to prominence as a statesman, than Sir John Gladstone was ambitious and hopeful that his son should prove an effective, if not unequaled champion of the Toryism which was as dear to him as his religious faith. Both these young men were prodigies in mental power and equipment, though in precocity Pitt outstripped Gladstone, having been made Chancellor of the Exchequer at twenty-three, whereas Gladstone did not reach that position until he was above forty. It must be said in favor of the latter, that he had no George III., whom he was speedily to teach by eloquent opposition, whom another Pitt could amaze by refusing office unless he should have a Cabinet seat under some Rockingham, nor had Pitt found, as did Gladstone, a master hand upon affairs, such as Sir Robert Peel, able to conduct a government with astuteness and power. Pitt came upon English politics after a revolution in France which had made English politicians look with something of prayerful concern for bright and patriotic young men, and he had entered his public career when another revolution, brought about by America, left a huge debt for England to pay which would have staggered anything but that kind of "youth," which, Disraeli says, "is genius." Gladstone, on the contrary, found these matters as quiet and settled as if they had belonged to the policies of Rome under Augustus, a consummate politician and adroit leader of men was at the helm, and before England stretched the golden days consequent upon the triumph of the Reform Bill. It is interesting to note, however, that Pitt's opposition to the Toryism

of the Crown and the Ministers, in fact, Pitt's Whiggery, was prophetic of Gladstone's Liberalism.

The former literally compelled Toryism to confess his general
usefulness, after he had antagonized the King's insatiable desire for war,
battled for retrenchment in public expenditure, championed Parliamentary Reform, struggled against the corrupt forces at the Court
and urged the abbreviation of Parliamentary sessions. Never, as many
historians remark, did Reform come so near to victory, before Gladstone's day, as it did on one of Pitt's motions.

Both of these men entered Parliamentary life as remarkable speakers. Classical training and close study of mathematics, enormous historical reading and rare familiarity with the poetry of ancient and
modern times were, despite Pitt's ill health, allied in each with supple
and impressive physical presence, excellent if not remarkable voice and
graceful manner, fervent imagination and taste for argumentation, to
furnish an orator of the highest type. Gladstone, however, possessed
a wealth of fancy and impulsive audacity in contention, characteristic
of Chatham rather than of his calmer and more resourceful son. Each
of these young debaters soon made St. Stephen's echo rotund and
stately sentences, and both Pitt and Gladstone had not to speak often
in the House of Commons until the imperial manner of their address,
the towering sarcasm of the one or the general loftiness of the other,
brought the charge of intolerable arrogance and haughty conceit. If
Pitt was cold and used a keener blade with dauntless equanimity, Gladstone was to be radiant and impassioned, even so hot, that his sword,
once bathed in fiery zeal, illumined while it burned in the air of discussion. If each had come panoplied with culture and masterful of
accomplishment in matters of Church and State, Pitt was more often
to treat the Church as a statesman, Gladstone was to deal with the
State more frequently as a churchman. Indeed, Gladstone never got
out of the mood which early beset him and made him desire to enter
holy orders. He often preached as well in the House of Commons, as
once he did, at King's College for his Episcopal friend. The home of
Pitt and the home of Gladstone were gymnasia for the development
of every noble characteristic of their eloquence and every generous

impulse of their souls. Music and illustrious friendships, the admiration of art and the love of high aims, had given to their youth the domain best calculated to foster the most exquisite taste and reverence for the good and true.

Pitt studied finance with Adam Smith as the apostle of a better political economy; Gladstone learned to formulate a Budget at the feet of that successful business-man, his father, Sir John Gladstone. The one could never see why Adam Smith's theories would not pay England's debt or secure England's financial ascendancy; the other could never comprehend why the principles which had made Sir John Gladstone's business career successful, should not, if applied to the commercial undertakings and problems of the English nation, produce sufficient revenues and enrich the realm. At first, it appeared strange to dull-eyed aristocrats that Pitt's cultured mind should bend so low as to deal with facts and figures; at first, Gladstone's lively imagination and classical lore appeared a team of racers trying to do the work of cart-horses in laboring with finance. But both these men knew that statesmanship is not altogether eloquence or poetry. In each of them was a spinal column of inflexible good sense, and England forgives much in them because they triumphed in finance.

Each came to public life, the one in Fox's time, the other in Byron's, to offer to his country what neither of these could present, the gift of pure personal character. Both had read much theology. Pitt had, it is said, found more questions started by Butler's Analogy than that excellent treatise answered; Gladstone spent his declining years in the pious labor of giving to it lucid exposition. Pitt, as a young man, was reverent and moral; Gladstone was always devoted and deeply religious. Morals without religion proved "broken cisterns which could hold no water." Intellectually, Pitt was ever a Cambridge man; Gladstone struggled, like Milton's lion, "to get free" from Oxford, and made a lifelong work of it, which was finally crowned with triumph, though only a Gladstone, even at the last, could have convinced him of this fact.

Gladstone never would have taken the post of Prime Minister, as did Pitt, when the latter was offered it for the second time and accepted

it for the first time, for it came to Pitt as the result of an act of royal
bad faith. Gladstone never took a Lord Temple upon his laborious
shoulders, as did Chatham's son. Pitt was Gladstone's equal in his
ability to withstand abuse. Everything, however, consists in *how* a
thing is done, and Pitt was Gladstone's inferior in possessing the moral
power from which assailants retire as cowards. The first was self-
confident, haughty and wary; the second was confident of the sure
basis of justice, inflexible as truth, and he risked all with an impulsive
carelessness which tried friend and foe alike. Pitt contrasted his indubitable purity in the Pells Clerkship case with the unblushing corruption of the Court. He was, perhaps, as sagacious, however, as he
was stainless. His defeat of foes which crowded to hurl him from
power can be matched only by Gladstone's overwhelming entrance
to power when Disraeli fell. He could handle a jumble of elements,
as Gladstone drove his famous "four-in-hand,"—and each confounded
Toryism with a noble disregard of privileged classes. Such a personal
quarrel as that of Pitt with Fox was impossible to Gladstone, but such
triumphs as his in finance were the glory of the later commoner. Each
stoutly protected the public credit; each hated magic in fiscal economy;
but while Pitt felt with no deterring force the fact that the future of a
country ought not to be mortgaged by the debts incurred in the past,
Gladstone insisted that the expense of the Crimean War should be paid
at once. No such indictment of the latter's career has ever been offered
as that which was framed against Pitt in these well-known words:
"Mr. Pitt's memory needs no statues. Six hundred millions of irre-
deemable debt are the eternal record of his fame." Pitt, however, was
a prophet. He foretold Cobden's victory; he hopefully looked toward
free trade. Gladstone came and made its statutes work with ease.
In both cases, the fathers of these sons, Chatham and Sir John Gladstone, had to be thrown overboard, for they were Protectionists. Pitt
might have written Gladstone's great words which helped to bind
France and England together, not as grappling foes, but as friendly
states, and, adopting Adam Smith's opinions, Pitt fought for free trade,
except in corn, for Ireland against her own Burke. On the subject of
Parliamentary Reform, high office made Pitt timid and Gladstone fear-

less. He created peers, seven scores of them. Gladstone also created peers, but he sent up to the Lords his measures which shook their House with peril. Pitt made them for votes; Gladstone defied them, refused to be made an earl, and was content with defeat. Gladstone honored the great men of literature, and educated the populace. Pitt did neither. Pitt taxed the newspapers; Gladstone removed the duty on paper. The former, however, reformed the shameless Libel Law, and gave Eldon to England, to reform other legislation, while he dealt unsparing blows against slavery, whose horrors Gladstone forgot when he said Jefferson Davis had created a new nation. The Tests Act, which he kept in force, Gladstone repealed. Catholic Emancipation, which Pitt at first favored, was to come in Gladstone's full noonday.

Greater still is the contrast, the one tottering to his grave, prematurely aged and worn, the other young, and buoyant at eighty. Pitt was affrighted at Liberalism as it came out of the wreck of the French Revolution, and at length he leaned toward war with France. The war came, but not as expected. He attacked the liberty of speech and writing in England. The Habeas Corpus Act was suspended. Ireland and Scotland knew a veritable reign of terror. Gladstone failed, it may be, as a War Minister, for he was a man of peace. William Pitt failed as a War Minister, without the loss of a single good intention. He at last disclaimed friendship for Catholic Emancipation. The war went on. In certain aspects it was a great war, but in the glory of Wellington's victory, it must be remembered that Pitt had lost faith in the powers which alone will conquer Bonapartism. Without the deepest confidence in them, and without the unswerving devotion to them which alone brings deepest confidence in the necessary and therefore ultimate triumph of the principles of free government, Pitt's heart was broken by the specter of Napoleon at Austerlitz; Gladstone, on the other hand, saw specter after specter appear in defeat after defeat, and so sure was he that the evolution under God of "the parliament of man, the federation of the world" is hastening that nothing could break that tireless, dauntless heart.

The Budget of 1862 again brought Gladstone to the front as a great Finance Minister, a greater orator, and a man more certain than ever that the House of Lords would make itself impossible in England if it continued in its career of obstruction. England was proud and almost self-glorious when, in early May, 1862, the great Crystal Palace Exhibition was opened. A deep shadow lay upon the British public mind, which came from the fact that the Prince Consort had suddenly terminated his career just when the prospects of this enterprise were most bright.

Early in 1863 Dean Stanley was his guest and the following account of the visit is taken, by permission, from "The Life and Letters of Dean Stanley," published by Charles Scribner's Sons:

"When I arrived, there were only the two little Gladstone boys there—at tea—Herbert and Henry—good little creatures. They were in some alarm at having dropped some jam onto the crystalline butter-bowl. But I managed to mop it up with my pocket-handkerchief.

"After dinner the subject of subscription was introduced. We went on discussing it till after the ladies were gone and on till 12:30 P. M. (sic). It was an immense relief to me. Gladstone was most satisfactory. If he were to say publicly what he said privately, the question would be settled. I was extremely glad to have the opportunity of giving him all my mind; and he, lending himself to it with the astounding readiness which he has, completely understood everything which I said.

"What made all this profusion of talk the more remarkable was, that he was full of the Budget, which comes on next Thursday."

CHAPTER XXI.

THE AMERICAN CIVIL WAR.

It would be a delight if an American student, rejoicing up to this point in that continuously advancing Americanism which was at last the salt that lost not its savor in Mr. Gladstone's politics and prophecies, might leave out of a chronicle such as this any account of a most strange wandering upon his part, when the life of the American Union was trembling in the balance and all the principles which later on Gladstone espoused and defended were waging a fierce battle against armed foes. Not only was the experiment of American self-government on trial, but the very chrysalis in which these energies were working for finer and larger results for all humanity was threatened. Gladstone's biographers in England have not truly estimated the righteous indignation felt by American lovers of constitutional government, when, from across the sea, there came such formidable prophecies of our national ruin as could only carry wildest hope into the bosoms of the foes of our Government. More than this was involved in the Civil War in America, for that contest was to decide whether the institution of slavery should be made into a cornerstone for a political temple, or whether, in the name of civilization and humanity, it should be crushed to pieces. The English Government had looked upon the election of Abraham Lincoln as an event of too slight importance to justify the Southern States in commencing war, but they had seen the South open hostilities. English publicists like John Stuart Mill and Thomas Hughes, writers like Harriet Martineau, and reformers like Clarkson, Wilberforce and George Thompson, had warned England that the curse of human slavery was determined to arrogate to itself new territory at all costs. Upon the proposition that no more territory should be given to slavery, Mr. Lincoln was elected. Sumter had been fired upon and the war of secession was begun. Lord John Russell, in the

House of Commons, on the 18th of May, 1861, announced that "after consulting the law officers of the Crown, the Government were of opinion that the Southern Confederacy must be recognized as a belligerent power." The Neutrality Proclamation was made May 13th. The Government of England warned all Her Majesty's subjects from enlisting on either side or giving aid or comfort to either contestant. The English Government did not wait for the arrival of the new American Minister, Mr. Charles Francis Adams, that they might be informed upon the merits of the question as to whether this proclamation ought to be issued. Even Mr. Forster made the mistake of supposing that this was an announcement of war, and if there were no war recognized, neither would the blockade of Southern ports by the Northern powers be recognized by anybody. The air became filled with a confusion of voices. Lancashire had the ear of Gladstone, and he saw mills, which depended upon the export of cotton from America to England, shut down, and the working people were in dire distress. John Bright saw more clearly than the philosophy of the soup-kitchens which were established all through Lancashire to relieve the working people whom the war in the United States had deprived of the opportunity of labor. He counseled and guided them until they arose with the spirit of humanity to a height not usually reached by our race. Lord Palmerston waited as long as he could, and at last took an attitude in which he exploded his wrath and displayed haughtily the banner of England in the face of America. Steadily America and England looked for Gladstone to speak, and he spoke not. At last, at Newcastle-on-Tyne, October 9th, 1862, he said, with more than his usual solemnity and dogmatism: "Jefferson Davis has made a new nation; he has made an army; he has made a navy," and he loaned his eloquence to the idea that the experiment of free government in America had so far failed. Gladstone's speech was of great service to the American people only in this, that it made the North review carefully the reasons for previous action, and settled without question the conviction of the advocates of the Union that, while a great man had gone wrong in England, they were right in America. It is not remarkable that at such a crisis in our affairs the spirit embodied in Charles Sumner should be perplexed at the attitude of England.　An excellent account of Sumner's mind and movements on this topic is given in the valuable biography of the American Senator by his friend, Edward L. Pierce.　Here we find that Sumner addressed Mr. Bright, July 21, as follows:

"I have read the debate of the 30th of June.　Your last words touched the whole question to the quick.　The guilt of this attempt is appalling; but next to the slave-mongers is England with a grinning neutrality.　My friend Mr. Gladstone dealt with the whole question as if there were no God.　Englishmen may doubt.　I tell you, there can be but one end to this war.　I care not for any temporary success of the slave-mongers, they must fail; but English sympathy is a mighty encouragement.　You will note our success in the Southwest; everything there is against the rebellion.　There is a pretty good reason to believe that Charleston will soon be ours.　Lee's army has lost thirty thousand men, and I am inclined to think now must be much demoralized.　We are too victorious; I fear more from our victories than our defeats.　If the rebellion should suddenly collapse, Democrats, copperheads, and Seward would insist upon amnesty and the Union, and 'no question asked about slavery.'　God save us from such calamity!　If Lee's army had been smashed, that question would have been upon us.　Before this comes, I wish two hundred thousand negroes with muskets in their hands, and then I shall not fear compromise.　Time is essential; so great a revolution cannot come to a close at once."

Men who had watched his growth from Conservatism in the direction of Liberalism were startled and deeply grieved at Gladstone's taking a position so indefensible.　Nothing better was expected of Palmerston, but it was thought that Gladstone would walk with Cobden and Bright in unfaltering fidelity to the interests of freedom.

Another great result helpful to the cause of the Union in America which Gladstone's unfortunate speech brought about was this, that every such orator as John Bright found his speech more intelligent and comprehensive in eloquence than ever before and gladly gave its richness and power to the cause of liberty.　Bright spoke in reply to Gladstone at Birmingham on December 18th, and among other things he said:

"I am very happy that, though the Chancellor of the Exchequer is able to decide to a penny what shall be the amount of taxes to meet public expenditure in England, he cannot decide what shall be the fate of a whole continent.

"I say, it is the home of the working man; as one of her poets recently said:

> 'For her free latch-string never was drawn in
> Against the poorest child of Adam's kin.'

"And in that land there is no six millions of grown men—I speak of the Free States—excluded from the constitution of their country and its electoral franchise; there you will find a free church, a free school, free land, a free vote, and a free career for the child of the humblest born in the land. My countrymen, who work for your living, remember this; there will be one wild shriek of freedom to startle all mankind if that American Republic should be overthrown.

"Now for one moment let us lift ourselves, if we can, above the narrow circle in which we are too often apt to live and think; let us put ourselves on an historical eminence, and judge this matter fairly. Slavery has been, as we all know, the huge foul blot upon the fame of the American Republic; it is a hideous outrage against human right and against Divine law, but the pride, the passion of man, will not permit its peaceable extinction. The slave-owners in our colonies, if they had been strong enough, would have revolted too. I believe there was no mode short of a miracle more stupendous than any recorded in Holy Writ that could in our time or in a century, or in any time, have brought about the abolition of slavery in America, but the suicide which the South has committed and the war which it has begun.

"I blame men who are eager to admit into the family of nations a State which offers itself to us, based upon a principle, I will undertake to say, more odious and more blasphemous than was ever before dreamed of in Christian or Pagan, in civilized or in savage times. The leader of this revolt proposes this monstrous thing—that over a territory forty times as large as England the blight and curse of slavery shall be forever perpetuated.   I can not believe, for my part, that such a fate shall befall that fair land, stricken though it now is with the ravages of war.   I cannot believe that civilization, in its journey with the sun, will sink into endless night in order to gratify the ambition of the leaders of this revolt, who seek to

> 'Wade through slaughter to a throne,
> And shut the gates of mercy on mankind.'

"I have another and a far brighter vision before my gaze. It may be but a vision, but I will cherish it. I see one vast confederation stretching from the frozen North in unbroken line to the glowing South, and from the wild billows of the Atlantic westward to the calmer waters of the Pacific main—and I see one people, and one language, and one law, and one faith, and, over that wide continent, the home of freedom, and a refuge for the oppressed of every race and of every clime."

For such a speech as this Gladstone had no rejoinder.

The aspect of things was transformed by the autumn of 1863. Mr. Bright wrote to Sumner, September 11th:

"It would be curious to have a speech from Gladstone now. Perhaps he is beginning to doubt whether Jeff Davis has made a nation. There is much cleverness mixed with little wisdom, or much folly, in some men, and our Chancellor seems to be one of them. I think I shall make a selection from the writings of the 'Times' and the speeches of our public men, and publish them, that their ignorance and folly may not be forgotten."

No one has more thoroughly regretted Gladstone's lapse from the high confidence to which he had been growing and which ultimately enabled him to adopt the ideas of Home Rule for Ireland than did Gladstone himself. Five years elapsed, and to a New York correspondent he made acknowledgment of his error. "I must confess," he wrote, "that I was wrong; that I took too much upon myself in expressing such an opinion. Yet the motive was not bad. My sympathies were then—where they had long before been, where they are now— with the whole American people. I, probably, like many Europeans, did not understand the nature and workings of the American Union. I had imbibed, consciously, if erroneously, an opinion that twenty or twenty-four millions of the North would be happier and would be stronger (of course assuming that they would hold together) without the South than with it, and also that the negroes would be much nearer to emancipation under a Southern Government than under the old system of the Union, which had not at that date (August, 1862) been abandoned, and which always appeared to me to place the whole power of the North at the command of the slave-holding interests of the South. As far as regards the special or separate interest of England in the matter, I, differing from many others, had always contended that it was best for our interest that the Union should be kept entire."

It is absurd to attempt an apology for Mr. Gladstone which does not at once invite the force of the usual remark, oftentimes made so justly with reference to him and his career: "Here is Oxford scholasticism in the role of an explanation."

It is a delight to turn from such a page as this in Gladstone's history, to one of the greatest of the American periodicals to which he afterwards contributed and find him face to face with the future of America, himself a thoroughgoing Englishman, but withal a philosopher and prophet of a statesmanship to which in 1863 he was partially a stranger.

"There were the strongest reasons why America could not grow into a reflection or repetition of England. Passing from a narrow island to a continent almost without bounds, the colonists at once and vitally altered their conditions of thought, as well as of existence, in relation to the most important and most operative of all social facts, the possession of the soil. In England, inequality lies imbedded in the very base of the social structure; in America it is a late, incidental, unrecognized product, not of tradition, but of industry and wealth, as they advance with various and, of necessity, unequal steps. Heredity, seated as an idea in the heart's core of Englishmen, and sustaining far more than it is sustained by those of our institutions which express it, was as truly absent from the intellectual and moral store, with which the colonists traversed the Atlantic, as if it had been some forgotten

article in the bills of lading that made up their cargoes. Equality combined with liberty, and renewable at each descent from one generation
to another, like a lease with stipulated breaks, was the groundwork of
their social creed. In vain was it sought, by arrangements such as those
connected with the name of Baltimore or of Penn, to qualify the action
of those overpowering forces which so determined the case. Slavery
itself, strange as it now may seem, failed to impair the theory however
it may have imported into the practice a hideous solecism. No hardier
republicanism was generated in New England than in the Slave States
of the South, which produced so many of the great statesmen of
America."

Coming to our Civil War, he said:

"The Civil War compelled the States, both North and South, to train
and embody a million and a half of men, and to present to view the
greatest, instead of the smallest, armed forces in the world. Here
there was supposed to arise a double danger. First that, on a sudden
cessation of the war, military life and habits could not be shaken off,
and, having become rudely and widely predominant, would bias the
country towards an aggressive policy, or, still worse, would find vent in
predatory or revolutionary operations. Secondly, that a military caste
would grow up with its habits of exclusiveness and command, and
would influence the tone of politics in a direction adverse to republican
freedom. But both apprehensions proved to be wholly imaginary.
The innumerable soldiery was at once dissolved. Cincinnatus, no longer
an unique example, became the commonplace of every day, the type
and mold of a nation. The whole enormous mass quietly resumed the
habits of social life. The generals of yesterday were the editors, the
secretaries, and the solicitors of to-day. The just jealousy of the State
gave life to the now forgotten maxim of Judge Blackstone, who denounced as perilous the erection of a separate profession of arms in a
free country. The standing army, expanded by the heat of civil contest
to gigantic dimensions, settled down again into the framework of a
miniature with the returning temperature of civil life, and became a
power well nigh invisible, from its minuteness, amidst the powers which
sway the movements of a society exceeding forty millions.

"More remarkable still was the financial sequel to the great conflict.

The internal taxation for Federal purposes, which before its commencement had been unknown, was raised, in obedience to an exigency of life and death, so as to exceed every present and every past example. It pursued and worried all the transactions of life. The interest of the American debt grew to be the highest in the world, and the capital touched five hundred and sixty millions sterling. Here was provided for the faith and patience of the people a touchstone of extreme severity. In England, at the close of the great French war, the propertied classes, who were supreme in Parliament, at once rebelled against the Tory Government, and refused to prolong the Income Tax even for a single year. We talked big, both then and now, about the payment of our National Debt; but sixty-three years have since elapsed, all of them except two called years of peace, and we have reduced the huge total by about one-ninth."

Thus he concluded:

"But I will not close this paper without recording my conviction that the great acts, and the great forbearances, which immediately followed the close of the Civil War form a group which will ever be a noble object, in his political retrospect, to the impartial historian; and that, proceeding as they did from the free choice and conviction of the people, and founded as they were on the very principles of which the multitude is supposed to be least tolerant, they have, in doing honor to the United States, also rendered a splendid service to the general cause of popular government throughout the world."

One of these great acts of forbearance was made easy by the development of Americanism in Gladstone himself.

On September 7, in 1864, we find Gladstone welcoming Garibaldi to London. Earlier than this, in a long and keen correspondence involving Lord Shrewsbury, Anthony Panizzi and Mr. Gladstone in controversy, this lover of liberty, perhaps recently trained to step to the larger music of freedom with his unfortunate experience with the American war, had given adequate expression to his sympathy for the struggles of the Italian people toward emancipation and unity. Gladstone had shown himself intelligent upon the general theme of Italian patriotism in a review on the Roman State, published years before.

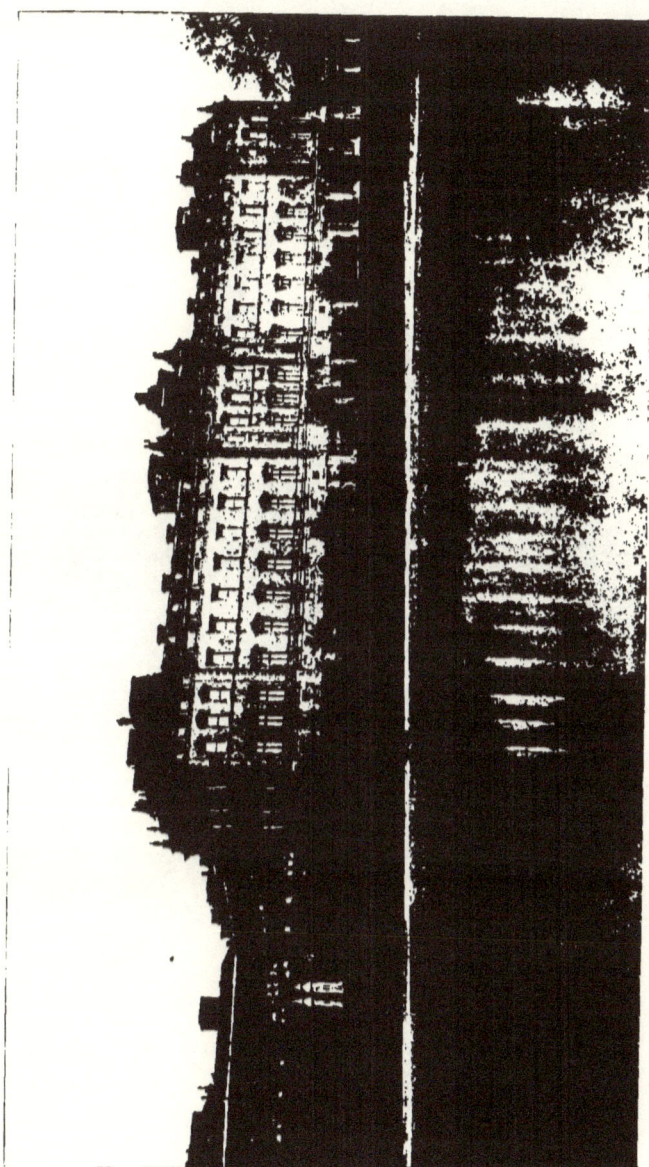

BUCKINGHAM PALACE

RIGHT HONORABLE—THE MARQUIS OF SALISBURY, K.G.

In all these years, Gladstone's mind was being trained to say of Garibaldi, Cavour and Victor Emmanuel: "These three names together form for Italians a tricolor as brilliant, as ever fresh, and, I hope, as enduring, for many and many generations, as that national flag which now waves over a united Italy." Years before, in his denunciation of the Neapolitan government, he had shown his intrepidity by snatching a phrase which he heard from the lips of an oppressed people: *"La Negazions di Dio Eretta a Sistena di Governo."* By his indomitable will and the force of his shining character, he had commanded the attention of civilization, until the world believed that his indictment against Italian misrule was proved in every count. It was but the beginning of a long crusade in which the Italian people themselves were most heroic, and which was now concluded amidst the acclamations of a free and united people.

It became certain that the genius of Lord Palmerston, assertive, narrowly British, and commanding as it was, no longer represented the widest vision of the modern Englishman. He was a bluff aristocrat, declining the appearance of enthusiasm by visiting it with the theories of the race-course. He blustered, and for a long time attracted ordinary citizens with the noise he made, and the ardor with which he unfurled the flag of England whenever something more important needed to be done for the honor and future of her growing life.

It began to be evident that England would no longer be bantered or dazzled or joked down, or even threatened by Palmerston. At eighty years of age, such a man as Gladstone may be still young, but this is not so with an intelligence such as Palmerston's. If he conceded anything to freedom-loving Lord John Russell, it must be a Reform Bill of 1860 of such thin consistency as to furnish nothing but an evidence that Palmerston had resolved that Reform was not in his line, and that it was not in England's line. It was at this moment that Gladstone felt that the people had been educated up to the point where, when Palmerston should terminate his career, England would demand a director of affairs whose unquestionable courage must be matched by the largest and most hopeful intelligence. Bishop Wilberforce, who

13

anticipated that Gladstone would be chosen Prime Minster at an early day, wrote in 1863:

"That wretched Pam seems to me to get worse and worse. There is not a particle of veracity or noble feeling that I have ever been able to trace in him. He manages the House of Commons by debauching it, making all parties laugh at one another; the Tories at the Liberals, by his defeating all Liberal measures; the Liberals at the Tories, by their consciousness of getting everything that is to be got in Church and State; and all at one another, by substituting low ribaldry for argument, bad jokes for principle, and an openly-avowed, vainglorious, imbecile vanity as a panoply to guard himself from the attacks of all thoughtful men. I think if his life lasts long, it must cost us the slight remains of Constitutional Government which exist among us."

Palmerston himself had said: "Gladstone will soon have it all his own way; and, whenever he gets my place, we shall have strange doings." Palmerston was the sort of man to take offense at intellectual and political liberality. In his cynical old age it was impossible for him not to feel that a sprightly, eager, and wide-eyed soul such as was Gladstone, was a menace to the England which he had served, and which he had tried to keep within the bounds of his own aristocratic temperament. Next to Bright was Gladstone in the circle of Palmerston's hate. It was impossible that they should understand one another, when it was the night struggling with the day, and even when there was external harmony prevailing, it was still the quiet harmony of that moment between day and night, when morning streams victoriously over the hills.

CHAPTER XXII.

THE SCHOLAR AND ORATOR.

As against the fading figure of Palmerston, distrustful of popular government at the last, rose the form of Gladstone, who had amazed England's Conservatism. All these things were treasured up against Mr. Gladstone by the learned and reactionary constituents who thronged about Oxford University and clung fast to the Toryism which Gladstone was certainly forsaking. They sought to defend the night against the morning by the scholastic methods which the most eminent of Oxford's modern sons ultimately outgrew. It was evident that his struggle to remain a representative of Oxford University in the Parliament of England was to be long and severe, and perhaps end in defeat.

It is a beautiful example of the way in which Gladstone's mind gave itself truest recreation and went forth to refreshment, returning with power from his excursions from politics into literature, that he now spoke so eloquently and wisely in presenting his concluding discourse as Lord Rector of the University of Edinburgh. In it, he added to the world's literature one of the most comprehensive and philosophic of the creations of his mind. His address had as its title, "The Place of Ancient Greece in the Providential Order of the World."

He was in the plenitude of his physical and intellectual power. The delivery of the address was calm and yet energetic, his genius kindling as he rose to supreme places in classic oratory.

Many phases of the theme he illustrated with abundant learning and graceful oratory. But he never seemed more deeply eloquent, for he was never more truly moved in all his soul, than when he turned to the Religion of the Bible and said:

"But indeed there is no need, in order to a due appreciation of our debt to the ancient Greeks, that we should either forget or disparage the function which was assigned by the Almighty Father to His most

favored people. Much profit, says St. Paul, had the Jew in every way.
He had the oracles of God; he had the custody of the promises; he
was the steward of the great and fundamental conception of the unity
of God, the sole and absolute condition under which the Divine idea
could be upheld among men at its just elevation. No poetry, no philosophy, no art of Greece, ever embraced, in its most soaring and widest
conceptions, that simple law of love towards God and towards our
neighbor, on which 'two commandments hang all the law and the
prophets,' and which supplied the moral basis of the new dispensation.

"There is one history, and that the most touching and most profound of all, for which we should search in vain through all the pages of
the classics,—I mean the history of the human soul in its relations with
its Maker; the history of its sin, and grief, and death, and of the way of
its recovery to hope and life, and to enduring joy. For the exercises of
strength and skill, for the achievements and for the enchantments of
wit, of eloquence, of art, of genius, for the imperial games of politics and
war—let us seek them on the shores of Greece. But if the first among
the problems of life be how to establish the peace, and restore the balance, of our inward being; if the highest of all conditions in the existence of the creature be his aspect towards the God to whom he owes his
being, and in whose great hand he stands; then let us make our search
elsewhere. All the wonders of the Greek civilization heaped together
are less wonderful than is the single Book of Psalms.

"Palestine was weak and despised, always obscure, oftentimes and
long trodden down beneath the feet of imperious masters. On the other
hand, Greece, for a thousand years,

> "Confident from foreign purposes,"

repelled every invader from her shores. Fostering her strength in the
keen air of freedom, she defied, and at length overthrew, the mightiest
of existing empires; and when finally she felt the resistless grasp of the
masters of all the world, them, too, at the very moment of her subjuga-
tion, she herself subdued to her literature, language, arts, and manners.
Palestine, in a word, had no share of the glories of our race; while they
blaze on every page of the history of Greece with an overpowering

splendor. Greece had valor, policy, renown, genius, wisdom, wit; she had all, in a word, that this world could give her; but the flowers of Paradise, which blossom at the best but thinly, blossomed in Palestine alone."

After nearly two hours of golden speech, he concluded thus:

"Everywhere, before us, and behind us, and around us, and above us and beneath, we shall find the Power which—

"Lives through all life, extends through all extent,
   Spreads undivided, operates unspent."

And, together with the Power, we shall find the Goodness and the Wisdom of which that sublime Power is but a minister. Nor can that wisdom and that goodness anywhere shine forth with purer splendor than when the Divine forethought, working from afar, in many places, and through many generations, so adjusts beforehand the acts and the affairs of men as to let them all converge upon a single point; namely, upon that redemption of the world, by God made Man, in which all the rays of His glory are concentrated, and from which they pour forth a flood of healing light even over the darkest and saddest places of creation."

Mr. Gladstone first appeared as an author on the great theme of Homer, at an hour when the proclamation of the theories of Wolf, Lachmann and Hermann had begun to lose a little of its jauntiness and to indicate the absurdity of its dogmatism. It is an interesting fact to note that the orthodox view of Homer and of the Homeric poems, in so far as it was advocated by Mr. Gladstone, is stronger to-day than it was when he wrote, whatever may have been the general opinions with respect to the value of his ingenious essays. He was already Doctor of Civil Law, as well as leader in the British Parliament, and was known as an erudite and eloquent man who touched every subject at least with cleverness and brilliancy, and who scarcely spoke or wrote without betraying an almost contagious enthusiasm and thus creating a love in his hearer or reader for pure and noble thought as well as musical rhetoric. These elements were expected by scholars, to enter and play no small part in the perpetual charm which the announced volumes would exercise over the reading public. It was an easy way of getting rid for a moment of Mr. Gladstone's influence in politics, to say that he could not reason without sophistry because bewildering sophisms were of the bent and tendency of his mind. The Whigs who were dissatisfied with him charged this up to his Oxford training, and the Tories insisted that they had acutely observed that it was innate and incurable. It was also urged that his was not a mind which realized vividly and deeply as by the divination of genius a great truth seen only from the watch-tower of the highest imagination. Scholarship was quite ready, however, to welcome the three volumes of excellent and eloquent writing, upon a subject beset with all manner of difficulties, each of which involved most accurate induction and profoundest scholarship for even its respectable treatment. Those who settled the business of particles, as did Browning's dead grammarian, were ready. Reviewers were not therefore surprised that Homer's own winged words had influenced Mr. Gladstone into a too energetic use of his own wings, and that therefore the three volumes, in which were collected the results of his studies of Homer, were unnecessarily long, marred by his usual brilliant plausibilities, and yet glorious with the radiance of an orator's mind. Indeed, in writing, it was always very difficult for Mr. Gladstone the scholar and expositor to get away from Mr. Gladstone the orator. He did love the effects produced by a sincerely eloquent man. His translations of the classics, especially of the ancient poets, indicate a poetical rhetoric, rather than imagination all compact and that inevitableness, as Emerson termed it, in the use of words, which characterize the poet and even the excellent translator of poetry. He has an abundance of force and skill, but they are the force and skill of the orator, not of the poet, not even of the best sort of ordinary literary man. Nothing that he has done lacks his ardor in *tempo* and melody, and in much of his work as a translator he reaches profound harmony. His work never suffers from weakness, but on the contrary, it is remarkably vigorous; yet the music and the power belong rather to the orator than to the true singer or the inspired translator. His imagination in this first study of Homer was as faithful to him as ever this unsurpassed power of his had been in the illumination of the apparently sordid concerns of fiscal science or in the handling of the thorny difficulties of Ireland's misgovernment. In his translations he did not disdain to give touches even of beauty and of suggestiveness, which came not from Homer's mind. Mr. Bentley said of Pope: "You have written a very pretty book, but you must not call it Homer," and Mr. Gladstone's translations of Homer are indications of how a generous, not to say supreme, imagination may amplify even upon the work of the blind bard "of Scio's rocky isle," while, because of the defect of that same imagination, it often fails to completely reproduce the truly Homeric atmosphere.

It has always been well-nigh impossible for Mr. Gladstone to do the trifling things of life with less of seriousness and strength than he employs in the performance of the most majestic task. He was not heavy but he was great, yet scarcely great enough to work with lightness and delicacy. Nothing was more evident in his recent volume of translations from Horace than this; that the lighter effusions of the Roman bard were simply trampled beneath the heavy onset of Mr. Gladstone's somewhat unsympathetic genius. Horace, perhaps, was too trifling and light-minded to be truly translated by a great English statesman resting upon his laurels in old age. Frolicsome as Mr. Gladstone has been, though he has declined to enter his second childhood and thus bear witness to the truth of the old statement "Twice a boy and once a man," he failed in this, perhaps because he was entirely unable to enter into the playful moods of some of the authors whom he has sought to translate, except in such a way as to put a stop to the humor of the situation entirely. The lofty and massive quality of his mind appeared in the book of translations in which he shared authorship with his friend Lord Lyttleton. But while this is to be said, it must also be held that there are few who have ever undertaken translation who surpassed Gladstone when he had to deal with the poetry of Greece and Rome in the higher flights of song. Quotation has often been made of the description of the Greeks as they go forth to war in the fourth book of the Iliad. Here Gladstone chose as his guide the Homer of English prose and poetry, Sir Walter Scott, and these are some of the lines:

"As when the billow gathers fast,
  With slow and sullen roar,
Beneath the keen north-western blast
  Against the sounding shore;
First far at sea it rears its crest,
  Then bursts upon the beach;
Or with proud arch and swelling breast,
  Where headlands outward reach,
It smites their strength, and bellowing flings
  Its silver foam afar;
So, stern and thick, the Danaan kings
  And soldiers marched to war.
Each leader gave his men the word,
  Each warrior deep in silence heard;
So mute they marched, thou couldst not ken
  They were a mass of speaking men;
And as they strode in martial might,
  Their flickering arms shot back the light."

As successful as Gladstone was in such passages, the rigor and stateliness of his muse made it impossible for him to handle the delicate tapestry of less serious-minded singers.

There can be no doubt that the enthusiasm of the English reading public over Mr. Gladstone's volumes on Homer and the Homeric Age began to decline after it was known that, marvelous and almost unmatched as were Mr. Gladstone's genius and laboriousness, neither or both of these could invent so many hours or supply so much strength, outside of the demands which a great statesman had placed upon him, as to give him the right to stand before the world as both the first of English statesmen and an accurate and profound Homeric scholar. Anybody knows that it is easier to write a long book containing a given amount of knowledge and philosophy than it is to write a short one. When Mr. Beecher once preached an hour and a half he smilingly said, "If I had had time to think this subject up, I would have left off the first hour of this sermon." Gladstone's three volumes on Homer are the witness of what an incalculably large draft was made upon a first-class intellect by the exigencies of his political life. It left him no time to put his thought briefly and clearly. Every page has its charms and no chapter is to be read without gaining the enthusiasm of the author. The cleverness of the treatise was surpassed only by its length. He had furnished a work which proved to scholars what a mighty man in learning he might have been if he had had the time, and he demonstrated to statesmen his unrivaled versatility. As we look upon Mr. Gladstone's Homeric studies from this later date, when he arises before us as the man Dr. Dollinger has called the greatest theologian of Europe, we cannot help thinking of the remarkable likeness of Gladstone the Homeric scholar and Gladstone the Theologian. He may see his Moses and Isaiah emerge from the Higher Criticism as did his Homer. In the latter domain as well as in the former, he leaves the impression, even after his greatest work is done, that human nature, after all, cannot be counted upon for accuracy, profundity and comprehensiveness in more than two or three of the supreme interests of human life. The atmosphere of plausibility does not permanently abide over statements which can not stand fire, nor do even the merits of Mr. Gladstone's work in both these domains count for full value in the neighborhood of the fact that sometimes he carries his strife for an assumed position by sheer force of fascinating speech, rather than by the power of coherent argument. The presence of the orator with his immeasurable powers of persuasion, glancing from his face or flowing melodiously from his lips, has much to do with gaining the day, though one may be a little conscious that the whole thing has been accomplished with a dexterity and ingenuity almost too fascinating. But alacrity in passing over the difficulties of a case with facile theorizing which half conceals problems as dark and tortuous as they are hidden, the light handling of difficulties in the presence of fancied analogies all of which would surely break if taken in a vigorous grasp—all this when put into print furnishes indubitable evidence either of unnecessary haste in the writing and publication or of great desire on the part of a skillful orator to appear as great a writer as he is a speaker. Gladstone's Homer was full of observations which might have made the fortune of any other literary man in English writing on the subject. In the glory of their philosophic light, however, his inaccuracies stood forth badly, and furnished the students of historical criticism with a case not easy to forget.

This great merit of the books can never be forgotten. England saw the scholarly statesman turning the eyes of Anglo-Saxon literary world again to a vast planet in the sky. Who had any right to suppose that Mr. Gladstone had ever gone to this planet and stood there long enough to be able to write concerning it, microscopically? His superb contribution lay in the fact that he, as almost no other man in the world, could and did look upon this matchless star, telescopically. But the difficulty with Mr. Gladstone was he had made such an exhibit of erudition as he was always likely to do, and had seen so many little things that nobody cared to attend to, that the things of medium size which were of importance to scholars and which he passed over or misunderstood greatly perplexed them. Questions as to when writing came into Greece, as to the unity of Homer's work were usually referred to the greater works of other scholars, but Gladstone's over-wordy statement on other matters unfortunately invited the clear, sharp intellect of Mr. Grote into the consideration of the problem and the result was that we often found ourselves preferring the terseness and completeness of Grote's description to his own. It is when Mr. Gladstone deals with the Homeric poems as compared with the Hebrew scriptures, or when analyzing the forces which have gone into the making of literature in the land of Pindar and Hesiod that we find ourselves borne along by eloquence as faithful to the facts as it is stirring to the imagination.

Whenever he touches such a subject as Homer's perception and use of numbers and color, all the best qualities of Gladstone's mind are manifested. We can see here the great intellect luxuriating playfully with a subject precisely to his fancy. Hasty he may be in many of his opinions and somewhat disputatious with reference to some of his deductions, but the Homer of Gladstone is a distinct gift, large, fullblooded, harmonious, awe-compelling, and that he has left the world more eager than ever to know this majestic figure is proof of the majesty and charm of his own genius.

CHAPTER XXIII.

CONTESTING FOR OXFORD.

In Gladstone's struggle to hold Oxford as his constituency, and in the attacks made upon him at that time, may be read perhaps the most interesting chapter in his career as a contestant for honors, where he accepted every challenge, and, after a hard battle, won glory in defeat. Toryism presumed to lecture him in its reviews, to weep over what it termed his moral lapse in its drawing-rooms, to execrate him with clumsy abuse in its newspapers. Dryasdusts emerging from the chambers where monasticism had given a peculiar hue to their thinking, wrote to the great reviews and made exposition elsewhere of the terrors with which Oxford again confronted the possibility that so dangerous a man should represent so much which had always been respectable, scholarly, and conservative. Palmerston had once advised that he be kept under the influence of Oxford, for he would be controlled in no other wise. He was appealed to on account of his father, and was reminded from what a consistent, steady, old-school baronet he had sprung. Contrasts were instituted between the brilliant and recalcitrant orator and Mr. Gladstone's good, Tory brother, to whom Sir John Gladstone had bequeathed his estate in Forfarshire. One enthusiastic person projected the plan of somehow providing William E. Gladstone with sufficient property, in the hope that the possession of an estate like his brother's might give him some like sense of responsibility and woo him back to the Toryism which now appeared unsatisfactory to him. Reminiscences were produced by those who had quarreled with him in childhood and youth, and, of course, these reflecting people remembered nothing except his stalwart obstinacy and his irritable temper, and especially the fact that, as a child, he would not play much with other children, but ordered them about, to their great disgust. Writers of letters to local papers asserted that England might have ex-

pected as much from him, for even while he was a boy, and ought to
have been engaged in sport, he stubbornly kept reading his books,
and acquired then that superiority of intelligence and unpleasant seriousness of mind which, in spite of the charms of the Arabian Nights,
Plutarch's Lives, Walter Scott's tales, Robinson Crusoe, and the stories
of Homer and Virgil, led him into the study of Thucydides, Cicero,
Dante and Plato, and made him so good and loquacious an historian
that nobody else wanted to talk with him.

Other critics maintained that they recollected him as a youth so
beset with the habit of writing poor but ambitious verse that it was
impossible to expect anything else than a most fanciful and dreamy
politician out of it all. The following quotation was made from one of
his early attempts at poetizing:

WAT TYLER.

"Shade of him whose valiant tongue
  On high the song of freedom sung;
Shade of him, whose mighty soul
Would pay no taxes on his poll;
Though, swift as lightning, civic sword
  Descended on thy fated head,
The blood of England's boldest poured,
  And numbered Tyler with the dead!

"Still may thy spirit flap its wings
At midnight o'er the couch of kings;
And peer and prelate tremble, too,
In dread of nightly interview!
With patriot gesture of command,
  With eyes that like thy forges gleam,
Lest Tyler's voice and Tyler's hand
  Be heard and seen in nightly dream.

"I hymn the gallant and the good
From Tyler down to Thistlewood,
My muse the trophies grateful sings,
  The deeds of Miller and of Ings;

She sings of all who, soon or late,
    Have burst Subjection's iron chain,
Have seal'd the bloody despot's fate
    Or cleft a peer or priest in twain.

"Shades, that soft Sedition woo,
    Around the haunts of Peterloo!
That hover o'er the meeting-halls,
    Where many a voice stentorian bawls!
Still flit the sacred choir around,
    With 'Freedom' let the garrets ring,
And vengeance soon in thunder sound
    On Church, and constable, and king."

And men went about believing that this boy's ironical production was the first fruits of his extreme liberalism!

One grave gentleman insisted that he was the victim, in early life, of what has been called the "fatal facility for extemporaneous utterance;" that oftentimes Gladstone found it impossible to satisfy his love of contention unless he were to take the wrong side of the question, which he promptly did, and that his superlative talents so irradiated and bewildered him that at last he convinced himself that he was on the right side, and he stayed there, with a pertinacity and doggedness unequaled except in the last session of Parliament. Oxford could scarce endure this.

It was a signal opportunity for Gladstone's critics to find the root of everything which they now disliked in him, in some anecdote relating somewhat of his past. Boys who had known him at Eton, and were not so strenuous as he, now rose to remark that he never was popular, but was cold and haughty, and yet he was smart enough to keep out of scrapes, and politic enough to be on the winning side, so that even then he was called "Popular Billy." No one dreamed in the confusion that the case against him had suffered from too much proof. It was the common complaint of these critics who were intent upon his defeat, that he had always been the dupe of his own impulsiveness of disposition, which led him into committing himself before he knew what he was about, and, possessing abnormally high self-respect, not to say egotism, he never could be persuaded to abandon his false position. He could extricate himself from apparently hopeless dilemmas, and meet with adroitness his own mistakes; and all this had developed within him, they said, a tendency which Oxford never in the world might suffer longer, namely, a bent of mind and a desire to argue eloquently, even against his own reason and conscience, rather than give up a proposition which in his haste and conceit he had adopted. Little did Oxford think that the thing objected to, so constantly misapprehended, was really a current of Gladstone's mind revealing the fact that he was at last escaping the dogmatism and scholasticism of his old University.

It was impossible, even in 1865, for these foes to forget that Gladstone had been an excellent churchman, and that he had written a book which left no ground visible for a Dissenter or even an unctious Evangelical churchman to stand on. Church Toryism took to itself with singular affectionateness this part of Gladstone which had insisted that one religious denomination could never be as good as another. It was very amusing to hear Church Toryism produce its lament that a young and brilliant statesman such as Gladstone, who had been a regular attendant at St. Mary's, Oxford, when John Henry Newman exercised his indescribable charm over the young auditors, and yet had not taken them all to the Church of Rome, should not have contented himself with a statesmanship which would have left him still a churchman as learned and redoubtable as Keble and as conservative as an Oxford don. That this same Gladstone had nevertheless appeared happy that the Reform Bill had swept away so many landmarks, so-called, that he rejoiced that the ten-pounds householders had a representative in the House of Commons, and that there were yet other things he might help to do in the same direction before the Government of England would appear perfect to him—this was incredibly bad. Mourners went about the streets reflecting that, if Gladstone had never come under the milder political sophistry of Sir Robert Peel, he might not have developed such a skill in manipulation, such prodigious powers of refining and making distinctions through which Toryism was constantly escaping, as now confounded them, and that he never would have dazzled plain people by the finesse with which he attained his purposes.

Unquestionably, Gladstone had behind him a record which gave great pain to the straightforward disciples of Toryism. His foes could not forget that Mr. Gladstone's speech on Lord John Russell's motion for applying the surplus revenues of the Irish Church to secular purposes had compelled the Earl of Derby to pronounce him the most eloquent young man he had heard since the beginning of his own long public life. Neither could Toryism forget that Gladstone had shown a business ability and a power for handling and solving financial problems, a master of the art of lucid exposition equaled but not surpassed by the younger Pitt; besides all this, he had the force of stainless personal character; but lo! these energies had gone with his dreadful aspiration to think for himself and to act for himself, thus, as one Tory general said, making it certain that he was "to mar a genius otherwise so brilliant and to detract from the value of a reputation so important to the party." "Party," indeed!—Gladstone has made partyism (as opposed to patriotism) as ridiculous as it is abominable. Oxford had noticed pretty carefully that Gladstone had not been as violent as his constitutionally bad temper ought really to have made him against such propositions as Duncombe's in 1840, "to bring in a Bill for exempting Dissenters, on certain conditions, from the payment of Church rates." Since that time Gladstone's sentimentalism in the direction of the wicked Non-Conformists has often horrified the guardians of the Ark of the Lord in England. Gladstone had even been caught coquetting with other Liberal notions. It is true he had so labored to change the commercial system of Great Britain as to make England solvent, but he was accused of unseemly vanity about his efforts, even in the presence of Sir Robert Peel, who had been chief in the pilot-house while the ship was thus taking its course. He had not, another observed, improved in the quality of his Toryism, but he had become more adroit and tumultuous in battle.

The opposition to him became positively humorous. His churchmanship, which had been once held to be more exacting and upright than that of Mr. Keble, was hotly attacked from another point of view, and the Oxford dons revolted at the assertion:

"For the last thirty years I have not been able to trace any danger to the Church of England arising from the political acts of Dissenters."

Every delicate ecclesiastical sensibility was shocked. The Book of Common Prayer might as well have been burned before their eyes. Besides all this, there had recently been some significant strikes upon the part of the laboring men, and Gladstone, who had been favorable to the extension of the Franchise, had not called them rascals,—the word "anarchists" had not then come into use—and he had further offended their perfumed respectability by recognizing Garibaldi and bringing himself into disrepute with people who could not understand the valor of the red-shirted hero.

Oxford had noted that Gladstone was speaking in South Lancashire, and Oxford insisted that this meant that Gladstone understood how unsatisfactory he must be to a cultivated community. It was only necessary for Oxford to reprint and circulate his speech at Bolton, in order to properly guard its refinement against the danger of voting for Gladstone.

If this had been all, some might have lapsed so far as to forgive him, but, just at the moment when he was intimating that there were times when a statesman became over-lively in his urging reforms, he said to the workingmen of Manchester:

"Gentlemen, permit me to express a hope that this great community will be upon its guard against what I may call the principle of political lethargy. That is not a sound or a healthy principle. There are times when I apprehend it would be the duty of any public man, in addressing a public assembly, to endeavor to moderate what might seem to him over-liveliness and excessive eagerness, even in the work of reform and improvement. But the time in which we live is not a time of that character; it is rather a time in which it is becoming we should recall to our recollection, that although so much has been done, and well done, to the honor of all parties concerned in this country during the last thirty years, yet it behooves us to continue cautiously, steadily, and justly but firmly, to continue in the same career. We cannot look

ST. JAMES PALACE—LONDON

CARDINAL NEWMAN

abroad over the face of our country without feeling that there is much that we have yet to desire. We cannot look across the channel to Ireland, and especially to the state of feeling in Ireland, and say that that state of feeling taken as a whole, is becoming for the honor and for the advantage of the United Kingdom. We cannot look upon our brethren and our fellow-subjects there without heartily wishing that they were more entirely united with us. We cannot say that their duty to the people has been discharged. I do not say that Parliament is to blame. I contend, indeed, that Parliament is the faithful steward of the powers which it has received. It is governed by an enlightened desire to promote the interests of the entire community. But that Parliament has more than once heard an expression of the desire that some extension should take place in the direct action of the people in the choice of its representatives. (Cheers.) There cannot, I think, be a doubt that, whenever the state of public feeling shall have matured for the satisfactory entertaining of that question, one of the great demonstrative facts of the moral claim of the people to have some extension of the franchise will rest with the conduct of the population of Lancashire during the distress of the last few years."

Surely even the impetuous and wily Gladstone could not be allowed by Oxford to go further. He went to Liverpool, and there, in spite of the recollection of his Tory father, and his lively consideration of the fact that the merchants of Liverpool were quite proud of him, and he was anxious to retain the honor they did him, he spoke freely with reference to the duty on corn and the further application of the principles he had espoused.

South Lancashire was vulgar and sooty and uncultured;—Oxford was about to say to Mr. Gladstone that he belonged to that sort of people. After Oxford had washed the hands of the aristocracy from previously-acquired defilement, and Gladstone was no longer her representative at Westminster, with the attention of England directed to him, as he might have desired, he gave a farewell address. He said, speaking to a vast audience in Manchester:

"After an anxious struggle of eighteen years, during which the unbounded devotion and indulgence of my friends maintained me in the

14

arduous position of representative of the University of Oxford, I have been driven from my seat. . . . I have loved the University with a deep and passionate love, and as long as I breathe that attachment will continue; if my affection is of the smallest advantage to that great, that ancient, that noble institution, that advantage, such as it is, and it is most insignificant, Oxford will possess as long as I live. But don't mistake the issue which has been raised. The University has at length, after eighteen years of self-denial, been drawn by what I might, perhaps, call an overweening exercise of power, into the vortex of mere politics. Well, you will readily understand why, as long as I had a hope that the zeal and kindness of my friends might keep me in my place, it was not possible for me to abandon them. Could they have returned me by a majority of one, painful as it is to a man at my time of life, and feeling the weight of public cares, to be incessantly struggling for his seat, nothing could have induced me to quit that University to which I had so long ago devoted my best care and attachment. But by no act of my own am I free to come among you. And having been thus set free, I need hardly tell you that it is with joy, with thankfulness, and enthusiasm, that I now, at this eleventh hour, a candidate without an address, make my appeal to the heart and the mind of South Lancashire, and ask you to pronounce upon that appeal. As I have said, I am aware of no cause for the votes which have given a majority against me in the University of Oxford, except the fact that the strongest conviction that the human mind can receive, that an overpowering sense of the public interests, that the practical teachings of experience, to which from my youth Oxford herself taught me to lay open my mind —all these had shown me the folly, and, I will say, the madness of refusing to join in the generous sympathies of my countrymen, by adopting what I must call an obstructive policy."

He added:

"Without entering into details, without unrolling the long record of all the great measures that have been passed—the emancipation of Roman Catholics; the removal of tests from Dissenters; the emancipation of the slaves; the reformation of the Poor Law; the reformation— I had almost said the destruction, but it is the reformation—of the tariff;

the abolition of the Corn Laws; the abolition of the Navigation Laws; the conclusion of the French treaty; the laws which have relieved Dissenters from stigma and almost ignominy, and which in doing so have not weakened, but have strengthened, the Church to which I belong—all these great acts, accomplished with the same, I had almost said sublime, tranquillity of the whole country as that with which your own vast machinery performs its appointed task, as it were in perfect repose—all these things have been done. You have seen the acts. You have seen the fruits. It is natural to enquire who have been the doers. In a very humble measure, but yet according to the degree and capacity of the powers which Providence has bestowed upon me, I have been desirous not to obstruct but to promote and assist this beneficent and blessed process. And if I entered Parliament, as I did enter Parliament, with a warm and anxious desire to maintain the institutions of my country, I can truly say that there is no period of my life during which my conscience is so clear, and renders me so good an answer, as those years in which I have co-operated in the promotion of Liberal measures. . . . Because they are Liberal, they are the true measures, and indicate the true policy by which the country is made strong and its institutions preserved."

Lord Palmerston, whose life had now closed in petulance and faithlessness, had said of Gladstone: "He is a dangerous man. Keep him in Oxford, and he is partially muzzled; but send him elsewhere, and he will run wild." Now at Liverpool, his old home, the unmuzzled man spoke, in part, as follows:

"During eighteen years I have been the representative of Oxford. It has been my duty in her name to deal with all those questions bearing upon the relations of Religion and Education to the State, which this critical period has brought to the surface. Long has she borne with me; long, in spite of active opposition, did she resist every effort to displace me. At last she has changed her mind. God grant it may be well with her; but the recollection of her confidence which I had so long enjoyed, and of the many years I have spent in her service, never can depart from me; and if now I appear before you in a different position, I do not appear as another man. .   . If the future of the University is to be as glorious as her past, the result must be brought about by enlarging her borders, by opening her doors, by invigorating her powers, by endeavoring to rise to the heights of that vocation with which, I believe, it has pleased the Almighty to endow her. I see represented in that ancient institution the most prominent features that relate to the past of England. I come into South Lancashire, and find here around me an assemblage of different phenomena. I find the development of industry. I find the growth of enterprise. I find the progress of social philanthropy. I find the prevalence of toleration. I find an ardent desire for freedom. . . .

"If there be one duty more than another incumbent upon the public men of England, it is to establish and maintain harmony between the past of our glorious history and the future which is still in store for her. . . . I am if possible more firmly attached to the institutions of my country than I was when, a boy, I wandered among the sand-hills of Seaforth. But experience has brought with it its lessons. I have learned that there is wisdom in a policy of trust, and folly in a policy of mistrust. I have observed the effect which has been produced by Liberal legislation; and if we are told that the feeling of the country is in the best and broadest sense Conservative, honesty compels us to admit that that result has been brought about by Liberal legislation."

South Lancashire adopted the stone whom the Oxford builders rejected at the very time when panic-stricken men, such as Lord Shaftesbury, were blind to the cynicism and antediluvianism of even as strong a personality as Lord Palmerston. "Lord Palmerston," said Lord Shaftesbury, lamentingly, "is the only true Englishman left us in public life." It was a sad time, indeed, except for prophetic souls.

He desired to rest, but England would not hear his plea.

CHAPTER XXIV.

LEADER OF THE HOUSE OF COMMONS.

February 6, 1866, found the new Parliament opened in a manner befitting the sad event which had left the Queen of England a widow and the nation mourning for the Prince Consort. Matters were not minced in the announcement that Parliament would be expected to deal with the Reform Bill. The speech from the Throne contemplated action in the direction of a broadening of the Elective Franchise. Four hundred thousand voters were to be added, and thus a larger suffrage was to be introduced; all adult males, who, in two years had deposited fifty pounds in a savings bank, could register; compound householders were to stand in a position relatively equal to that of the rate-payers; the clauses of the Reform Act were to be abolished, admitting voters above the line of ten pounds; and the Occupation Franchise was to include houses at fourteen pounds rental and attain as high as fifty pounds.

Every thoughtful man in England watched Gladstone's appearance with interest as the leader of the House of Commons. He had been splendidly trained in the past, and his cause was now finely reinforced by excellent men who would stand by his side. Gladstone was in his best form. He stood in his own manly strength,

> "A pillar of state; deep on his front engraven
> Deliberation sat and public care;
> With Atlantean shoulders fit to bear
> The weight of mightiest monarchies."

He spoke with impassioned strength on the Reform Bill before the House:

"We cannot consent to look upon this large addition, considerable although it may be, to the political power of the working classes of this country, as if it were an addition fraught with mischief and with danger. We cannot look, and we hope no man will look, upon it as some Trojan horse approaching the walls of the sacred city, and filled with armed

213

men, bent upon ruin, plunder, and conflagration. We cannot join in comparing it with that *monstrum infelix*—we cannot say:

> "——Scandit fatalis machina muros,
> Fœta armis: mediæque minans illabitur urbi."

I believe that those persons whom we ask you to enfranchise ought rather to be welcomed as you would welcome recruits to your army, or children to your family. We ask you to give within what you consider to be the just limits of prudence and circumspection; but, having once determined those limits, to give with an ungrudging hand. Consider what you can safely and justly afford to do in admitting new subjects and citizens within the pale of the Parliamentary constitution; and, having so considered it, do not, I beseech you, perform the act as if you were compounding with danger and misfortune. Do it as if you were conferring a boon that will be felt and reciprocated in grateful attachment. Give to these persons new interests in the constitution, new interests which, by the beneficent processes of the law of nature and of Providence, shall beget in them new attachment; for the attachment of the people to the Throne, the institutions, and the laws under which they live is, after all, more than gold and silver, or more than fleets and armies, at once the strength, the glory, and the safety of the land."

Gladstone was tenderly regardful of his personal obligations to his friends, and his love for Sir Robert Peel always commanded his chivalrous speech. While he never made much of a figure in the world of fashion, Gladstone took it suddenly by storm in the year 1866, by appearing at the christening of Sir Robert Peel's descendant—an event which assembled the rank and fashion of the metropolis. Gladstone made a speech which produced a profound impression. It was his to propose the health of the infant, and some of his rotund and graceful sentences the audience had a right to expect. But he struck out into a new line for himself and for his audience, and thereby captivated fashionable London. The speech, it was said, "set two colonels crying, and disturbed the equanimity of a brace of bishops." It was chronicled by an observer of note, in March, 1866, that this orator had begun to speak with a certain air of command, and that so imperious and yet fascinating was his manner that it seemed perfectly right for such men as Sir George Grey,

John Stuart Mill and John Bright, to be dominated as well as charmed by him.

In this session John Stuart Mill had, no doubt, his greatest influence upon the thought and tone of Mr. Gladstone.   Up to this date, Mill was thought an indifferent speaker, because he was a philosopher; and it was usually arranged, at least at the first, that he should be through his speaking before Gladstone arose.   Mill's was a unique service in that body of legislators which has been spoken of as possessing "all the vices of a mob, with none of its virtues."   Nobody had any doubt that he was the greatest authority in England on logic and political economy. Now he was to shine as a persuasive speaker.   At sixty years of age he won a distinct triumph in the annals of British speech, and no one was more happy than Gladstone himself in the unmistakable victory accredited to this scholar and philosopher.   It was needful that the Liberal party at that time, having use for Gladstone in other parts of the field, should enlist in the advocacy of its opinions some one whose personal character and abundant information might unite with powers of persuasion, to place before the House of Commons the Liberal view of such subjects as were involved in the question, for example, whether "the redundancy of revenue should be applied, not to the remission of the Malt Tax, but to a payment of the national debt."   Mr. Mill had been serious in study-ing the House of Commons from the opening of the session.   The peri-patetics of that body went flitting about in the lobbies or lounging in the refreshment rooms—in short, doing anything and everything to escape the dullness of a tedious debate; but Gladstone and Mill might always be found present and patient in listening to the dreariest of Par-liamentary bores.   Mill had already attracted the attention of the think-ers in the Assembly.   His voice was feeble and somewhat uninteresting in the quality of its tone, his figure slight and delicate, appearing small enough in comparison with the hearty John Bright, who sat in front of him at the upper end of one of the Independent Liberal benches, and ap-pearing very ungraceful, also, in comparison with the lithe and upright form of Mr. Gladstone.   Yet Mill's face was exceedingly sensitive, and it always glowed with the indwelling intellectual force with which his whole personality was surcharged; and, at once, the House of Commons saw a man thinking keenly and deeply on his feet, and evidently putting the reasoning of the moment into words as inevitable as the thought itself.   His own book on Political Economy was as much on trial as Gladstone's book on Church and State had ever been on trial in other quarters.

Mill had attracted the lance of Mr. Robert Lowe, and a finer play of swords in the British intellectual arena had not been seen for a long time.   Mr. Lowe met a foeman worthy of his steel, and by his own dexterity and the fierceness of his thrust in the onset, he simply proved that his antagonist, John Stuart Mill, had brought unsurpassed intellectual skill to the House of Commons.   The debate on the Revenue and the National Debt was wearisome in the extreme, until Mill rose to defend the position he had taken that an effort be made by this tax to reduce the National Debt.   He lacked the mental excitement which the presence of Bright, Lord Stanley and Disraeli might have given him. Gladstone and Bulwer-Lytton had been long before wearied out, and they seemed to vie with each other in gymnastics, one of them "unfolding a greater variety of sprawling postures than anyone would suppose the human form, even of an acrobat or a financier, capable of assuming;" the other an eminent man "whose long, meager, uncouth form had writhed and twisted impatiently upon his seat," and who, upon the appearance of Mr. Mill, "bent far forward with his chin in his left hand and the elbow resting on his knee, while his eyes glared intently from beneath the shadow of his broad-brimmed hat."   These, with perhaps seventy men of indifferent standing, had remained when Mill began to speak.   There could be no doubt of the magic of the spell he exercised. The whole subject was illuminated by a man of genius, not rhetorical, far from verbose, but fluent and sincere and resistless by the clear force of his compact thinking and classic utterance.   It was an hour before he concluded his peroration.   Mr. Gladstone was the most delighted man in England.

He had already adopted into such friendship as ideas alone may make immortally powerful, this timid scholar, whose gentle and unassuming oratory, carrying superlative wisdom, had placed him in the front rank of the really effective speakers of England.

It was Gladstone's characteristic that he drew from every such man his highest and best contribution for the general cause of Liberal statesmanship. Differ as Bright and Mill might from Gladstone, he taxed their utmost powers and obtained their richest devotion to a cause more important than their differences. Mr. Gladstone was in the midst of the fight for reform. "Society," which John Stuart Mill and such men had despised, was against the Bill. Gladstone himself had spoken, both at Liverpool and at Manchester, and it was still a question as to what England meant to do. Gladstone doubted if the agitation for the measure had been strong enough and long and widespread enough. Brooking no antagonism, he had startled the House of Commons by turning around upon his antagonists and hurling upon them his scorn at their horror of admitting the workingman to the Franchise, as if they were foreign foes instead of being, as he said, "our fellow subjects, our fellow Christians, our own flesh and blood." In the swiftness and breadth of his eloquence, his auditors almost forgot whether they were to vote on this particular Bill, or on the broader question as to the right of the working classes to exercise their share of electoral strength. The Liberal party kindled under the influence of his speech, and even those who were disposed to rebel against the imperiousness of Gladstone, concluded to put off deserting the cause until they heard from the country. Everybody began to say that it was "the citizen against the aristocrat." Bright shared with Gladstone the labor and honor of addressing monster meetings in Lancashire. When Gladstone was badgered by those who said he had not been able to state openly what it was hoped to effect by a more democratic Parliament, he stood upon his dignity, and hurled back the charges of indecision with as much success, and with more reason, than Disraeli could hurl back the charges of his foes by his old tone of insolent triumph. No doubt the Liberal party, as a party, was weaker than Mr. Gladstone, because Liberalism at that time was very anxious to prove that it never could become very democratic. The truth is that it took a long while for Gladstone and his Liberal friends to realize that in their sympathy with the South in the Civil War in the United States, they had stabbed their own cause in England. They had been shouting that democratic institutions would go to pieces, and now they had the English public suddenly to educate and to be convinced that this, which was a movement in the direction of democracy, was a wise thing for England.

England never has cared to learn much from her daughter, America. It is obviously true that she had to learn, at that time, that democratic principles were gaining ground in England because of the success achieved by the American democracy in handling the Rebellion. Mr. Gladstone's adroitness, his unmistakable ability to conceal an idea amidst high-sounding and fascinating phraseology, even his unmatched gifts as an orator, were needed to make things appear palatable to the British mind. On the first night of the debate, as long before the time of which we are writing as was early March, Gladstone had supported the Bill with dexterous power. It is doubtful if he ever appeared to better advantage physically. His voice rang out like a trumpet, and every tone indicated the superb health of his vital organism. His handsome face appeared so transparent that the burning soul looked out through every feature upon his audience. The supple, fairly tall, spare figure, marked a little by the scholar's stoop until the moment came when he lifted himself to his full height and thundered forth his resistless periods, held its volume of excitement fairly well, while he shook his rather large and fine head, crowned, as it was, with hair which was turning from black to gray, and destroyed the arguments of the Opposition by a glance from the piercing eyes, or the announcement of some unanswerable argument, to which the firm, strong chin and finely moulded mouth loaned all their power.

Mr. Gladstone always gave undeniable evidence, by his utterance and its character, when his mind was not quite made up, or when he saw difficulties which he knew were stronger than his antagonists supposed. This state of mind manifested itself in his finding four or five terms with which to express his meaning, and three or four phrases which only served to indicate how unsatisfactory to himself was his own thought on the subject. Time after time, in this speech, which was two hours and a half long, Gladstone demonstrated the fact that he could take more sideroads and find more interesting scenery in taking them, and still get back upon the main road, than any man in England.   He was not quite clear to himself, although he spoke with vigor.

It was very apparent that Mr. Robert Lowe, with his vitriolic analysis and instinctive doubt as to the value of Mr. Gladstone's oratorical productiveness, could ask no finer opportunity to win the triumph over his old Oxford friend.   Gladstone and Lowe could never understand one another.   Lowe was as predestined a failure as Gladstone was a predestined success, in a political career.   Gladstone had genuine sympathy for the people, Lowe had none.   Gladstone trusted his sentiments, and loved to dally with his own reasons and study their subtleties; Lowe despised sentiment, and his mind was too hard and logical to tarry long in a web of finely spun distinctions.   No doubt his speech that night accentuated the defects of Gladstone's advocacy of the Reform.

Everyone who met Gladstone at this time discerned a resiliency of intellectual and spiritual fiber remarkable in any man.   Lord Houghton writes of him at this moment:

"I sat by Gladstone at the Delameres'.   He was very much excited, not only about politics, but cattle-plague, china, and everything else.   It is indeed a contrast to Palmerston's Ha! ha! and *laissez-faire.*"

Even after the Reform Bill had begun to shrivel as a blossom in a time of frost, Gladstone's pluck and skill for confounding his enemies did not forsake him.   He had the disadvantage of finding that everybody could say when the Reform Bill proved a failure: "I told you so." Bishop Wilberforce had written in his journal March 12th:

"Gladstone has risen entirely to his position, and done all his most sanguine friends hoped for as leader.   .   .   .   There is a general feeling of the insecurity of the Ministry, and the Reform Bill to be launched to-night is thought a bad rock."

And that was the sentiment of all thoughtful England.   The Gladstone who was urging England toward democracy was paying for his blunder with respect to the ability of American free government to perpetuate itself against rebellion.   It was hard to argue against the past.

John Bright has described the collection of half-hearted Liberals who organized themselves against Gladstone as a political "Cave of Adullam," but this did not answer their contention.

CHAPTER XXV.

GLADSTONE AND DISRAELI.

It was remarkable, if not disheartening, to Gladstone, that this association of malcontents was growing larger day by day. Its most polished weapon he saw when the son of his father, Sir Robert Peel, spoke in opposition to the Bill. No doubt Mr. Gladstone's speech was saved from much that was wandering and inconclusive, by the fact that Disraeli so bitterly taunted him concerning his past. The thrust roused him to noblest eloquence. Disraeli was more than ordinarily patronizing and insolent when he reminded Gladstone that once the latter had made a speech in the Oxford Union against the Reform Bill of 1832. Gladstone leaped at him with terrific force in these well-known words:

"The right hon. gentleman, secure in the recollection of his own consistency, has taunted me with the errors of my boyhood. When he addressed the hon. member for Westminster, he showed his magnanimity by declaring that he would not take the philosopher to task for what he wrote twenty-five years ago; but when he caught one who, thirty-six years ago, just emerged from boyhood, and still an undergraduate at Oxford, had expressed an opinion adverse to the Reform Bill of 1832, of which he had so long and bitterly repented, then the right hon. gentleman could not resist the temptation. He, a parliamentary leader of twenty years' standing, is so ignorant of the House of Commons that he positively thought he got a parliamentary advantage by exhibiting me as an opponent of the Reform Bill of 1832. As the right hon. gentleman has exhibited me, let me exhibit myself. It is true, I deeply regret it, but I was bred under the shadow of the great name of Canning; every influence connected with that name governed the politics of my childhood and of my youth; with Canning, I rejoiced in the removal of religious disabilities, and in the character which he gave to our policy abroad: with Canning, I rejoiced in the opening which he made towards the establishment of free commercial interchanges between nations; with Canning, and under the shadow of that great name, and under the shadow of that yet more venerable name of Burke, I grant, my youthful mind and imagination were impressed just the same as the mature mind of the right hon. gentleman is now impressed. I had conceived that fear and alarm of the first Reform Bill in the days of my undergraduate career at Oxford which the right hon. gentleman now feels; and the only difference between us is this—I thank him for bringing it out—that, having those views, I moved the Oxford Union Debating Society to express them clearly, plainly, forcibly, in downright English, and that the right hon. gentleman is still obliged to skulk under the cover of the amendment of the noble lord. I envy him not one particle of the polemical advantage which he has gained by his discreet reference to the proceedings of the Oxford Union Debating Society in the year of grace 1831. My position, sir, in regard to the Liberal party is in all points the opposite of Earl Russell's. . . . I have none of the claims he possesses. I came among you an outcast from those with whom I associated, driven from them, I admit, by no arbitrary act, but by the slow and resistless forces of conviction. I came among you, to make use of the legal phraseology, *in formâ pauperis.* I had nothing to offer you but faithful and honorable service. You received me, as Dido received the shipwrecked Æneas—

> Ejectum littore egentem
> Excepi,

and I only trust you may not hereafter at any time have to complete the sentence in regard to me—

> Et regni demens in parte locavi.

You received me with kindness, indulgence, generosity, and I may even say with some measure of confidence. And the relation between us has assumed such a form that you can never be my debtors, but that I must forever be in your debt. It is not from me, under such circumstances, that any word will proceed that can savor of the character which the right hon. gentleman imputes to the conduct of the Government with respect to the present Bill."

More and more rich became his eloquence, as he concluded:

"Sir, we are assailed; this Bill is in a state of crisis and of peril, and the Government along with it. We stand or fall with it, as has been declared by my noble friend Lord Russell. We stand with it now; we may fall with it a short time hence. If we do so fall, we, or others in our places, shall rise with it hereafter. I shall not attempt to measure with precision the forces that are to be arrayed against us in the coming issue. Perhaps the great division of to-night is not the last that must take place in the struggle. At some point of the contest you may possibly succeed. You may drive us from our seats. You may bury the Bill that we have introduced, but we will write upon its gravestone, for an epitaph, this line, with certain confidence in its fulfillment:

Exoriare aliquis nostris ex ossibus ultor.

You cannot fight against the future. Time is on our side. The great social forces which move onwards in their might and majesty, and which the tumult of our debates does not for a moment impede or disturb—those great social forces are against you; they are marshaled on our side; and the banner which we now carry into this fight, though perhaps at some moment it may droop over our sinking heads, yet it soon again will float in the eye of Heaven, and it will be borne by the firm hands of the united people of the three kingdoms, perhaps not to an easy, but to a certain, and to a not far distant, victory."

Perhaps never had Gladstone so moved the English nation by his eloquence, and it is a question, if, in modern times, any single utterance in a hall of legislation has so instantly and widely commanded the enthusiasm of a people as did this speech. The future England—indeed "the parliament of man, the federation of the world," for an hour, hung, not as a dream, impossible of realization, in the sky, but as a reality to be soon reached and enjoyed—and this vision, at the moment, actually thrilled the somewhat heavy and stolid intelligence of John Bull, shopkeeper. Disraeli's remark, that the English are, after all, an enthusiastic people, would have been taken as sober truth, by a chance visitor from abroad, who, next morning, tried to get a hearing at table or at the railway station upon the subject of his breakfast or his ticket. Crowds of excited men were listening to another full-voiced Briton as he read Gladstone's speech—the tears and shouts mingling, as sentence after sentence came upon their eager ears. Drawing rooms, not yet disenchanted by the "society" whose fantastic prerogatives such a philosophy as his would inevitably sweep away, gave themselves up to his praise. His house was filled with a host of admirers and his eye looked out upon crowds who had seen from afar but who were yet sure at least for the present, to be cheated out of the better day he prophesied. It would not be fair to say that Gladstone's eloquence was the only product of oratory and genius in that debate. Mr. Robert Lowe, as Conservative in this hour as he was likely to be Liberal the next, a man who profoundly distrusted the people and who saw that Americanism had at last captured Gladstone, uttered a brilliant protest. He was soon to be made Lord Sherbrooke and his speech was characteristic:

"Monarchies," said he, "exist by loyalty, aristocracies by honor, popular assemblies by political virtue. When these things begin to fail, it is in their loss, and not in comets, eclipses and earthquakes, that we are to look for the portents that herald the fall of States." And again: "We are about to exchange certain good for more than doubtful change; we are about to barter maxims and traditions that never failed for theories and doctrines that never succeeded. Democracy you may have at any time. Night and day the gate is open that leads to that bare and level plain where every ant's nest is a mountain and every thistle a forest-tree. But a Government such as that of England is the work of no human hand. It has grown up by the imperceptible aggregation of centuries. It is a thing which we only can enjoy, which we cannot impart to others, and which, once lost, we can not recover for ourselves."

Against such Conservatism not even Gladstone could lead John Bull at that hour.

There was no possible use in Russell and Gladstone attempting to carry the Bill unless some concessions were made. After a bare majority of five had carried its second reading, these conciliations were offered, but they were offered in vain. On the anniversary day, when the English spirit congratulated itself on the victory obtained over Napoleon at Waterloo by Wellington, a motion was carried against the Government. Rating for rental was substituted as the basis of the Franchise in boroughs. Lord Macaulay's nephew gave to the public a poem which made its place in the history of the time. Tribulation increased for the "Gladstone coterie," so-called, and it was driven to resign. A financial panic came, the European continent quivered with alarm; Queenstown saw an American monitor in the harbor, and excitement was intense from one end of the realm to the other. The one fact which left its mark was the Austro-Prussian conflict, of which Gladstone afterwards said:

"Never was there a war shorter than that of 1866, but its consequences were immense. It restored the national existence of Germany, and brought within view its complete consolidation. It consummated the national unity of Italy. It put an end to all possibility of refusing the demands of Hungary. As part of the Hungarian arrangement, it secured free government for the whole Austrian Empire, and, lastly, in thus restoring the power of utterance and action to that country, it shattered the fabric of Ultramontanism which had been built up by the Concordat of 1855. Such were the results, in the South, of those few weeks of war."

Gladstone was at least satisfactory to the Radicals. Would they go too far for him? Bright was satisfied.

"Who is there in the House of Commons," he demanded, "who equals him in knowledge of all political questions? Who equals him in earnestness? Who equals him in eloquence? Who equals him in courage and fidelity to his convictions? If these gentlemen who say they will not follow him have any one who is equal, let them show him. If they can point out any statesman who can add dignity and grandeur to the stature of Mr. Gladstone, let them produce him."

Radicalism had frightened sober John Bull. It seemed to be a poor time for reforms, when Trafalgar Square was made riotous by more than 100,000 people passing resolutions in its favor. Yet Gladstone was holding his own. The music of Mr. George Trevelyan's poem was turned into truth, and Mr. Gladstone's house was surrounded by a

GLADSTONE AND HIS SON HERBERT

LORD BEACONSFIELD

throng of Englishmen who sang hymns in his honor.   Nothing could have added more signally to the popularity of the Chancellor of the Exchequer than the fact that as Lord Russell's Government went down, the stalwart conviction and unquestioned genius of Gladstone became manifest to Great Britain.   Every one of his friends believed that a year or two of opposition would strengthen him, and they were right.

Meantime Mr. Gladstone's sobriety and good sense appeared to the best advantage.   His were small as contrasted with the difficulties which Mr. Robert Lowe's sharp sword had produced for himself, in the fact that the laboring people of Great Britain were more indignant as to his scorn of them than they were credulous as to the truth stated in Mr. Gladstone's eloquence, or in John Stuart Mill's reasoning.   It is certain that Gladstone lost no opportunity to take advantage of the popular sympathy which was aroused when Mr. Robert Lowe's strange talent for saying the wrong thing led him to utter his bitter attack upon the working classes and led them to believe that theirs was Gladstone's cause.   This added significance to the vast assemblage in Trafalgar Square.

Mr. Gladstone was now a public figure of such prominence that it was entirely impossible for him to move without creating curiosity and remark.   He had been a long loved and honored friend of Cardinal Manning, and Newman had influenced his thinking and religious life. Now he and his family went to visit Rome and they called upon Pope Pius IX.   For eighteen months thereafter, from whisper to public proclamation, "the accusation growing bold and true," the report gained currency that he had gone to Rome to arrange with the Pope to destroy Protestant Church Establishment in Ireland, and to consult with respect to other matters of like importance, he being at heart a Roman Catholic. It is easy to imagine what Philistinism and bigotry in England made out of a report so delicious to its taste as was this one.   We doubt very much if Gladstone ever got over the effect of the report that he either had been intending to join the Roman Church, or was intending it now, or was going to intend it in the future.   It has been continually embarrassing to his career as he has dealt with the problem involving the destinies of the Irish people.

15

At this time Gladstone gave a great deal of attention to what was called the Ritualistic Movement in the Church of England. Americans have, at one time, been called upon to face the question as to whether a special denomination of Christians should arrogate to themselves the name of "Church of America." The Ritualistic party in America was in the lead during this discussion, and perhaps educated the American mind into some interest as to the general drift of Ritualism elsewhere. Gladstone's high churchmanship led him at once into an appreciation of the symbolism and poetry of ceremonial and worship. It was at the time of the Church Congress that the Ritualists gave their exhibition of clothes used in their services. Seven large rooms were filled with copes, stoles, chasubles and the like, and this display, while it fascinated the antiquarians and tickled John Bull in so far as he was a manufacturer of ecclesiastical millinery, and whatever else they needed, excited an intense feeling of antagonism to the whole Ritualistic movement. Gladstone's famous essays on the general subject were being prepared.

The only other subject upon which Gladstone talked at all times and with everybody in the course of these autumn days, was the Elective Franchise. True, the Reform Bill had failed, but the justice and the expediency of a wider suffrage was most apparent to Gladstone. For the common people not to desire it and for England to be glad, was for England to agree to their voluntary degradation. Gladstone saw the educational value of suffrage, subject to such qualifications as an intelligent man would propose. There was a growing feeling now that it was fair to admit men into the processes of civilization if it was meant to civilize them, and that this was wiser than to leave them out where their interests and prejudices could have no voice or vote. The astonishing success of the American Union began to fill the mind of England with larger hopes for democracy everywhere. The ten-pound householder stop-and-brake had not hitherto kept England from corruption. No wise man would say that the morals of a voting class, each having an income of 10,000 pounds, would be higher than the morals of a vot-. ing class having an income of 100 pounds per annum. Of one thing Gladstone was convinced, the burden of proof lay upon the advocates of an exclusive franchise. The tests ought to be rational, not arbitrary.

Permanence of residence and education were better and sounder tests than wealth and a fine pedigree. A Constitutional Government depending upon the loyalty of all its citizens could not be carried on by shutting out a large proportion of the community and compelling them to believe that the cherished interests of a few always controlled legislation. John Stuart Mill stood by him again and again, in urging the fact that popular suffrage has a most stimulating effect on the popular mind. As democracy grew in England, such men as Gladstone did not fear the excitement of an election.

The consideration of public affairs by the public involves an immense educational movement, and on this educational movement Mr. Gladstone was relying more day by day.

Meantime the English radicals and the Irish Democrats, under the influence of Mr. Bright and the Roman Catholic bishops whom he met at Dublin, were forming as much of an alliance as was possible with the turbulent Irish agitators, who entered the combination and who now saw that Gladstone, with Mill and Bright, were sure to do something soon with the Land Tenure and the Irish Church.

A conspicuous figure now arose who called himself "The O'Donoghue." He was almost as eloquent as Mr. Bright, and as handsome as Gladstone, and he refused to use the title "Mr." and was called "The" because he had descended from an Irish king. He was ubiquitous, wily and able, and had to be reckoned with.

It was anticipated that Disraeli had persuaded the Conservative Ministry to a proposition looking toward Household Suffrage. He had craftily left a path open to this concession by his recent speech.

And now, peace-defending John Bright was heard sounding strange tones from beneath his broad, Quaker hat. It is possible that if Mr. Bright had known to what extent his words would have been quoted at a later date, he would not have labored for the regeneration of Ireland by intimating that the item of physical force should have something to do with the settlement of the question. It was an anomalous thing for John Bright to do, but it was a time when physical force had been appealed to on other matters. At the meeting at Trafalgar Square, in which Gladstone and Bright had been praised by the workingmen, much must have reminded Gladstone and Bright how that the same governing classes which were resisting reform had before resisted almost everything but physical force in 1832. At a famous meeting in Birmingham now Bright received with delight the announcement that 100,000 workingmen and artisans would again pledge to march on London. In 1832 the threat of creating a new company of lords who could handle the old peers who had resisted Reform brought the Throne and the Upper House to terms. Now the House of Lords, having declined to be led by Gladstone toward a broadening of the suffrage, looked out upon the scene and saw the possibility of 100,000 workingmen marching on London, and raising such a tumult in other ways as either to ultimately fill the House of Lords with undesirable occupants or to abolish it. Noisy indeed were the peasantry of Ireland whenever the Irish question touched their Church or State. They were learning from other lands. Stein had raised the Prussian peasantry from wretchedness and ignorance and revolt, to comfort and intelligence and political power, and it was upon the lips of men who would willingly have granted Gladstone's contention on Disestablishment, that things must go no further until Ireland was civilized, not by physical force, which, either in England or in Ireland, had done so much to uncivilize her, but by some such radical change as would contemplate the possession of land by the citizens of Ireland in fee simple. Fenianism arose out of its grave, and the specter horrified the country. The London Times and the Morning Post warned the Irish people that the rebellion would be disastrous. The Reform Administration meanwhile had met in London. At this time John Bright's eloquence had reached a height altogether unmatched, even by Mr. Gladstone's versatile powers. Ordinarily Bright had to struggle, in the House of Commons, and out of it, with an audience which did not agree with him. He spoke to monster meetings in London and elsewhere. Within the sound of St. Stephen's debates, his audience carried him on into unwonted realms of oratorical splendor. The Tory policy with reference to the evils of Ireland had received more cautious, more just, and therefore more terrible and unanswerable antagonism from the calmer and more skillful oratory of Gladstone. But never before had severity joined with genius to cast upon the Tory party an odium so overwhelming as came from Bright's address at this time.

Meantime Gladstone was taking thoughtful notice of the fact that a strong feeling had arisen among workingmen that the State Church was not worthy of the place which it at least held, if it had not usurped, and that the property which belonged to all the nation ought not to be used for a particular class of people. The opposition of the House of Lords to reform, and the discussion of Irish Church Disestablishment had led to this feeling, and now Mr. Gladstone set his great energies to the task of influencing the body of clergy in the English Church to discharge their high functions in regard to education and the general treatment of social grievances, so that the institution which, as we have seen, he loved so much, and which was so vital to the larger interests of England and humanity, might worthily stand in the front rank of the forces of progress.

Such always was the statesmanship of Gladstone, that no biographer can state, for none can calculate, the conservative influence he has exercised in labors like these. Institutions may be preserved only by statesmen who make them worthy of themselves.

Early in February Parliament was opened, and the Lord Chancellor stood by the side of the Queen and read the speech. Everybody waited for Disraeli to redeem the promise that the Government should do something about Reform. Gladstone appeared to see, as everybody else saw, that Lord John Russell was failing in physical power and intellectual energy, and Gladstone himself was more brilliant and industrious than usual. He promised to help his opponents, if they would deal honestly and progressively with the questions before them. Perhaps Gladstone's impulsiveness was never more counted upon by his antagonists than just at this time. His versatility had now and then added to his difficulties by giving him a reputation for bad temper and arrogance. He was in a trying position. His High Churchmanship made the Dissenters unsatisfied with him. His leaning toward the people inflamed such men as Lord Cranborne to compare him to a pettifogging attorney, and, next day, to apologize to the attorneys of England for doing so. The old Whig families hated him because he gave so much talent to the cause of the plebeians.   But he had genius, and he was in the right.

Just at this time, when the Fenians were attempting to raise a revolution in the neighborhood of Hawarden Castle, Gladstone's home, Mr. Disraeli arose to present the Government scheme of Reform.   His deep and sonorous voice quivered as he threw taunt and challenge to those who had stood for Reform, and his manner was irritably lofty and serious as he uttered admirably phrased commonplaces apparently charged with the deepest political wisdom.   Theatrical in the extreme, his pompous sneer accompanied him as he strode forth, dealing out tinsel and drops of burning sarcasm, never attempting the heights of eloquence visited by Bright or the more rigorous paths of statesmanship toward which Gladstone was leading England.   He spoke of Goldwin Smith as a "rampant lecturer," and coolly proposed that every such man as he should be willing to think Reform a measure above party, and he hinted that he and his party alone ought to determine about the Franchise, the redistribution of seats, and whatever else the Liberal party was aimlessly talking about.   Soon the Government scheme of Reform was published, and the Conservative party found itself hopelessly at war with itself.

It was John Bright who gave Mr. Disraeli a name which followed him to the last.   What Bright had said now appeared truer than ever:

"Now, Mr. Disraeli is a man who does what may be called the conjuring for his party.   He is what, amongst a tribe of Red Indians, would be called 'the mystery man.'   He invents phrases for them—and one of the phrases, the last and the newest, is this lateral extension of the franchise.   Now, Mr. Disraeli is a man of brains, of genius, of great capacity for action, of a wonderful tenacity of purpose, and of a rare courage.   He would have been a statesman if his powers had been directed by any noble principle or idea.   But, unhappily, he prefers   a temporary and worthless distinction as the head of a decaying party, fighting for impossible ends, to the priceless memories of services rendered to his country and to freedom, on which only in our age an enduring fame can be built up."

Disraeli kept England waiting for some deep and wise scheme of policy to unfold itself.   Gladstone watched carefully, expecting to see his own Bill, changed sufficiently to satisfy the prejudice of aristocracy and the demand of the rabble, offered by Mr. Disraeli. At last Disraeli showed his hand, and he spoke in introduction of a Reform Bill which his party despised because it was a Reform Bill, and which the Liberals laughed at. Gladstone had already triumphed so far that the Cabinet had to offer a bolder scheme, and a device was added to the scheme of Household Suffrage, and Disraeli solemnly warranted it all to work. Meantime the more orthodox Conservatives resigned, before the "mystery man," and the silent advance of Gladstone's prudent and self-restrained battalion. The man who had been accused of arrogance and bad temper, who was simply and nobly angered at the folly of his friends and the audacity of his foes in the presence of a supreme question, beheld his opponents dispirited in the meantime.

The "Cave of Adullam," in which the discontented of Liberalism gathered, with Mr. Lowe posing as a Liberal in everything else but the one thing for which Liberalism had the right to exist, felt the humiliation. Gladstone's followers, who were led farther than they wanted to go in the direction of popular government, were swept on by the enthusiasm of the victor. Nobody knew what would be the end of the controversy. Disraeli had only a remnant of his own party, but he had the support of a large fraction of the opposition who were in favor of Reform. Was it possible that this athletic magician, who was a Conservative only by accident, as Gladstone was a Liberal by conviction, could unite a fragment of the Tory party with the mob on the streets and make a Reform Bill desirable to England? Mr. Gladstone was certainly rising to a place in the admiration of England to which he had never before attained. Henry Fawcett, afterwards to be his Postmaster General, now the blind and beloved member for Brighton, the author of excellent works on political economy and a laborious ally, with Thomas Hughes, of Rugby fame and of philanthropic enterprises, represented the sort of men who were rapidly coming to speak of Gladstone with enthusiasm, and even the old Whigs regarded the vehemence of his speech as a witness to the eagerness of his soul.

Never were Gladstone and Disraeli more unconsciously leaving ineffaceable portraits of themselves for the eyes of England to look upon.

Gladstone's eloquence suffered oftentimes from his cleverness in the handling of words, but it suffered more from the tendency of his mind to see interesting distinctions which are important only to a scholastic mind and for which words are the names, and then it was that words mastered him, and he waded uneffectively through his too elaborate and sonorous sentences.   Never until his conscience and heart were stirred so that his intellect had no time for subtleties, did the impetuous stream carry its full burden of meaning, and his fervid imagination yield its resources to his fully conceived purpose as an orator.   Gladstone's ardent temperament shines through these 'best appeals, and one can easily understand how much more popular Disraeli must have been in what Thackeray calls "society," where a cold cleverness means so much and where an imperious moral aim means so little.

Gladstone appeared to be leading his party, when Disraeli's Bill proposing to establish Household Suffrage came up.   Gladstone objected to the establishment of unequal suffrage as Disraeli proposed, and to the leaving of the distribution of the franchise to be handled by whimsical parish vestries. He proposed a substitute for Mr. Disraeli's qualification, and he advocated an instruction to the committee embodying the scheme of a uniform rate giving the franchise to all occupiers of holdings rated at five pounds. Gladstone's enemies saw that a race was in progress between him and Disraeli, and he was accused of going too far "toward the mob," in admitting a far larger number of persons to the vote than even Disraeli proposed.   Besides, the Liberal leaders were afraid their constituents would say that this amendment would create an arbitrary line, making a man's right to vote rest on the value of his house, and not on the size of his taxes or the amount of his intelligence.

The famous "tea-room meeting" of the Liberals occurred.   Gladstone was told of their refusal to support him.   The vote showed a victory for Disraeli, and the Tories were jubilant.   Gladstone could only say to to his friends: "I have deferred to the opinions of others; I abandoned the instruction I proposed; I have been accused of arrogance and imperiousness.   Had I been imperious in this case, my very defeat would have been a victory."

CHAPTER XXVI.

THE DERBY-DISRAELI GOVERNMENT.

The Derby-Disraeli Government had been constituted in February, and Disraeli's plan for the reduction of the Franchise in Boroughs had come before Parliament in the shape of resolutions. At length Gladstone succeeded in forcing Disraeli to offer the plan in the form of a Bill. Even this did not produce a political paradise. But Gladstone was not through with public life. He gave notice of amendments to the Bill which Disraeli insisted were so vital that if they should succeed the Government would decline further responsibility. The discussion revealed great diversity of ideas. Gladstone's first resolution was rejected, but after the Easter vacation, in the hey-day of their power, and in the confident expectation upon the part of the Government that the Bill would pass and be satisfactory to his following of Conservatives, in spite of the modifications urged by the Liberals, Disraeli saw his measure utterly transformed. Gladstone had succeeded in getting his ten Modifications adopted, with the single exception of the second, which was subsequently taken in, and the Conservatives had surrendered. It was the most unprecedented struggle in length and severity in which Gladstone and Disraeli ever took part, each calling forth the reserve energy and unsuspected dexterity of the other in the exciting duel. On and on these debates led them, confronting ministerial crises, pushing responsibilities from one side to the other, until the House of Commons grew weary, and in July, 1867, passed the schedules, and called for the third reading of the Bill. Meantime Lord John Russell had definitely withdrawn from politics and given the leadership of the party into Gladstone's hands.

In November, 1867, Mrs. Disraeli fell ill. The Abyssinian difficulty came before Parliament in the short session before Christmas. Mr. Gladstone, naturally, was interested, and desired to talk on the address, but he declined, under the circumstances, to speak on any subject which might challenge Mr. Disraeli to contest with him in debate at such a time.

Disraeli was now as much of a turncoat, in the eyes of the Conservatives, as Gladstone had ever been. It was not necessary for Gladstone to visit his wrath upon his old foe, even if he had any to visit, which was not the case in the present instance. Lord Cranbourne and Mr. Lowe could attend to Disraeli. It is sufficient to quote Lord Cranbourne's last remark, which was surpassed in severity by Mr. Lowe's longer reference to the subject:

"I should deeply regret to find that the House of Commons has applauded a policy of legerdemain; and I should above all things regret that this great gift to the people, if gift you think it, should have been purchased at the cost of a political betrayal which has no parallel in our parliamentary annals, which strikes at the root of all mutual confidence, which is the very soul of our party government, and on which only the strength and freedom of our representative institutions can be sustained."

Disraeli replied to little purpose. The Bill passed the House of Commons, and after some amendments and characteristic speeches by Earl Russell and Lord Derby, the Bill was adopted. After Disraeli's record on the Reform Bill there was little else for him to do but to make a grand play, such as amused Great Britain, when, at the end of the year, he declared at a dinner given in his honor in Scotland, that he had always been a reformer, and, above all, the champion of the granting of the broadest Elective Franchise. He said in explanation of his previous history: "I had to prepare the mind of the country, and to educate— if it be not arrogant to use such a phrase—to educate our party. It is a large party, and requires its attention to be called to questions of this kind with some pressure. I had to prepare the mind of Parliament and the country on this question of Reform."

After all that might be said of Gladstone's "intellectual intricacy," Disraeli's cleverness had not kept him from appearing before the country as a man who had been beaten with the very ideas in his keeping against which he had fought so long. Meantime, on other subjects,

Gladstone had pronounced strongly.   There could now be no doubt about his position of antagonism to the Established Church in Ireland, and he had favored the opening of the Universities to all sects.   The argument against the State supporting a religion which in Ireland had only a small minority, was put by Gladstone most clearly.   Gladstone was already beginning to feel sure of the bigotry of Dissent, which saw in the contest against the Irish Established Church the appearance of a "rag of Popery."   He had been criticized by Tory gentlemen because he had gone toward the "Americanization" of England,—and a most remarkable specter was this!   Now this same timorous respectability beheld him adopting a course of conduct which would ultimately lead, they thought, to the disestablishment of all kinds of privileged institutions in the realm.   The well-paid Bishops saw that what has been called "the religious department of the British Government," namely, the Church of England, was also threatened, and Gladstone's High Churchmanship, which had been suspected of leaning toward a Church in absolute control of the State, was now sadly discredited, for was it not certain that he had acknowledged, in a public way, the valuable services of the Dissenters on the Franchise question, and had he not lately given an address to a body of Nonconformists?   Besides, the Churchmen could not forget that the Church no longer had its old hold upon the Universities to the exclusion of Dissenters, and Mr. Gladstone was held in blame for this state of things.

Really, it was too bad that all this should be occurring at a time when Mr. Huxley was writing review articles overthrowing ancient dogmas and that even Gladstone could not satisfactorily contend against these unchurchly fulminations, and Max Müller was composing addresses on comparative religion, to be delivered within the walls of Westminster Abbey or at Oxford.   No wonder Conservative Churchmen, well fed and trembling for their benefices, looked toward the House of Lords as the only breakwater against such a flood.   It was not remarkable, at such an hour, that one excited believer should propose to call Omnipotence in to protect the defense itself.

Now came a peripatetic orator named Murphy, who led a crusade amongst the lower classes against the Romish priests.   It was followed

by the murder of a man named Brett, and this fact indicated such a
state of things as would demand the consideration of some scheme
which would make Fenianism the name of a less dangerous force in
politics. Not even the trades-unions question, which was the cause of
a general controversy, could attract Gladstone from this subject.

London could hardly enjoy Christmas because of the explosion at
Clerkenwell and the revelations made by Fenianism, and the irritation it caused showed that something must be done immediately with
regard to removing the causes of Irish discontent. A Government was
in power called the Derby Government, whose interests Disraeli was
practically managing, and nothing but coercion could be expected
from them. On the 25th of February (1868) Lord Derby had resigned.
Disraeli had formed a new Administration, and now he could look back
upon the period when his speech was received with shouts of derision
and speak with his accustomed satire of those who had laughed at him.
He had struggled, single-handed and alone, from being the despised
Jew in politics to a position of glory and power. He was now Premier
of the Realm.

March 30th Gladstone moved the following resolution:

"1. That in the opinion of this House, it is necessary that the Established Church of Ireland should cease to exist as an establishment, due
regard being had to all personal interests and to all individual rights to
property. 2. That, subject to the foregoing considerations, it is expedient to prevent the creation of new personal interests by the exercise
of any public patronage, and to confine the operations of the Ecclesiastical Commissioners of Ireland to objects of immediate necessity, or
involving individual rights, pending the final decision of Parliament. 3.
That an humble address be presented to Her Majesty, humbly to pray
that, with a view to the purpose aforesaid, Her Majesty will be graciously pleased to place at the disposal of Parliament her interest in the
temporalities, in archbishoprics, bishoprics, and other ecclesiastical dig-
nities and benefices in Ireland and in the custody thereof."

The spirit in which the reform was proposed had been revealed in a
debate on a previous motion.

"If we be prudent men," Gladstone said, "I hope we shall endeavor, as far as in us lies, to make some provision for a contingent, a doubtful, and probably a dangerous future. If we be chivalrous men, I trust we shall endeavor to wipe away all those stains which the civilized world has for ages seen, or seemed to see, on the shield of England in her treatment of Ireland. If we be compassionate men, I hope we shall now, once for all, listen to the tale of woe which comes from her, and the reality of which, if not its justice, is testified by the continuous migration of her people; that we shall endeavor to

> Raze out the written troubles from her brain,
> Pluck from her memory the rooted sorrow.

But, above all, if we be just men, we shall go forward in the name of truth and right, bearing this in mind—that when the case is proved, and the hour is come, justice delayed is justice denied."

He now followed up his resolution by a long discourse, brilliant, learned, denunciatory of the Irish Church Establishment, and containing such passages as this:

"There are many who think that to lay hands upon the national Church Establishment of a country is a profane and unhallowed act. I respect that feeling. I sympathize with it. I sympathize with it while I think it my duty to overcome and repress it. But if it be an error, it is an error entitled to respect. There is something in the idea of a national establishment of religion, of a solemn appropriation of a part of the Commonwealth for conferring upon all who are ready to receive it what we know to be an inestimable benefit; of saving that portion of the inheritance from private selfishness, in order to extract from it, if we can, pure and unmixed advantages of the highest order for the population at large; there is something in this so attractive that it is an image that must always command the homage of the many. It is somewhat like the kingly ghost in 'Hamlet,' of which one of the characters of Shakespeare says:

> "We do it wrong, being so majestical,
> To offer it the show of violence;
> For it is, as the air, invulnerable,
> And our vain blows malicious mockery.

"But sir, this is to view a religious establishment upon one side only—upon what I may call the ethereal side. It has likewise a side of earth; and here I cannot do better than quote some lines written by the present Archbishop of Dublin, at a time when his genius was devoted to the muses. He said, in speaking of mankind:

> "We who did our lineage high
> Draw from beyond the starry sky,
> Are yet upon the other side
> To earth and to its dust allied.

"And so the Church Establishment, regarded in its theory and in its aim, is beautiful and attractive. Yet what is it but an appropriation of public property, an appropriation of the fruits of labor and of skill to certain purposes, and unless these purposes are fulfilled, that appropriation cannot be justified. Therefore, sir, I cannot but feel that we must set aside fears which thrust themselves upon the imagination, and act upon the sober dictates of our judgment. I think it has been shown that the cause for action is strong—not for precipitate action, not for action beyond our powers, but for such action as the opportunities of the times and the condition of Parliament, if there be a ready will, will amply and easily admit of. If I am asked as to my expectations of the issue of this struggle, I begin by frankly avowing that I, for one, would not have entered into it, unless I believed that the final hour was about to sound:

> "Venit summa dies et ineluctabile fatum.

"And I hope that the noble lord will forgive me if I say that before Friday last I thought that the thread of the remaining life of the Irish Established Church was short, but that since Friday last, when, at half-past four o'clock in the afternoon, the noble lord stood at the table, I have regarded it as being shorter still. The issue is not in our hands. What we had and have to do is to consider well and deeply before we take the first step in an engagement such as this; but having entered into the controversy, there and then to acquit ourselves like men, and to use every effort to remove what still remains of scandals and calamities in the relations which exist between England and Ireland, and to make our best efforts at least to fill up with the cement of human concord the noble fabric of the British Empire."

In the latter part of the year 1868, after the General Election, Mr. Gladstone published his famous "Chapter of Autobiography."

He agreed that autobiography ordinarily should be posthumous, but he saw that the cause, namely, the Disestablishment of the Church of Ireland, was likely to suffer "in point of credit, if not of energy and rapidity, from the real or supposed delinquencies of a person," and that person was himself. He thoroughly appreciated the heavy fire under which the Liberal party was then standing.

But this was only introductory to his most skillful and elaborate defense. He referred to the fact that he had published a book which Lord Macaulay had reviewed, and that he applied the theories of that book to the case of the Irish Church. He knew the paradox which confronted him, and says that then he "erroneously thought we should remove this priceless treasure from the view and reach of the Irish people," and further, he then believed it would be meanly to purchase their momentary favor at the expense of their permanent interests, and establish "a high fence against our own sacred obligations." He proceeded to point out inconsistency and immoderateness in his book, and to say that the main proposition of that book, "The State in its Relations with the Church," bound him hand and foot, and hemmed him in on every side. He acknowledged at once that he had retreated from an untenable position, and in this Chapter of Autobiography he proceeded to prove that it was not a sudden retreat, it was not "performed with indecent levity," it was not "made to minister to the interests of political ambition," the gravity of the case was not "denied or understated," it was not "daringly pretended that there had been no real change of front," and that many had misunderstood him and his position.

Never did Gladstone appear to better advantage than in this interesting piece of literature. The whole domain of recent Church history and his personal relations to it, was traversed carefully.

He proceeded to prove that he did not leap to the conclusion that the Established Church of Ireland must, at no distant period, cease to exist as an Establishment. He added:

"I was not sorry, I was glad, that while Ireland seemed content to have it so, a longer time should be granted her to unfold her religious energies through the medium of an active and pious clergy. My mind recoiled then, as it recoils now, from the idea of worrying the Irish Church to death. I desired that it should remain even as it was, until the way should be opened, and the means at hand, for bringing about some better state of things."

He rehearsed the chronicle of her history and his own. Year upon year was examined and correspondence printed which showed how continuously Gladstone's Liberalism had been growing, how certainly erroneous impressions were passing away, and how healthfully a large view of statesmanship had developed in his mind. Solidly and brilliantly his defense at last arose as an argument, until his conclusion came as follows:

"An establishment that neither does, nor has her hope of doing work, except for a few, and those few the portion of the community whose claim to public aid is the smallest of all; an Establishment severed from the mass of the people by an impassable gulf, and by a wall of brass; an Establishment whose good offices, could she offer them, would be intercepted by a long unbroken chain of painful and shameful recollections; an Establishment leaning for support upon the extraneous aid of a State, which becomes discredited with the people by the very act of lending it; such an Establishment will do well for its own sake, and for the sake of its creed, to divest itself, as soon as may be, of gauds and trappings, and to commence a new career, in which, renouncing at once the credit and the discredit of the civil sanction, it shall seek its strength from within, and now at length learn to put a fearless trust in the message that it bears."

Disraeli read the elaborate essay and quietly remarked: "Mr. Gladstone is an Italian in the custody of a Scotchman."

PORTRAIT OF GLADSTONE PAINTED BY HAMILTON

(Luxembourg)

JOHN BRIGHT

CHAPTER XXVII.

DISESTABLISHMENT.

Gladstone scented victory from the beginning of this fight. The vote in the House of Commons put a stop at once to the appointments to livings in the gift of the Government, and no more vacant bishoprics could be filled. Bright's speech in the debate was so fine that even the "Saturday Review" declared that no Liberal Ministry could be complete without him. Disraeli took an attitude of chivalrous defense for the institution, and advertised a long and bitter struggle. He did not know how much he ought to do in what he called the "education of the party." Acute in all his maneuvers, he had fascinated the mob by tinsel and attracted the loyalty of the democracy. He was sparing no expenditure of power to get it into line with the Conservatives on Church matters. Paradoxical and satirical, Disraeli battled like a gladiator against threats of dissolution, until, just as he had once adopted Household Suffrage, he began to make mysterious suggestions after his own manner and in the same direction. The conjurer sat, relying upon his hope that out of the mass of voters whom he had brought into being there had come a new strength to the Tory party. Disraeli's visit to the Queen, which led to the announcement early in May that he would neither resign nor now dissolve Parliament, but would hold on until new voters had an opportunity of expressing their opinion, was the cause of unfavorable comment, and it seemed certain that a vote of want of confidence, even though it was advertised that the Queen proposed to have more to do with what Parliament was considering than hitherto, was likely to be suggested.

Arthur P. Stanley, now Dean of Westminster, who had been Gladstone's old friend in the early schooldays, spoke against Irish Disestablishment with great force, though his audience at last roared him down. Disraeli encouraged his followers. Many such men as Principal

Tulloch failed to approve the Gladstone method. In his journal, the scholar of St. Andrews said:

"May 27, 1868: I cannot see, on the whole, that Mr. Gladstone's is a policy of pacification. The evils and miseries of Ireland, however originally connected with the Irish Church, have undoubtedly long since extended beyond it. They are no longer specially connected with it. The disestablishment of the Irish Church will not very directly touch the present evils and miseries of Ireland, while its immediate effects may be in some respects very disastrous. The Irish Church has, after all, been a civilizing agency in various ways, and it is impossible to doubt that you cannot withdraw this agency in a sudden manner without certain social evils resulting. Religious parties will indeed be placed on an equality, and, as I think, a great historical wrong will be expiated, because the Irish Church has ever been a historical wrong. Any man who goes into its history will be more and more convinced of this. But still the evil passions fostered by religious inequality will remain; and I fear the results of these passions will be more disastrous when once the controlling force of law is withdrawn.

"Secondly, Mr. Gladstone's policy appears to me not so much in itself, as in reference to many who are supporting it, to be an anti-Establishment policy, and the probable result of it will extend much beyond what he anticipates.

"It is all very well to say that there is no logical connection between the Church of Scotland or the Church of England and that of Ireland. There is no logical connection; but political movements do not move by logic. Unquestionably when you think of the principles that are moving many parties who strongly support Mr. Gladstone, you cannot but apprehend grave results from them. As there are dogmatic State Churchmen, so there are dogmatic anti-State Churchmen. There are men who look upon the State Church principle as an irreligious principle, a principle for the destruction of which they are bound to contend. I think these men are profoundly mistaken. I look upon the connection between Church and State, rightly regarded, as a great blessing. . . . It is not my business to indicate here what I would have considered a wiser policy. But I may say frankly that my own view would have been to continue in a greatly modified and reduced form the Established Church of Ireland, and apply its superfluous revenues to the general religious uses of the Irish people. I know it is in vain to speak of that in this Assembly; I know that the very name of Popery excites such a feeling that it is in vain to speak of supporting it in any shape. But nevertheless, this has been the policy of all our great statesmen, the traditional policy of the great political minds of our country since the time of Pitt; and I believe that if the feelings of the country had permitted it to have been carried out, Ireland would have been this day in a state for which every one would have reason to rejoice."

It was impossible for Gladstone to avoid seeing the difficulties, which, however, he would grandly master. An idea of these obstructions to his success is conveyed in a letter of Lord Houghton: "Gladstone is the great triumph; but he owns that he has to drive a four-in-hand, consisting of English Liberals, English Dissenters, Scotch Presbyterians, and Irish Catholics; he requires all his courage to look these difficulties in the face, and trust to surmount them."

Dukes and earls, the Archbishop of York, the Bishop of Oxford, and the Bishop of London, might address public meetings to their hearts' content; Gladstone saw that the day of his triumph was coming. Disraeli taunted Mr. Gladstone's disagreeing party with conducting an unseemly fight over expected plunder. The excitement in the House of Commons was intense, and Lord Derby was foolish enough to declare that the House of Lords would throw out the Bill if it came up from the House of Commons. This was the chance of a lifetime. Of course, Gladstone's denunciation was vehement and indignant and crushing. Disraeli mysteriously hinted that the Queen had told him something which he could not tell, and the conjuror again trusted to magic. He was chafed and wounded in the eager assault of his foes. The moral height upon which Mr. Gladstone stood was discernible by all, even though he discharged volleys of wrath against the hollow Conservatism which pretended to be wise and patriotic. Disraeli's position was more serious, because he was so much alone, and he could not afford to lose his coolness. He was adroit, subtle, dexterous, and held his ground with remarkable strength.

Until July 31st Parliament was not prorogued. After an appeal to the country, Disraeli announced that his colleagues had resigned their offices. The Queen summoned Gladstone to Windsor to constitute a new Government. He was at last Prime Minister of England, and behind him was a majority representing the sentiments of human progress. No longer was he the servant of Dukes of Newcastle or otherwhere, or the voice of timorous and scholastic Oxford. He had become instead the Tribune of the people.

Gladstone made Mr. Bright President of the Board of Trade, and otherwise made himself strong in his lieutenants. He had announced his purpose at least to test Ireland and to demonstrate, if possible, if Ireland could be governed according to Irish ideas. He was met by unsuspected difficulties. Three-score years had poured their wealth of experience and culture into him, and he confronted his problems with astonishing vivacity. By his side was Mr. W. E. Forster as Vice-President of the Council, as incessant a worker as Gladstone himself. Many of his closest friends knew that the question of disestablishment involved and would lead to a consideration of the Irish problem in genera'

March 1st had come, and Gladstone had introduced his measure for the Disestablishment of the Irish Church. So intense was his thought, and so impetuous was his stream of reasoning, so clearly did Gladstone understand himself upon this subject, that Disraeli, who was accustomed to say that Gladstone was likely to be "inebriated by the exuberance of his own verbosity," declared that the oration, three hours long, had not a sentence which any thorough consideration of the subject could have marked out as superfluous.

The proposition of Gladstone was that what had hitherto been a State Establishment should become a free Episcopal Church. He concluded his speech in the following memorable sentences:

"I do not know in what country so great a change, so great a transition, has been proposed for the ministers of a religious communion who have enjoyed for many ages the preferred position of an Established Church: I can well understand that to many in the Irish Establishment such a change appears to be nothing less than ruin and destruction; from the height on which they now stand the future is to them an abyss, and their fears recall the words used in 'King Lear,' when Edgar endeavors to persuade Glo'ster that he has fallen over the cliffs of Dover, and says:

> "Ten masts at each make not the altitude
> Which thou hast perpendicularly fallen;
> Thy life's a miracle!

"And yet but a little while after the old man is relieved from his delusion, and finds he has not fallen at all. So I trust that when, instead of the fictitious and adventitious aid on which we have too long taught the Irish Establishment to lean, it should come to place its trust in its own resources, in its own great mission, in all that it can draw from the energy of its ministers and its members, and the high hopes and promises of the Gospel that it teaches, it will find that it has entered upon a new era of existence—an era bright with hope and potent for good. At any rate, I think the day has certainly come when an end is finally to be put to that union, not between the Church and religious association, but between the Establishment and the State, which was commenced under circumstances little auspicious, and has endured to be a source of unhappiness to Ireland and of discredit and scandal to England. There is more to say. This measure is in every sense a great measure—great in its principles, great in the multitude of its dry, technical, but interesting detail, and great as a testing measure; for it will show for one and all of us of what metal we are made. Upon us all it brings a great responsibility—great and foremost upon those who occupy this bench. We are especially chargeable—nay, deeply guilty—if we have either dishonestly, as some think, or even prematurely or unwisely challenged so gigantic an issue. I know well the punishments that follow rashness in public affairs, and that ought to fall upon those men, those Phaetons of politics, who, with hands unequal to the task, attempt to guide the chariot of the sun. But the responsibility, though heavy, does not exclusively press upon us; it presses upon every man who has to take part in the discussion and decision upon this Bill. Every man approaches the discussion under the most solemn obliga-

tions to raise the level of his vision and expand its scope in proportion
with the greatness of the matter in hand. The working of our constitutional Government itself is upon its trial, for I do not believe there ever
was a time when the wheels of legislative machinery were set in motion,
under conditions of peace and order and constitutional regularity, to
deal with a question greater or more profound. And more especially,
sir, is the credit and fame of this great assembly involved; this assembly
which has inherited through many ages the accumulated honors of brilliant triumphs, of peaceful but courageous legislation, is now called
upon to address itself to a task which would, indeed, have demanded all
the best energies of the very best among your fathers and your ancestors. I believe it will prove to be worthy of the task. Should it fail,
even the fame of the House of Commons will suffer disparagement;
should it succeed, even that fame, I venture to say, will receive no small,
no insensible addition. I must not ask gentlemen opposite to concur
in this view, emboldened as I am by the kindness they have shown me in
listening with patience to a statement which could not have been other
than tedious; but I pray them to bear with me for a moment while, for
myself and my colleagues, I say we are sanguine of the issue. We
believe, and for my part I am deeply convinced, that when the final
consummation shall arrive, and when the words are spoken that shall
give the force of law to the work embodied in this measure—the work
of peace and justice—those words will be echoed upon every shore
'where the name of Ireland or the name of Great Britain has been heard,
and the answer to them will come back in the approving verdict of
civilized mankind."

Disraeli kept the way brilliant with explosive generalities and the
ground was hot with his sarcasm, which ran like a fire amidst dry leaves,
while he trained his heavier cannon upon Gladstone's propositions. He
talked about the importance of religion, and handed out tawdry imita-
tions of cloth of gold with commonplaces regarding trust-money and the
Protestant Church which he was so heroically defending, and he closed
by reminding Mr. Gladstone of the certain effect of this legislation on
the position of the Church of England. Here perhaps he erred not.
The only blood he now drew was when he indicated that the effect of the

Bill was to give the landlords a large amount of the spoils of the Church. Gladstone's proposition to spend this sum upon eleemosynary institutions hardly withstood the shock of Disraeli's attack. The second reading of the Bill was carried by a majority of 118. Lord Stanley, whose silence was thought to indicate that he was willing for a compromise, gave England a phrase which set many men going about saying that they were in favor of "saving as much as possible out of the fire." At last Stanley spoke in excellent phrase, offending the Conservatives because he went so far from hereditary creeds, and antagonizing the Liberals because he did not follow the logic of his convictions in the direction of Disestablishment.

It cannot be denied that the Irish people behaved badly, and that fresh outbreaks of agrarian outrages annoyed Gladstone exceedingly. Warren and Costello, two released Fenians, eulogized the murder of the Duke of Edinburgh, and rejoiced that Gladstone was going to "abolish the Church." Ireland's gratitude to Gladstone never had a very wise or honorable way of exhibiting itself, and just now the Liberal leaders feared that Ireland's agitations and repeated acts of lawlessness would create a feeling in England which would not permit justice to be done in the case of the Church. Mr. Gladstone's associate in office, Mr. Forster, offered valuable legislation to correct abuses which had undoubtedly produced barbarism and ignorance.

There was one subject alone commanding superlative attention. Everybody looked to the House of Lords. The opposition had gathered again and privilege arrogated the right to put down progress. John Bright warned them of the probable results of their obstinacy. The Bill passed, and July 29, 1869, saw the Irish Church disestablished.

Ireland had at last gained the ear of Parliament. O'Connell had not prophesied vainly and Ireland was certainly not likely to lose the opportunity, now that she had England's attention fixed upon her. John Bright suggested that they would better hold a good long session in Dublin, and that, there and then, all the Irish questions should be submitted and Irish domestic matters attended to comprehensively and at once. The land was reverberating with the cry from Ireland asking for fixity of tenure, and that cry would have been heard more certainly if there had not come from the same hot-headed population demands for wholesale confiscation, and expressions of the general expectation amongst the peasantry that things would culminate in every Irishman's having a little farm of his own.

Gladstone's Bill for the reform of the system of Land Tenure in Ireland was taking its form in his mind, while the landlords, who had hitherto been undisturbed, were volcanic in their expressions of wrath, and, while also, at a meeting in Ireland a tenant gravely advocated the British Government's providing every family with enough free-hold land to give them support. John Stuart Mill, Henry Fawcett and other political economists sought a means of establishing peasant proprietors in Ireland. A confusion of opinion reigned; stormy seas were before Mr. Gladstone. He was meantime resting himself in reading the reviews of his book called "Juventus Mundi," and entering into pleasant controversies as to whether Athene is, in accordance with the idea of Sanskrit scholars, The Dawn; or as to whether he ought to have insisted, as he did, upon an antagonism between Pelasgian and Hellenic. He followed this program by bringing upon his head a fierce opposition, because, in sympathy with his broad view as to the functions of the Church of England, he had selected Dr. Temple, one of the essayists in the famously liberal book known as "Essays and Reviews," to be Bishop of Exeter.

Lord Derby died in October, and no one regretted his loss more than Mr. Gladstone. They had studied together on various topics, including Homer, and each had been accused of political inconsistency. Their roads had crossed, for Derby had begun as a Whig and ended as a leader of the Conservatives, and Gladstone had remarked upon his consenting to the trick by which Disraeli caught the Tories who passed so democratic a bill as the measure broadening the Elective Franchise. Lord Derby, at length, represented the fading yesterday, as Gladstone represented the dawning to-morrow. While Gladstone was seeking to put before England so comprehensive and prophetic a measure as his Irish Land Bill, Lord Derby was standing in the House of Lords, almost weeping over the resistless progress of the reforming spirit. Gladstone had found no easier way of amusing the British public than getting into a controversy with Lord Derby on finance, for the latter knew almost nothing of the subject, and yet he was an admirable debater, and he had what Gladstone did not possess in debate, a gay and rich humor. Gladstone and he had furnished classical quotations in Parliament, when almost every one else had forsaken the practice of offering information understood by only a few, and no one more than Gladstone honored the incorruptible and brave gentleman. Lord Stanley, his son, was now elevated to the House of Peers.

The spirits of Gladstone at this time reflect their light and warmth in this letter extracted from Mr. Fagan's delightful biography of Panizzi:

"My Dear Sir:
    " 'Like a good fellow,' I will certainly dine with you on Tuesday, the 25th instant.
    "There is an Italian opera buffa, in which a gentleman who wishes to become a poet, and takes lessons as to the mechanism of verse from a poet, wishing to ask his master to dine with him, tries to convey his invitation in an hendecasyllable, and begins, 'Volete pranzare meco oggi?' (Will you dine with me to-day?) but it would not do, so he changed, 'Volete pranzare meco domani?'(Will you dine with me to-morrow?) It would not do either, and the poet suggested at once, 'Volete pranzare meco oggi e domani?' (Will you dine with me to-day and to-morrow?) a very good line, and so it was settled. Now I have made a line for our dinner here, of which you must approve. 'Pranzate meco il ventitre e quattro' (Dine with me the 23rd and 24th.) The poetry is not good; have patience, and, 'like a good fellow,' come both days.   Yours ever,
                                        "A. PANIZZI."

Too soon, indeed, Gladstone was to sit by the bedside of his beloved friend, who thanked the Premier for a friendship which forgot affairs of State while he guided Panizzi through the Valley of the Shadow.

CHAPTER XXVIII.

TRIUMPHANT LIBERALISM.

We are now confronting an era in Gladstone's life and in the development of the new movement in English Government. Never did an administration astonish a country with such a succession of nobly conceived and eloquently advocated measures as was now about to be introduced. Gladstone infused his own party with his supreme conviction that these measures were the logical outgrowth of all that the centuries of constitutional monarchial government in England had brought forth, and the Liberal party, for the four years following, caught and reflected the luminous quality of his mind and the magnetic influence which his spirit exercised upon all who came in contact with him.

England's navy was made more certainly mistress of the seas than ever before. Gladstone had spoken of England and her relation to the sea many times. No more significant words than these concerning England's supremacy on the ocean have been spoken:

"Shakespeare saw, three centuries ago, that a peculiar strength of England lay in her insular and maritime position. And yet no long period had then elapsed since that little arm of ocean, which France still calls the Sleeve, had been from England into France, if not from France towards England, the familiar pathway of armed hosts. The prevision of the poet has been realized in subsequent history. Three hundred more years have passed; and if during that long period, we have, some three or four times with no great benefit to our fame, planted the hostile foot in France, the shores of England have remained inviolate, and the twenty miles of sea have thus far been found, even against the great Napoleon, an impregnable fortification.

"It may be said the case is now different. It is; and the differences are in our favor. Now, as then, the voyage is a danger; now, as then, leagues of sea, regarded as mere space, do not yield, as an occupied country may be made to yield, the subsistence of an invading army. Now, as then, the necessary operation of landing affords a strong vantage-ground of resistance to the defending force. Now, as then, the sea details some uncertainty in the arrival of supplies.   But now, as it was *not* then, maritime supremacy has become the proud, perhaps the indefectible, inheritance of England."

It was not strange therefore that he should introduce reforms in the management of the Navy of Great Britain. Abuses in the Army, especially in the direction of promotion to command by purchase had grown to be scandalous and chronic. A complete reorganization was made and that system was finally destroyed. Education had its championship, school-boards were established in every district, and local rates were assessed for their support. A new system of balloting which put an end to abominable corruptions was carried. Liberalism was in the plenitude of its power. We may look at each one of these as a separate point upon which the genius of Gladstone exhibited its strength and luminousness.

On the 15th of February, the House of Commons was crowded in every part. It was in the air that a great and definite step was to be taken that day, by the leader of the party in power, in the direction of constitutional government. The fact that this athlete was willing to grasp so many momentous questions at once amazed and delighted English pluck. He proposed his Land Bill.

Whatever might be the practical effect of the introduction of this measure upon the country, every well-informed Englishman knew that the hour had come when a consideration of its principles was likely to commence working out in Anglo-Saxon civilization a result unsurpassed in the history of human political affairs. The principle of Gladstone's Bill was in harmony with all the ideas which, from Alfred to Victoria, had conspired to the development of the institutions of popular government. It was impossible to look upon that principle for a moment without being convinced that it was right, and that the whole system of land-holding in Ireland rested upon a principle utterly opposed to it, and entirely wrong. A feudal baron, whose personality had shrivelled in the course of centuries now seemed to vanish, as the theory that any landlord could possess legally a limitless right over the land in Ireland faded like an ugly dream. Before that breathless and crowded auditory, his face white with the excitement of thought, his eyes burning out with their gem-like intensity as he spoke, Gladstone took these relics of a barbarous past which still lingered in the body of British law, and pulverize'd them to dust in the presence of the luminous statements he made, founded upon principles which have provided the foundation of modern statesmanship. There has been no better abridgment of Gladstone's speech than that contained in the history of these times written by Mr. Bright's friend, Mr. Molesworth, and this ran as follows:

"In the first place," he said, "the bill proposes the enlargement of the power of the limited owner in regard both to lease and rate. Assistance will be given by loans of public money to occupiers disposed and able to purchase the cultivated lands now in their occupation where landlords are willing to sell. Facilities will also be given landlords, by means of loans, to prepare waste lands for occupation, by making roads and erecting necessary buildings; and to assist purchasers of reclaimed lands upon the security of an adequate nature. These transactions will be managed by the Board of Works in Dublin. With regard to occupation, the new law will be administered by a court of arbitration and a civil-bill court, with an appellate tribunal consisting of two, and in case of necessity three, judges of assize; the judges having power to reserve a case for a court for land causes in Dublin, to be composed of equity and common-law judges.

"At present there are four descriptions of holdings in Ireland which I have thought it my duty to keep specially in view. The first of these is known as the Ulster custom. This custom, where it exists, the bill will convert into a law, to which the new courts will give effect. The second class of holdings are those which prevail under customs and usages other than that of Ulster; and these, too, are to be legalized, subject to the restriction that the tenant may claim the benefit of them only in cases where he is disturbed in his tenancy by the act of his landlord, if he has not been evicted for non-payment of rent, and has not sublet or subdivided his holdings without the landlord's consent. All arrears of rent and all damages done by the tenant to the farm may be pleaded by the landlord as a setoff, and the landlord may bar the pleading of any such custom, if he chooses to give his tenant a lease for not less than thirty-one years.

"Where the buildings are not connected with any custom there will be a scale of damages for evictions. In the case of holdings above fifty

pounds a year, the parties may contract themselves out of the scale of
damages, on the landlord giving a thirty-one years' lease, and undertaking to execute necessary improvements.

"In cases of eviction the following will be the scale of damages: If
the holding is not valued in the public valuation over £10 a year, the
judge may award the holder a sum not exceeding seven years' rent;
between £10 and £50 a year, a sum not exceeding five years' rent; and
above £100 a year, not exceeding two years' rent.

"In addition to this, the question of permanent buildings and the
reclamation of land will have to be dealt with.

"For the purpose of promoting improvements, advances of money
will be authorized to landlords, to enable them to defray any charge raised
against them in the way of improvement in the case of tenants retiring by
an act of their own. The principle on which I propose to deal with
improvements is, that they must have a rentable value and be suitable
to the holdings, and the burden of proof will be laid on the landlords;
and the measure will not be limited to future improvements, but will
extend to those already made. No claim will be allowed for any improvement made twenty years before the passing of the act, unless it is an improvement of the nature of a permanent building, or a reclamation of
land; nor if the tenant holds under an existing lease or contract which
forbids it; and in the case of past improvements the court may take
into consideration the terms for which, and the terms on which, they
have already been enjoyed by the tenant. No claim will be allowed in
respect of improvements contrary to a future contract voluntarily entered
into by the tenant, and which are not required for the due cultivation of
the farm.

"As to lands under lease, a landlord may exempt his lands from being
subject to any custom except the Ulster custom, provided that he agrees
to give his tenant a lease for thirty-one years; but the lease must leave
to the tenant at the close of that term a right to claim compensation under
three heads—namely, tillages and manures, permanent buildings, and
reclamation of lands.

"From the moment the bill is passed every Irishman will be absolutely responsible for every contract into which he enters. Non-payment of rent will be held as a bar to any claim on the landlord, reserv-
ing, however, discretion to the courts in certain cases. Notices to quit
will have to be for twelve months instead of six, and date from the last
day of the current year; and the notice must have a stamp duty of two
shillings and sixpence.

"The bill also proposes to deal with the question of the county cess, which it will assimilate to the poor-rate. In every new tenancy it will have to be paid in moieties by landlord and tenant, as the poor-rate is now paid, and in every old tenancy under £4 a year the occupier will be at once relieved."

At the conclusion of Gladstone's exhaustive speech on this occasion, he met with the most enthusiastic congratulation, even by his foes. He had redeemed his pledges to the country; the Tory had shuffled off his Tory habits and become a thorough Liberal. Oxford scholasticism had been consumed at last by the fire of an intense devotion to humanity and justice,—the true Gladstone was delivered—and he now proceeded to overstrain the mental and moral machinery of John Bull. He was irritating to the people who wanted only a quiet and motherly family physician. The "Saturday Review" acknowledged his genius, but said:

"It may also happen that a doctor who, from his daring and determination in the use of heroic remedies, is especially serviceable at the critical moment of a desperate disorder, is not the best man to do the work of the ordinary family attendant, and to deal with the small ailments of everyday life. A weakness for heroic treatment is apt to become a dangerous passion. It has more than once happened that a skillful surgeon has been suspected of a predilection for amputation, just as a 'daring pilot in extremity' has been accused of whistling for a wind—

"Pleased with the danger, when the waves went high,
He sought the storm; but, for a calm unfit,
Would steer too nigh the sands to boast his wit."

Mr. Forster's measure looking toward national education for all, on a plan which should prevent England from lapsing into ignorance as she progressed toward Liberal policies in Church and State, became a law. It was perhaps well for Gladstone, who, later on, had to rely upon the services of Dissenters for any sort of successful championship of his plans for Ireland, that he had comparatively little to do with the management of the Bill, and that therefore he did not offend hopelessly the Non-Conformists who were greatly annoyed at the attitude of the Government toward their religious bodies. Forster's Bill was tolerant of the Roman Catholic Church and her position on education. The cry went up: "No State aid to any but undenominational schools." This cry was repeated most earnestly by the very people who were most in favor of the principle that a popular government ought to look out after popular education. Many of Gladstone's friends trembled for his future. The Roman Catholics never would forget what Mr. Forster and Mr. Gladstone were ready to do to satisfy their consciences, and it was equally sure that a large section of the Liberal party called Non-Conformists never would forget what Mr. Forster and Mr. Gladstone failed to do to satisfy theirs. He was again accused of being at heart a Roman Catholic. After all the tumult, it became apparent very soon that a great step had been taken by the Gladstone Administration in the direction of intelligence and the safety of popular institutions. By and by, doubtless, the Dissenters would remember, however, that their sentiments had been outraged in this matter. In the course of the discussion of Mr. Forster's bill much bad feeling was engendered. An intense opponent averred that Gladstone had led one section of the Liberal party through the Valley of Humiliation, adding, "once bit, twice shy, and we can't stand this sort of thing much longer." Gladstone was almost sublime, as he said: "I hope that my honorable friend will not continue his support to the Government one moment longer than he deems it consistent with his sense of duty and right. For God's sake, sir, let him withdraw it the moment he thinks it better for the cause he has at heart that he should do so. . . . We must recollect that we are the Government of the Queen, and that those who have assumed the high responsibility of adminstering the affairs of this Empire must endeavor to forget the parts in the whole, and must, in the great measures they introduce into the House, propose to themselves no meaner or narrower object,—no other object than the welfare of the Empire at large."

If ever a man found himself heavy laden with the peculiarities of those who were placed, or who placed themselves, in positions of influence and trust, Mr. Gladstone had been that man. He had loaded up with the prejudices and passions, the contentiousness and bigotry of the Irish people, at a time when their liberty was in sight, and when they were most apt at eclipsing even their unenviable record as belligerents on general principles, he had on his back a crowd of his own party, the Dissenters, who were out of sorts with him and he soon had another section of Liberals who opposed him on another matter of great importance.

There can be no doubt that Gladstone's eager nature looked forward with much hope to the abolition of the purchase system in the British Army. It was an abuse of long standing and had grown flagrant with the lapse of years. Officers dreamed not of such a thing as promotion according to merit, in the regular troops. True, there were certain branches of the service, and there were certain regiments in which this obnoxious system of obtaining commissions and promotion by purchase, did not exist. But except in a few regiments of the army of England, it is now almost incredible, but it was the rule that these things were practically on sale. A commission had been bought and could be sold at an advance, just as any other ware. The law of supply and demand controlled the price of the same, and the Horse Guards might mention one price, but if the holder valued it at another, and somebody wanted to remain in the English Army with a commission, or to obtain a promotion, as the case might be, badly enough to pay a very much larger price, this circumstance fixed the sum. It was amazing to find how much of respectability arrayed itself against any change. The haughty and influential classes had beheld Lord Stanley, Mr. Trevelyan and Sir DeLacy Evans laughed out of Parliament, or at least silenced and defeated, when, at other times, they had urged this reform. But Gladstone was determined, and his government defied the aristocracy. Never were the drawing-rooms of distinguished members of the Army, dukes, earls and the like, more chilly to Gladstone than when this democratic idea stood on its feet in Parliament and fought against caste and privilege and corruption. To easy-going, fashionable gentlemen, it seemed positively dreadful that a man should have a promotion just because he merited it, or that a nobleman, who had obtained personal property in the form of a commission in the Army, should not be able to sell it just as he would a horse which someone wanted more than its present owner. The cry that this whole crusade was "another fit of Americanism introduced as an abomination into English military life," was repeated by lords and ladies, and it was almost pathetic to witness

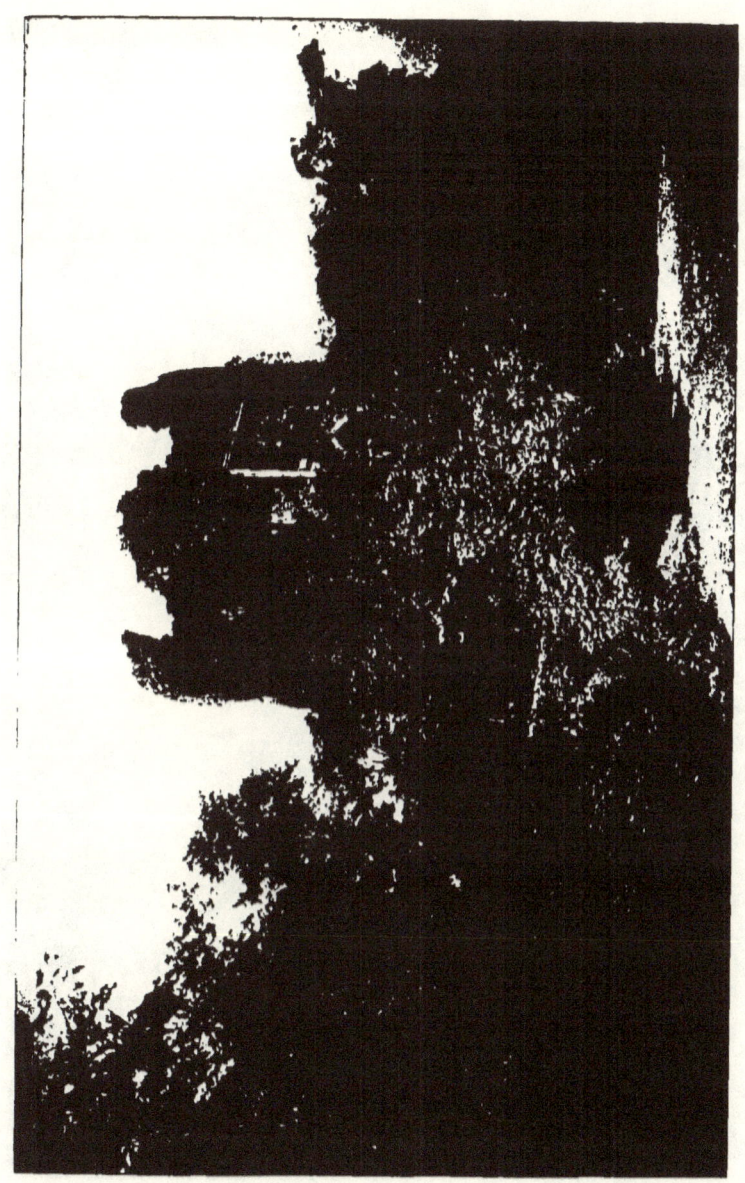

THE OLD CASTLE AT HAWARDEN

GLADSTONE DELIVERING A FAMOUS SPEECH

the effusiveness with which men who had never been suspected of caring much about "economy in governmental affairs" pleaded that this measure would take out of the hands of private dealers in commissions a kind of business, the absence of which would compel the Government to give compensation to the leaders of the army, who, of course, now no longer might conduct their enterprise of buying and selling these wares.

Gladstone's government had run up against the terrible word "economy," and, as he was unable to save all the cargo of his ship, Army reorganization was thrown overboard, but, with a fixed determination that the system of purchase should be overthrown, the Government carried the Bill on the third reading in the House of Commons, early in July, 1871. Of course the House of Lords was horrified at having to consider such a measure, and fought it with unwonted strength and shrewdness. Fearing, however, the doom which this persistent opposition of just measures might invite, and which was likely to fall some time upon the head of this party, an amendment was shrewdly invented, which, by the efforts of the Duke of Richmond, was carried, and which relieved the House of Lords of the Bill, for the time being.

Now Gladstone did a bold thing. He persuaded the Queen to cancel the Royal Warrant which made purchase in the Army possible under the law—for the truth was that only under the Royal Warrant had the system of purchase been carried on. An annulment of the Royal regulation, therefore, completely settled the question.

November 1st came. The Royal Warrant was issued, and the House of Lords had no question of importance before it. They passed the Bill with a graceless and angry spirit, publishing, however, the causes of their discomfiture.

Whether this was a triumph of Liberalism, pure and simple, is not a question now, but soon it became a question in England. There are some victories which even a Gladstone may scarcely afford. The Lords had censured the Government because it had attained its end by the "exercise of the Royal prerogative and without the aid of Parliament." It was an hour in which Mr. Disraeli's lofty sneer strode forth with unwonted vigor, and most fiery was his denunciation of the action of the Ministry. Henry Fawcett, one of the most noble-minded and capa-

17

ble members of Parliament, called Mr. Gladstone's attention to the fact that he had done just the sort of thing a Liberal Government ought to condemn. Doubtless Gladstone had also played unfairly with the delicate lords. It was ungraceful in him, and unworthy of him to have defeated them in this manner. It might be constitutional and all that, as his adviser, Sir Roundell Palmer, agreed, but Gladstone had persuaded Queen Victoria to do a thing in the exercise of her Royal prerogative which only a Puritan like Cromwell, in a different manner, or a Royalist like Charles the First, in a manner peculiar to himself, might have done. It was all really too bad, but it was done.

Gladstone's Government could not be blind to the fact that this was a good time for repealing the Ecclesiastical Titles Bill, to which attention had already been called, as a most ludicrous and inefficient monument of affrighted bigotry, emanating from the genius of Lord Russell when the Protestants were in fear of the Pope's taking England unto himself twenty years before. The quiet way in which this Bill was repealed contrasted favorably with the tumult in which it was passed.

More important, however, in the direction of true Liberalism was Gladstone's position on the University Tests question. It was an old question, and had been discussed for many years in England. Nearly forty years before, a motion had been offered, asking leave to bring in a Bill for the admission of Non-Conformists to both the Universities, and Lord John Russell had spoken in its defense. From time to time this demand for justice to Dissenters had reappeared, and more than a score of years before, he who was now Dean of Westminster, Arthur P. Stanley, Gladstone's school friend at Seaforth, presented a prayer for the appointment of a Royal commission of inquiry. Commissioners were appointed, and a report was made in 1832. In 1854 the recommendations of the commissioners were so far adopted that a Bill for the reform of the University of Oxford was brought in by Lord Aberdeen's Government, and one hundred members of the House of Commons prayed Lord John Russell to introduce clauses abolishing the religious tests of Oxford. After repeated refusals, and after overcoming great difficulties, in various years, after incessant opposition upon the part of

Conservatives, the principle in Gladstone's University Tests Bill was triumphant and Oxford and Cambridge opened their doors to lay students of any and every faith. Of course this long step forward in the direction of pronounced Liberalism exiled from Mr. Gladstone the timorous and the unfaithful.

He saw, early in his career as Prime Minister, that something must be done in England to make the ballot more sacred and effective. Mr. Forster's Bill, introduced February 20, 1871, was conceived upon the philosophy that where suffrage meant so much as it must always mean in England, the abominations of the system hitherto in vogue ought speedily to be cleared away. Bribery must be prevented and intimidation rendered impossible, yet these outrages had been constantly growing in English political life. The Bill proposed to abolish disorder at the time of the nomination of candidates, by providing that registered voters alone should nominate candidates by means of a paper upon which a proposer, a seconder, and eight assenters had placed their names. The Bill was carried, but the struggle was intense and bitter. It seems now almost incredible that such a measure should have been so ardently opposed. Surely Liberalism was lifting the conscience of England to unsuspected heights of endeavor. Gladstone had worked incessantly in the past for a broader Franchise. He was now convinced that if England was to retain any fragment of her power as a secure constitutional monarchy, voters must be protected against the emissaries of corruption of every sort. The House of Lords had fought it, but they had only delayed its progress. The system of secret voting commended itself to such men as John Bright and their followers, though John Stuart Mill opposed it on the ground that "concealment is unmanly." The amendment introduced in the House of Lords, which proposed to make the ballot optional, was thrown out by the Commons. The privileged classes were determined that landlords might still exercise authority over tenants; the House of Commons was determined that secrecy should be granted to the tenant and protection as he voted. The success of this measure has laid the foundation for a vast reform in the electoral system of England.

Mr. Gladstone, however, was certain to more truly offend the sensibilities of Conservative England in the course of a debate in which he said something on woman's suffrage. It was sure that this subject would come up after the ballot had been so purged and guarded as to make a woman independent of all influences whatsoever, if she might be allowed to vote. Gladstone frankly said that he did not see any harm in allowing women to vote. Toryism shuddered at the prospect. He soon had opportunity, however, for the proving of his conservatism on other points.

It was impossible that Gladstone should succeed in the disestablishment of the Irish Church, especially because it was Protestant, and not invite the activity of those who, like the busy and able Mr. Miall, had been thinking that the disestablishment of a National Church even in England might be a good and desirable thing to undertake. So no one was much astonished when that redoubtable Non-Conformist offered his motion to use the policy adopted and executed on the Irish Church upon the English establishment. Gladstone's churchmanship met the challenge at once and with unwonted zeal. He warned the belligerent dissenter as to the size of the job he had proposed, and said:

The question of the Irish Church sinks into insignificance—I mean material insignificance—beside the question of the English Church. It is not the number of its members or the millions of its revenue; it is the mode in which it has been from a period shortly after the Christian era, and has never for 1,300 years ceased to be, the Church of the country, having been at every period ingrained with the hearts and the feelings of the great mass of the people, and having intertwined itself with the local habits and feelings, so that I do not believe there lives the man who could either divine the amount and character of the work my hon. friend would have to undertake were he doomed to be responsible for the execution of his own propositions, or who could in the least degree define or anticipate the consequences by which it would be attended."

The motion was overwhelmingly defeated. Perhaps Mr. Miall's cause may also be able to wait.

Gladstone's Government could not forget the workingman, and Oxford was proven clearly right when in 1865 she prophesied that this statesman was really in earnest about helping the unprivileged majority in England.

The Trades-Union Bill was introduced, and laws which outraged justice and imposed exceedingly heavy burdens upon the workingmen were repealed or moderated. However, Mr. Gladstone had no Gladstone to propose his Budgets and explain them in such a manner as to fascinate, if not thoroughly inform, the waiting people, and he was soon deeply embarrassed by his Chancellor of the Exchequer, Mr. Robert Lowe. He could far more easily bear such abuse as the following than the effect of such a mistake as Lowe's, for Gladstone knew that hate in the breast of the rhymester had overshot the mark:

"When the G. O. M. goes down to his doom
   He will ride in a fiery chariot,
And sit in state, on a red-hot plate,
   Between Satan and Judas Iscariot.
Says the Devil, 'We're rather full, you see,
   But I'll do the best I can;
I'll let Ananias and Judas go free,
   And take in the Grand Old Man!'

   Gone from the cares of office!
   Gone from the head of affairs!
   Gone in the head, they tell us!
   Gone—whither, no one cares!"

CHAPTER XXIX.

COMPLICATIONS AND PERILS.

Lowe was an antagonist or an ally so brilliant and resourceful at many points that his very weaknesses accentuated his own particular powers. He appears with Gladstone as a boy at Eton, and even there, in some fugitive writings, he gave evidence of that power of statement, affluence of thought, and resources of almost vitriolic sarcasm which served him well as a really great leader-writer, if not a forceful speaker, in later days. He was a vigorous debater and an indomitable defender of principles which he never forsook up to the last. Without oratorical gifts, he yet wielded an opposition to popular suffrage with which Gladstone had to reckon whenever the latter dealt with the elective franchise. Tenacious to the last degree, his contempt was visited upon the reformers who cared for the toilers and the philanthropists who sought legislation favorable to the poor. In this year, as in 1867, his powers of acute thinking, joined with bitter invective, well-nigh overcame the defects of weak and tuneless utterance and a somewhat cold and too literary manner, and no one felt that the most searching and perhaps impressive argument had been made on these questions until Lowe had spoken. But he now blundered, brilliantly as was his wont.

He came to propose a scheme to supply England's treasury with the income, to be received in part from the tax on matches. He calculated on 550,000 pounds from this source. His brilliant mind advocated the words: "*Ex luce lucellum*" as a proper phrase to appear on every match box. People went about for explanation of the phrase. It was too much for John Bull's risibility, and while the manufacturers of lucifer matches rose in opposition to the tax imposed, the English people had a good laugh, whether they understood the Latin device or not.

No man can well resist the antagonism of the children, and Palace Yard was one day crowded with processions of boys and girls whose business had been the selling of matches. It was only one of Mr. Lowe's unlucky hits. But it did not help Mr. Gladstone's Government with a class of people who were likely to think that Mr. Robert Lowe, as a Chancellor of the Exchequer, ought to have been engaged in larger business. It dwarfed the size of the whole administration in the public mind.

When Lord Granville had succeeded Clarendon upon the death of the latter, June 27, 1870, he felicitated himself and the nation that everything was peaceful in all Europe. Within two weeks the Franco-Prussian war had broken out, and Gladstone's Government had an opportunity to prove its fidelity to the Premier's well-known convictions with reference to non-intervention. The English Government did all that a brave, self-centered and successful political enterprise might do to maintain and cultivate peace. While generally the people sympathized with Prussia, one only need glance rapidly through the newspapers of the period to see how, in spite of the previous policy of Napoleon, when the Empire fell, England believed that Prussia had gone far enough. Gladstone was wise, calm, pacific, while Trafalgar Square rang with the shouts of a sympathetic multitude whose heart throbbed with France. On the 21st of July, Gladstone had told England that both of the contesting powers had made assurances that Belgium, Holland and other territory should be respected in their neutrality, and he explained to Disraeli the efficient condition of England's defenses.

Now the sentiment arose in England that the Government ought to help the French because they were down. It looked at one time as though England would have to interfere to defend the neutrality of Belgium. Mr. Bright promptly placed his resignation in the hands of Mr. Gladstone, to be made use of in such a case. Gladstone had published an important article in the Edinburgh Review on Germany, France, and England, and it clarified the atmosphere.

A Treaty had been made in 1856, which declared that the Black Sea was open to the ships of every nation, but Russia might have upon that sea only six small ships of war at the most. Prince Gortschakoff's famous circular, in which the Russian Government announced, in the

name of the Emperor, that it would not stand by the provisions of the
Treaty which at that time were most important, between France and
Germany, came to the seats of diplomacy in Europe with startling force.
England telegraphed a vigorous protest, and Lord Granville and Mr.
Gladstone found themselves in firm association with Prussia and Austria and Italy on this delicate subject. A conference of the Great Powers
was proposed, and its date was delayed only until the gates of Paris might
open, and the French Minister be permitted to go to London to attend
the meeting. The Prussian Government, however, refused safe conduct
for him, and the conference, in the absence of the French representative, abrogated that portion of the Treaty of 1856 which made the
Black Sea neutral, and it permitted the ships of all friendly and allied
powers to sail through the Dardanelles and the Bosphorus whenever
peace was threatened.

Keen was the criticism of the Government at this time. Sir Robert
Peel made England think for the moment that the Gladstone Government was doing very little else but venturing, for he read numerous
extracts from the foreign correspondence in which the word "venture"
was used. Gladstone's foes said that this was the Gladstonian and
Granvillian way of talking at a thing, and all England laughed. It was
Peel's delight to call up the shadow of Lord Palmertson, who had a very
bluff manner, and England remembered Gladstone's almost intemperate
attack on Palmerston at an earlier date, when the noble lord was
coquetting with France, and England laughed again.

Meantime Gladstone, serene in the confidence of full information
and adequate power, perceived how foolish were all these alarms.
Punch, week by week, was representing France as a glorious maiden,
wounded and chained, and yet ardent with revenge. Every other nation
was as anxious for peace as was England. But there were hundreds of
orators who had caught Disraeli's thundering phrases, "the honor of
England," and "a spirited foreign policy," which were but two of the
high-sounding bits of speech which were passed, as by enchantment,
from lip to lip. The result of it all was that Gladstone's Government
was more successful than it could have been otherwise, in making efficient the British Army. "The honor of England" took that turn.

CHAPTER XXX.

THE "ALABAMA CLAIMS."

We have spoken with the utmost freedom of Mr. Gladstone's failure to understand the true situation, when the war between the States in America brought to the side of freedom and republican government not only John Bright, but also Benjamin Disraeli, and led Gladstone to solemnly announce the breaking-up of the American Union. It is pleasant to turn from that blunder of Gladstone's to his attitude toward America when it was demanded of England that settlement be made for the losses suffered by American commerce at the time when Gladstone's hastily formed opinions were so far adopted by the English people as to permit the ravages of the Alabama and other British ships. Never did the Earl of Derby show his sagacity and humanity to better advantage than when he promptly avowed his faith that this question might be settled by arbitration. Perhaps the United States Senate, which rejected Reverdy Johnson's scheme for a convention empowered to settle this difficulty, never found itself legislating on loftier grounds. But it was a time when a little foolish talk, taking the form of unnecessary praise of things English, offended men, some of whose children have since become Anglo-maniacs, and it took the genius of Motley, the historian, and the calm statesmanship of Hamilton Fish, to properly renew negotiations which had thus been broken off. Gladstone's magnanimity and honorable conduct in this affair, of course, offended both the upper classes and the rabble on the streets of London, who forgot the humiliation and sufferings of the United States, in a time of grave peril, at the hands of the five privateers which roamed the seas, capturing more than three score of our vessels, and committing outrages under the British flag, even after the British Government had been warned by the representative of America. For twenty-three months, at the crucial moment in the life of the American Republic,

England had permitted the nefarious and outrageous pursuit of our vessels by her own. President Grant's stern will, demanding a settlement of the question, was now allied with Gladstone's equally indomitable refusal to be moved from a course of justice by British criticism. Nothing could have been more certain than that Gladstone's popularity at home was to pass from him rapidly when England was made to admit that the devastation caused by her blockade runners and piratical ships was to be regretted. As the Board of Arbitration sat at Geneva, it was entirely impossible for Gladstone and the most eloquent and sincere lovers of peace to get England to perceive that a majestic era had been entered, in which the victories of peace and arbitration should at least equal those of bloody contention and strife. It was nothing whatever to Gladstone's foes that he had avoided war with America, and it was of still less consideration to them that he had done right. The conference at Geneva agreed that it should be governed by such rules of international duty as must always be recognized as marking a new age in international politics. Fifteen millions of money and interest came from England to her wronged daughter over sea. Nearly a decade afterwards, Gladstone had an opportunity in the House of Commons to make reference to this subject. A resolution had been moved demanding that the British Government urge on all the Great Powers "a simultaneous reduction of armaments." Among other things Gladstone said this:

"There is a third way, however, in which I think it is in the power of the Government to qualify itself for becoming a missionary for those beneficial purposes which are contemplated by my honorable friend—that is, by showing their disposition, when they are themselves engaged in controversy, to adopt these amicable and pacific means of escape from their disputes, rather than to resort to war. Need I assure my honorable friend and my right honorable friend behind me (Mr. Baxter) that the dispositions which led us to become parties to the arbitration on the Alabama case are still with us the same as ever; that we are not discouraged; that we are not damped in the exercise of these feelings by the fact that we were amerced, and severely amerced, by the sentence of the international tribunal; and that, although we may think the sentence was harsh in its extent and unjust in its basis, we regard the fine imposed on this country as dust in the balance compared with the moral value of the example set when these two great nations of England and America, which are among the most fiery and the most jealous in the world with regard to anything that touches national honor, went in peace and concord before a judicial tribunal to dispose of these painful differences, rather than resort to the arbitrament of the sword."

Even Tennyson remonstrated with Gladstone and his desk was piled high with letters against "paying the money to the Yankees." Peace herself might have used Doyle's words, and not in vain:

> "One of a long-oppressed insulted crew,
> At length, dear Gladstone, I appeal to you;
> I do not mean the warrior of the State,
> Clothed in bright armour at the temple's gate,
> Set in front of battle, to uphold
> The truth that streams in glory from of old;
> To praise thy bearing in that arduous fight,
> Proud friends and unresentful foes unite,
> And the hushed spirits of the future see
> Even now, a lord of humankind in thee."

Now was an excellent opportunity afforded those persons who had watched intelligently the development of Mr. Gladstone's conduct with reference to religious affairs, to accuse him of being secretly in league, if not, indeed, a member of, the Roman Church. He had looked kindly toward Ireland and had undertaken the onerous task of curing her chronic ills. A certain Mr. Whalley, who was also a member of Parliament, drew him into a correspondence which is now ludicrous for the very seriousness with which it was conducted, the upshot of which was that Gladstone convinced England that he had met with no change in his faith. The cry of "Home Rule for Ireland" was making itself heard everywhere, and that Gladstone was not ignorant of the difficulties any reforming statesman would have on his hands in trying to help the Irish people, is made evident by an address he made on receiving the freedom of the city of Aberdeen. He showed what he and others had tried to do for Ireland, and he then contended that Wales and Scotland were much more favorably placed than Ireland for demanding and wisely using the gift of Home Rule.

That Gladstone himself had not grown to his full height as a reformer of abuses even in Ireland, was made evident by what was contained in the question he asked at that time:

"Can any sensible man, can any rational man, suppose that at this time of day, in this rational condition of the world, we are going to disintegrate the great capital institutions of this country for the purpose of making ourselves ridiculous in the sight of all mankind, and crippling any power we possess for bestowing benefits, through legislation, on the country to which we belong?"

The Treaty negotiated by Mr. Cobden between France and England was now about to expire, and Gladstone was deeply interested in what England wished to do with reference to the maintenance of what had recently been a warm friendship. He was all the more interested, because he was touched by the pathetic condition of France laden with unparalleled debt and stricken to the heart at the loss of territory. No act of his Administration is grander than that continuous exercise of intelligence and will with which he brought England at last into just understanding with the humiliated nation across the Channel.

Discontent on the part of the laboring populations, a state of war between labor and capital in England, especially the demand on the part of the toilers for shorter hours and larger wages, led to a consideration, upon his part, of the causes for this discontent and of possible remedies to be suggested. Both the laboring classes and Mr. Gladstone missed the presence of John Bright at this time, who had fallen desperately ill from overwork, and whose straightforwardness of character, coupled with his influence upon Mr. Gladstone, might have saved the latter from making two appointments—at least they were charged to him—which could not add to his popularity amongst the classes most anxious that privilege should not obtain over merit in the Government. Sir Robert Collier was lifted to a position by the use of a technicality, and this did not please the common people to whom Mr. Gladstone had to look for his staunchest friends.

A vote of censure was moved in the House of Lords, but, fortunately for Gladstone, it was rejected. In the other case, which was known as "the Ewelne scandal," a certain Mr. Harvey was made a member of the Oxford Convocation by Oxford itself, for the purpose of qualifying him for the Rectory of Ewelne. These appointments were unfortunate incidents in the career of the head of a Government attempting to maintain his influence over English Liberalism.

Meantime he was preparing to get everybody who cared much for gin and beer in opposition to him. The trade in liquors had as much hold upon England and as much influence in her politics as ever that trade has had in America and that is much. Sir Wilfred Lawson, who was a man of genuine moral enthusiasm and persuasive speech, organized an agitation whose end was to give England what we call in America "local option," with respect to the public sale of intoxicating drinks of every kind. It was very certain that the war against drink in England had revealed the fact that there were many localities which wished to stop the traffic in intoxicating liquors altogether. The Bill contemplated an extra penalty for drunkenness, and it shut the doors of gin-shops and other drinking houses at hours when they had commonly been open.

Gladstone had always seemed too pious and upright for the rabble to like him deeply. Besides this, he had appeared once to favor the upper classes in their vice, if vice this might be called. He had proposed legislation which allowed the people who could afford to go to certain houses to drink wine, and he failed to offer legislation which would permit anybody else to have his usual glass. Now these public-house keepers were against him, and the fact that the present measure made a wholesale attack upon all houses where drink could be obtained, led to the massing of the most reputable and the most abominable of the liquor dealers in a league against the Government. Here was the very rabble to which Disraeli could hand a phrase accepted by the upper classes in their parlors and drawing-rooms, passed from lip to lip by the people who constitute "society," and very soon the English people, neglecting to look upon the greatness of Gladstone's aims and the largeness of the results obtained in the direction of popular freedom, looked abroad and concluded that there was no "spirited foreign policy," and that the "honor of England" was not being well looked after.

Meantime Gladstone was delivering addresses on matters theological and literary; he had given to the reviews essays of astonishing vigor and calm consideration, and he was carrying on a large correspondence with men of every class upon subjects of the first importance to legislation. When he arose to speak at the beginning of his term of office as Prime Minister, England remembered that he had said in the campaign leading to his election, that there was a certain "Upas tree" which had cursed Ireland, and that one of the main branches of this tree was the system of public education in that country. Concluding the speech he had said:

"For the House, for us all, for the country, I ask what is to be the policy that is to follow the rejection of this bill? What is to be the policy adopted in Ireland? Perhaps the bill of my honorable friend, the member for Brighton, will find favor, which leaves the University of Dublin in the hands of Trinity College, and which, I presume, if passed, will only be the harbinger of an agitation fiercer than that which we are told would follow the passing of the present bill. It will still leave the Roman Catholic in this condition, that he will be able to obtain a degree in Ireland without going either to the Queen's College, to which he objects, or placing himself under examinations and a system of discipline managed and conducted by a Protestant board,—a board composed of eight gentlemen, of whom six are clergymen of the Disestablished Church of Ireland. The other alternative will be the adopting for Ireland of a new set of principles which Parliament had repudiated in Ireland and has disclaimed for Great Britain, not only treating the Roman Catholic majority in Ireland as being the Irish nation, but likewise adopting for the Irish nation the principles which we have ourselves overthrown, even within the limits of our own generation. I know not with what satisfaction we can look forward to these prospects. It is dangerous to tamper with objects of this kind. We have presented to you our plan, for which we are responsible. We are not afraid, I am not afraid, of the charge of my right honorable friend that we have served the priests. (Mr. Horsman: "I did not say so.") I am glad to hear it. I am ready to serve the priest or any other man as far as justice dictates. I am not ready to go an inch further for them or for any other man; and if the labors of 1869 and 1870 are to be forgotten in Ireland—if where we have earnestly sought and toiled for peace we find only contention—if our tenders of relief are thrust aside with scorn—let us still remember that there is a voice which is not heard in the crackling of the fire, or in the roaring of the whirlwind or the storm, but which will and must be heard when they have passed away,—the still, small voice of justice. To mete out justice in Ireland, according to the best view that with human infirmity we could form, has been the work,—I will almost say the sacred work—of this Parliament. Having put our hand to the plow let us not turn back. Let not what we think the fault or perverseness of those whom we are attempting to assist have the slightest effect in turning us even by a hair's breadth from the path on which we have entered. As we have begun, so let us persevere even to the end, and with firm and resolute hand let us efface from the law and the practice of the country the last,—for I believe it is the last—of the religious and social grievances of Ireland."

The year 1873 had come, and Gladstone's scheme for the settlement of this most annoying and complex question was offered. It was his aim to unify and pacify the antagonistic desires of the Romish and Protestant populations, and to so adjust things that there should be a University so conceived and conducted that the convictions of neither party would be seriously injured. Surely he might well appeal to the consciousness of civilization, and ask if there could be a higher or nobler task attempted than thus to nourish and enlarge human intelligence and at the same time to protect the consciences of men. Irish Protestantism again stood forth in opposition. Roman Catholicism uttered its denunciations. The Irish Protestants wanted to retain their University, which had stood so long as their safeguard, and the bishops of the Church of Rome were not satisfied with what they were to obtain in exchange for what they were to give up. A short time before, Mr. Gladstone had made his appeal to the people, and in that turbulent auditory—as large an audience as he ever had addressed, even in the open air—at Blackheath, where he wrestled for hours with a mob hooting at the first, then cheering, then groaning, then storming with approving applause, then howling with derision, he had discerned the attitude of the people of Greenwich toward himself, his methods, and perhaps his political ideal. At last, on that chilly October day, he had conquered the audience, and he came back home feeling that the same cause in its general aspects advocated with the same resolution, argument and courage, would succeed elsewhere.

But now Disraeli unsheathed his sharpest sword, and he was more than ordinarily brilliant in his sarcasm when he saw that a large number of the Liberal party were arrayed in opposition to Gladstone, and that Gladstone's former friends, the Irish members, utterly forgetful of every reason for loyalty to him, were shouting and voting against him. Never was Gladstone more athletic and resourceful in debate than on that night in March, 1873. He was badgered on all sides and taunted by those who had been closely attached to him on other measures, and he was mercilessly attacked by those whose habit it was to condemn unsparingly his statesmanship. Everything that he had touched in the last three years was labeled that night as a failure or a curse for England.

On January 9th, the Emperor Napoleon had died, and England had manifested a warm feeling of sympathy for the Empress and for France, but now the Treaty of Paris was heralded as a victory for Russia with English interests abandoned, while the rise of Republican France made the haters of Republicanism in England more violent than ever against everything and anything in Gladstone's career and conduct which looked toward "the Americanization of the British Isles."

It is hard to say where things would have gone, even before this, if the motion made by Sir Charles Dilke in the House of Commons a year before, in which that lively statesman proposed to inquire as to how the allowances and income of the royal family were expended, had accomplished its purpose. As we all remember, the Prince of Wales became ill, and Mr. Gladstone's reply to Sir Charles Dilke, in which he vehemently demonstrated what no one has ever doubted,— his attachment to the Queen and her family, and even to the ancient institution of monarchy itself,—brought to him the gratitude and admiration of a large section of people who had begun to stray away from him and who had foolishly joined in the old cry, that Gladstone cared nothing for English institutions and would willingly see the

GLADSTONE AND HIS FRIENDS

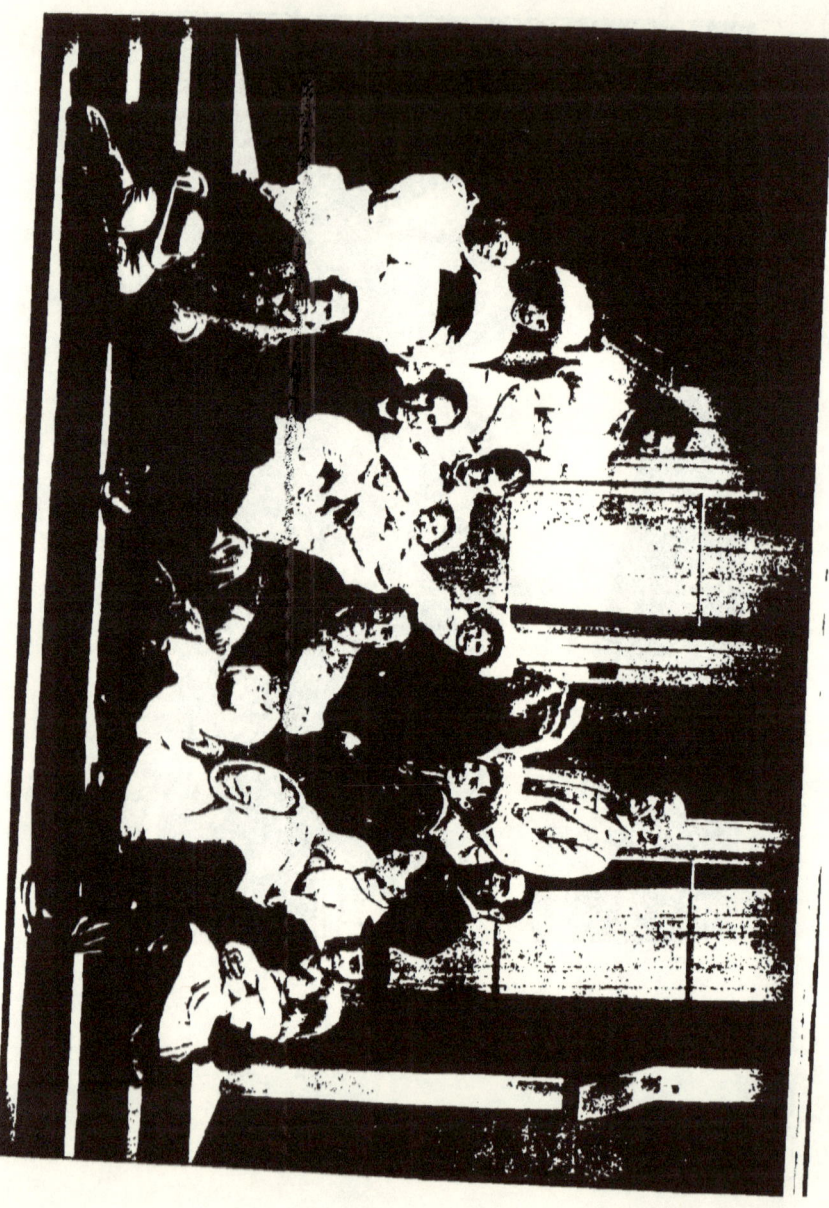

GLADSTONE AND HIS FAMILY

whole machinery go to pieces. Here, however, in the debate on this measure for the settlement of educational affairs in Ireland, Gladstone was to find that nothing could save the day. The unenfranchised classes in the rural districts were heard from in a singular way, for they had not gotten over their wrath at being left out of the functions and responsibility of government by the last Reform Bill. But here the glittering steel of Disraeli was backed by powers much more demonstrative and serious than this. He also had felt the pulse of the country, and while he was feeling the patient's pulse, he had got him on his feet, and in many places throughout the realm he had organized an opposition to Gladstone and his plans which now was resistless. He made England laugh as he spoke of his rivals under Gladstone as "a range of extinct volcanoes." Master of that kind of rhetoric which is most happy in opposition, the supreme incarnation of a gravity upon which his own somewhat gaudy ornaments of speech appeared to be gems indeed, with everything to gain and with nothing to lose, playing to the classes most privileged on the one hand and to the classes most hopeless of advancement on the other, he enforced his criticisms with such strength and certainty of stroke, that there was nothing now but defeat for Gladstone.

Disraeli was soon sent for by the Queen, but, having a minority in the House of Commons, Disraeli declined and Mr. Gladstone was persuaded to remain in office.

Now, having been wearied with arduous labors and feeling a decline in his health, yet loyal enough to his Queen to retain office under such embarrassing circumstances, he saw Mr. Fawcett's measure for dealing with the educational question in Ireland carried, and Mr. Disraeli faltering as to whether he dared go to the country and to squarely make his appeal on the Irish University question. The circumstances were such that neither Gladstone nor Disraeli wanted office. The Fall Elections declared against the Liberal party. Mr. Lowe, one of whose blunders we have recorded, was succeeded by Gladstone himself as Chancellor of the Exchequer in his own Cabinet. At length Mr. Gladstone resolved to appeal to the people. He dissolved Parliament. In an address marvelous even for Gladstone, he

18

appealed to his constituents, but the address was too long for the people to read. Gladstone's colleagues opposed his action, and, this fact being known, there was a great popular disapproval of his speedy resolve, and it was easy for his foes to make ignorance and lawlessness agree that he had proved, in any event, that he was not a statesman. The magnanimity, the trust he showed in people themselves, the sublime carelessness with which he did the right—all of these now were made evident. The fight before the constituencies was exciting, turbulent and long continued. Every malcontent in England, every vested interest, every privileged class, every indolent aristocrat, every mob-loving democrat,—the whole mass of dullness and mediocrity, ever strong,—rose against the one man who in recent times, had led England to do a sublime thing. John Bull had been overstrained by the earnest Gladstone. He was weary of the strenuousness and the heroism of this open-eyed and progressive spirit. Men forgot that he had brought to a successful close the Ashantee war, of the very existence of which England ought to have been ashamed. They passed over the fact that he had dealt wisely and humanely with the famine in Bengal, and the countrymen who had been offended because they had not been able to get into step with an ever advancing statesmanship which had so often refused to honor their petty criticism, rejoiced in the downfall of one of the most earnest and self-sacrificing champions of constitutional government who ever lived.

Greenwich placed him second on her poll, for the first man returned was an inconsequential distiller.

If ever Gladstone's enthusiasm took possession of his whole life, intellectually and physically, it was discerned in the course of that unmatched progress toward Republicanism to which he urged, but could not lead, his party, between 1870 and 1874. So thoroughly did he seem to believe in the capability of John Bull to receive regenerating influences that when, in 1874, after thirty years of absence, the Conservatives swept into power, his confidence in principles stood firm, even though his vision of the fact stunned him. For these years Gladstone had been running a race with himself in proposing to the English people measure after measure calculated to place the Government of Great Britain upon the broadest human foundation, and make her the leader of the world's civilization. As has been well said, every one of his measures was a capital piece of legislation, and to have carried any one of them through would have made a man of ordinary genius sure of immortal praise. He had disestablished and disendowed the Irish Church; he had given to the realm the Irish Land Act, in which reside the forces of statesmanship which shall finally create a truly united kingdom; he had reformed the abuses of the Army; he had garrisoned and guaranteed the safety and sacredness of the ballot; he had given England a scheme of education which meant the defeat of popular ignorance throughout the entire realm, and, as we have said, because he had overstrained the capacity of the English people to accept and apply the most important political ideas of modern times, his Government was overthrown by the Licensed Victualers, and the publicans routed an administration the most mighty since the days of the younger Pitt. The slight promise of legislation contained in the speech from the Throne when Parliament was opened in 1874, indicated how willing everybody was for a rest. It was the hour for well-groomed people to poke coarse fun at a generous and prophetic enthusiast. Even the "Saturday Review" could say:

"Mr. Gladstone, in a speech delivered to his Greenwich constituents, extemporized in his well-known fashion a general proposition that Governments always decline in popularity after three years of office. If it had suited his purpose, he might have accounted for the result which he acknowledged without resorting to arbitrary theories."

And that caustic sheet added:

"It has been said that soldiers prefer a leader in battle who invites them to come on to one who merely orders them to go on. Mr. Gladstone in a great Parliamentary contest gives neither direction, but like one of his favorite Homeric heroes, he prefers to fight alone in front of his army."

This is not fair to Gladstone. His faith in ideals was sublime. He was trying to bring his army up to the color-bearer; he did not and would not take the flag back to the halting army.

CHAPTER XXXI.

SEEKING REST AND FINDING NONE.

Now came the opportunity for Gladstone to insist that he had earned the right to rest, after a long series of years devoted to public business and to the proclamation of the principles of Anglo-Saxon freedom. His health was certainly affected, and although he was only sixty-four years of age, he desired the companionship of his books, the quiet of his home, opportunity for travel, and, above all, the wide audience of the world which he might instruct and inspire with his pen. He felt himself that he had carried England to a point where she might see the promised land of a larger political life, and just at that moment England had expressed her desire to return to the flesh-pots of Egypt. On the 12th of March he sent a letter to Lord Granville containing these words:

"For a variety of reasons personal to myself, I could not contemplate any unlimited extension of active political service; and I am anxious that it should be clearly understood by those friends with whom I have acted in the direction of affairs, that at my age I must reserve my entire freedom to divest myself of all the responsibilities of leadership at no distant time. The need of rest will prevent me from giving more than occasional attendance in the House of Commons during the present session.

"I should be desirous, shortly before the commencement of the Session of 1875, to consider whether there would be advantage in my placing my services for a time at the disposal of the Liberal party, or whether I should then claim exemption from the duties I have hitherto discharged. If, however, there should be reasonable ground for believing that, instead of the course which I have sketched, it would be preferable, in view of the party generally, for me to assume at once the place of an independent member, I should willingly adopt the latter alternative. But I shall retain all that desire I have hitherto felt for the welfare of the party, and if the gentlemen composing it should think fit either to choose a leader or make provision ad interim, with a view to the convenience of the present year, the person designated would, of course, command from me any assistance which he might find occasion to seek, and which it might be in my power to render."

The Liberal party arose as one man, and insisted that their Moses had led them forth too far from Egypt for them to return, and now were they to be left to die so far this side of Canaan?

While the discussion was going on, the Public Worship Regulation Bill, which was aimed at the abolition of Ritualism in the Church of England, was introduced by Archbishop Tait. The old war horse, Gladstone, heard the bugle and the sounds of battle. He had spoken on the subject of Ritualism elsewhere, urging that ritual had its value but ritual must not be mistaken for holiness.

The whole House favored the Bill. It passed, as did the Ecclesiastical Titles Bill of Lord John Russell many years before, which was tenderly repealed by Gladstone twenty years after its passage, during which twenty years it had been a dead letter in the statute-books of England. And this Bill, which was read the second time in the House of Commons, and was so manifestly popular that Gladstone withdrew his resolutions against it, was to furnish another example of the same sort. Meantime, in the Committee, Mr. Gladstone came into hottest contention with the man who had been his Solicitor-General a year before, Sir William Harcourt, and with two or three strokes of his sword, he laid Sir William low, after the latter had poured forth the following intemperate words with reference to both Disraeli and Gladstone:

"We have a leader of this House who is proud of the House of Commons, and of whom the House of Commons is proud. Well may the Prime Minister be proud of the House of Commons, for it was the scene of his early triumphs, and it is still the arena of his later and well-earned glory. . . . . We may well leave the vindication of the reputation of this famous assembly to one who will well know how to defend its credit and its dignity against the ill-advised railing of a rash and rancorous tongue."

The ill-advised Sir William had ventured to measure swords with Gladstone on matters of ecclesiastical jurisprudence and polity.

Disraeli proposed to go on with a Cabinet of twelve. He had already perceived the capabilities and relied upon the industry of Lord Salisbury, who was now in the Indian department, and Lord Cairns, with whom also he had been closely associated in debate and in the conducting of public business, was created Lord Chancellor, and everybody whom Gladstone had ever offended by his brilliancy was made peaceful and acquiescent with the appointment of Lord Derby as Foreign Secretary. It is true that Salisbury and Disraeli had quarreled years before, but now the former was evidently in training for a position which Disraeli would some day leave to him. Mr. Gathorne Hardy, who now represented Oxford as Gladstone did not represent her, was given charge of military affairs, and Mr. Gladstone's former private secretary, who was now Sir Stafford Northcote, and whose training under Gladstone so well fitted him for the position, was made Chancellor of the Exchequer.

Here is an interesting page from the Life and Letters of Dean Stanley:

"Stanley was invited to meet the Czar at luncheon at Marlborough House. Lord Beaconsfield, who had lately become Prime Minister, sat in a post of honor, whilst Mr. Gladstone, whose fall was still recent, and who had lately forsworn public life, sat, in a less prominent place, near the Dean. When the company rose to leave the luncheon room, Mr. Disraeli, as he then was, came down from his lofty position, and passed in front of the place where Stanley and Mr. Gladstone were standing. He turned to his political rival, and said, in allusion, to the latter's absence from Parliament, with a mixture of comedy and tragedy expressed on his countenance:

"'You must come back to us; indeed, we cannot possibly do without you.' Mr. Gladstone, with more than usual severity, answered, 'There are things possible, and there are things impossible; what you ask me to do is one of the things that are impossible.' Upon this Disraeli turned to me, as the nearest representative of the public present, and said, 'You see what it is—the wrath, the inexorable wrath of Achilles.'"

Mr. Gladstone had indeed come back and he had been complimented by Mr. Disraeli upon his re-appearance in the House, when the former entered into the debate on the Church Patronage Bill, and it really seemed as though the patronage of his rival was tempered by kindly friendship. Sir William Harcourt's somewhat extemporaneous erudition on Church affairs received serious shocks when Gladstone opposed the Bill, whose aim was to upset the right of veto on the part of a bishop, and to give to the archbishop in one diocese the power to begin suit in another. Salisbury and Disraeli were making things interesting as they crossed their slender and brilliant blades, and the people of England were resting from the lofty-mindedness of Gladstone, while he looked on, beholding the absurd pretentiousness and utter uselessness of a measure which was intended to put down Ritualism. The Ritualists gathered around Gladstone and regarded him as their savior and friend, though his argument amounted to showing that they had proposed too much of what he thought a good thing. Whenever Sir William Harcourt attempted to be learned on ecclesiastical matters, he met the energetic Gladstone, and his learning dissolved into thin air. Gladstone's manner was irresistible, as at one time he spoke of Sir William in the following words:

"I confess, fairly, I greatly admire the manner in which he has used his time since Friday night. On Friday night, as he says, he was taken by surprise. The lawyer was taken by surprise, and so was the professor of law in the University of Cambridge; the lawyer was taken by surprise, and, in consequence, he had nothing to deliver to the House except a series of propositions on which I will not comment. I greatly respect the order and the spirit of the order of the House which renders it irregular, as, in my opinion, it is highly inconvenient, especially when there is no practical issue, to revive the details and particulars of a former debate. Finding that he has delivered to the House most extraordinary propositions of law and history that will not bear a moment's examination, my honorable and learned friend has had the opportunity of spending four or five days in better informing himself upon the subject, and he is in a position to come down to this House, and for an hour and a half to display and develop the erudition he has thus rapidly and cleverly acquired. Human nature could not possibly resist such a temptation, and my honorable and learned friend has succumbed to it on this occasion."

It was now a delight for Mr. Gladstone to use something like leisure in contributing to the reviews his articles on ecclesiastical, literary, and especially theological subjects.

Again he tried, in the winter of 1875, to get the Liberal party to release him from leadership. But it was impossible to find another to bend the bow of Ulysses. With a sublime carelessness as to the matters usually affecting what Mr. Gladstone has been termed,—a shrewd politician,—he created a furore among the Roman Catholics in his controversies with regard to the Church of England and the Church of Rome. It was gravely insisted by those who could not understand Gladstone, that he had grown tired of the Irish cause, and was willing now to offend the whole body of Catholics wherever they lived.

He had added to the tumult thus created, for now he published his famous pamphlet called "The Vatican Decrees in Their Bearing on Civil Allegiance." More than 100,000 copies of the pamphlet containing his vigorous treatment of this topic, were sold at once, and an army of controversialists arose to answer him. Manning and Newman drew their polished swords against him with characteristic force. No power of mind which he had shown in his handling of a financial Budget, or in his defense of a great political measure, forsook him in this debate. His friends insisted that he was digging more deeply his political grave with every stroke of his shovel, though they admitted that from a literary point of view the edge of the shovel gleamed like gold. His enemies, especially those who desired him to become as unpopular in Ireland as possible, were overjoyed at the fact that he was smiting the assumption of the Roman Catholic Church to rule in civil affairs hip and thigh, and rendering its position uneasy, and its communicants angry at him. He paid no attention whatever to the beseechings of his old colleagues, or to the vituperation, mixed with hilarity, on the part of his foes. With almost unwonted seriousness and inflexibility, he pursued his way serenely. He knew he was treading a lofty "path which the vulture's eye hath not seen."

CHAPTER XXXII.

GLADSTONE AND "THE MYSTERY MAN."

When Gladstone was leading his Government on the subject of education in 1870, he met a most heated opposition on the part of the Roman Catholics, with whom, it began to be said in 1875, he was settling his account in his controversy with Cardinal Newman, and he confronted also the Nonconformists, who, it was hoped, had settled their account with Gladstone by helping to overthrow him in the General Election of 1874. To both of these opponents Gladstone had made reply when he said to the leader of the Nonconformists, Mr. Edward Miall: "We are the Government of the Queen, and those who have assumed the high responsibility of administering the affairs of this empire must endeavor to forget the parts in the whole, and must, in the great measures they introduce into the House, propose to themselves no meaner or narrower object than the welfare of the nation at large." If these offended parties had expected to cling to Disraeli, he was ruthlessly to disappoint them. The very constituency at Greenwich, which had refused to support Gladstone, was now angered beyond expression at the behavior of him whom John Bright had called "the Mystery Man." Disraeli had not only shown himself careless, if not indolent, as to any improvement in domestic affairs, but he had whiled away his time and expended his energies in showy appearances in political debate, out of whose tumult came nothing but vague and formless phantoms. Disraeli had laughingly said: "History never repeats itself! She is the least original of all the Muses,—a spun-out tautology." Now he was about to furnish a strange commentary on this remark. The Oriental elements in his blood never more truly exhibited themselves in his speech and demeanor than at this time. He strode on magnificently, gorgeous in his rhetorical apparel and confident in the strength of the overwhelming majority with

281

which he accomplished whatever pleased him. Gladstone's steel was resting in the sheath, while he was warring with his pen with the chief militants in the controversy in the realm of theology and Church policies. John Bright was laid aside by physical weakness, and the world was Disraeli's. His vast phrases, in which the word "imperial" shows forth abundantly, resounded over England, and a Jingo policy had taken possession of the hearts and ambitions of his followers. Yonder in Egypt was the Suez Canal, the construction of which the British Government for a long time had antagonized. Now, however, that it had become a fact, and that the Khedive of Egypt was in financial straits, and nearly half of his holdings of the shares in the Canal, which amounted to nearly one-fourth of the total number of shares, was for sale, Disraeli bought them.

Hardly a month had passed away when it was evident, in the spring of 1875, that Disraeli's mysterious expressions were meant to signify that somehow England had saved the world from another strife between France and Germany. By the beginning of the year 1876 Bismarck had shown the English people that the British magician had really nothing to do with such a possible event, for war existed as a probability only in his luxurious imagination. It was necessary for Disraeli to make some sort of show against this disappointment, and Lord Salisbury gave voice to the desire for a new sensation, and again mounted the old phrase of Disraeli, which he gave to the Electors of Buckinghamshire in his reply to Gladstone's address to the Electors of Greenwich two years before: "A little more energy in our foreign policy, and a little less in our domestic legislation." Disraeli said with reference to the Suez Canal operation:

"I have always and do now recommend it (the purchase of the Canal shares) to the country as a political transaction, and one which I believe is calculated to strengthen the empire. That is the spirit in which it has been accepted by the country. . . . . . They are seasick of the 'silver streak.' They want the empire to be maintained, to be strengthened; they will not be alarmed even if it be increased."

The Dock Yards were made unusually active. Estimates for the Army and Navy were increased, and "the imperial instincts of the nation were tempted forward into unwonted display." Gladstone saw the darkness from the East and waited.   He was not bewildered, though England was bedazzled.

It seemed that the old days, when *Civis Romanus* Palmerston made every Englishman defiant of every other country on earth, had come again.   Lord Derby, who never was a great speaker, but was regarded as, on the whole, the most sensible man in England, had wit enough to reduce a little toward its proper form the rhetoric of Disraeli with reference to England's policy and to prepare for the less torrid feeling of later days.   James Anthony Froude, who often did, in writing alleged history, what Disraeli was doing in practicing politics, was sent out on a South African enterprise, the Prince of Wales was sent as a visitor to India, the emotional author of "Lucille" was made Viceroy over that people.   More was to follow.

At the beginning of January, 1876, England looked upon the new peers which had recently been created.   Mr. Gladstone had added forty peers in the course of six years to the Upper House, and Mr. Disraeli had created twenty-four in half the time, slightly outdoing Mr. Gladstone, and taking a good deal of effectiveness out of the charge against the latter that he had strengthened his party in the Upper House in this way.   Disraeli's mind, turning naturally to dukes, was not satisfied with less than three.   When Disraeli came to handle the question of Pitt's peerages, he said: "He created a plebeian aristocracy. He made peers of second-rate squires and fat graziers.   He caught them in the alleys of Lombard Street and clutched them in the counting-houses of Cornhill."   It was evident that Disraeli was likely to eclipse Pitt in his effort to be strong in the House of Lords, and he had the disadvantage of having neither a Wellington or a Nelson, as Pitt had, for these lofty positions.   Yet, on the whole, they were a good lot of men, harmless enough for promotion, and Disraeli lost nothing by lifting them above their fellows.   He was soon to be in their company.

Perhaps nothing more thoroughly exemplified Mr. Disraeli's love of splendor, which fortunately had the effect of holding Gladstone's opulent fancy more soberly in check, than the former's proposal of

the Royal Titles Bill. Disraeli had fascinated even the footlights of
the theater in which he was playing, by proposing to add to the august
title of his sovereign an oriental and grandiose phrase,—"Empress of
India." With what Bright described as "a mixture of pompousness
and servility," Disraeli waved off annoying questions with reference
to what the Government had in store and proceeded to prepare the
country for this majestic designation. While all this charlatanism was
going on, the Prime Minister had no ear for the cry which had already
pierced the scholarly calm at Hawarden and found for broken hearts
an inimitable and chivalrous champion. The contrast was complete
as the news became more and more sadly true from the Balkans.

Disraeli lost nothing by the fact that he was able to fairly crush
Mr. Robert Lowe, who made another of his interesting blunders by
asserting that the Queen had tried to induce two earlier administra-
tions to add this title to her already august name. Lord Hartington,
the somewhat heavy and always slow-going leader of the Liberal
party, could not even apologize for the interesting mistake.

And now the figure of Russia arose, dread and specter-like as
ever, when she appeared before the mind of England. It was true
that Turkey had proved reactionary and had refused every suggestion
of progress. Insurrections had followed upon outrageous misgovernment, and while blood was shed freely, Turkey became more barbarous
and cruel. There could be no question in the mind of England,
however, because England's mind had a constitutional and chronic
fear of the effect of Russia's ambition, that Russia now, having gone
further into Asia with her territorial lines, meant to take advantage of
the situation in Turkey and of the revolts which followed one another
incessantly and build a new future for herself, doubtless on the ruins of
the Ottoman Government. In Herzegovina and Bosnia insurrections
had broken out. The Government at Constantinople complained that
the first insurrection had been aided by Russia and Montenegro, as well
as, perhaps, by Austrians and Servians. Lord Derby was cautious and
procrastinating, if not weak, and he did not opportunely answer the
appeal made to the Government of England that it should urge
Austria to refuse help. Finally the Austrian minister formulated a

declaration that it was time for the Porte to interfere and compel Turkey to change her course. He was right in saying that Servia and Montenegro could no longer be resisted in their desire to take a hand in the insurrection. In this plan of Count Andrassy, Italy and France were ready to join, but Lord Derby was silent, until the Porte itself actually besought the English Government to unite with the others.

By this time Turkey came to believe that England was on her side, and, although the note which England finally signed with the rest of the powers, was irritating, Turkey made some excellent promises which were capable of being twisted into meaningless assertions by Oriental craft. A meeting of the Powers was proposed. The Berlin Memorandum came, and Turkey was told that unless these promises were speedily redeemed, combined action on the part of the Powers might be expected. Again Lord Derby hesitated about joining in the Berlin Memorandum. England naturally believed that Russia was behind this whole enterprise, stirring up a religious war, if such a thing were possible, in order that she might seize more valuable territory. Turkey took hope at this, even though her Sultan had outdazzled Disraeli's Orientalism when he was received in London, and had ended his career by taking his own life, after having been dethroned.

At this moment there broke forth in Bulgaria a powerful insurrection. It was a noble rebellion against intolerable tyranny. It was met by incredible violence, and hideous massacre reigned in the Balkans. Disraeli had flashed in a most spectacular manner, when he told Parliament that the English Government would have nothing to do with the Berlin Memorandum. Now stories came to London of unparalleled suffering and crime, led on by the Turkish Government against the Bulgarians, while the British fleet was said to be moving toward Besika Bay. The "spirited foreign policy" was certainly brilliant and bloody enough in its undoing. Hate of Russia, the stupid reiteration of the word "imperial" to England's bewildered mind, fascinated as it was for a moment by the glitter of Disraeli's rhetoric and promises, could not, however, stop the ear of humanity.

The Daily News, which was a Liberal organ, and, therefore, was not to be regarded, much less believed, by a Tory such as Mr. Disraeli, poured upon the Government information which the Government would not heed, but which revealed a chapter of atrocities unparalleled in the history of the race. Never was there an hour when civilization, shuddering at horrible and wholesale murders, bound by an ambitious and apparently heartless Government, so needed a heroic hand to loose her that she might deal justly with insensate barbarism.

CHAPTER XXXIII.

THE KNIGHT ERRANT.

Sitting in Hawarden Castle and poring over the Iliad of Homer or the Analogy of Bishop Butler, or felling great oaks in Hawarden Forest, or reading the lessons, as was his custom, in the morning service at the parish church, entertaining distinguished artists, illustrious poets, or eminent theologians, the stalwart spirit of Gladstone could not be satisfied or acquiescent. He heard the cry of beleaguered and outraged humanity, and while the words of Disraeli describing the reports of these atrocities as "coffee-house babble" were still defiling the air of St. Stephens, and while London was reading with emotions of horror the report of the English Consul confirming previous statements as to the shameless crimes of the Bashi-Bazouks, Gladstone suddenly made his appearance in the House of Commons. An imperialism of genius utterly unlike that of Disraeli's rhetoric, a profound faith in justice, triumphantly glowing in his face, and a sublime passion for righteousness beaming from those deep-lit eyes, took possession of the House, while a stream of fiery eloquence poured from his agitated soul. Every facility which his eloquent tongue and scarcely less eloquent pen might employ was used in the unparalleled crusade. A Saint Bernard spoke again. He organized and led against the policy which now stood revealed in all its satanic features, as the merciless light of Gladstone's mind and conscience played upon it. He was called sentimental, and he was said to be preaching "Sunday-school politics." Once on a time an excellent Bishop had been expected to address, on an important occasion, a distinguished body of students at King's College, but failed to appear; Mr. Gladstone supplied for him, as we would say, and proved himself a preacher indeed who might have rivaled Jeremy Taylor or Canon Liddon. Now, however, Gladstone's eloquence was like that of Savonorola of

Florence in which the crown of Lorenzo de Medici was consumed. Speech followed speech, monster meetings succeeded an address of denunciation in the House of Commons, and the realm trembled under the spell of his genius. He was called "the friend of Russia," which has always been enough, in England, to condemn an archangel. In the midst of his crusade he had talked intemperately, some of his friends said, and many were led to believe that he wanted the Turks, men, women and children, thrown bodily out of Europe. A reaction sprung up. Disraeli attitudinized as the only friend of England's foreign or domestic interests. He stood in the House of Commons one day, directing his stinging arrows at Gladstone the Crusader, and poured a torrent of scorn and ridicule upon the opponents of his own Government. Next day he was a member of the House of Lords, and had entered a new era in his history as the Earl of Beaconsfield.

Still, however, Gladstone's appeal was echoed and re-echoed throughout the realm. He said:

"I am far from supposing—I am not such a dreamer as to suppose that Russia, more than any other country, is exempt from selfishness and ambition. But she has also within her, like other countries, the pulse of humanity, and, for my own part, I believe it is the pulse of humanity which is now throbbing almost ungovernably in her people. Upon the concord and hearty co-operation—not upon a mere hollow truce between England and Russia, but upon their concord and hearty, cordial co-operation—depend a good settlement of this question. Their power is immense. The power of Russia by land for acting upon these countries as against Turkey is perfectly resistless; the power of England by sea is scarcely less important at this moment. For I ask you what would be the condition of the Turkish armies if the British Admiral now in Besika Bay were to inform the Government of Constantinople that from that hour, until atonement had been made—until punishment had descended, until justice had been vindicated—not a man, nor a ship, nor a boat should cross the waters of the Bosphorus, or the cloudy Euxine, or the bright Ægean, to carry aid to the Turkish troops?

"Let us insist that our Government, which has been working in one direction, shall work in the other, and shall apply all its vigor to concur with the other States of Europe in obtaining the extinction of the Turkish executive power in Bulgaria. Let the Turks now carry away their abuses

GLADSTONE AND LI HUNG CHANG

CATHERINE GLADSTONE

in the only possible manner—namely, by carrying off themselves. Their Zaptiehs and their Mudirs, their Bimbashis and their Yuzbachis, their Kaimakams and their Pashas—one and all, bag and baggage, shall, I hope, clear out from the province they have desolated and profaned. . . . If it be allowable that the executive power of Turkey should renew at this great crisis, by permission or authority of Europe, the charter of its existence in Bulgaria, then there is not on record since the beginning of political society a protest that man has lodged against intolerable misgovernment, or a stroke he has dealt at loathsome tyranny, that ought not henceforward to be branded as a crime."

And England more clearly understood him. Gladstone was never more patriotic or effective. He had doubtless saved England from going into war and placing herself on the wrong side of the contest. It was a disheartening day, however, in the life of the great statesman, when even Disraeli could be applauded as he spoke of the "sinister ends" which the followers of Gladstone and their chief were seeking to accomplish, and stigmatized their conduct as "worse than the Bulgarian atrocities." It was impossible for Gladstone to safely appear on the streets of London. Mr. Lucy's famous "Diary of Two Parliaments" furnishes but one of the many pages written by publicists and historians perpetuating the memory of those militant days:

"Scene, division lobby of the House of Commons; date, 12th April, 1878; time, 9:20 p. m. Gladstone is walking along the lobby, having recorded his vote against a hasty proposal to conduct the business of Parliament in secret. The Conservative majority in the other lobby observe him through the glass door and suddenly set up a yell of execration which could scarcely be more violent if the murderer of Lord Leitrim, flying for sanctuary to Westminster, were discovered skulking in the lobby. The crowd increases till it reaches the proportions of forty or fifty English gentlemen, all well educated, many of good birth who, with hand held to mouth to make the sound shriller, howl and groan, while some even shake their fists. Gladstone, startled at the cry, looks up and sees the crowd. He pauses a moment, and then, advancing close up to the glass door, calmly surveys the yelling mob. On the one side the slight figure drawn to its full height, and the pale, stern face steadfastly turned towards the crowd. On the other the jeering, mocking, gesticulating mob. Between them the glass door and the infinite space that separates a statesman from the partisan."

19

The windows of Gladstone's house were broken; he received threats of personal violence, and often found himself under the necessity of seeking police protection; but during it all there walked by his side, in beautiful majesty, his faithful wife. Meantime, in the presence of a world slowly turning to the side of humanity and justice, Disraeli and Gladstone were grappling in debate. The distance from the House of Commons to the House of Lords could not make peace between them. It was the fiercest controversy in which these political duelists had ever been involved, and it furnished England and civilization a lesson never to be unlearned.

Lord Salisbury, however, was sent to Constantinople to demand that an end be put to the atrocities, while Gladstone was still rousing England. He was in sight of victory. Gladstone's review article on Montenegro, published in 1877, will always remain like a mirror in which the face of the author himself may be seen and studied. His unsurpassed zeal for down-trodden men and women furnished many witnesses to itself in that long controversy. Every element of his physical strength, and every energy of his indignant soul, every accomplishment of his fertile mind, every dearest friendship—he consecrated all to this cause. In the autumn of November, he visited Ireland. This visit was to prove of the utmost importance to him and to the Irish people in a short period. He came closer to the Irish problem than ever before, and his visit, while very enjoyable, accomplished something more than to prove to him the warmheartedness of the Irish people. It gave him an insight into some of the difficulties which finally came to him from that population, in his attempted solution of the problem years afterward. He said, speaking in Dublin:

"I could not describe the tumult almost of thought and emotion that a visit to Ireland brought into my mind. I saw from its antiquities, which formerly I knew the existence of only in the abstract, how remarkable was the position which Ireland occupied in those days, and I may say in those centuries, when she had almost a monopoly of learning and piety, and when she alone held up the truths of civilization, of true, Christian civilization, in Northern and Western Europe. They made a very deep impression on me, and they enabled me the better to understand the intense feeling with which the Irishman loves his country."

However, this was not Ireland's time for Gladstone's impassioned oratory. It is doubtful if ever her cause so commanded a certain kind of eloquence as the state of affairs in the East drew from the experienced speaker. Certainly Gladstone's grandest days as an orator were these. A certain Mr. Chaplin sought to vex him, if not compel him to cease, before a volley of questions. They were such as only roused Gladstone to a hotter onset. He thus disposed of the inconsequential Chaplin who had been stupid enough to intimate that Gladstone had not been honorable in meeting his antagonists. Said the high-spirited Gladstone:

"He says, sir, that I have been an inflammatory agitator, and that, as soon as I have got into this House, I have no disposition to chant in the same key. But before these debates are over—before this question is settled—the hon. gentleman will know more about my opinions than he knows at present, or is likely to know to-night. I am not about to reveal now to the hon. gentleman the secrets of a mind so inferior to his own. I am not so young as to think that his obliging inquiries supply me with the opportunities most advantageous to the public interest for the laying out of the plan of a campaign. By the time the hon. member is as old as I am, if he comes in his turn to be accused of cowardice by a man of the next generation to himself, he probably may find it convenient to refer to the reply I am now making, and to make it a model, or, at all events, to take from it hints and suggestions, with which to dispose of the antagonist that may then rise against him.

"I will tell the hon. gentleman," added Mr. Gladstone, "something in answer to his questions, and it is that I will tell him nothing at all. I will take my own counsel, and beg to inform him that he shall have no reason whatever to complain, when the accounts come to be settled and cast up at the end of the whole matter, of any reticence or suppressions on my part."

He then rose from his prostrate foe, to the level of his great theme, concluding thus:

"We have, I think, the most solemn and the greatest question to determine that has come before Parliament in my time. It is only under

very rare circumstances that such a question—the question of the East—
can be fully raised, fully developed and exhibited, and fully brought
home to the minds of men with that force, with that command, with
that absorbing power, which it ought to exercise over them. In the original entrance of the Turks into Europe, it may be said to have been a turning point in human history. To a great extent it continues to be the cardinal question, the question which casts into the shade every other question, and the question which is now brought before the mind of the country
far more fully than at any period of our history, far more fully than even
at the time of the Crimean War, when we were pouring forth our blood
and treasure in what we thought to be the cause of justice and right.
And I endeavored to impress upon the minds of my audience at Taunton,
not a blind prejudice against this man or that, but a great watchfulness
and the duty of great activity. It is the duty of every man to feel that he
is bound for himself, according to his opportunities, to examine what
belongs to this question, with regard to which it can never be forgotten
that we are those who set up the power of Turkey in 1854; that we are
those who gave her the strength which has been exhibited in the Bulgarian massacres; that we are those who made the treaty arrangements
that have secured her for twenty years from almost a single hour of un-
easiness brought about by foreign intervention; and that, therefore, nothing can be greater and nothing deeper than our responsibility in the matter. It is incumbent upon us, one and all, that we do not allow any
consideration, either of party or personal convenience, to prevent us from
endeavoring to the best of our ability to discharge this great duty, that
now, at length, in the East, has sprung up; and that in the midst of this
great opportunity, when all Europe has been called to collective action,
and when something like European concert has been established—when
we learn the deep human interests that are involved in every stage of the
question—as far as England at least is concerned, every Englishman
should strive to the utmost of his might that justice shall be done."

He soon proposed a series of resolutions which most comprehensively attacked the Government, and he supported them in a powerful
speech which he thus concluded:

"Sir, there were other days when England was the hope of freedom.
Wherever in the world a high aspiration was entertained or a noble blow
was struck, it was to England that the eyes of the oppressed were always
turned—to this favorite, this darling home of so much privilege and so
much happiness, where the people that had built up a noble edifice for

themselves would, it was well known, be ready to do what in them lay to secure the benefit of the same inestimable boon for others. You talk to me of .the established traditions and policy in regard to Turkey. I appeal to an established tradition, older, wider, nobler far—a tradition not which disregards British interests, but which teaches you to seek the promotion of these interests in obeying the dictates of honor and justice. And, sir, what is to be the end of this? Are we to dress up the fantastic ideas some people entertain about this policy and that policy in the garb of British interests, and then, with a new and base idolatry, fall down and worship them? Or are we to look not at the sentiment, but at the hard facts of the case which Lord Derby told us fifteen years ago— viz., that it is the populations of those countries that will ultimately possess them—that will ultimately determine their abiding condition? It is to this fact, this law, that we should look. There is now before the world a glorious prize. A portion of those unhappy people are still as yet making an effort to retrieve what they have lost so long, but have not ceased to love and to desire. I speak of those in Bosnia and Herzegovina. Another portion—a band of heroes such as the world has rarely seen—stand on the rocks of Montenegro, and are ready now, as they have ever been during the 400 years of their exile from their fertile plains, to sweep down from their fastnesses, and to meet the Turks at any odds for the re-establishment of justice and of peace in those countries. Another portion, still, the 5,000,000 of Bulgarians cowed and beaten down to the ground, hardly venturing to look upwards, even to their Father in Heaven, have extended their hands to you; they have sent you their petition, they have prayed for your help and protection. They have told you that they do not seek alliance with Russia or with any foreign Power, but that they seek to be delivered from an intolerable burden of woe and shame. That burden of woe and shame—the greatest that exists on God's earth—is one that we thought united Europe was about to remove, but to removing which, for the present, you seem to have no efficacious means of offering, even the smallest practical contribution. But, sir, the removal of that load of woe and shame is a great and noble prize. It is a prize well worth competing for. It is not too late to try to win it. I believe there are men in the Cabinet who would try to win it if they were free to act on their own beliefs and aspirations. It is not too late, I say, to become competitors for that prize, but be assured that whether you mean to claim for yourselves even a single leaf in that immortal chaplet of renown, which will be the reward of true labor in that cause, or whether you turn your backs upon that cause and upon your own duty, I believe for one, that the knell of Turkish tyranny in these provinces has sounded. So far as human eye can judge, it is about to be destroyed. The destruction may not come in the way or by the means that we should choose; but come this boon from what hands it may, it will be a noble boon, and as a noble boon will gladly be accepted by Christendom and the world."

One night the House of Commons was thrown into confusion by the startling report that the Russians were in sight of Constantinople. It was a clamorous and wild scene. Although the report was wrong, it carried the English fleet through the Dardanelles, and brought the navy of England within sight of the Turkish capital. It seemed impossible that negotiations between Russia and England could prevent a more serious strife; Russia had entered into negotiations with Turkey in the Treaty of San Stefano; but England would have none of this arrangement. Russia insisted that while her difficulties with Turkey were for herself and Turkey to settle, she was willing to have a congress of the Great Powers. England replied by calling her Indian troops west, and placing them on the Syrian coast and occupying Cyprus. Lord Derby declined to remain with the Ministry, for all his efforts in behalf of peace had failed, and Lord Salisbury took his position. Now a "spirited foreign policy" was made evident by his circular announcing that England would go into no congress in which the Treaty of San Stefano could not be fully considered. Prince Bismarck now interposed. A congress was to be held in Berlin, and the Powers were invited to participate in the discussion which was to involve all the provisions of the San Stefano Treaty. Here was the moment for Lord Beaconsfield, and he seized it with that avidity which he always showed for a dramatic situation. Lord Salisbury was pushed aside, and Beaconsfield strode to Berlin amidst acclamations and scenic glory. Back from Berlin he came, and the crowds which had cheered him on his way thither had doubled in multitude, until their shoutings actually bewildered the supreme actor on that occasion. He had reached the height, and from that moment on, the applause slowly but surely died away.

Lord John Russell had died on the 28th of May, and the depression in trade, coupled with the growing feeling that Beaconsfield's domestic policy had been a steady neglect of the interests of England at home, conspired with disturbances in Ireland to discredit the Government. There was no one in the House of Commons who could attend to Mr. Gladstone in debate, and especially to one other man who had exhibited extraordinary resources and skill, great calmness and assurance in managing the interests of his party, and an all-consuming devotion to his cause,—Charles Stewart Parnell.

The invasion of Afghanistan, directed in a large part by the author of "Lucille," and possessing none of the better characteristics of that sentimental production, added nothing, but took away much from the credit of the Government. The South African war, into which the English Government had gone with the somewhat romantic energy of James Anthony Froude as advisory leader, proved even less wise. A Zulu chief and king, Cetewayo, invited the rivalry of Sir Bartle Frere, and war was declared, and the king finally put on exhibition in London. In the country suffering was increasing constantly. A very severe winter had caused great distress among the working classes, and Ireland was on the edge of a famine. Gladstone had trained Sir Stafford Northcote for many years in debate, and later Disraeli, now Lord Beaconsfield, had coached him as a Tory gladiator, but he could not give him that fortitude and inflexible strength which he so much lacked when he came into the contest with the foes of the Government. Gladstone had defied the ministers to let the constituencies decide as to its worth or worthlessness.

CHAPTER XXXIV.

THE MEMBER FROM MIDLOTHIAN.

The autumn of 1879 came. Gladstone himself was determined to allow Midlothian to decide as to the advisability of his remaining in Parliament. Now began a series of speeches from Gladstone, unexcelled even in the history of that great Commoner. Could he control and conquer a vast assemblage?—his friends even questioned the man of three score and ten. He proved that he was not more out of place on the platform before five thousand people at the Corn Exchange in Edinburgh, or even at the open-air monster meeting in Perth, than he had been in the comparatively small auditorium known as the House of Commons. On the 4th of December he showed something of the versatility of his power as an orator, for at one hour on that day he was addressing an enthusiastic assemblage of 6,000 Scotchmen on politics, while at another hour he had spoken with grace, dignity and elegance, his address as Lord Rector of the University of Glasgow. The Scotch people were wild in their admiration of a Scotchman, who, they said, had only the misfortune of having been born in England. March 8, 1880, the dissolution of Parliament was announced. An overwhelming wave of popular sentiment led on by Gladstone had swept over the ministry. Beaconsfield rose to the occasion and said: "There are some who challenge the expediency of the Imperial character of this realm. Having attempted and failed to enfeeble our colonies by their policy of decomposition, they may now perhaps recognize in the disintegration of the United Kingdom a mode which will not only accomplish, but precipitate that purpose." Gladstone's reply was characteristic and powerful. Lord Derby seceded from Conservatism. The three kingdoms prepared for an intense struggle, and on the 10th of March, Gladstone began his second conquest of the Midlothian country. It was remarkable with what dignity he dealt with the bitterness and apparent malignity of Disraeli's attack. Referring to his opponents, he said:

"I give them credit for patriotic motives; I give them credit for those patriotic motives which are so incessantly and gratuitously denied to us. I believe that we are all united, gentlemen—indeed, it would be most unnatural if we were not—in a fond attachment, perhaps in something of a proud attachment, to the great country to which we belong—to this great Empire which has committed to it a trust and a function given from Providence as special and remarkable as ever was entrusted to any portion of the family of man. Gentlemen, I feel when I speak of that trust and that function that words fail me; I cannot tell you what I think of the nobleness of the inheritance that has descended upon us, of the sacredness of the duty of maintaining it. I will not condescend to make it a part of controversial politics. It is a part of my being, of my flesh and blood, of my heart and soul. For those ends I have labored through my youth and manhood till my hairs are gray. In that faith and practice I have lived; in that faith and practice I will die."

In 1880, during his tour in Scotland, Gladstone's versatility and eloquence were demonstrated by masterly speeches on the finances of the country, and if ever there had been doubt that the younger Pitt was eclipsed by the brilliant display of extraordinary powers of statement and exposition, these speeches settled the question forever. Before audiences excited to exuberant manifestations of patriotism on every hand, Gladstone stood with commanding force, and with unrivaled lucidity explained the finances of the country.

In April, 1880, Lord Beaconsfield dissolved Parliament, producing a result as unforeseen and as destructive to his hopes as was that produced by Gladstone in 1874, when suddenly and against the advice of his colleagues, he persisted in dissolution. Many Liberals still believe that Gladstone's Government in 1874 might have held on and regained the confidence of the country. Nobody thought that Lord Beaconsfield's Government at Easter, 1880, could be far away from a necessary defeat. When the new Parliament came, the uneasy gentlemen who had occupied the "Cave of Adullam," the band of discontented ones under Gladstone's leadership, found that their places knew them no more. Gladstone himself had come back, after having performed a feat uneclipsed in the history of human eloquence. It was evident that the liquor interests had not reappeared with the old sneer and power to obstruct or embarrass the Government. A large number of journalists had become members, and what John Stuart Mill had called the stupidity of the Tories, was set off in contrast with the brilliant literary skill of these new figures in official life. Herbert Gladstone, the son of the statesman, sat for Leeds. The great houses were notably absent, and while questions as to agriculture and the tenure of land were sure to come up, the landed proprietors were now to be associated by representative tenant farmers, who knew at least something about the subject. Fashionable society, of course, which had made Toryism a step to its drawing-room, regarded the whole collection as countrified and generally unpleasant. There sat Mr. Fawcett and Sir Charles Dilke, ready with Radical plans not quite to the liking even of Lord Hartington and Lord Granville, who were undoubted Liberals, but the differences between the elements in the party were bound up with something of amity by the strong hand which led them to this triumph. Since the days of Sir Robert Peel when the Reform Bill had swept England as by a flood, no man had so completely overturned his foes as had Gladstone. After Lord Beaconsfield had gone to Windsor and resigned the seals of his office, Her Majesty sent for Lord Granville to constitute a Government. It was a graceful and perhaps necessary thing to do, but England did not expect Granville to be the Premier, and Granville told the Queen that this was the case. She then sent for Lord Hartington, who was an excellent gentleman, having sense enough, in spite of his general heaviness, to know that one man alone had overturned Beaconsfield and his party, and that his name was not Hartington. She then sent for William Ewart Gladstone, and that night he returned from Windsor once more Prime Minister of England.

Mr. Gladstone found himself in office to meet unexpected problems. He found the Irish question overwhelmingly significant at the very moment when he was trying to deal with the Indian Budget, which latter presented the difficulty consequent upon the fact that fifteen millions, instead of six millions, was the debt made by the Afghan war. The Queen's speech had called attention to the Berlin Treaty, and there were conditions in that document which had not been met. On the 1st of June, it was understood that what was known as the Peace Preservation Act for Ireland would expire. The announcement came that there was no intention on the part of the Government to renew this legislation. The workingmen were told that legislation would be had, making employers liable for certain accidents, and the Irish people were interested to know how far the Borough Franchise was to be extended in their country. Everything was interrogatory, but it could not remain so.

To any persons who met and knew Mr. Charles Bradlaugh during his visit to America, in which he delivered masterly and most eloquent lectures on "Cromwell and Washington," "Republicanism in England" and other kindred subjects, it is unnecessary to speak of the picturesqueness and ineffaceable charm which he brought with him. He always spoke of Mr. Gladstone in most friendly terms, and rehearsed with great interest the story of Gladstone's development from Toryism to Liberalism, dwelling especially upon his attitude toward the Jews in Parliament, the Disestablishment of the Irish Protestant Church, and his manifest sense of justice toward those who differed from him in religious opinions. But it was impossible that Bradlaugh could avoid being a serious thorn in the side of the great Liberal leader. His very genius and love of liberty, which allied him to Gladstone, made it less easy for Gladstone to handle him as he might have done. There were enormous differences between them. Bradlaugh was an atheist and Gladstone the most devoted of churchmen. Bradlaugh had risen from penury and ignorance through countless difficulties to a position in England from which he exercised his marvelous powers of eloquence and the charm of his interesting though somewhat militant personality. He had been a successful lecturer, before audiences whose numbers and enthusiasm had increased as he unfolded his negative and somewhat revolutionary doctrine. He had successfully edited a secularist sheet devoted to the propagation of his theories. He had now been elected to Parliament for Northampton. Nobody had the slightest idea that this magnificently-formed creature was to employ the fighting qualities which had already commended him as a member of the British Army, and that these qualities had open before them a new era, at the moment when he presented himself to be sworn in as a member of the House of Commons. He urged his claim that he be allowed to affirm or declare his allegiance, in place of taking the oath, as was customary. Time after time he had appeared in the highest courts of England, and had been permitted to affirm rather than take the oath under the law known as the Parliamentary Oaths Act of 1866. The Speaker was dumfounded, as he was to be many times afterwards, by the boldness of Bradlaugh's argument, and he asked the House of Commons to decide the matter. A select committee was appointed to report their opinion on the problem and to suggest a way out of the difficulty, and everything appeared to be settled when they reported against Bradlaugh. The latter immediately announced that on the 21st of May he would present himself and offer to take the oath. This was unexpected, and still more unexpected was his defense of his position, in which he insisted that he would regard himself bound only by the spirit which would have been conveyed by an affirmation, for he could not regard seriously the letter of the oath. When that day came he was opposed by Sir H. Drummond-Wolff, who presented a careful and able argument, insisting that Bradlaugh's new position showed that no binding effect on the conscience would be exercised by an oath. At this moment Gladstone proposed the selection of a committee, but he was seriously opposed by those who wished the matter decided at once. Gladstone insisted that it ought to be treated with care and wisdom. His opponents claimed that Bradlaugh had proposed an act of blasphemy. Gladstone and Bright, opposed by Sir Stafford Northcote and Mr. Gibson, argued that religious opinions ought not to be involved in the debate, but that the question ought to be discussed as a question of statute and of justice. At length Mr. Gladstone succeeded, and a committee was appointed.

In the latter part of June, the sprightly and always entertaining editor of Truth, Mr. Henry Labouchere, who also came from Northampton, proposed that Bradlaugh be allowed to affirm or to declare, instead of swear, as was the custom. He moved a resolution on the ground that the statute gave Bradlaugh this right.   All the fearful and extraordinarily religious persons in the House of Commons thronged about Gladstone, and beseeched him to avoid giving comfort or encouragement to so dangerous an infidel as was Bradlaugh.   Gladstone arose in the debate, far above the tumult of religious or irreligious clamor, and made a speech which will be considered a monument in the history of religious toleration. The vote showed that the House of Commons was unwilling that Bradlaugh should be permitted either to swear or to affirm or declare.

At this time they had only begun to be weary of him. The next day Bradlaugh was before the table of the House, asking to be sworn. Being ordered to withdraw, and refusing to obey, the sergeant-at-arms took him into custody on the motion of Sir Stafford Northcote, and he was placed in the clock tower. In twenty-four hours the freed atheist was abroad again in the world, and on July 1st, the piety of England breathed more freely because a resolution had been passed which permitted any person who claimed to be one allowed by law to affirm, to do so, instead of swearing, but leaving him to the consequences of prosecution on a statute making members liable. Of course Bradlaugh affirmed, meanwhile keeping his seat in the House of Commons. Now began a series of lawsuits against him, which left him day by day more and more deeply involved in debt, for every case went against him.

With Bradlaugh's case, for the moment, a little out of the way, Mr. Parnell arose as the fearless and resourceful champion of Ireland. Gladstone had taken his measure at an early date, and with wonderful astuteness he led Parnell into an ever-increasing influence in the House of Commons. Parnell had established the Land League. Mr. Michael Davitt, who had commended himself to Ireland by having been incarcerated in jail as a Fenian, willingly seconded Parnell in his upbuilding this association of tenants in Ireland, and this was done just at the moment when Irish landlords were pursuing a policy of wholesale eviction in the very districts which had suffered most from famine. When the House of Commons had made an heroic effort to legislate in the direction of compensation for these penniless and suffering tenants, the House of Lords, with its usual conservatism, crushed the plan.

Early in January, 1881, it was evident that a struggle was on hand arising from the use of obstruction as a Parliamentary weapon. What was called the "Irish Protection of Property Bill" was to be brought up, and the Queen's speech had already opened a struggle which involved the discussion of the condition of Ireland, and it lasted eight days. Unprecedented as was the length of this debate on the Queen's speech, the most wonderful thing about it was the fact that Mr. Gladstone held his temper in the midst of the most vexatious circumstances. Parnell and his friends repeated uninteresting statements and rehearsed ancient arguments until the members of the House of Commons found that they knew them by heart. Some of the representatives of the English boroughs participated in the discussion and there was almost no opposition on their part to the Bill. After a little time the extremists of the Home Rule party took entire charge of the talk and prosecuted the scheme of putting in the time, and they held to it with a tenacity unparalleled. Adjournments were moved repeatedly, harangues conceived with ingenuity for consuming time were offered, and from night to night the expected division was put off because of the interposition of a new and long-continued speech. Even the usual hour for adjournment made no difference. It was passed and repassed. All night and all day motions and speeches joined with amendments and resolutions continued the sitting. Sometimes Mr. Forster had a sharp tilt with an Irish member, and sometimes a little wit illumined the dullness and hopelessness of the situation. The Government stood with its majority, able to defeat Mr. Parnell and his colleagues in everything but this, while Mr. Parnell and his crowd supplied a speaker whenever one was needed. A systematic effort was made to rest the thirty or forty Home Rulers who had begun to grow weary. Some went home and slept, being careful to return on time and relieve the others who had talked during the night. Then they went to bed. Never before had the House of Commons sat so long, and on Tuesday night the excitement was intense. From every part of London where the lamp could be seen shining still in the high chamber of the tower of the Houses of Parliament, indicating that the House of Commons was still in session, men were gazing in wonder or in wrath that the obstructionists could hold things so long. They were surpassing every like success they had achieved in the past and were emboldened by their triumph. Whips were walking about in the early morning, taking hold of this sleepy member and that and urging them to remain, for it was certain that human nature could not hold out much longer. The ire of those who had endured this persistent obstruction had now arisen and they must speak. There was no slightest indication that the Home Rulers could not have talked on another day or two, but anger was evident upon the faces of those who saw Mr. Gladstone, who had been vainly endeavoring to master the situation and lead the House in the discharge of public business. At the usual breakfast time a highly irritated crowd of members were speaking most bitterly over their morning repast in the breakfast room, into which daylight was coming. The whips suddenly hurried in and the company broke up and rushed to the House. Gladstone, worn, pale and undaunted, had unexpectedly reentered. The Speaker of the House arose and stopped the debate in words that have become famous in the history of Parliamentary proceedings, and asked a vote on the question. Mr. Justin McCarthy, who was leading the Home Rulers in the temporary absence of Mr. Parnell, protested, but he was silenced. Out of the House he strode with his colleagues, all of them shouting "Privilege! Privilege!"

Now those who had endured for so long this method of obstruction expressed their pent-up rejoicings in repeated cheers. Gladstone arose at once and gave notice that he would move resolutions, next day, enabling the House of Commons to proceed with business under the order of the Speaker, who should be invested with new powers for the control of debate. It had taken a great amount of courage on the part of the Speaker; it now remained for Gladstone to use his majority in wisdom. Next day Mr. Parnell and his colleagues, after having thrown the authority of the Speaker to the winds, placed the Government under the necessity of removing them. London was excited and England looked forward to the day when a less sensible and fair presiding officer might abuse the authority with which Gladstone's motion, on that day, had invested the Speaker of the House of Commons. There was no question but that Gladstone emerged from the difficulty to the admiration of all England. He had shown fairness and patience, now he showed decisiveness and strength.

He spoke thus at Leeds, as he spoke elsewhere:

"The way to make England great in the estimation of foreign countries is to let it be known by every one that England desires above all things to be just, and will not seek to impose upon them any laws of action, or any principles for the interpretation of their conduct, except those to which she herself submits."

Referring to Parliament, he said, in another speech:

"The twelve Parliaments in which I have sat have surpassed all their predecessors in the amount of devotion, measured by time and actual expenditure of energy, which they have given to the public service. I know not whether the half-century that is to come—and to it most of you who are here assembled may reasonably look forward, although I may not—will be one which will record upon its annals as many real triumphs, as many records of evil mitigated and of good achieved for the benefit of the Empire and of mankind. God grant it may be so; but of one thing I feel assured, and that is, that the same pride which has conducted and animated the nation during the half-century that is now for me expiring, will continue to subsist in the breasts of my fellow-countrymen under circumstances equally favorable, and will not fail to produce at least equally favorable results."—Speech at the London Guildhall, Oct. 14.

Large and international hopes were making him England's "Old Man Eloquent."

GLADSTONE AND HIS GRANDCHILD

PRINCE OF WALES' VISIT

CHAPTER XXXV.

THE IRISH PROBLEM AGAIN.

Now even Gladstone's heart was faint at the unexpected behavior of the Irish people, while murder followed murder in that unhappy country. It was impossible that Gladstone, pledged as were his heart, intellect and conscience to redeem Ireland, could avoid favoring a Coercion Bill, which, in turn, simply provoked the Irish people to more outrages. He was at work on a Land Bill, which, at a later time, was to be offered and its wisest provisions to be torn out ruthlessly by the House of Lords. Ireland arose against him in the rural districts and at Dublin, and Mr. Parnell, aided by powerful colleagues, pursued the policy of obstructing everything in the House of Commons, until the cry of Ireland for self-government should be heard. Years afterward, Mr. Gladstone admitted that he had inherited so much of embarrassment and labor consequent upon the misgovernment under Beaconsfield, that he had no just conception of the Irish problem at that moment. He had done much for Ireland, but he had done just enough to get Ireland on the way in the evolution of righteous government, or in a revolution which they seemed willing to undertake. He had so far believed that the Irish question was settled that the Queen's speech did not mention the subject. Mr. William E. Forster, a most sagacious, well-meaning and able gentleman, was Chief Secretary for Ireland, and his Bill, known as the Compensation for Disturbance Bill, had been rejected by the House of Lords, leaving the peasant farmers of Ireland to make their own fight against the landlords who persistently evicted them.

In August, 1880, Mr. Forster said that he did not think the Houses "would expect him to remain the instrument of that injustice." More than 17,000 persons were evicted, and in most cases the farms upon which they had lived had been greatly improved by them; in

20

some cases the Fen-country had been redeemed and made valuable and productive soil by their labors. The League attempted to do what they believed the Government ought to have been doing, and crime was rampant everywhere. Under the influence of Mr. Forster, prosecutions were ordered which reached Mr. Parnell and his colleagues. Now the Gladstone Government and the Irish contingent, led by Mr. Parnell, were at swords points in the House of Commons. Surely the Coercion Bill of Mr. Forster, which enabled him, by signing a warrant, to put any man in jail if he suspected him to have committed an offense, and all this without trial, was a hard thing for the Irish people to bear, and a difficult thing for Gladstone to defend. Murder so followed upon the heels of outrage in Ireland that it may be said the Irish people forced Mr. Gladstone, at the very hour they ought to have awaited his evident design to help them, to make this formidable legislation effective. Never was Mr. Gladstone placed in such an unhappy position. He rushed forward with all his energies to the introduction of his Land Bill, and on April 7th he offered this conciliatory legislation. At last he defended the proposition that the State ought to stand between the domineering landlord and the half-crushed tenant and do justice to both. Of course he had been urged so rapidly by events to this measure that it lacked perfection, and it could not represent all the wisdom and humanity in his nature. But the Bill remains as a most heroically conceived page in the statutory progress of mankind. It seemed a brighter day had come when the Land Commissioners, which the Government appointed under this Act, assembled in Dublin Castle, where they were selected, and confronted the bitterness which had grown in Ireland from the fact that it had been asserted that landlordism would choose these Commissioners. Parnell had advised the selection of a few special cases, out from the multitude which the farmers wanted, to place in the hands of the land courts. He wished in this way to test the good faith of the Government. Of course the Government regarded this as equivocal and demagogic. Even Mr. Gladstone labored with Mr. Parnell and insisted that the action gave the appearance of wishing to keep the people from the benefit of his Act.

Mistake followed mistake on both sides. In October Parnell and several of his colleagues in the House of Commons, with numerous other leaders elsewhere, were arrested, the Land League was declared an illegal association, and everywhere was confusion. Ireland would not wait a moment for Mr. Gladstone, though at that hour Mr. Gladstone was making such speeches as should indicate his lack of sympathy with the policy of coercion, and his deep study on the subject of Ireland's woes. He said to the representative of Ireland:

"My Lord Mayor, it is not with the people of Ireland that we are at issue. . . . It is not on any point connected with the exercise of local government in Ireland—it is not even on any point connected with what is popularly known in that country as Home Rule, and which may be understood in any one of a hundred senses, some of them perfectly acceptable and even desirable; others of them mischievous and revolutionary. . . . I for one will hail with satisfaction and delight any measure of local government for Ireland, or for any portion of the country, provided only that it conform to this one condition—that it shall not break down or impair the supremacy of the Imperial Parliament."

Hardly less fortunate was the position of Mr. Forster, the Chief Secretary. There is no doubt that Mr. Forster's failure to help Ireland broke his heart. From early life he had interested himself in her relief. No man had given more freely of his time and money and labor, and he sincerely believed, when he became Chief Secretary, that something could be done definitely to conclude the unpleasantness between Ireland and England. He counted too much upon the suspicion that Irish agitators were misrepresenting the people of Ireland and were leading the tenant-farmers to desire and demand what otherwise they would not care for. He had too much faith in the jail as a means of repressing free thought on political subjects. Every priest and poor-law guardian whom he locked up was one more man of the many who were thus taken from the communities which they might have controlled and restrained from acts of violence. Ireland was a camp, and Mr. Forster rode away dispirited and broken.

If ever the great heart of one, set upon devising liberal things for a hot-headed yet wronged people, was struck in the moment of his deepest hope for them, it was Gladstone; when the news came to London that Lord Frederick Cavendish, the new Chief Secretary, and Mr. Thomas Burke, an official in Dublin Castle, had been foully assassinated in Phœnix Park, Dublin. Mr. Parnell was just out of jail, and Gladstone had then arranged to bring in what was called an Arrears Bill which offered great relief to Ireland. At this moment civilization was made to shudder before the prostrate and hacked bodies of these two representatives of law and order. The storm which raged around Gladstone grew in fierceness, and it almost seemed at one time that the opponents of his Government could not be responsible for his life. Parnell generously offered to retire from Parliament and public life, if Gladstone said the word. With equal magnanimity and with dauntless heroism Gladstone stood in the midst of the tempest like a pillar, against which Parnell was commanded still to lean, and the pillar moved not while the tumult raged. Of course the effect of this most cruelly conceived and executed murder was inimical to Ireland, yet at that moment Gladstone took hold of the wronged and needy country with more affection and hope than ever.

It is at this time that some old and affectionate friends departed from him. Many upon whom he felt he had the right to count failed to indorse his course. Principal Tulloch's biography furnishes a portrait of a really noble mind perplexed, if not outraged by Gladstone's policy:

"Did you hear yesterday," (May 7, 1882,) he says, "the appalling news from Ireland?

"It came to Eton at midday, just as we were coming out of the chapel. Professor Knight had come down from town, bringing an 'Observer' with the dreadful announcement. Everybody was excited beyond measure. There is something diabolical in the business, and you may imagine the state in which London has been, and still is. It will cover the end of Gladstone's career with disastrous disgrace, and, I should think, break to pieces the Liberal party. The sooner, in fact, this is done, the better. The first article in the 'Times' expresses my views about the matter better than anything I have seen elsewhere. They may say what they like about the 'Times,' it rises to a great occasion, and I have seen no writing on the subject at once so justly indignant and yet so controlled. Of course the

Government acted for the best; but nothing can excuse their course in breaking with Mr. Forster, and if the result was brought about, as the best informed here believe, by a Radical intrigue within the Cabinet, it could only end in disgraceful ruin, as it has done. W. E. G. is no doubt a great man, but he is both perilously facile and self-willed, which is a disastrous combination of qualities for a statesman; and that his star should sink, as I have little doubt it must, in such a miserable and awful collapse, is pitiful indeed. And yet who can take his place? The whole party business has worked itself out, and what the country needs is a combination of wise and sensible men on both sides, which the Radicals, of course, would do their best to prevent."

Meantime Mr. Gladstone's greatest rival, Lord Beaconsfield, had terminated his career. It was Gladstone's proposition that the ashes of his most distinguished political foe should be buried in Westminster Abbey with proper ceremonies, but Lord Beaconsfield's will had given other instructions, and he was buried at Hughenden. Mr. Gladstone, on the 9th of May, made a motion that Her Majesty be presented with an address asking her to direct the erection of a monument in Westminster Abbey to Lord Beaconsfield. In spite of the opposition of the Liberal party, after a noble speech, Mr. Gladstone carried his motion.

On May 15th Gladstone introduced the Arrears Bill, in which the Irish Church surplus, and, in the case of its failure to furnish enough money, a Consolidated Fund was to supply the amount necessary to pay the landlords half the remaining arrears after the tenant had paid his year's rent due for 1881, in so far as he might, the holding being under thirty pounds valuation. By this Bill either landlord or tenant could apply to the Land Court for justice. After a stormy time in the House of Commons, where it was much changed in unimportant particulars, and a fight in the House of Lords, this legislation was passed.

Now stepped into the arena of debate the towering form of Charles Bradlaugh. Sir Stafford Northcote's motion had prevented his taking the oath on the 7th of February. The effort to obtain the issue of a new writ for Northampton had failed, even though the editor of "Truth" had urged it with singular powers of persuasion. There seemed nothing else for Bradlaugh to do but to swear himself in, and one day the Speaker and the House of Commons were amazed to behold this undesired presence before the table, where he proceeded to administer the oath to himself. Still Gladstone would not interpose against Bradlaugh, though the scene was becoming ludicrous in the extreme. The House expelled him, and Northampton re-elected him, and, for a little time, Bradlaugh reposed upon his questionable honors.

One of the inheritances from the Government of Jingoism under Beaconsfield which annoyed Gladstone seriously, was the Eastern question. In August, 1877, Mr. Gladstone had written an important article in the "Nineteenth Century" called "Aggression on Egypt and Freedom in the East."

He thus wrote of the material greatness of England, saying:

"The root and pith and substance of the material greatness of our nation lies within the compass of these islands; and is, except in trifling particulars, independent of all and every sort of political dominion beyond them. This dominion adds to our fame, partly because of its moral and social grandeur, partly because foreigners partake the superstitions, which still to no small extent prevail among us, and think that in the vast aggregate of our scattered territories lies the main secret of our strength."

He continued, saying:

"Nations are quite as much subject as individuals to mental intemperance; and the sudden flash of wealth and pride, which engenders in the man arrogant vulgarity, works by an analogous and subtler process upon numbers who have undergone the same exciting experience. Indeed, they are the more easily misled, because conscience has not to reproach each unit of a mass with a separate and personal selfishness. With respect to the Slav provinces, the 'strong man' of British interests, of traditional policy, and of hectoring display, has been to a great degree kept down by a 'stronger man;' by the sheer stern sense of right and wrong, justice and injustice, roused in the body of the people by manifestations of unbounded crime. But it may be very doubtful whether, in questions where ethical laws do not so palpably repress the solicitations of appetite, the balance of forces will be so cast among us as to insure the continuance of that wonderful self-command, with which the nation has now for so long a time resisted temptation, detected imposture, encouraged the feeble virtues, and neutralized the inveterate errors of its rulers."

CHAPTER XXXVI.

GLADSTONE AND BRIGHT.

Egypt, however, had been occupied by English troops, and under the leadership of Arabi Pasha, an insurrection had sprung up against the Khedive. Soon the English guns were heard bombarding Alexandria.

Before this action had been taken an event occurred in the history of Mr. Gladstone's friendships which touched his heart deeply. On the 17th of July, John Bright came into the House of Commons, and his very manner betokened that his relations to Mr. Gladstone's Government had been changed. On the second bench below the gangway he sat, pale and yet massive in his nobility, and every eye was upon him. It was almost impossible to proceed with the disposition of the usual questions, and as soon as this matter was disposed of, the room was full of cries for Bright. He rose with great dignity, and with perfect sobriety of utterance and evident sorrow addressed the House, to which Gladstone replied in excellent taste.

Mr. John Bright was something more than an orator of highest quality and of widest popularity, more than a statesman of profound sagacity and constructive force, even more than an assailant of respectable iniquity and a champion of neglected justice; he was an influence, a spiritual guide in practical affairs, a serene presence in stormy hours, a fortress of belief standing for a divine and eternal order, a pillar of fire radiant and even warm,—brilliant, genial, and pervasive—as he moved on toward the dream and reality of the measureless peace. Indeed, his career and his message may never be understood, except as one recognizes at the first that he was above all a man of peace and what sort of peace he stood for. His peace was not the peace of weakness awed and crushed by power, not the peace of surrender to haughty evil, not the peace of brainless stagnation and thoughtless acquiescence, still less the peace of hopelessness and death; but his was the peace of power. "My peace I leave with you!" said his Master, and Him this affectionate disciple always obeyed. He trusted truth; he believed in ideas; he risked all upon principles; he was sure of the victory for peace, because they were and are for peace, and theirs is the only triumph men or nations can afford to seek or to have. He detested war, because war is an abandonment of the conviction that ideas rule. He knew that military glory is barbarous, and he saw that a nation sheathed in steel is and must be a weak nation, having lost confidence in the power of truth to make its way in the world, or, worse still, having truth against her, and vainly thinking to resist such a divine antagonist. He had been reared in and he represented an industrial constituency, and war paralyzes industry and cheats the laborer. He was one of the common people, a friend at their firesides, and war runs its red desolation through the homes of the poor and the middle classes; theirs is the agony and catastrophe of battle urged on, too often, by the favored classes who leave no widows and orphans by the bellicose cnaracter of speech or act, who also succeed in arranging it so that the taxation consequent upon the triumph of hate and the well-nigh intolerable burdens resulting from the anger they have fomented, must be borne and cared for by the common people. Therefore the phrase "honor" did not mean "war" in his or in the true vocabulary of England. When England went to war with China and with Russia, England must have his condemnation and Manchester his seat. When the South fired on Fort Sumter to protect slavery, he knew she had lost faith in truth or truth was against her, and he gave his eloquence to the other side, whose captain cried out: "Let us have peace!" When the guns of his own dear England discharged their missiles upon Alexandria, he vacated his lofty seat and broke his official relationship with his great and loved friend, Gladstone. He feared and loved God absolutely, as he did and could none else. He had no use for Jingoism, be it born in any quarter whatsoever. "The sword," said Hugo, "is a flash in the darkness; right is the eternal ray." And Bright believed this without faltering.

What had united Gladstone to him in bonds of secure and deep friendship was not learning, for, in the sense in which Gladstone was,

Bright was not, a learned man. He was educated in the lore of God, and he did know and believe in the possibilities of human nature ultimately to see and to do the truth. Not many, but some languages were his; not a multitude, but several philosophers he had mastered; not all the patristic writers, but some and all the evangelists and apostles, prophets and heroes he knew with profoundest sympathy; not the whole classical world and its chief figures were his study, but he knew the lowly, the needy, and the helpless in his own time; not Æschylus, Euripides, Homer and Horace, so much as Dante, Shakespeare, Milton, and freedom-loving Whittier, fed his soul; but above all these, he so loved and understood the Bible, and he so nourished his mighty spirit on its poetry, its worship, its hope, that Bright and Gladstone found a companionship of spirits as perfect as it was beautiful and blessed. Deep were the streams of religious aspirations running through both natures, though Gladstone was a High Churchman of the Episcopal order, and Bright was a plain Quaker. Each of these men saw light in His light from different points of view. Gladstone's almost immeasurable catholicity of mind is illustrated in the letters written to John Henry Newman, who went to Rome, and John Bright, who "stood on a tombstone in Rochdale Churchyard and denounced Church Rates," and wanted no Bishop in the House of Lords, maintaining that the Lord's Supper, which, to Gladstone, was invested with sacramental graces, could be only a friendly meal with no authority as to its recurrence. In all his relations with Bright, Gladstone knew that he was dealing with one of the most sincerely religious, as well as one of the most courageously independent men in all the kingdom. He was aware that this man had no use whatever for his own doctrines as to the relations of Church and State. A Christianity needing a State's support is the King of Kings on a crutch of wood, and a State needing an established Church is a government leaning on a well-paid phantom. Bright had always maintained that a majority of the nation had forsaken the English Church, and he thought that to be taxed to support it was a proposal worthy of opposition. He never felt that a Dissenter ought to be treated as an outlaw. But Gladstone must always be reckoned upon as a man of too deep piety and too earnest devotion to God to fail in appreciating and calling to his aid a man who possessed the manly vigor of faith, the uncasuistical zeal, the robust austerity of conduct, the affectionateness of devotion, the power of discerning and obeying the highest revelation of truth, characteristic of the nature and temper of John Bright.

For the greater part of the career of each, they were sworn allies in the fight for the victory of that true and just Liberalism which is bound to rule the future. Gladstone felt with Bright, and would have acted with him in the matter of the Crimean War, if the former had not been of that impressionable and agile nature which yielded perhaps enough to his Oxford training. Gladstone's father had used slavery to advance his interests as a merchant; the Quakers violently abhorred slavery, and Gladstone and Bright parted on the question of the Civil War in America, although it must be remembered, as we have said, in justice to Gladstone, that he favored the education of the slaves held by English interests, and hoped, in that way, to help them to freedom. They were bound to part on the Irish question, and Bright had opposed the bombardment of Alexandria. Greater than their differences were their alliances, for each of these men could pronounce the word God, in the flood of splendid eloquence, and not feel it necessary to tell a nerveless and materialistic England that he felt bound to offer an apology for his belief that the secret of all true statesmanship lies in finding in what direction the Almighty One is going. These men had the faith that God moves to great ends by means of and through human advancement, and statesmanship is the art of getting things,—trade, art, institutions, social forms, and whatever else—out of His track, or, better still, getting them all into His chariot, that they may not be crushed beneath the wheels; nay, rather that they may be borne on to His ends.

We have it from Gladstone's own lips that he admired and relied upon Bright's oratorical gifts and the exercise of their power as much as Bright did upon his own. In eloquence, they were as different only as their natures and methods of culture. Gladstone drew from fountains unknown to Bright's limited knowledge. Bright drank from streams unvisited by Gladstone's unsurpassed and somewhat aristocratic

erudition. The human soul Bright knew, and it is greater than all the
literature or history it has produced; the fairest and most luminous page
it has written or inspired Gladstone knew, but these alone he knew as
Bright knew the soul of man, and, therefore, while Gladstone surpassed
him by reaching laterally the length and breadth of man's concerns and
treating them with lucidity and learning, Bright surpassed Gladstone by
reaching depths of passion and power, and heights of aspiration and
hope which he alone, of modern English orators, saw and understood.
When Bright poised himself for flight, when the concerns of suffering
humanity had no other voice amidst the din of ignorant sovereignties
clashing themselves to fury, or the patronizing silence of intelligence
softly resting in its fancied security, England at last recognized the fact
that he had a realm all his own, and so easily masterful then was his
intellect and conscience of even his great physical powers that he rose
to heights not reached by men of less lofty spiritual capability of imagination.

Disraeli alone sparkled, as did he, in lively epigram, and burned,
as did he, in caustic irony or penetrative wit. Not even Disraeli surpassed him in scorching sarcasm, and Bright possessed a world of
humor, sweet and wide, to which the great British phrase-maker was a
stranger. Speaking of Disraeli's high-sounding plan for Irish pacification, he said:

" . . . . It reminds me of an anecdote, which is related by Addi-
son. Writing about the curious things which happened in his time, he says
there was a man who made a living by cheating the country people. I
do not know whether it was in Buckinghamshire or not. (Laughter.)
He was not a cabinet minister—he was only a montebank—(great laughter)—and he set up a stall, and sold pills that were very good against the
earthquake. (Roars of laughter.) Well, that is about the state of things
that we are in now. There is an earthquake in Ireland. Does anybody
doubt it?"

As the champion of Gladstone, he answered Disraeli's complaint
that the former had "harassed every trade, worried every profession,
and assailed or menaced every class, institution or species of property
in the country." Bright caught the word "harass," as he often found a

term and invested it with an unexpected force by placing it to a surprising use. He said in reply, concerning the Tories: "Without doubt,
if they had been in the Wilderness they would have condemned the Ten
Commandments as a harassing piece of legislation, though it does happen that we have the evidence of more than thirty centuries to the wisdom and usefulness of those commandments." He never permitted
himself to use the weapon of scorn which showed its edge now and
then, and he preferred to match Disraeli's air of superiority, when he
sneered, with imperturbable dignity or gay humor. Gladstone's personality, Disraeli's personality, if he really had one, were no more truly
set forth in their speeches than was Bright's in his own. In tacking
ship, as we have indicated, there are moments when the sailor himself
seems to depend on a most tricky wind, and Gladstone's mind often
seemed quite uncertain as to just what he would do with the sails. He
says "perhaps," "one might say," "possible view of the case," and numerous other phrases which make one feel that he does not grasp the lines
with any clear plan as to the next movement. But he is handling a ship
on board of which is a noisy lot of people who have to be consulted—
he is feeling of them, feeling of the sea, feeling of the air itself. When
he knows, his every nerve is lightning, and his slightest touch has the
assurance of measureless strength allied with a purpose as inevitable
as gravitation. Bright had only the greatest admiration for Gladstone's
ability to do this and for his boundless industry and happy fortune in
keeping in with the crew, wind, and tide, and yet ruling them. But there
it ended, for Bright was as little laborious as even a poetic and eloquent
commoner could be. Gladstone scarcely ever withdrew from the windows of himself,—his eyes shone with the soul looking out, eager to
flash its message or to scan the situation. He almost never seemed other
than intense and interested. Bright often went far behind those blue
eyes of his and retired from the fortress-like countenance, and, having
found a good soft place, he rested. When he came back he saw straight
before him, and had not a moment for an ambiguous phrase; the foe
was clearly beheld; the stroke was brilliant and sure as fate.

CHAPTER XXXVII.

EGYPT AND DEFEAT.

Meantime the British Government was attempting to put down the rebellion, and an important expedition under General Wolseley had routed the Egyptians out of Tel-el-Kebir. There can be no question that Gladstone had been forced into despatching this army, and that, as Prime Minister, he was following up an initiative which his own brain and heart and conscience never would have made, but for which he was now to bear the responsibility, and for whose unfortunate issue he was to carry odium to the end of his career. The Jingo policy of Beaconsfield had gotten into the blood of the present Government, and it was impossible for Gladstone and other Liberal leaders to get it out until the war was on, and everywhere in England Tories and dissenting Liberals were taunting Gladstone for having adopted a policy as fantastic and belligerent as Beaconsfield's, both toward Ireland in Acts of Coercion and toward Egypt in prosecuting strife in the Soudan. London opinion was noisy and uncontrollable under the leadership of the "Pall Mall Gazette." It had previously demanded that at once no less a prominent figure and brave soldier than Charles George Gordon should be sent to handle the difficulties at Khartoum. Sir Garnet Wolseley's expedition was now pressing on to his relief. Never were two men more deeply trusted than were Gordon and Wolseley. The former had always carried the heart of the British nation. In 1880 he had visited Ireland and had written to the "London Times:" "I have lately been over the Southwest of Ireland, in the hope of discovering how some settlement could be made of the Irish question, which, like a fretting cancer, eats away our vitals as a nation. No half-measure acts," he added, "which left the landlord with any say to the tenantry of these portions of Ireland, will be of any use. They would be rendered, as past Land Acts in Ireland have been, quite abortive; for the landlords will insert clauses to do away with their force. Any half-measures will only place the Government face to face with the people of Ireland as the champion of the landlord class." He proposed that £80,000,000 be spent to transform the southwestern portion of Ireland into Crown Land, where landlordism should not reign.

England had heard him and admired him unreservedly for his heroism, his high personal character, and, above all, for that glowing chivalry which his presence kindled in the hearts of those who knew him. Wolseley as a soldier had proven himself able to carry through other daring achievements such as this. Far away from the scene, England watched day by day, hoping that Wolseley might be able to relieve Gordon.

At the instant when Gordon was most dear to the heart of the realm, and when Wolseley was thought to be on the point of relieving him, the news came to England that Gordon had been murdered at Khartoum. In this awful calamity the people of England almost forgot that Gladstone had concluded the war with the Boers in South Africa in a way that afterwards brought honor to his name. His Government blundered here. London was wild with wrath against Gladstone for the failure of his Government to relieve Gordon. He was the subject of scorn and severest censure on almost every hand. Even a year after the sad event, Andrew Lang found an echo in the English heart for such a sonnet as this:

"To-morrow is a year since Gordon died!
  A year ago to-night, the Desert still
  Crouched on the spring, and panted for its fill
Of lust and blood. Their old art statesman plied,
And paltered, and evaded, and denied;
  Guiltless as yet, except for feeble will,
  And craven heart, and calculated skill
In long delays, of their great homicide.

"A year ago to-night 't was not too late.
  The thought comes through our mirth, again, again;
Methinks I hear the halting foot of Fate
  Approaching and approaching us; and then
Comes cackle of the House, and the Debate!
  Enough; he is forgotten amongst men."

There can be no doubt that Englishmen will be divided for many years to come as to the value of Mr. Gladstone as a minister in foreign affairs. Americans have a point of view with reference to this topic which is not shared by our English friends. There has never been a spirit in America, and there never can be, let us hope, such as England experienced during those days when a Jingo policy was a passport in British society, and when any most stupid man who talked about Imperial plans and Imperial interests, and Imperial enterprises, was supposed to possess a sagacity to which men of the intellectual caliber of Mr. Gladstone, could not, by some unhappy fault of nature, attain. The truth is that Gladstone's indiscretions as a foreign Minister have all been owing to his yielding somewhat to a Toryism from which at last he entirely freed himself. He did not have use for their word "Imperialism;" he was the famous opposer of their schemes. No man had a more serious or complicated problem that he, an English statesman living in the time of Benjamin Disraeli, who found that characteristic and pestiferous demand amongst Englishmen to have a hand in everybody's affairs and to reduce the islands of the sea and the States of both continents, if possible, into a sort of federation which shall have its chief loyalty at Westminster and its chief glory in the sovereign of the British Isles. The conception of peace which has ruled in England for many years has not been such as would allow a man like Gladstone to be thoroughly trusted. He found endless difficulty in going as far as he did toward peace with all the world, because of the fact that the little Island gets crowded, and that Jingoism, in one form or another, contaminates the air. Certainly no one can condemn Gladstone,—perhaps with a single exception, when Gordon was not relieved at Khartoum in time, and we reverently believe that there may have been insuperable difficulties before Gladstone in this case; he had been slow to get into trouble, but powerful and rapid enough when the strife was on. Surely his treatment of Russia gave the conscience and business sense of England a noble example of calmness, and Gladstone was surrounded by as much bellicose talk as ever annoyed a British statesman.

It is hard to say whether the Tory party has always wanted war because Gladstone was a man of peace, or has always hated Mr. Gladstone because it wanted war for the sake of seeming to be patriotic and thoroughly British.

There is no doubt that Gladstone was a man of large sentiment, and that John Bull is not particularly sentimental except in minor matters. Disraeli could not hesitate with reference to what ought to be done in view of the Bulgarian atrocities, for Toryism did not believe much in atrocities that would annoy its Administration, and Disraeli could not vacillate. He was cock-sure, as Toryism is always cock-sure of what is to be done. The few phrases of his with regard to an Imperial policy might have lifted Tory England to her feet in antagonism to some people who would fain keep their own territory and maintain their own Government, but Toryism would never lavish a taking phrase in the name of humanity. Inhumanity never vacillates; it goes at things with a bludgeon. It is a remarkable fact that nothing else hits the rabble on the street and tickles the fancy of one of those relics of feudalism safe in his castle, so certainly as opposition to a foreign policy conceived by a man of peace. When convictions and ideas are the basis of a man's action, he may be supposed to hesitate and to consider, as did Mr. Gladstone. When he believes in persuasion and is such a master of debate as was Gladstone, he is perhaps likely to argue too long and to seek to win over a foe while the foe is preparing to deal him a death-blow. But the error in this direction is certainly less ignoble than the error in the other direction. Gladstone's powerful personality had stood for peace and for ideas. He had undertaken the enterprise of Government with the faith that men must be reasoned with and persuaded from wrong causes to right causes. Whenever any nation in weakness has looked toward England's strength, it has believed also that, with Mr. Gladstone at the helm, England could be reasoned with, and perhaps persuaded. No small nation has ever thought that her Toryism had any such qualities. So long as Gladstone held sway it was evident that his remarkable abilities, his regard for the opinions of others, and his high personal character, as well as his confidence in Christian principles, made it possible to accept justly from the nation of which he was a single citizen, some such reasonable adjustment of difficulties just arisen as would postpone and perhaps nullify the barbarism of war. Mr. Gladstone always believed in and practiced the noble art of educating his party. Of course, he influenced his party by the impetuosity of his eloquence and the richness of his imagination, and he added to the impulse and imaginativeness of the English people. But he did not train them to yield to the impulse for contention, nor to imagine reasons for strife where none existed. A "vigorous foreign policy" is not Gladstone's phrase, and taken alone, it is a very silly phrase from any one. A reasonable foreign policy is much nobler, even though such a policy should pause and reflect and argue and seek to persuade one moment too long, in a given case. An unreasoning man—that is, a man who is not open to anything which may change his opinion—is always sure that the reasoning man is fickle and incompetent; and a soul able to poise and consider, as was the soul of Gladstone, is very certain to be accused of procrastination.

Gladstone's policy in Egypt was not "vigorous," either in the direction of annexation or in the direction of a protectorate. He had already asserted that he would be true to the Liberal opinion of England in 1880, that he understood the principles on which that victory was won, and that victory did not contemplate a Tory program. To assume supreme authority in Egypt was not what Gladstone's conscience or intellect meant to do. The Beaconsfield ministry had been condemned. Whenever Gladstone has failed to follow out a Tory policy with reference to a foreign country, as he did in this case, he has been called a man indifferent to the honor of the British Empire. "The honor of the British Empire" is a phrase, and a poor phrase, in a case like this. The Disraeli Government was dishonorable to the

21

ideals of the English nation worthiest of English loyalty and devotion.
Still more, when he was leader in the House of Commons in 1877, he
offered resolutions upon the action of the Government relative to Turkey. He wished to avert the war which Beaconsfield was fomenting.
Great Britain and Russia, however, could not discipline or advise Turkey successfully. But Gladstone was anxious that the trial should be
made. He was therefore not to be condemned because, afterwards,
when a war broke out, he could not follow up that war with his personal enthusiasm. It may seem like a plea for Sunday-school politics,—
but, after all, Sunday-school politics have civilized most of the planet,—
if we say that Mr. Gladstone had been a Christian and believed that the
blessings of peace are greater than the triumphs of war. Extension of
territory for the sake of Imperial England is not commending itself
to the greatest or best of English thinkers. Annexation is not a
victory for civilization in every case. Gladstone's relations to
Egyptian affairs had been imposed upon him by inheritance, and by
the fact that then there was no different policy which would not have
wrought greater disaster. No Englishman in 1886 could say that he
was particularly proud of the fact that England had meddled with
Egyptian affairs. But England demanded that Gladstone should do
something. He adopted a policy in the face of the fact that another
policy would have abolished the liberty of Egypt, and that it would
have imperiled England's advance in the Indian Empire. There is no
question that Gordon's personality, chivalrous, saintly, heroic, gave
Mr. Gladstone's good name a more serious difficulty out of which it
should come unscathed, than if he had been less knightly and beloved.
One must ask what would have been the case if a more practicable and
less romantic nature had entered into the service of the Government,
before Gladstone is condemned in a wholesale manner. It is doubtful
if even Gladstone's imagination might have anticipated the difficulties
which Gordon's own genius created. Surely the expedition into the
Soudan by General Hicks was not very wise, and Gladstone was not
responsible for it. The trap into which Gordon walked was made
certainly not less fatal by his own peculiarities of nature. He ought

perhaps never to have been sent on the mission. The garrisons could have made their own adjustments as well as he, and they could have made them better than he, who, as the most fascinating and admired figure of the moment, was offered as the one who ought to go, largely because the excitement of party feeling had been lifted to that point by an unpatriotic opposition to the ministry. Here was Mr. Gladstone's mistake. He yielded to public opinion in London, and it seems almost as theatrical a thing as Lord Beaconsfield could have done. It was a moment in which the most unscrupulous lovers of money slipped into partnership with unselfish chivalry, and the sacrifice was made. Here Mr. Gladstone was working for peace. He might have stepped down from office rather than agree to the shout of London: "Send Gordon!" But then it would have been to let in upon the Parliament a party whose policy was opposed to the every truest interest, both of England at home and Egypt abroad. There is no real reason why England should consider some of her own citizens unpatriotic and Americans Anglophobists because it appears to them that she is not created by destiny or Providence to dictate to all the world. Gladstone's idea of what constitutes a great nation will never be satisfactory to those who believe that British sovereignty ought to grow by extension of territory. And it was with these ideas in mind that a large number of Nonconformists, who had been exiled from him, gave Mr. Gladstone their unswerving support in his later dealings with Russia.

Never had a man worked more definitely and self-sacrificingly for honorable peace. This was the refrain in all he said:

"War for a bad cause has this apology, that the bad cause may in good faith be mistaken for a good one; and in this case it is preferable to a war for no cause at all. The blind fanaticism which calls evil good and good evil, and which includes something besides self in the scope of its desire, is less ignoble than the cynical indifference which accepts war and all its horrors without watching or caring how lie the weights in the scale of justice. Men talk as if we were free to fight, as a Scotch lord would fight in Edinburgh three centuries ago for the centre of the causeway; or as a boy fought at Eton in my time to determine whether he could or could not 'lick' another boy; or as in Ireland, at a fair, shillelahs were flourished, and heads cruelly mauled and broken, for the simple preference of one name to another; or for the pleasure of that excitement which fighting brings. If we are to revive, in the present daylight, the levities of childhood, the manners of a semi-barbarous age, or the excesses pardonable in an over-driven people, it is high time to take heed and make some inquiry concerning the paths of honour and of shame. A war undertaken without cause is a war of shame and not of honour."

Thus and thus only did he look with hope on England's future.

Gladstone's Government was now trembling under the shock of the repeated attacks made by the Opposition from points of view which these facts supplied them. On the 13th of December, 1882, however, his house was opened, and friends, postmen and telegraph messengers brought countless messages while he was celebrating the fact that, fifty years before, on that day, he had entered Parliament.

In the course of the year 1883 his health was seriously affected, but a month or so at Cannes, and the delight of having his family and books about him at Hawarden Castle reinvigorated the old statesman, and he was soon back in Parliament, introducing an Affirmation Bill which was aimed at settling the Bradlaugh controversy. In this debate he uttered eloquence which for brilliancy and force was not surpassed by any effort of his life. The Bill failed, and he turned his attention to the Agricultural Bill and the Corrupt Practices Bill. He advocated a Franchise Act* which gave the counties Household Suffrage, and a new law for the redistribution of seats in Parliament. But the fate of his Government was decided. On the proposal of the Budget he was defeated, and while the streets of London were still echoing the words: "Bradlaugh and Gordon," Mr. Salisbury was made Prime Minister of England.

---

*Mr. James Russell Lowell talked with him at this time on the Franchise Bill, and congratulated him that he had included Ireland. He said to Lowell: "I had rather the heart were torn out of my breast than that clause out of the Bill."

CHAPTER XXXVIII.

CALLED AGAIN TO POWER.

It was evident in the early autumn that England was again disappointed with Toryism. The battle was now on and speakers were discoursing everywhere in the Kingdom. It was clear to all Englishmen when Parliament was prorogued August 14th, that any appeal to the country would cause widespread enthusiasm and profound interest on both sides. Mr. Gladstone's manifesto was an address characteristic of his spirit and its increasing intensity of conviction, and Midlothian was asked again to help him to "maintain the supremacy of the Crown, the unity of the Empire, and all the authority necessary for the conservation of that unity." He trusted that the Electors believed with him that this was "the first duty of every representative of the people." There was one sentence in his manifesto charged with unsuspected and irrepressible significance. He said: "Subject to this governing principle, every grant to portions of the country of enlarged powers for the management of their own affairs, is, in my view, not a source of danger, but a means of averting it, and in the nature of a new guarantee for increased cohesive happiness and strength."

Scotland had been Gladstonian, but it must not be supposed that all Scotch people were pleased now. Principal Tulloch's biographer, writing of that time, says:

"In the Highlands there was nothing to be heard of but Mr. Gladstone's triumphal progress, and the fictitious devotion of the people everywhere. That such a cheap enthusiasm should make the Queen 'less careful of the notice and applause of the multitudes' was what the Principal feared; while he was himself much irritated and annoyed to hear that the Premier, who encouraged and accepted these demonstrations 'as never Premier did before,' had, contrary to his pledge not to hear one side without hearing the other, received a deputation from the Disestablishment party. 'It was mean of him,' says the disgusted champion of the

Church, who thought the quasi royal progress 'very vulgar-minded,' as well as in very bad taste. When he was brought into direct contact with the hero of these ovations some days later, his commentary was no doubt sharpened by these causes of offense."

"September 17.

"The weather is perfectly lovely here today, and Mr. Gladstone has been planting a tree—not cutting one down. It is really amusing the kind of incense offered to him. It does not excite respect, although I dare say it is genuine. I had a talk with him last night, and this morning I had the amusement of sitting next Mrs. ———, who can hardly say a dozen words without introducing his name. There is really an absurd simplicity or want of humor about it. 'He is so simple,' this is the 'noble feature of his character.' Sancta simplicitas! is all one can say. If he is simple, who is double? But, really, I must not mock."

In December, some one, who did achieve the feat at least of getting a hearing, little knowing the mischief he did, or else calculating shrewdly to create an excitement in which it was impossible for most people to think clearly, published a paragraph, over no name, announcing that Gladstone was ready to deal with the demand of the Irish for Home Rule in a liberal spirit, should he be returned to power.

The manifesto to which reference has already been made contained also this passage: "History will consign the name of every man who, having it in his power, does not aid or prevent or retard an equitable sentiment between Ireland and Great Britain."

Gladstone's enemies and Gladstone's friends pointed to this statement, and his foes cried out immediately that the Grand Old Man had adopted the policy of Home Rule for Ireland, and must henceforth be regarded as its champion. A volley of questions was poured upon Mr. Gladstone's head, to which he gave no answer. He was sure of his own position; when the right time came there would be no question as to his plan and the method by which he expected to defend it. The Tory Government felt the ground-swell beneath it. Their representatives were horrified and many good people feared that the downfall of the British Empire was imminent. Such sane and progressive men as John Morley were full of hope that a career so splendid and prophetic as Gladstone's would crown itself by giving Ireland a just government.

The air was full of rumors. It was believed by many that Lord Beaconsfield's wily successor, Lord Salisbury, had shrewdly arranged things with the Irish National party. It was believed by another large section that the Parnellites were for Gladstone and his program. Gladstone's speech at Edinburgh made it clear that he believed that a majority must be returned great enough to get on without the Irish vote, else the Irish question could not be properly treated. It is true that the Irish National League called upon all Irishmen to vote for the Tories. Parnell was in a strange position, and the Irish National Party was in Salisbury's hands, when Gladstone was elected by a tremendous majority. Meantime the Irish began to understand Gladstone, and the Irish Nationalists saw that their hope was with the Liberal party. Later on it was seen that the Liberal party itself, to which they had come, was disunited and feeble.

In January, it was no longer possible, with what was no doubt a complete Liberal triumph, for the Tory Government to stand; the Queen sent for Mr. Gladstone to come to Osborne, and he was there made Prime Minister of England again. He had hardly been, as it was in this case, for the third time, called to this position of authority, until many of his friends and companions in office declared that if they understood his policy, they could have none of him. Only the three hundred that lapped, as in old Israel, stayed with Gideon.

It seems strange to an American student of English public opinion and its development, and especially to those acquainted with the vital quality of Mr. Gladstone's mind and his unwavering faith that no subject is truly within the limits of political discussion, and especially of political action, until the people are educated upon that subject, that there should have been horror of his past conduct on the Home Rule question expressed on the part of men like Lord Hartington, Lord Derby, and Lord Selbourne. It is no less remarkable that any one should have been unduly excited when Gladstone announced that five years' study had brought him to look with favor upon the project of Home Rule in Ireland, and that he believed the topic had at last come into the realm of political discussion, if not of political action.

We have tried in this biography to sketch the causes which operated upon this receptive and excursive intellect to produce this conviction. He and his idea were not even yet out of the woods, as we say. Gladstone was not now able to see quite clearly how the Imperial Parliament and its ultimate control of questions could be maintained while Ireland conducted her own business. He was not even sure that Ireland demanded Home Rule, and especially he doubted that the noisiest of her citizens represented the great majority of her people. Certainly the new popular suffrage which had been active since the Reform Bill of 1884 had broadened the sense of responsibility among Irishmen, and it had not indicated, as yet, that Home Rule was the thing that the majority of the intelligent and self respectful Irish people wanted. Now, however, things took a turn, and Ireland had declared unequivocally. It is impossible for us to share in any other feeling than that of admiration for an English statesman who so carefully and patiently as Gladstone had walked with the people, and set popular government so securely upon its broad base as to make it the utterance and embodiment of popular demands. Gladstone's ideas of the necessity for generous education of the people made it incumbent upon him to make them intelligent, especially on such an important matter as this, and surely, from time to time, in his treatment of Ireland, he had inspired and guided the English conscience and brain to deal justly with this subject. Perhaps it was true that his own eager and deeply moved intelligence and moral sense had outrun those of the public. Never until this moment did his prophetic vision deem it possible for Home Rule to be anything but a failure in Ireland; now he thought England and Ireland capable of making such a project valuable and victorious. It was the highest act of statesmanship, which is faith.

In the year 1886 the British public was offered the pamphlet of Mr. Gladstone called "The History of an Idea." It was very like the address which he issued in the course of his labors for the disestablishment of the Irish Church, and it gives testimony to what we have been trying to indicate all along—the fact that in dealing with Mr. Gladstone, one is having to do with an almost unmatched congeries of vital processes,—a restless, plastic mind, never regarding any avenue of thought, except perhaps the one that led and yet leads churchwards, as permanently closed to human entrance, never believing that the last word has been spoken upon any great question, never failing in hope for the federation and complete sovereignty of all just and comprehensive ideas. Less daring intelligences, and consciences less vitality related to his abundant faith in man might well fail.

Here Gladstone lost from his side two able men. The one was Mr. Joseph Chamberlain, and the other, Mr. John Bright. Perhaps he cared less for the fact that he was forsaken in this moment by Lord Northbrooke, Lord Carlingford, and Sir George Trevelyan.

It was a great moment in the history of one powerful man's faith in the ability of weaker men to enter into the processes and triumph of civilization by way of self-government, when this once haughty Tory rose, and breathless interest centered on an old man radiant with the fadeless youth of his principles, and Mr. Gladstone had offered his Bill for the Government of Ireland, and the Bill for making purchase of the lands and improvements from the Irish landlords. It was the signal for a declaration of hostilities against him and his policy by thousands of Liberals of every degree of talent and influence. Away went a large Liberal vote, and there came to him what he was never quite able to control—the Irish vote. One hundred years before, on another April day, in America, men "fired the shot heard round the world," attesting the fact that a revolution against the idea of taxation without representation had been inaugurated. Here was no revolutionist, but an evolutionist as practical as Darwin was philosophical, uttering calmly a word heard also round the world, and, swordless but firm, Gladstone stood fast by the same principle which had guarded our forefathers.

It was impossible for Gladstone to deal with any topic without passionateness of devotion and the completest manifestation of inner loyalty to its aims manifesting itself in every act, especially in his industry and eloquence. This intensity can never be understood by people who have no intensity.

Every element of his nature which had received the precious precipitate of experience from long years of debate, every sensibility of spirit which had been played upon and made vibrant by a thousand winds from the decades of controversy, every reach of imagination which had been enlarged by the fact that he had witnessed the dawn of an ever-increasing day for the people, every force of his genius which had been trained to suppleness and potency in serving causes which had first come to him begging upon their knees and left him crowned with sovereign triumph, seemed now to rise refreshed from long dwelling in his soul and to engage again with a domination almost superhuman, as he laid upon the altar of constitutional government and freedom the remaining years of his illustrious career.

He had fought in every part of the field. At the beginning of 1886 Mr. Gladstone again gave his mind a holiday, by entering into a long controversy involving enormous learning and great dialectical skill, as well as those resources of debate of which he was the easy master, meeting such antagonists as Professor Max Müller, Mr. Huxley and Dr. Albert Reville. Each of these men wrote from his quiet study; and he had no Irish question or any of the other half-dozen great questions which beset Mr. Gladstone, to deal with. His versatility of mind is illustrated in the fact that on the very day upon which he received the "Nineteenth Century" containing his article entitled "Proem to Genesis; a Plea for a Fair Trial," he began to write upon, as the only man in England who could adequately discuss Sir Henry Thring's "Thoughts of Imperial Federation," and Barry O'Brien's "Federal Union with Ireland." Mr. Gladstone had kept his craft alive where many seas have met.

Serious opposition was organizing itself against Home Rule. Mr. Gladstone was being quoted as a false man. His old phrases were conjured up and he had to again explain the fragment of an old speech— "so that with fatal precision the steps of crime dogged the footsteps of the Land League." Gladstone was accused of a desire to create the Irish Parliament, because he had found out that England regarded Irish members in the House of Commons as a nuisance and that therefore relief ought to be afforded, even if a grave danger were encountered. Even those who agreed so far with Gladstone as to admit that some kind of Home Rule would be the best thing for Ireland, now animad-

verted upon Gladstone's ability or willingness to fulfill Liberal principles, "and to permit the majority of the Nobodies of Ireland to govern
themselves." No doubt there was an honest fear that, if Home Rule
were granted, loyal men in Ireland would be exposed to the Irish wrath
which had been bottled up for centuries, and outrages and murder
would be rampant on every hand. Wise friends of Mr. Gladstone fell
from his side, because they held it was impossible for him to say that
absolute protection for the loyalists would be made a condition pre-
cedent to Home Rule. England feared the use of cruelty—the very
weapon which England had so long used against Ireland. Thoughtful
men knew that no single act of Parliament could abolish the memory
of ages of misgovernment in that Island, even if these thoughtful men
did not sympathize with Mr. Shaw-Lefevre when he called the Parnell
movement "a shameful, audacious and gigantic act of robbery." No
doubt Gladstone was confronted with the misgivings of men he respected deeply. He knew justice must be done to Ireland, yet he knew,
and he was to know still more certainly, in the future, that a nation once
so long under the heel of wrong as Ireland had been could hardly avoid
an outburst of plundering, cruelty and revenge. The last five years
had taught him as much. What guarantees could he give? Here were
a lot of Irishmen who had done faithful service in enforcing the laws of
the Realm—they were laws of the Realm even if they had been bad
laws—and now they saw themselves about to be handed over to the
ruffians they had controlled—to men against whom England could not
protect them. Large investments had been made by Englishmen in
Ireland, and if these men were turned out or persecuted, they would
have the right to have pecuniary relief. The awful lesson of the Phœnix
Park murders had compelled Parliament to pass the Crimes Act, but
the crime had gone before, and the victims could not be reached. The
Land League always had the appearance of a base conspiracy to a large
section of English people. Terrorism in Ireland had been too closely
associated with some of the men most anxious for Home Rule, for
many voters to forget that with an Irish Parliament criminals might be
holding the lives and property of loyalists in hands bloody already.
"For five years," said Arnold-Forster, "Gladstone held Parliament in

the hollow of his hand and he gave no single word of encouragement or hope to the sorely tried loyalists of Ireland." Of course this was not true, but many a man believed it.

The Irish of the Molly Maguire and Tammany Hall were offered as evidence that no good could come out of Ireland. Such men as James Bryce, while sharing none of these opinions, looked upon the situation more calmly.

Yet Bryce insisted that "no scheme of Home Rule or local self-government is admissible which would leave the landowners at the mercy of Irish elective bodies, and that no such scheme as aforesaid is admissible which does not recognize and provide for the case of the Ulster Protestants." Although he admitted the fact that these propositions might suggest more difficulties than they saw, he would not despond, least of all would he believe that democracy "at which it is now fashionable to rail, is the cause of present perplexities, for," he added, "these were as great under the oligarchy before 1832, and during the period of middle class rule that followed."

He had a word to say, however, to the Nationalists, and it was this:

"It is to be hoped that the Nationalists in Ireland and America will not mistake this spirit, which has borne many provocations quietly, for a want of firmness or of courage. If they do, they will be fatally mistaken. England will yield nothing to menace; but she is strong enough to be magnanimous. Recognizing the novelty of the present situation, recollecting the lamentable errors of the past, contrasting her own peace and prosperity with the miseries of distracted Ireland, she is prepared to give a calm and patient consideration to any and every scheme which offers a prospect of alleviating those miseries and of creating a better feeling between peoples whom nature meant to be friends, and whose friendship is essential to the welfare and the greatness of her empire."

William Ewart Gladstone had brought men of this quality, at least, to speak calmly, and honestly consider his plans for Ireland.

CHAPTER XXXIX.

TRIED AND FAITHFUL.

It was sufficient to discourage confidence in popular government through representation to behold the violence with which Gladstone's foes treated his presence and conduct in the House of Commons at this time. Perhaps Mr. Gladstone never met so angry and vociferant an opposition as he met in the new Parliament of 1874 on the 18th of May. The Conservative party seemed to remember the former glory and the height of popularity from which this Lucifer had fallen, and now they were having their jubilee. Disraeli then looked upon the noisy and excited mob as if felicitating himself upon the fact that it was the hour of his triumph and that of his rival's humiliation. This was the time when Gladstone received nothing else than discourtesy and even malignant treatment whenever he arose to speak. The habit of his enemies grew more fierce as the years went on from 1874 to 1880. The Conservatives kept reminding him that he was not only out of office, but he was not even the leader of the Liberals whom they affected to despise. Further, they insisted, he continually kept coming and going like a jack in a box, at one time retiring entirely out of sight and leaving notice that he was not at all responsible for Liberal leadership, then popping up and intimating by some flash of genius that nobody else could lead the Liberal party. He was attacked by one member of Parliament as a man who was guilty of almost every improper and unworthy method of gaining power, and, at this, the Conservatives went wild with rejoicing. No wonder that Gladstone in 1882 had done all he could to make this disorder impossible of repetition. He said himself that they had come upon a condition of affairs which "struck a fatal blow at the liberties of debate and the dignity of Parliament." Certain it is that at the time we are now considering, May, 1885, it was almost impossible for Gladstone to rise in his place and to begin to speak without being met by noises of every sort and especially by groans. Perhaps it is true that Mr. Gladstone himself had met more serious opposition amounting to personal antagonism when on the 7th of May, 1877, he proposed to offer his resolutions on the Eastern Question. For more than one and one-half hours he stood, as Beecher had stood at Liverpool in the course of our civil war, before a mob of English Conservative Members of the House of Commons, but he conquered them.

While Gladstone was waiting for England to make up her mind what she would have him do, he published alongside with these articles and others which had to do with Welsh Disestablishment, Radicalism and Socialism, Moderate Liberalism and immoderate Liberalism, Turkish and Land questions, an essay on "Dawn of Creation and of Worship," which was written as though there could be no tumult in earth or heaven, and he fought out his controversy as though the only serious question on a planet like this was the origin of religious activity in the form of worship on the part of man. The mobility and largeness of Mr. Gladstone's mind, its passion for utterance, and its love of disputation are nowhere more remarkably exhibited than in an article such as this. Without doubt, the advice of Lyman Beecher to a young man who had been told not to put too many irons in the fire, in which the excellent minister said to him, "put all your irons in, tongs, shovel and everything else," had in some form come to Mr. Gladstone and had been adopted in early life; and the result was that he always had a hot iron on hand and did not get weary, as many do, of having to use one burning instrument. Here is the same wealth of information and fullness of statement associated with the same tendency to verbose statement and reiteration of ideas which was characteristic of nearly everything he did, either in oratory or in letters, when his mind was not poised with the thought of his guardianship and championship of convictions important for the immediate destiny of nations and men. He thus refreshed himself and then re-entered the debate to prove the untruth, at least in one instance, of Pulteney's remark to Walpole: "Political parties are like snakes, which are not moved by their heads, but by their tails." Here truly the head was leading.

CHAPTER XL.

THE AGED WARRIOR.

Gladstone was now an old man, and yet one of the youngest old men the world has ever seen. The courage which in earlier years had never forsaken him was now alert and open-eyed and true. The amazing information which three-quarters of a century had brought to him appeared to be arranged for this special conflict. The quick eyes which had not then begun to lose their pristine brilliancy,—if indeed, like the sightless eyes of Milton, Gladstone's fading eyes did not to the last seem to be radiant and penetrating,—flashed their morning-tide upon the dark phases of this angry subject. The conviction of the righteousness of his matured plan, which had at least none of the acidity of unripeness in it, but had rather grown mellow and rich as he had considered and developed it, now satisfied the hunger of his moral nature. He believed in it at the center of his being, and in the full possession of his superb energies of mind and spirit, he threw aside all "judicious mixtures," all thoughts that intimidation could be a just or wise method of civilizing human beings, and entered his consummating work with a fresh and buoyant hope. The Tory Government had gone out. He did not want anybody to come over to his side with such rapidity as would prevent his bringing his intellect and conscience along with him. He had long ago said to those who were likely to be rash: "I would tell them of my own intention to keep my own counsel, and reserve my own freedom, until I see an occasion when there may be a prospect of public benefit in endeavoring to make a movement forward; and I will venture to recommend them, as an old Parliamentary hand, to do the same." This slow and steady pace he never forsook, until he was compelled to march with the speed of his ideas rushing to their accomplishment.

A new party came under the leadership of Lord Hartington and

335

Mr. Chamberlain. This party was composed of the Whigs and Radicals who went in with the Tories. Gigantic was the opposition. All England was astir, and London had only a single voice in the morning and a single voice in the evening which did not join in the chorus of the newspapers against Gladstone. He could still grow; his power to reason even with an antagonist never vanished. No doubt Gladstone was badly advised with regard to his hope that the Home Rule bill would pass at its second reading in the House of Commons. No doubt he was misled with reference to the amount of horror England conceived at the idea that cut-throats and knaves would hold office in Ireland if the Home Rule bill prevailed. No doubt he overestimated the Irishman's willingness to be orderly, even under the best auspices. It is questionable if the intense and progressive spirit of Gladstone seriously missed the slow-going and lethargic Lord Hartington, but it was impossible for Gladstone not to feel keenly the secession of Joseph Chamberlain. The latter had come into the Government as the President of the Board of Trade. He certainly had read Mr. Gladstone's address to the Electors of Midlothian in which he said: "The hope and purpose of the new Government in taking office was to examine carefully whether it is not practicable to try some method of meeting the present case of Ireland, and ministering to its wants, more safe and more effectual, going nearer to the source and seat of the mischief, and offering more promise of stability, than the method of separate and restrictive criminal legislation." One man was sure to be missed,—for William Edward Forster had recently died. Gladstone could not be indifferent to the lessons to be learned from the life of Forster and his effort at administration in Ireland.

Gladstone was not a man who could have been bewildered into a false conception as to the strength of his position with the English people, by the fact that he had been so warmly received when he introduced the Bill. Before this he had heard cheers for him which shook the House of Commons, but he had never had such an enthusiastic greeting from the tumultuous crowd who followed Mr. Parnell and the somewhat miscellaneous company of Radicals from whom the man from Oxford had rarely received anything but admiration for his talents and sneers for his earlier political respectability. For three hours and a half in the course of a speech in which every element of his nature contributed its special strength and glory to his eloquence, he had had the chance of feeling and studying England's mind and heart in the House of Commons. It was a speech containing less of that metaphysical quality which often had wearied his friends by adding distinction to distinction and laying him open to the charge of disingenuousness, than any other speech he had made on any other equally important subject. It was not unusually oratorical, for this master of the art—indeed, here he mastered it—and it was not all rhetorical, which has been said to be the defect in Mr. Gladstone's manner and method as a public speaker. There was nothing of the Oxford scholasticism in the way in which he spoke to the House of Commons on that occasion, while yet his frame trembled with the excitement which he had caught from the vast and tumultuous crowds in the street. Surely no expressed admiration—and nobody in the House failed to pay him the highest tribute when he concluded his speech—no congratulations even from his opponents had won him away from that clearsightedness which gave him to understand that a long and terrible conflict lay before him and the ideas he had uttered. But it is true that so certain were some of his closest friends of defeat, on the day of division, that they began to console him soon with the hope that they could at least appeal again to the country. Mr. Russell tells us that some devotee went so far as to agree to move the vote of confidence on general grounds, with the idea that "this would be supported by many who could not vote for the Home Rule bill." It was true, the defeat was imminent. All this eloquence and wisdom, statesmanship and humanity, hopes and fears commingled, went down before the vote, when, on June 8th, a majority of thirty rejected the bill. Mr. Gladstone had not educated his public, and the public was not ready for so complex a measure. In love of humanity, he had outrun Peter to the sepulchre. His ideal was not dead. Abroad in the world, it would some day be recognized. He could wait. The Irish Nationalists alone were fairly pleased with the scheme, because it was a scheme in their general direction. Mr. Parnell from the first did not like the idea that Ireland

22

would not be represented at Westminster, and England did not like the idea that Ireland would have a Parliament of her own.

Long ago Mr. Gladstone's plan of Home Rule has become so familiar to American readers that it is only necessary here to say that the measure for the buying-out of the Irish landlords, which came along with the Home Rule bill, offended those who wanted not to sell and those who wanted not to buy; and England, Scotland and Wales, with their large Irish populations, joined with the Roman Catholics in the demand that some Irishmen should represent them in the Imperial Parliament at London.

Mr. Chamberlain's opposition was directed against Gladstone, because of the land scheme. Perhaps it will always be thought that Mr. Chamberlain would have felt better about things if his own scheme of Home Rule had been adopted. Certain it is that he has been a severe critic and a powerful antagonist to a man who put into his scheme what Chamberlain's scheme did not possess,—recognition of Ireland's nationality. Gladstone's poetic mind had clearly appreciated the genius of the Irish people.

Lowell, however, wrote to his friend Norton (See Letters of James Russell Lowell, Copyright, by Harper's, from which this extract is taken by permission:)

"The political situation continues to be interesting, and opinion about the fate of Mr. Gladstone's bill varies from hour to hour. I for a good while thought the second reading would be carried by a small majority, but believe now that it will be defeated. I hear that Mr. Gladstone said to the Duke of Argyll: 'I hoped in my old age to save my country, but this is a bitter, humiliating disappointment.' The fate of second reading depends somewhat upon the fear of a dissolution of Parliament, but the general opinion now is that the Government, if defeated, will dissolve. I asked Mr. Chamberlain day before yesterday if he thought the G. O. M. was angry enough to dissolve, and he said yes. I met Mr. Gladstone a few days ago, and he looked as gay as a boy on his way home from school. From what I hear, I am inclined to think that what is called Irish public opinion in favor of Home Rule is nearly as factitious as that of our American meetings and resolutions."

And he wrote again:

"From Osterley I went to Holmbury (Leveson Gower's), where I spent a couple of days very pleasantly with Mr. and Mrs. Gladstone and other guests. Mr. Gladstone was in boyish spirits. He told me, among other things, that 'in the whole course of his political experience he had never seen anything like the general enthusiasm of the country for Home Rule in Ireland.' I asked slyly 'if it was not possible that a part at least, of this enthusiasm might be for the Prime Minister?' 'Oh, no, no, not a bit of it!' he answered with eager emphasis. And I am inclined to think he persuaded himself for the moment. This is one secret of his power as a speaker, that he is capable of improvising convictions. He left us to go down to Scotland, and I couldn't help remembering that I first met him at a dinner at Lord Ripon's, in March, '80, when he was on the eve of starting for Midlothian on his first Scottish campaign. He was very confident, and the result justified him. Perhaps it will again, though the general opinion (as one hears it) is the other way. But I still think the people strongly with him."

Later Lowell, who had perhaps lost some of his vision in later years, wrote:

"It amuses me to see the Grand Old Man using the same arguments against this bill that I vainly urged against 'his' bill five years ago. You know that I am 'principled agin' indulging in prophecy, but I made one at that time which has been curiously verified. I used to ask, 'Suppose the Irish nation should strike, what are you going to do about it?' They have struck, and I am still at a loss. I am glad to see that their tone over here is much more moderate than it was. 'Studiously moderate,' you will say. But I think they begin to see the difficulties more clearly than they did. Meanwhile, the coercion policy is crowding the immigrant ships to this country, and we have already as many as we can digest at present. We are really interested in your Irish question in more ways than one. It is really we who have been paying the rents over there, for we have to pay higher wages for domestic service to meet the drain."

John Bright's opposition had been the most serious met in the progress of the debate. Lords and dukes had no hearing with the people of England, for it was suspected that they were not particularly anxious for reforms which broadened the base of the pyramid of government. But John Bright had a hearing with that strong middle class who rule the realm. Besides, he was well known as a friend of Ireland. In season and out of season, he had labored for her honor and her well-being. The intemperate and often outrageous action on the part of the Irish leaders and misleaders had given him grave doubts as to the ability of the Irish people to use Home Rule save as a curse to England and to themselves, and no persuasions of his old friend, Gladstone, could lead him to revise the opinion that the Irish he cared for did not really want Home Rule. The Bill, as we have said, was defeated, and yet in the defeat it was evident that an ultimate triumph was sure to come. The Queen labored in vain to get Mr. Gladstone to remain in power, and on June 26th, Parliament was dissolved. An appeal was made to the country, and the Conservatives triumphed; but it was a kind of triumph in which Gladstone saw hope for the principle he had espoused. Things were in a hurly-burly, so far as parties and leaders and constituencies were concerned. Even the classes appeared seriously separated one from another. Drawing-rooms began to close their doors to Mr. Gladstone. Fierceness of controversy never went further in the history of British politics. Hate and rage strove with ignorance and passion to pour out vials of vituperation upon Mr. Gladstone. He had hitherto born with equanimity and beheld with a smile the political cartoons which had represented him in the form of a bird, beast or denizen of the sea; he was now to be advertised from one end of the country to the other as an inhabitant of hell, and no abuse was too foul or insult too stinging for the Grand Old Man. Art—if the coarsest sort of malignant opposition may be said to produce anything like art—exhausted its resources in describing him as a being unfit for earth and hopeless of even the mercy of the God whom British aristocrats talked of glibly as they turned the friends of Gladstone from their mansions. May 3d Lowell wrote home to America to this effect:

"The editor of the 'Contemporary Review' has just gone out, having vainly endeavored (at the instigation of John Morley) to persuade me that I should be doing a public service by giving my views on Mr. Gladstone's Home Rule project in that periodical. But I prefer to keep clear of hot potatoes—and Irish ones are apt to be particularly hot. Pretty nearly Everybody who is Anybody here is furious—there is no word for it—and de-

nounces the G. O. M. as a kind of baser Judas Iscariot, all the more contemptible because he will be cheated of his thirty pieces. The Irish themselves are beginning to feel the responsibility of governing Ireland, and Mr.
———— has said that they should 'want an alien act to enable them to deal
with those ———— Irish-American scoundrels.' (This is confidential.) The
'situation' is a very grave one, and everybody who isn't excited is depressed."*

Through the whole of this fearful ordeal Mr. Gladstone walked
erect, serious-minded, unmoved by the rancor of enemies or the adula-
tion of his associates, sure-footed and certain that he was engaged in
bringing without doubt a result worthy of the loftiest mind.

Of course his enemies rejoiced to see the men of the Liberal party
quarreling among themselves as to the bill, though Gladstone believed
they differed only on details and not on the great principle involved.
As he saw the spirit of intolerance directed against himself, he appreciated more strongly than ever what Ireland had suffered in the centuries of her humiliation. He saw how far injustice and unreason could
go in a refusal to remedy the terror of suffering borne in the past, and
to continue the course of conduct in England which simply solidi-
fied the ignorance of England with respect to the whole Irish question
and made it a weapon enforcing coercive measures which could never
remedy Irish evils. No doubt the upper classes, so called, really believed
that Gladstone was ready to destroy England's greatness, for the upper
classes of England are notoriously ignorant. No doubt respectable
bishops and well-fed ecclesiastics thought that this illustrious Protestant
wished to uproot Protestantism in the British Isles, for churchmanship
in England is not necessarily intelligent; it is only flavored with antiquity. No doubt England was ready to think that Gladstone had lost
his ability as a financier, and was likely to lose his mind, for the
English shop-keeper could never understand Gladstone's financial ability, and he was not always proven an omniscient judge on the latter
subject.

Certain it is, that during the whole of that campaign, and for long
afterwards, Gladstone's name was a name of execration and despite,

---

* From the "Letters of James Russell Lowell," copyright, Harpers,
N. Y.

whenever those who ought to have trusted him most, ventured to speak of him in public.

When the Tories came into power a most interesting and bumptious scion of the house of Marlborough leaped to the front, and, as in the Bradlaugh debate, he completely overshadowed men of greater genius and larger views, so here the former leader of the House under the Conservative Government had to stand back, and the new Chancellor of the Exchequer, Lord Randolph Churchill, became leader of the House. A certain sort of ability he possessed in a very remarkable degree. He had a profound belief that he ought to be heard, and he had a remarkable gift in the direction of making himself heard. Salisbury had constituted the new Tory Administration, and his active lieutenant in the House of Commons found himself opposed to a man seventy-six years of age and a cause as old as liberty and as young as her fondest hope.

Soon Lord Randolph Churchill added to the list of his brilliant surprises by resigning from the Salisbury Government and declining a career as Chancellor of the Exchequer, which appeared brilliant indeed. The truth is that Lord Salisbury and the ardent young Lord could not agree. Things never went with sufficient rapidity, not to say vivacity, to suit Lord Randolph. It got to be the habit of the English public to think of him as one who wanted to stir up the old fellows at Westminster and have a great and jolly time with them. When Lord Randolph wanted the public to laugh at him they persisted in thinking him a very bright and valuable man; when he wanted the public to regard him with seriousness, they laughed. The fact is that he had the faith of Disraeli, that it is possible to gather into one interest and make a sort of trust out of Toryism and its superciliousness on the one side, and democracy, its ignorance and prejudice on the other. He said in the House of Commons on the land subject:

"The system of a single ownership of land in Ireland we believe may be the ultimate solution of the difficulties of the Irish Land Question. Mr. Gladstone has been defeated in order to prevent Land Purchase, and here were his conquerers proposing Land Purchase the moment they appeared before Parliament. But this was not all. The main argument, as has been seen, against Mr. Gladstone's proposal, was that it would impose taxation on the British taxpayer. Mr. Gladstone entirely denied this, and agreed with his opponents in thinking that any burden on the British taxpayer for the payment of the Irish landlord would be monstrously inequitable. But the turn of his conquerors had come, and the chief among them laid down that not only would the British taxpayer have to pay for the Irish landlord, but that he ought. Lord Salisbury was dealing with the judicial rents fixed by the Land Courts, and with the demand that these rents should once again be revised. Such a general demand he described the Government as resolved to reject. But if it should come out that the Courts have made blunders, and that there is that impossibility in any case of paying rent, I think it is not the landlords who should bear the loss. I think this would be one of the cases for the application of the principle of purchase by the State, and that the State, and not the landlords, must suffer for the errors that have been made."

Of course it was impossible for him to make this theory work, for Ireland would not admit, as Mr. O'Connor says, that the rent of the landlords "had been fixed as to time through blunders." To adopt this and reject the land proposal of Mr. Gladstone was out of the question. The Irish party was up in arms at once. Mr. Parnell met the proposal which Mr. Chamberlain might have been expected to agree to, but Chamberlain was not heard from. Mr. Gladstone was meanwhile sitting with Dr. Döllinger in Germany and recuperating his energies by discussing theology and philosophy with that famous athlete in both. Back to Parliament he came and gave his voice to the old cause. Mr. Parnell's bill was rejected. The fact is that there was disorder in the ranks, and what is known as the Plan of Campaign was adopted and published to the world October 23d, 1886. It is too long to reproduce here, and is perhaps well understood by our readers. The Government had appointed a commission to inquire into the condition of the Land Question and also as to intimidation and unlawful conspiracy. The Irish party took such ground as to justify Mr. Parnell rather than Sir Michael Hicks-Beach, who was the representative of the Government. It was very certain that the latter had to confess that crime had been decreased by the Irish people themselves. Things were getting on very well, and Ireland was learning to like Sir Michael Hicks-Beach, when he resigned, and Mr. Arthur Balfour became Chief Secretary. Here was a man persistent, able, scholarly, and he had the whole Tory tradition and Government behind him. Six years before he had begun to antagonize Mr. Gladstone and his proposals. Without Gladstone's physical strength, and with none of Gladstone's intensity of conviction or utterance, this languid and well-mannered relative of Lord Salisbury, sharing, by the way, Gladstone's love of theological lore, roused himself from that lassitude and indifferentism of which he often gave a picture in the House of Commons, and proved himself one of the firmest and most vigorous of men who ever undertook to rule Ireland. But he was not powerful, except along lines which prophesied nothing for the future.

Such men as James Russell Lowell thought, with England, that Gladstone did not know his own mind. Lowell writes (see "Letters of James Russell Lowell," copyright, Harpers, N. Y.), May 22, 1887:

"At dinner, by the way, I was glad to meet John Morley for the first time since my return. He welcomed me most cordially but looks older and a little worn with the friction of politics. But the cheerful fanaticism of his face is always exhilarating to me, though I feel that it would have the same placidly convinced expression if my head were .rolling at his feet at the exigence of some principle. He knows where he stands on the Home Rule question better than Gladstone, for his opinions are more the result of conviction than of sentiment."

He writes again, May 26:

"I have seen Gladstone several times, and he is lighthearted as a boy —as lightheaded, too, I might almost say. I am amazed at the slowness of people here in seeing that the ice they have been floating on is about to break up—nay, will at the first rough water. The Irish question is only incidental to the larger question of their whole system of landholding, and the longer they delay settling that the more inevitable is it that this should' stir itself. It is a misfortune and not a crime to be entangled in an anachronism, but if one won't do what he can to break loose, one must share its fate without complaint or hope of compensation."

No doubt Balfour's position was one which could not have been filled satisfactorily by any man in England who was willing to administer the affairs of Ireland on the Tory philosophy. Whatever reason Gladstone had for opposing coercion as a scheme of civilizing Irishmen in the past, Balfour's career in Ireland had furnished him with countless other reasons why it was not to be thought of as the scheme of the future. Balfour's reign was denominated a reign of terror, and his career in Ireland was called a regime of brutality. England and Ireland could hardly have warred more seriously or foully. Bayonets and policemen made Ireland look like a besieged territory. Gladstone's administration had permitted police reporters on the platform where Irishmen spoke, and none had made objection. Indeed, the speakers themselves had arranged for the police reporters; but now the latter came in a warlike fashion; the crowd resisted usually, and law and order were despised and trampled under foot. A single occasion of this sort furnished Balfour with matter which was laid before the House of Commons. He was singularly unfortunate because his information was ludicrously inaccurate, and very soon the Irish people believed that English Government in Ireland meant armed injustice.

The Coercion Act was signed by the Queen on the 17th of July, 1887. Within a few days, armed with this new instrumentality and relying on intimidation, he proclaimed the greater part of Ireland as territory to be governed under the most stringent clause of this act. The National League was declared dangerous. He had started out to put down what he called "crime," and the National League was not considered by the Irish people to be a criminal organization. On the charges of inciting acts of violence and the promotion of interference with the administration of the law, the League found two hundred of its branches suppressed by the first of October. Tenants were evicted by landlords everywhere, and the Irish press was muzzled. Distinguished and honorable Irishmen were sentenced to imprisonment, and it came to be romantic, as any such incident of martyrdom will, to spend some time in one of the prisons, in obedience to the English Government. Indictments were presented against editors, lawyers and speakers of every degree of importance who denounced coercive measures. In one case, Mr. Balfour's indifference to humanity had been so great that Gladstone himself had described the occurrence of certain deaths, concerning which no adequate inquiry had been made, as inhuman in the extreme, and he said the three men were treated "as though they had been three dogs." Cases were brought before Mr. Balfour involving young boys who would have been incapable of giving offense to any justly strong Government, but he administered unchecked the provisions of the Coercion Act. The Irish people could not quite see, as one of the best of them explained, the difference between their own boycotting societies and the highly respectable association of Tories in England called the Primrose League.

During all this time grosser outrages were growing more frequent in spite of the Coercion Act and the pitiless execution of it by Mr. Balfour. In one famous case Mr. Gladstone took such interest as to enable him to declare that the whole affair was "a travesty of justice, as gross, as palpable, and as shameful as any that ever disgraced even the career of Judge Jeffreys." Gladstone asked if Balfour was not going to dismiss certain cases of injustice. Balfour replied that he was not. The conscience of England was becoming more sensitive with reference to these horrors. Landlords were beginning to see that Ireland was growing to be a hotbed of deep and permanent rebelliousness, and that extremity of disorder would come unless something could be done to make the relationship between landlords and tenantry more satisfactory. The whole enterprise under Balfour made the Coercion Act, as Frederick Harrison said, "an instrument which could be applied only to evict."

The Irish people demanded the same power granted to the Land Commissioners in Ireland as was granted to the Land Commissioners in Scotland. Here were unjust arrears, and here were also unjust rents. It was one problem with two sides. To deal with it justly would save Ireland from turmoil and England from danger.

Every nerve was strained in England to uphold the system of coercion. Parnell and his following must be put down at all costs. The London Times, in its foolish ardor, blundered into publishing with a flourish of trumpets, a forged letter attributed to Mr. Parnell. It was as follows:

"May 15, 1882.

"Dear Sir: I am not surprised at your friend's anger, but he and you should know that to denounce the murders was the only course open to us. To do that promptly was plainly our best policy.

"But you can tell him and all others concerned that though I regret the accident of Lord F. Cavendish's death, I cannot refuse to admit that Burke got no more than his deserts.

"You are at liberty to show him this, and others whom you can trust also; but let not my address be known. He can write to House of Commons.   Yours Very Truly,

"CHAS. S. PARNELL."

One may easily imagine the sensation created by such a publication, at such a crisis as this. After a long and fearful trial, Mr. Parnell's cowardly antagonist was crushed, and the forger of the letter committed suicide. Through it all, Mr. Gladstone stood holding fast to his faith and rendering such service to those who were watching with him the growth of a better sentiment. The popular revolt against Balfour's method and the treatment given to Parnell and the Irish cause swept against the Government, and when Mr. Balfour spoke, he was coldly received by the masses of honest men who were indignant at the senseless antagonism to the Irish people and at the "Times" in its conduct toward Parnell. Toryism flagged throughout the debate. Dr. Tanner, having escaped arrest, made his appearance, and Gladstone delivered a masterly speech. When Mr. Parnell arose, Mr. Gladstone exultantly joined with John Morley and Sir William Harcourt and the crowd of Liberals who cheered him vociferously. At length the Grand Old Man addressed the House. The echoes of Gladstone's speech rang through the House of Commons and re-echoed through England. His description of the character and conduct of the Government, which was then falling to pieces, was an awful denunciation of power haughtily used by unrighteous hands. He saw the coming of Home Rule, and he spoke like a prophet and seer. These were his concluding words:

"You may deprive of its grace and of its freedom the act which you are asked to do, but avert that act you cannot. To prevent its consummation is utterly beyond your power. It seems to approach at an accelerated rate. Coming slowly or coming quickly, surely it is coming. And you yourselves, many of you, must in your own breasts be aware that already you see in the handwriting on the wall the signs of the coming doom."

CHAPTER XLI.

THE GRAND OLD MAN AGAIN IN POWER.

With the last decade of his life our readers are doubtless familiar. At the general election of 1892 Mr. Gladstone was again given the reins of government, and he stood triumphant over the combination of Tories and Liberal Unionists, with a majority of two Home Rulers, England and Ireland, to make him sure of his position. For the fourth time he was asked and consented to constitute a Government under Her Majesty, and he became the Prime Minister. Dauntlessly true to the ideas to which he had consecrated the last years of his increasingly glorious career, and never more sure of the certainty of triumph for those principles which he had embodied in his plan for Home Rule than at that moment, he introduced a Bill on the 13th of February, 1893. Everything that Gladstone had done in the past for Home Rule appeared to have been a seed which blossomed into fullest fragrance in this public measure. What was called a "Parliament of Broken Pledges" lay as an ugly wreck behind him, but it gave such a lesson to England that it was easy for Gladstone to obtain a hearing for his wider and juster conceptions of the mission of constitutional government. He, himself, had grown, and Ireland was to be represented at Westminster by the action of this new Bill. It was a vast improvement over any previously proposed statute. Mr. Parnell no longer appeared as the leader of the Irish Nationalists, but Mr. Asquith, who had moved the vote of want of public confidence in the Tory Government, early in June, 1892, had risen before England as something else besides the successful and learned orator at the bar, which he undoubtedly had been for years, and Gladstone was ably assisted by his great and various Parliamentary talents. He made Mr. Asquith, Home Secretary, and this gentleman was not long in demonstrating to England that Gladstone's power of finding the right man and putting him

348

in the right place had made answer to the query: "Why Asquith?" This gentleman now showed himself to be a man of vast administrative capacity.

Gladstone also called to his aid such men as Bryce, who has written the best book, in any language, on our own American institutions from a foreigner's point of view; and an old friendship received undeniable and worthy witness in the fact that Mr. Arthur Ackland was placed in charge of public education. Sir William Vernon Harcourt was made Chancellor of the Exchequer, and Lord Rosebery, upon whom Mr. Gladstone's eye had already rested as his immediate successor, was placed in charge of foreign affairs. Gladstone made his old friend and literary companion, Lord Houghton, Lord Lieutenant of Ireland. It was perhaps wise that the sharp sword of Mr. Labouchere, editor and proprietor of Truth, was not made an active instrumentality of Cabinet life. These were the men closest to Gladstone when he came forward with his Home Rule scheme, in which England learned that one of the main features of the earlier scheme, namely, a separate Irish Parliament, with no representative for Ireland in the Imperial Parliament at London, was left out. Nothing, however, which he proposed in this measure could win back Mr. Chamberlain, but Sir George Trevelyan joined himself to Mr. Gladstone's party, and the latter thus found himself again officered by this genial and able lieutenant.

He had gone through a long struggle with reference to the question as to whether Parnell, who had suffered from a damaging experience in the Divorce Court, in a case which had gone against him, should be allowed to lead the Irish contingent, and, indeed, make any sort of figure in English life. Ireland had never been kind to her best friend and champion. Gladstone's loyalty to principle had, however, never wavered, in spite of this fact. But Parnell had disappeared, and the Home Rule cause was freed from this embarrassment, and Gladstone's Bill swept through the House of Commons. Never has a man who tried to do something valuable and just for a wronged people, in any era of human history, been more embarrassed, annoyed and outraged by the behavior of those who connected themselves or were numbered with the defenders of that people, than was William Ewart Gladstone, the friend of Ireland, when he stood with the Irish party hopelessly at war within itself and when England looked on laughingly and tauntingly as the Kilkenny fight among them proceeded. Thousands of men who were led by Gladstone's faith to believe in the capacity of even that section of humanity for self-government beheld the wretched and dismaying exhibition which the Irish people made of themselves, and to the sorrow, and often to the consternation of Gladstone and his followers, they pointed out what they believed to be traits of Irish character, or at least conditions of the Irish mind, which made Home Rule appear only a fantastic vision generated by a brilliant mind now coming to its dotage. The antagonistic sections of the Irish people did not fail to supply a most sickening picture to the heart of the greater leader. At unexpected times, and in entirely unforeseen ways, crime lifted its scaly form in Ireland; and it must be admitted that there was great sympathy even for the House of Lords, when it was known that they hesitated to pass Gladstone's Bill which had been successful in the House of Commons. But the Lords did more than hesitate; they rejected the Bill by an enormous majority. This was the last fact which could in any way bewilder the brain or extract the courage from the heart of a Commoner like Gladstone. He knew the House of Lords represented the vanishing tradition which had organized that body too often into opposition against measures whose passage through Parliament the English people demanded. He saw another thing which is sure to come to pass in England, that Anglo-Saxon freedom under Anglo-Saxon law will at length demand the most thorough reform or the total abolition of the House of Lords.

This, however, was not the time for Mr. Gladstone to inaugurate such a far-reaching movement as would disrupt and perhaps destroy the Upper House. That crusade must be led by another. He was a worker who had earned his right to rest, if only by the fact that in recent years he had undertaken such gigantic labors and carried them through with such infinite tact and toil. He had been incessant in labor in and out of season. None of his party could ever persuade him that he might be absent from sessions of the House of Commons while his projects were in the fire of debate. His enormous passion for work in

the cause of law and liberty took him into the closest study of all sorts
of subjects which were likely to appear before the mind of the Lower
House.   Punch has made a picture of Gladstone which almost every
visitor to the House of Commons will recognize as vividly true,—the
eager, radiant-eyed, flushed old man, sitting on the edge of his seat,
either trying to catch the eye of the speaker at the moment when he
might furnish the House some information, or expose some ignorance
of which he alone was aware, or anxious to call to himself some lieutenant who would execute his orders.   Like a sleepless general, he always
directed the battle.

As a young man, he had trained himself to answer every question,
discuss every clause, give amazing patience and careful knowledge to
any less strenuous ally, or more querulous member, and now, even while
some one else was expected to look after Financial Budgets, he pursued
the same method in handling doubtful friends or dangerous foes, in con-
ciliating those whom he had provoked by his straightforwardness, and
in supplying the defenders of the measure of which he was the champion
with all the resources with which he himself came and triumphed in
debate.   Never was a great man more lavish in bestowing his gifts and
intelligence upon those who could only be his lieutenants.   He had
been especially careful to note the appearance of every really noble and
rising young man; and it was his habit to grant to him complete possession of the large stores of knowledge and the lessons of his long
Parliamentary experience; and even when ingratitude showed itself, or
jealousy exhibited its less hideous features, the Grand Old Man acted
as though he had no power of control or weapon of argument which
he would not willingly give into the hands of some one else, if, by that
means, the measure initiated for public good might be made victorious.
The House of Commons, though he was opposed for long years by
Disraeli, sharply attacked by Lord Randolph Churchill, forsaken by
John Bright, mercilessly fought by Joseph Chamberlain, became a
school for young debaters, who have profited by beholding how much
of patient generosity and gentility may be allied with unprecedented
skill and boundless resource in such a figure and influence as Gladstone.
Young men were put to shame, oftentimes, by beholding this redoubta-

ble old man holding in his firm, yet courteous grasp, a beaten minority or a half despairing majority, until he could, by persistent appeal and adroit maneuver, win the day for his party. At the last of his career in the House of Commons, the exquisite modulations of that voice which would have given him distinction as a singer, fell upon the ears of friends and foes alike, in its subtle and resistless music.

Age had transformed the passion of his antagonists into something like respectful admiration of the unprecedented talents and superb courage, if not the large statesmanship, of one whose name is the pride of Anglo-Saxon civilization. Men seemed to know that he had fought his fight, and that it had been a noble one, that he had withstood the noise and severity of personal encounter with the mob, had showed the opposition a hundred times that he knew no such thing as fear, and was, in the eventide of life, as clear in his comprehension of the truth he wanted to state as ever before, and that the genuine reverence in which the dauntless old orator was held, became witness, not only to his unique talents, but also to the generosity of his lifelong foes. There can be no question that Gladstone, the once haughty and thoroughly equipped Tory, had an imperiousness of manner when he was in the fray, which bore down hard, sometimes, upon friend and foe alike. He had taken everything in his life seriously. He had been in dead earnest from the beginning to the very end of his career; and yet, with the mellow evening there came a sweetness of temper and a glowing beauty diffusing itself from his very presence, with which it was impossible to contend and in whose influence it was delightful to stand.

The Grand Old Man was about to place the reins of government in other hands. It was now impossible for him, as it had been in 1860, to carry his Bill over the House of Lords. He might have denounced them with the same resistless force of appeal and lofty arguments with which he disdained to scorn their action when his Bill for the abolition of Duty on Paper had been rejected. His friends urged him to appeal to the country, after dissolving Parliament. They still saw in the aged Commoner the potencies for a triumph such as might take from the machinery of English political life a good deal of unnecessary and antiquated material. Radicalism beseeched him to make the fight against the House of Lords. But there were reasons, which Gladstone himself never made public, but which ultimately led him even to deny the Liberal party the prestige and force of his own leadership, and the great leader went to the ranks as a follower in the House of Commons.

After a brief respite from public cares to which latter, even as an ordinary member of the House of Commons, he gave his usual laboriousness and power, he found himself, in 1894, on the Treasury Bench, his Home Rule measure having been rejected by the House of Lords. His face was still radiant with the hope that, by and by, and in other hands, it would achieve its triumph. It was interesting to watch him in those days as he came up against the fact that the House of Lords only had obstructed the progress of what he believed to be most important legislation in the interests of the British Empire. Once more they now unrighteously interfered. It was on a small matter,—the Parish Councils Bill,—but Gladstone spoke one word, which lifted the Liberal party to its feet. He seemed to see the people of the Empire rising in revolt at its dogged Conservatism and its jaunty reappearance as an obstructionist. He said:

"For me, my duty terminates with calling the attention of this House to a fact which it is really impossible to set aside—that we are considering a part, an essential and inseparable part, of a question enormously large, a question which has become profoundly a truth, a question that will demand a settlement, and must at an early date receive that settlement from the highest authority."

If Gladstone had been a Disraeli, theatrical as well as eloquent, loving to explode a sentiment as well as to put himself before the English people as their only deliverer and proper guide, he would have taken advantage of that hour, echoing still with the storm of cheers and witnessing to the growing quality of his statesmanship at the very last. He would have said some word of farewell which might have remained in the history of eloquence and patriotism, unique and prophetic. Perhaps he did not do that thing for the reason that through all his soul there moved the consciousness that his Cabinet and he were not in such harmony as might justify his speaking from such a position in the manner usually required by the necessities of the case. He was great

23

enough to move from out the light beating against the throne of his power without an attitude or gesture which could be misinterpreted. He was willing to retire at an hour when the British nation knew how perilous was the existence of the House of Lords, as at present constituted, in a crisis like this.

There was really no one for Gladstone to select as successor but Lord Rosebery. A crisis had come in the life of the Liberal party, and it was sure that Rosebery's abilities, his connections, and the attitude of the Liberal leaders toward him constituted him the best man for the place. He shared many of Gladstone's studies, though his own contrasted with Gladstone's regularity of conduct, for he was in the habit of giving his intervals of leisure not to the theology, either of Abraham or Homer, but to the interests of the turf.

The young Lord and Gladstone had often chatted together about old china, or the most recently obtained picture from the brush of an old master acquired for the National Gallery. They had been interested likewise in orators, novelists, historians, poets and essayists, and Rosebery, like Gladstone, was possessed of immense information. He was ambitious to be a great orator and an excellent writer, and in both of these ambitions he has obtained, especially in the latter, a fair measure of success.

Gladstone, who had fought under Lord John Russell, Lord Palmerston and Lord Derby, could see no objection to him because Rosebery was a lord. Gladstone knew the immense benefit which should accrue to him by having at his hand such abilities as were represented by Sir William Harcourt, Mr. Asquith, John Morley, Arthur Morley, Lord Kimberley and Mr. Fowler, who was already a fine swordsman in debate. His successor was left to appoint his own followers. He was to have the richest blessing of Mr. Gladstone, and he was duly inducted into the office, with Mr. Leonard Courtney as one of his efficient lieutenants, and a large number of able friends as his followers.

CHAPTER XLII.

GLADSTONE THE MAN.

It was impossible for such an eventide as threw its calm and beauteous light on Gladstone, to have visited upon a less noble figure its complete and serene glory. We have seen the statesman as a student of Christian theology and of Homer, and soon we behold him as the translator of Horace, adding to that branch of literature a contribution as characteristic as he has ever given to the world. At Hawarden Castle he lived in the sweet companionship of his books. His library, by the way, is a witness to the many-sided intellectual and spiritual life of the deceased statesman. No one has better understood the value and significance of books than he. To have seen him at Quaritch's, in Piccadilly, roaming about amidst that unique collection of rare volumes, was to see the most delighted of human beings in the most charming environment. Master of many tongues, he would pick up a rare edition of Dante and discourse upon the seriousness and message of the austere Italian singer, or, having lit upon the earliest printed edition of Homer, he would find a page which started his mind into scholarly utterance, or, attracted to a set of volumes by Racine, or a volume by Lacordaire, he would state with discrimination and fullness his views of the position of the one in poetry and of the other in churchmanship, and thus, from old missals glorious with gold and color or yellow with age, and interesting from previous associations, through tomes of church fathers and exhibits of bindings, which latter always demanded his careful and thorough appreciation, he would stray over to the Latin authors, or perhaps to a Hebrew Bible, and, thinking at that moment of a review which he was writing on the latest important novel, he would say: "Send me all the new books." Thus Hawarden Castle had as its point of central interest to this scholar, the magnificent collection of books which he had made in the flight of more than a half century. Every villager had been permitted to borrow books from this collection, and oftentimes one might see a young hired man on the estate journeying away from Hawarden Castle with a volume of most precious importance, both to the lender and borrower. The large tables in the library were each of them devoted to special subjects, and, in late years, Gladstone returned with affection to the Homer table, from which the storm of public life had so often driven him, and to which, as often, he went back with joy. In that library such authors as have created literatures for their own exposition had their separate places, thus enabling Mr. Gladstone and the members of his family to study them with ease; and there was no more interesting sight for a bibliophile than the Horace table, or the theology table, or the Armenian table, as these subjects, one after another, came before him in the days of his respite from arduous labors.

More interesting than any or all his books to Gladstone was the woman who sat with him through so many days and nights, whose father's castle became his home,—the daughter of Sir Stephen Glynne— Mrs. William E. Gladstone. The relationship in which these two souls have stood, labored, sorrowed, triumphed, has furnished an ideal chapter in the history of human marriages. Mrs. Gladstone has been his inspirer and guide, his closest and best friend, his sincerest appreciator and profoundest critic, his companion in soul and intellect, since that lovely day in which they found themselves man and wife in Hawarden Castle. She has matched his almost measureless capacity for work with her own. She has equaled his with her own intensity of conviction and her own comprehensiveness of intellect. She has gone with him through severe campaigns in Midlothian, attending to his wants as a mother might care for a child, partaking of the excitement of approving cheers and sharing with him the dangers of threatening mobs; at his right hand supplying him with this needed help or that note of manuscript, nursing him through colds, and arranging for his hours of sleep, relieving his mind, if possible, from the thousand cares which come with a family of children—loved and nurtured as have been Gladstone's children, going with him to the little graveyard, and standing with him by the empty cradle, traveling to the last from place to place on the planet, that her espoused and heroic husband might gain relief from torturing pain,—always the wife and mother, the friend and counsellor, his soul's veritable mate.

It would have been impossible for Gladstone to have accomplished anything like the measure of success in so many realms of human progress, if he had been otherwise associated in his family life. Mrs. Gladstone has met and managed the vast number of visitors clamoring for her husband's precious hours, and rarely, if ever, has the humblest been pained by too little, or the loftiest allowed too much, of his time and power, by the firm and intelligent administration she has conducted. Together with him she has walked almost daily to the little church in the village where the English Premier has often read the lesson, and where he was delighted and uplifted by the ministration of his own son. That little footpath leading from the Castle to the church has been trodden by them both in hours when British and international statesmanship was receiving its best inspiration from the churchgoing of this indissoluble couple. When he went forth, as was his habit, with axe in hand, to strengthen his already superb physical organism by cutting trees in Hawarden Forest, there was one eye which followed him with the love which she conceived when first they met in Italy.

Yet his favorite exercise was only one of the many ways in which his tremendous powers were employed. He would as likely take a companion, and, while pouring out from the wealth of his intelligence musical speech on religion, art, or politics, he would persist in walking ten or twelve miles, or set himself about the preparation of an address as Lord Rector of the University, or answer the command of his Queen to present himself at St. James' Palace, or Osborne, or begin his reply to the editor of the "Nineteenth Century" or the "Contemporary Review," or the half dozen other great periodicals in England or America to which he contributed; or perhaps he would be found at the station, meeting Robert Browning, or the Chancellor of the University of Oxford, or even his old friend Cardinal Manning; or he would join with one of his sons or daughters in making a visit to some helpless or unfortunate one among the many who lived in the cottages on the estate. In all these and in a hundred other ways, Gladstone lived his life, and it was shared most profoundly by the woman whom Providence gave to him as companion.

He always insisted upon his right to his Sunday, and he attributed a large measure of his health and good spirits to the fact that no one was able to steal from him this golden day. · He usually attended daily the service at Hawarden, or elsewhere, and those who have heard him read from the Scriptures in the village church know something of that feeling which was possessed by the great historian who averred his belief that Gladstone would have been the most fascinating, as well as vigorous power in English church life, if he had taken orders and had, as naturally he would have had, a career closing in the Archbishopric of Canterbury and Primacy of all England.

England has lost nothing, the world has gained much by the picture which is left to a materialistic and agnostic age—of the Premier of the British Empire standing at the reading-desk and filling the sacred house with the tones which bore to his hearers the vision of the prophet, the sigh of the saint, the prayer of the sinner, and the wide hope of the Evangelist. The Harley street house in London, and surely the Downing street house, never entered into successful rivalry with Hawarden as Gladstone's home. Mrs. Gladstone's brother added a new wing to the castle which he called the Gladstone Wing, dedicated to the author, orator and statesman. It has been what the title bestowed upon the library would indicate, "The Temple of Peace." Here and at a church Gladstone had found the deepest influences coming into his life. It must not be forgotten at any point in Gladstone's career, that, great as he was as a man of letters and sure and powerful as was that stream of literary power enforcing arguments and illuminating statements in his speeches as a politician, he was still more great as a churchman, and he seemed never to get over the disappointment at not having been allowed, in his youth, to pursue the career of a minister. Whatever peculiarity of mind Mr. Gladstone has shown, may be traced,—at least it has been influenced largely by—the fact that he has relied upon his religious convictions as the sole foundation of the political structure he would build. He has lived a singularly upright and blameless life. But he has done more than this, he began and continued his career in the belief that every strong man ought to feel, as he has felt, that he is an agent for the carrying out of the Providential designs of God. Nothing else will explain Gladstone's utter disregard of consequences apparent to other men,—consequences flowing from a course of action upon which he had decided.

He believed God would not forsake him, and if he had an imperiousness equal to Cromwell's, he fell back upon the faith of the prophet which he believed himself to be, and he trusted God as he conceived Him. We have pointed out that it is a churchman's conception of God which controlled Gladstone. Other men about him had no such faith, even in their own conception of God, still less did they feel his confidence in the God whom he conceived. Yet never even Disraeli sneered at Gladstone's religiousness. On the other hand, the former's foreign policy went down before the attack made by Gladstone upon it, in the name of those interests which are usually called religious.

Sunday evening at Hawarden Castle commonly closed the day of meditation and prayer and reading, with the singing of familiar hymns, in which Gladstone often joined. Monday came and found him in Parliament or elsewhere, refreshed and surer than ever that there is ever a God in Israel. Doubtless he oftentimes mistook his somewhat churchly view of God, his scholastically conceived opinions about what God wanted to do, for these sacred things; but to stand on his feet at all, such a man as Gladstone must have such a rigorous and even imperious faith. Other men might spend Sunday as they would; here was a man whose lips were glowing with the coal from God's altars, and, rested and inspired as he was, it is little wonder that he brought a keen intellect and an almost awful laboriousness to Downing street, and, then, every official in the Government knew that the conscientious and industrious statesman would know what he believed to be the truth about all the affairs of the Government. An intellect having such a grasp, and ranging over such territory as did Gladstone's intellect, could find nothing else upon which to rely in the varied moods and in the multitudinous paths it must know, save such a religious life as he has lived. This religious enthusiasm has been shared by his wife and family, and it has enlivened many pages of otherwise dry controversy.

Gladstone's home was always a resort of poets, artists, theologians, and politicians, from every quarter of the world. Even Gladstone's abhorrence of tobacco yielded to Tennyson, in order that the two great friends might enjoy happy days together.

John Ruskin had called himself a Tory such as Homer and Walter Scott, and he had violently berated Gladstone, and his biography, by Professor Collinwood, furnishes no more delightful page than this:

"During this term, 1883, he was prevailed upon to allow himself to be nominated as a candidate for the rectorship of the University of Glasgow. He had been asked to stand in the Conservative interest in 1880, and he had been worried into a rather rough reply to the Liberal party, when after some correspondence they asked him whether he sympathized with Lord Beaconsfield or Mr. Gladstone. 'What in the devil's name,' he exclaimed, 'have you to do with either Mr. Disraeli or Mr. Gladstone? You are students at the University, and have no more business with politics than you have with rat-catching. Had you ever read ten words of mine with understanding, you would have known that I care no more either for Mr. Disraeli or Mr. Gladstone than for two old bagpipes with the drones going by steam, but that I hate all Liberalism as I do Beelzebub, and that, with Carlyle, I stand, we two alone now in England, for God and the Queen.' After that, though he might explain that he never, under any conditions of provocation or haste, would have said that he hated Liberalism as he did Mammon, or Belial, or Moloch; that he 'chose the milder fiend of Ekron as the true exponent and patron of Liberty, the God of Flies;' still the matter-of-fact Glaswegians were minded to give the scoffer a wide berth. He was put up as an independent candidate in the three-cornered duel; and, as such candidates usually fare, he fared badly. The only wonder is that three hundred and nineteen students were found to vote for him, instead of siding, in political orthodoxy, with Mr. Fawcett or the Marquis of Bute."

Yet Ruskin changed his opinion.

After his leaving public life, it became much more easy for Mr. Gladstone to spend time with his correspondence, and to make play of literary work. But he has known so well the use of time in all his life, that he has been exceedingly productive as a letter writer, and many volumes attest the delight of his studies in the form of essays. As an example of his use of time, Mr. Lucy, writing, in 1882, tells us:

"One night last session, when the Irish members were in high spirits, and were leading the high court of Parliament through a continuous series of perambulations round the division lobby, Mr. Gladstone got through an immense amount of correspondence. He wrote on his knee whilst seated on the Treasury Bench. When the bell rang for the division he went on writing rapidly. As soon as the Speaker dispatched 'Ayes to the right' and 'Noes to the left,' the Premier adroitly sprang up, and displaying the agility of a young buck, made his way out into the division lobby before the crush came. In recesses of the lobby there are providentially set forth writing-tables, and here, whilst the throng of members pressed forward, the Premier sat, taking up the thread of his discourse, and writing as if the immediate object of his life was to earn the tenpence an hour doled out to the minions of the Foreign Office. As soon as the last member approached the wicket, Mr. Gladstone rose, passed through, resumed his seat on the Treasury Bench, and went on writing as before, going through the process with undiminished energy as often as it pleased the obstructionists to trot out the Saxon Parliament through the lobbies. In these circumstances, when the House is unequally divided, a minority of ten or a dozen going into one lobby and a majority of two or three hundred into the other, a division occupies at least a quarter of an hour. But Mr. Gladstone had saved every moment except those occupied in rapidly walking over the uncrowded course."

It is supposed that once Gladstone found himself giving too much time to old china, and in 1874 the excellent collection was sold. Of its rarity and value one may have some idea, if he has made studies of the fragment of the collection of ivories and antique jewels exhibited at the South Kensington Museum and the cabinets still containing countless objects of interest in Hawarden Castle.

In 1895 Mr. Gladstone sent a note to one of his friends containing this passage: "Above all present purposes, indicate the right of the House of Commons as the organ of the nation; and re-establish the honor of England, as well as consolidate the strength of the Empire by conceding the great and institutional claims of Ireland." This was signed and sent July 5th. It furnished evidence that the Grand Old Man still had a program, even if others were to carry it out. He dipped into theology at this period with even more than his wonted interest, and he wrote articles for the reviews, oftentimes eclipsing his former studies

by the brilliancy of his style and the affluence of his learning. The great
world which he had taught and in which he had acted for so long a time,
he could not wholly forsake, and, up to a recent date, if one was fortunate
enough to find him at Biarritz, or in the Riviera, he was sure to see
Gladstone amidst publicists, diplomatists, statesmen, literary men, artists
of other countries, leading the conversation and surpassing any or all
by the interest of his remarks. He was constantly turning to his old
authors and finding his early love well placed. His treatment of the
author of the "Analogy of Natural and Revealed Religion" is a tardy
piece of justice which came at last to the great Bishop of Durham, and is
a witness of Gladstone's piety, thorough scholarship, and conscientious
industry. He delighted himself and his readers with graceful and incisive studies of Sheridan and the English poets. But his deeper thought
ran toward the great subject of the unity of Christendom.

The present occupant of the Papal chair has, by his piety, learning,
and philanthropy, endeared himself to all Christians throughout the
world, and it was impossible that the letter which the Pope addressed
to the English people should not produce a great impression upon the
public mind. It furnished evidence that Leo XIII. deeply desired the
unity of Christ's flock in the world. Gladstone had for a long time been
in correspondence with the old Catholics, so-called, and with men who
stood in the position occupied by Dr. Döllinger and Cardinal Manning,
and he was sincerely interested in bringing about a union of the dis-
severed ranks of Christianity into one great army of the Lord. It is
doubtful if Gladstone would have done much to please the Dissenters,
although without the Dissenters in England we could hardly conceive of
Gladstone's having won some of his greatest victories for righteousness.
The discussion turned upon the point of the validity of orders in the
English Established Church. Gladstone's letter was worthy of his truly
comprehensive and profoundly irenic intellect. He acknowledged his
joy in noting "the progressive advance of a great work of restoration
in Christian doctrine." He was glad that it was not confined to his
own communion. He had faith in the future of the English Church, but
he indicated that if the Catholic Church might agree that the Anglican

ordinations are valid, a mighty step forward would be taken toward Church unity.

Of course this has no surpassing interest to many Americans, but it must ever be remembered as one of the consummate flowers in a garden glorious with eventide.

All England united at last to do honor to the Grand Old Man, and nothing was more beautiful than the speech of the Prince of Wales when, as Chancellor of the University, he spoke of Mr. and Mrs. Gladstone, upon the former of whom he had just conferred an honor.

"You will all join with me," the Prince said, "I am sure, in thanking the veteran statesman and eminent scholar, Mr. Gladstone, who, notwithstanding his advanced age, has undertaken a journey, necessarily fatiguing, in order to pay a compliment to the University of Wales and to myself as its Chancellor. I may truly say that one of the proudest moments of my life was when I found myself in the flattering position of being able to confer an academic distinction upon Mr. Gladstone, who furnishes a rare instance of a man who has achieved one of the highest positions as a statesman and at the same time has attained such distinction in the domain of literature and scholarship. His translation of the Odes of Horace would alone constitute a lasting monument to him even had he not accomplished so much besides which has rendered him illustrious. Nor do we extend a less warm welcome to Mr. Gladstone's ever faithful companion and helper during the many years of his busy life."

Nothing was more characteristic of Mr. Gladstone than that the powers in him which responded to the cry of Bulgaria should respond quickly to the equally pathetic cry of Armenia, or the weaker plea of Crete. No picture of the Grand Old Man is more interesting than that which he left upon the mind of the realm when he stood in his own birthplace, Liverpool, and made such an appeal as reached the fortress of the Oriental assassin, whose cruelty amazed the intelligence of Europe. Gladstone saw the terrible fact that the brutality of the Turk had set itself to the extinction of Christianity, and to the overturning of any rights which the Armenian subjects of the Sultan might have acquired. Gladstone knew that there was little which England might yet do, in comparison with what England ought to have done at an earlier date, but that little was much, and he said: "That coercion, which ought long ago to have been applied to him (the Sultan) might even now be the means of averting another series of massacres, possibly even exceeding those which we have already seen." Gladstone, the man of peace, had uttered the word which for the moment meant war, if necessary, and Lord Rosebery, with his party in a small minority, had found an opportunity for retiring from the leadership of the Liberal party.

But Gladstone's Liverpool speech was only one of many on the same subject, and his pen was as mighty as ever it had been in denouncing Bulgarian atrocities. He wrote in the "Nineteenth Century" and elsewhere, and the Sultan was pressed closely by public opinion in England, roused and heated by Mr. Gladstone to the point of making such demands as would satisfy the conscience of civilization. He proposed that England, on her own responsibility, should do righteousness. When it was suggested that England should listen to the siren voices, Gladstone said:

"However we may desire and strive to obtain the co-operation of others, is it possible for us to lay down this doctrine: England may give for herself the most solemn pledges in the most binding shape, but she now claims the right of referring it to some other person or persons, State or States, not consulted or concerned in her act, to determine whether she shall endeavor to the utmost of her ability to fulfill them?

"If this doctrine is really to be adopted, I would respectfully propose that the old word 'honor' should be effaced from our dictionaries, and dropped from our language."

The very presence of Gladstone in England, laying bare the peril of Christian civilization in the Orient, and pleading with intelligence and earnestness for humanity, is a fact never to be forgotten, even in the reign of that sordid materialism which answered it not.

Never was there a moment in Gladstone's career when a halting policy and vested interests chafed in Lombard Street, on the Exchange, and more sympathetically uttered the old criticism of Lord Aberdeen: "He is too obstinate. If a man could be too honest, I should say he is too honest. He does not think enough of what other men think. When he has convinced himself, perhaps by abstract reasoning, of some view, he thinks everyone else ought to see it as he does, and can make no allowances for difference of opinion." There is really nothing so stubborn or impractical, in the eyes of a politician, as the unbending convictions of a statesman.

Gladstone at this moment was a sick man, and his physician was urging him to avoid labor, and especially to keep out of unnecessary controversy. But his physician labored in vain. He said:

"Here is a man who, at the very end of a long life honorably spent in the service of his country, in possession of everything a mortal can desire, risks fame, position, the love, nay, the esteem, of his country and his Sovereign—everything, in fact, worth living for,—in order to carry out what he is profoundly convinced to be right. And how that man is vilified! But mark my word, no man will be more regretted or extolled when he is gone."

Always from these turbulent scenes Mr. Gladstone had gone into the peace and defense of Hawarden Castle. Ten years before his death, the fiftieth anniversary of his marriage with Miss Glynne had been celebrated; and the last ten years of his life, closing as they did in that remarkably tender and almost thrilling farewell when death came, were the answer to his prayer that he might spend the tranquil eventide and close the day of his life at Hawarden. Here he had loved and shared his life with the mate of his soul; here he had seen his children reared to manhood and womanhood, or from the little church yonder he had followed them to the grave. From the time they had bade farewell to the little girl, early in the fifties, to the time when the old man followed to the grave the son upon whom he most leaned as his friend and helper, the lights and shadows of life had mingled most significantly here. Here he had talked with Tennyson and Browning, with Ruskin and Dean Stanley, and from this library he had sent forth his views in controversy with the redoubtable antagonists of the Christian faith in every country. Out of this library had gone his words of fine optimism in his reply to Alfred Tennyson's "Locksley Hall Sixty Years Afterward," and it was but a specimen of that music which he sounded from the high moral and mental point of view he had in his own home. He said, speaking of the attitude of a thoughtful man toward the past and the future:

"Each generation or age of men is under a twofold temptation: the one to overrate its own performances and prospects, the other to undervalue the times preceding or following its own. No greater calamity can happen to a people than to break utterly with its Past. But the proposition in its full breadth applies more to its aggregate, than to its immediate Past. Our judgment on the age that last preceded us should be strictly just. But it should be masculine, not timorous: for, if we gild its defects, and glorify its errors, we dislocate the axis of the very ground which forms our own point of departure."

Nothing is more charactertistic of Mr. Gladstone's old age than the fountain of perpetual youth bubbling up its liquid jewels of thought from the very secrets of his soul. Other men might be delighted to see a country with an income so much more vast than its expenditures as to astonish the world; Gladstone knew that there is another basis for true national prosperity, and when he went to Wales to speak, he said:

"A country is in a good and sound and healthy state when it exhibits the spirit of progress in all its institutions and in all its operations; and when with that spirit of progress it combines the spirit of affectionate retrospect upon the times and the generations that have gone before, and the determination to husband and to turn at every point to the best account all that these previous generations have accumulated of what is good and worthy for the benefit of us, their children."

Such persistent vitality of thought was associated in Gladstone with a charm of manner and a reality of faith so comprehensive as to gather into its friendship some of those who had been most strongly antagonistic to him in other years. No one, for example, paid a more touching tribute to Gladstone after his life had closed, than Mr. Balfour, leader of the Tory Government, who, rising from a bed of sickness, sought to do himself and his party the honor (for he could add nothing to the laurels of Gladstone) of placing upon record his opinion of that great man. Lord Salisbury's address alone, in which he made special mention of the fact that Gladstone must be known as the incarnation of

Christian statesmanship, equaled the address of Balfour, and it eclipsed, by its radiance of affectionate regard, all the flashings of the swords in years agone. It all reminded one that, after all, there was in Gladstone something far greater than what any difference of opinion could possibly effect.

Once John Ruskin, who had been visiting at Windsor, was persuaded to go to Hawarden, and Ruskin used to say of his Toryism that it was firm and implacable. No man in England had furnished such bitter pages with reference to Gladstone as had Ruskin. But they met and loved each other. The history of human apologies is not complete without that page from "Fors Clavigera," in which Ruskin chronicles the fact that he had completely misconceived Gladstone. When the time for the reprinting of the old magazine came, Ruskin would not permit the passage in which he had scored Mr. Gladstone, to reappear, but in the blank space he left a little note, calling it "A Memorial of Rash Judgment."

Gladstone himself once quoted Browning's "Sordello" to this effect:

"Upgathered on himself the fighter stood
  For his last fight, and wiping treacherous blood
  Out of his eyelids, just held ope beneath
  Those shading fingers in their iron sheath,
  Steadied his strength amid the shock and stir
  Of the dusk hideous atmosphere."

And the aged man, always desiring the love of the best of men, remarked half sadly as he brightened with hope: "I know I have appeared like unto that; but 'time is on our side,' and I will be understood fully perhaps before my career ends here."

CHAPTER XLIII.

AT EVENTIDE.

One of Gladstone's earlier biographers has told us a story that, at one time, in the history of that home where argumentation was as much a staple of its life as religion was, the young William Gladstone and his sister Mary were disputing as to the proper place on the wall for a picture loved by both of them. The old Scotch servant, standing upon the ladder, was useless, but interested in the discussion, while the two argued about the momentous matter. William was chivalrous, and Mary was possibly weary, but certainly she did not yield, until the brother paused and the contest was ended without convincing him. The servant was directed to hang the picture as Mary desired, but he knew young William, and that his power of argument was unexhausted. Possibly he knew, also, that William was right. At any rate, he went across the room and drove a nail in the place William had suggested. When questioned as to his reason for this course of action, he said: "Awell, miss, that will do to hang the picture on when ye'll have to come round to Master Willie's opeenion."

The fact is that the spirit of human progress has heard with no little interest the contention which William Ewart Gladstone has urged, and the argument which he has used against what is perhaps least objectionably characterized as fear, ignorance and political bigotry. He has seemed to be the Great Defeated, and he certainly closed his life, after England's voice had joined in the chorus of praise for his earlier achievements, with the great desire of his heart unaccomplished in the form of legislation. This spirit of progress has been patient and yet far-seeing. After Toryism has hung its picture as it pleased, there has been a nail hammered into the opposite wall, and when Conservatism objects, the spirit of progress may say, with the old Scotch servant: "Awell, that

368

will do to hang the picture on when ye'll have to come round to Master Willie's opeenion."

The moral influence of such a man as Mr. Gladstone rose far above any anticipation his youth suggested, in the range and quality of its achievements. In November, 1844, Lord Malmesbury wrote in his journal:

"November 7th: Dined with the Cannings and met Mr. Gladstone and Mr. Phillimore. We were curious to see the former, as he is a man who is much spoken of as one who will come to the front. We were disappointed at his appearance, which is that of a Roman Catholic ecclesiastic, but he is very agreeable."

The priesthood of such a spirit has been more than any church could hold or any condition of politics could control. His effect upon public morals, as these were to be performed by a nobler Christian ministry, has been immeasurable. He himself said:

"It was, I think, about the year 1835, that I first met the Rev. Sydney Smith, at the house of Mr. Hallam. In conversation after dinner he said to me, with the double charm of humor and good humor, 'The improvement of the clergy in my time has been astonishing. Whenever you meet a clergyman of my age, you may be quite sure he is a bad clergyman.' "

No man has done more to create and re-create the clergy of Anglo-Saxon Christendom than has Gladstone. A soul with less glorious light shining out from its windows, and undertaking such tasks as he did in Ireland and in England, with rough peasants and useless ecclesiastics, would have seemed ludicrously incompetent. It was his moral strength which confounded his foes. The Ireland he attempted to deal with would have offered a complete resistance to merely intellectual power.

Sidney Smith was humorous and accurate as to the spirit of things when he described "those Irish Protestants whose shutters are bullet-proof; whose dinner-table is regularly spread out with knife, fork, and cocked pistol, salt-cellar and powder flask; who sleep in sheet-iron night-caps; who have fought so often before their scullery-door, and defended the parlor passage as bravely as Leonidas defended the pass of Thermopylæ."

24

If ever this Ireland has been made reasonable, it has been by a man who, horrifying Protestantism on the one hand by his insistence that Catholics should be fairly treated, and making Catholics indignant, on the other hand, by his searching criticism of the Vatican, could splendidly fling out over all the discussion, the illumination of a moral genius. This spiritual element abided like a twilight from another world, and in it no man could seriously deny the sovereignty of celestial elements.

That Mr. Gladstone was boundlessly charitable, and therefore stringently economical in the expenditures of himself and his family, is attested by thousands of causes he relieved, once even going so far as to sell a portion of his library, and cease gathering rare specimens of old china. That Mr. Gladstone exercised the height of an energetic oratory and thus controlled men who were opposed to him in political opinion, is instanced a hundred times by his Parliamentary achievements. That an intellectual splendor, gorgeous if never dry, diffused itself by the processes of reflection and refraction in countless streams of fascinating influence, is demonstrated in review articles, almost without number, in orations which have already taken their place with the eloquent utterances of Burke and Chatham, and in discussions of literary problems as comprehensive and keen as any written in his time. But all of these are greater by the fact that they were associated with and partly derived from a spiritual energy, the like of which has not manifested itself in another personality in our century. Mr. O'Connor Power furnishes us with a single incident of its influence. He says:

"The division lobby is often one of the most interesting sights of the House of Commons. There are huddled together for a brief space all the strange and varied personalities of the House. Even in the lobby, however, the great personality of Mr. Gladstone stands out. It is his usual custom to rush to one of the writing tables, and, after his fashion, on which the grand symmetry and orderliness of his great life have been planned and relentlessly pursued, he will not wholly lose even the brief space of time which is there expended. Accordingly he is to be seen writing away for dear life—sometimes holding the blotting-pad on his knees when he goes back to the House, and often calmly pursuing his work amid the shouts of hatred or triumph around him.

"But on Tuesday night, for a moment, he allowed the natural man to conquer. Selecting a seat in a quiet corner, he fell into a brief, hurried, but profound slumber, and was lost to the world of teeming and shouting life around him. The pallid look on the face told of the fatigue of the day, but the splendid mouth, firm set, was there—with that look of unalterable determination which conquers all things. It was a beautiful and impressive picture, and, by a quick and electric communicativeness, all its pathos and splendor and historic significance were gathered by the crowd. The usual noise of the lobby was stilled. Silently, reverently, members paused for a moment as they went by, whispered a comment in low accents, and passed on with hearts stirred silently, but profoundly, to reverence, awe, love."

As he came toward the end of his life, this moral power enabled him to clearly understand, as he could not understand in earlier days, the moral importance of such an experiment as our own in self-government. Dry as the subject might appear, the moral power shone over it all. In the autumn of 1889, in a speech delivered at the opening of new reading and recreation rooms at Saltney, Gladstone indicates how much he had learned from America. He said:

"My last recommendation to the student is one I have been in the habit of making for the last fifty years, because I then adopted the sentiments upon which it is founded, and I now make it therefore with greater confidence after the lapse of fifty years. That recommendation is, to those who are able to carry it out, to study the history of the American Revolution. That is an extraordinary history. It is highly honorable to those who brought that revolution about; but also honorable in no insignificant degree to this country, because it was by this country that the seeds of freedom were sown in America, because it was by imitating this country that America acquired the habits of freedom, and the capacity for more freedom. In this country we have happily had to a great extent, and I hope we shall have it still more, what is called local self-government—not merely one government at a certain point, composed of parties and exerting a vast power over their fellow-citizens, but a system under which the duties of government are distributed according to the capacities of the different divisions of the country, and the different classes of the people who perform them, in such a way that government should be practiced, not only in the metropolis, but in every country, in every borough, over every district, and in every parish. And that has tended to bring home to the mind of every father of a family, a sense of the public duty which he is called upon to perform. That has been the secret of the strength of America. The colonial system in which America was reared was in the main a free colonial system. You had in

America these two things combined: the love of freedom and respect for law, and a desire for the maintenance of order; and where you find these two things combined, love of freedom together with respect for law, and the desire for order, you have the elements of national excellence and national greatness."

At the Victoria Art Gallery, in Dundee, he indulged in quite different considerations, which, however, have been equally impressive to him. He said:

"Beauty is an element of immense pecuniary value. The traditional cultivation of taste and production of beauty in industrial objects, is better known in Italy, and very well known in France. We may still be some steps behind in many departments in that respect, but there is not a doubt that in the enormous commerce of France, the beauty of the objects produced counts from year to year for a great many millions sterling, and those millions sterling would fade into thin air, were the appreciation of beauty and the power of producing beautiful objects to be taken away, which, happily, it hardly can from such a people. It is an element of immense commercial value. Let us look abroad—let us take our lessons from nature, for, after all, we cannot go to a better source, or as good a source, as to the works of God. The Almighty has provided this earth with the beautiful, and has made the beauty of the land in which we are appointed to be born, and in which we live, an important instrument in stirring up in us and for confirming in us that devoted attachment to our country, which, I hope—under the name of patriotism or whatever other name—which, I believe, always has been a pointed characteristic of individuals, and which, I trust, always will be a marked and pointed characteristic of those who will succeed them in following generations. The Almighty has given us a lesson in this respect in making His works beautiful, showing that He suggests to us to make our works beautiful, humbly and reverently, but yet believing that if in every department of life we are following that example He will regard it with favor, and crown it with His blessing."

What he said of Bright when that life closed, may be said in a still higher way, of himself:

"Thus it has come about that he is entitled to a higher eulogy than is due to success. Of mere success, indeed, he was a conspicuous example. In intellect he might claim a most distinguished place. But his character lies deeper than intellect, deeper than eloquence, deeper than anything that

can be described or that can be seen upon the surface. The supreme eulogy
that is his due is that he elevated political life to the highest point—to a
loftier standard than it has ever reached. He has bequeathed to his country
a character that cannot only be made a subject for admiration and gratitude,
but—and I do not exaggerate when I say it—that can become an object of
reverential contemplation."

Out from the narrowing atmosphere of his individuality he looked,
and gave that atmosphere every wind of heaven, as he opened great subjects under the light of this moral faculty. No doubt he was deeply
disappointed in the attitude of the Irish people toward himself at various
times, and toward the cause to which he gave the best and truest devotion of his life. More heroically than in any diffculty with English
opinion, did Gladstone pursue his path with the unfortunate divisions,
and oftentimes unrelenting criticism of the Irish people themselves. The
present writer remembers hearing him, after he had read Mr. Barry
O'Brien's article on "Irish Wrongs and English Remedies," rehearse the
story there told, and every word of Gladstone's indicated that his faith
in humanity had endured much, but that it had triumphed over all. He
felt that he had the right to the confidence and loyalty of the Irish
people. It was a well-known saying of a great political philosopher
that his achievement in 1869, his carrying through Parliament his
measure of disestablishment, marked for English legislation the "only
complete measure of justice passed for Ireland since Catholic emancipation." But it was not to be wondered at that Ireland distrusted England's disposition and ability to do anything to remedy wrongs which
had been visited upon her, and which had produced chronic irritation.
Englishmen, on the other hand, saw how nearly impossible it was to
conciliate a people who believed that they had suffered centuries of
humiliation and outrage, with now and then a year or so of kindness
and an act of brotherly love. It had all been described in the phrase
which was applied to English rule in Ireland—"an alternation of kicks
and kindness, kicks freely given and kindness grudgingly bestowed"—
and a phrase like this has a marvelous power for traveling from cottage
to cottage in a land like Ireland. In Gladstone's time ignorant Catholics had been kept ignorant, because they would not conform to the

stated religion; he had seen that policy abandoned. From the eighteenth century charter schools, which existed only to make Protestants out of Catholics, drew their financial support from Parliament at the very time that Parliament declined to give a penny for the support of schools which would have reached the vast majority of the population; he had seen National schools open their doors to Catholic children, although they were superintended by a board in which Protestants appeared to Catholics as four to two, while the population indicated Catholics to Protestants as ten to two. To make this less pleasant to the Catholics, a Scotch Presbyterian clergyman had charge of it all. Their very school books made an effort to crush Irish patriotism, and Mr. O'Brien referred to the fact that the little Irish children were graciously permitted to sing the following words:

> "I thank the goodness and the grace
> That on my birth have smiled,
> And made me in these Christian days
> A happy English child."

In 1860 Gladstone had seen this happily transformed. The year 1832 came and went, leaving Ireland and O'Connell utterly dissatisfied with Reform measures, and Bright himself declared, in 1860, that the representation of Ireland in Parliament was virtually extinguished. Gladstone saw the Irish Reform Bill carried through in 1868, and the right to vote given in Irish boroughs to four-pound rate payers, and in 1884 the English and Irish franchises were granted alike to both peoples. He had entered public life at a time when Ireland was asking for the removal of tithes to support a church in which Irishmen had no religious interest, and when they objected they were coerced by law with the aid of the military and police, who had come to collect the tithes. He had watched Sir Robert Peel's bill, in 1835. and the amendment of Lord John Russell, and he had seen the amendment overthrow the bill, and "the surplus revenues of the established church applied to the purposes of general education in Ireland." Up to 1837 public opinion in England had given only such concession as was necessary to such schemes of coercion as its military force could apply. In spite of the Irish members, the Poor Law of 1838 had been carried, and it was put into operation, as the Irish expected, by Scotch and English officers. The Irish Municipal Reform Act of 1840 disenfranchised the municipalities. Up to 1869, a Protestant State church had been maintained by England, while it contained 800,000 communicants, and 6,000,000 of other people were unaided. On this topic the Peel government of 1844 refused to grant an inquiry. In 1846 Lord John Russell admitted that it ought to be reformed, but that the church must not be disestablished. In 1853 the same statesman announced his immovable opinion. Over and over the refusal was made. Disraeli's government in 1867 seemed as firm as was Peel's government in 1844, refusing to grant an inquiry. Then it was that Gladstone said "the time is not far distant when the Parliament of England, which at the present undoubtedly has its hands full of most important business and engagements, will feel it its duty to look this question fairly and openly in the face." In 1869 Gladstone had seen disestablishment accomplished. In 1842 the Times said:

"The tenant in Ireland has not the shadow of the character of a voluntary contractor. It is with him to continue on the quarter of an acre which he occupies, or to starve. There is no other alternative. Rack rents may be misery, but ejectment is ruin. And yet in this state of things estates are farmed out to middlemen; and ejectments are then brought, because the unhappy tenant is behind with his rent, or, what is still worse, upon some trivial breach of covenant, merely because possession would be convenient to the person seeking it. What has been the result? Conspiracy, hatred, revenge, and murder—most cold-blooded, most brutal murder."

And in 1850 it added:

"Are we to stand by with folded arms (writing after the murder of a land agent in the North of Ireland), looking on in mute despair, as if these events were an inevitable necessity—an evil beyond the reach of law or public opinion? Surely we are not justified in adopting such a listless course. If the proprietors of the soil, in maintaining the rights which the law has given them, thus recklessly inflict misery without stint upon the helpless and unfortunate peasantry; if they say that without the perpetration of barbarities which would disgrace a Turkish Pasha their rents cannot be collected; if they are to bring in the attorney multiplying process, and with process multiplying costs and reducing the peasantry to hopeless slavery; and if they are thus to convert the country into a battlefield for the landlords and process-servers, and sheriffs and sheriff officers on the one side, and the furious peasantry and banded assassins on the other—then we say it is the bounden duty of the Legislature to interfere, and either to enforce upon the present landlords the duties, while it maintains the rights, of property, or to create a new landed proprietary, whose intelligence and wealth will enable them to secure the peace of society, and thus lay the foundation of national prosperity."

The year 1852 came with a new spirit, but it was not until Gladstone introduced his bill in 1870 that the cause of the Irish tenants made a substantial gain. It is true that in 1835, 1841 and 1852, Gladstone, having learned much from Thomas Drummond, kept close company with Lord Stanley, afterwards Earl of Derby, on this subject. Lord Palmerston in vain tried to hold back the current of popular reform in 1865, but Gladstone was alert and ready when the moment came and his bill achieved "compulsory compensation for improvements effected against the will of the landlord." Swift and sure was the progress from 1870 up to this time, and now Mr. Gladstone stood with the phrase "Home Rule" quivering still upon his lips.

Not intellectual energy, but moral strength alone, kept the tribune of an often recalcitrant people ever faithful to their cause, because, whether that people heard or forbore, he knew the cause itself was right.

CHAPTER XLIV.

CONCLUSION.

For two years, according to Dr. Dobie, Mr. Gladstone's heart had been so weak as to be liable to fail suddenly; yet it was impossible for a man of Mr. Gladstone's out-of-door habits and immense vitality to come to the conclusion that he was a dying man. He took a trip to Scotland, and wandered over the heather, braving the Scotch rain and mist, and enjoying himself thoroughly with his friend George Armistead.

Presently there developed an irritation in his face and head which robbed him of all sleep. An examination of the distinguished patient proved that the mucous membrane had swollen, and that no surgical operation would be likely to relieve Mr. Gladstone. He obeyed his physician and went to Cannes, where he had enjoyed many a pleasant day with distinguished foreigners in an atmosphere hitherto most beneficial to him. He was a little relieved, and, indeed, resumed his old habits of reading, which earlier he had been compelled to give up. He turned again to Sir Walter Scott, and read his works with the keenest satisfaction. All the new books, and many of the old ones on theology were packed up and sent to him, in the hope that his health might so far be restored as to enable him to write more as a student of religion. Now and then grave symptoms appeared, and the physicians and Mrs. Gladstone were much alarmed.

It was thought best that he should return to England, and he passed a few weeks at Bournemouth, where he endured extreme pain. Now his whole desire was to get back to Hawarden Castle. He had been kindly in his attentions to the lowliest of his tenants in the hours of their suffering and sorrow, and the atmosphere of the beloved shire, in which he had passed so much of his life, was itself a welcome to the dying man.

It was most touching, during the last days of Mr. Gladstone's life, to observe the extreme tenderness with which the whole population round about Hawarden Castle watched the progress of the case of "the old gentleman," as they called him. Representatives of families whom he had visited in times of darkness and distress, came up with their simple offering of profound love, and left the castle in tears when they found that their great and good friend was suffering intensely.

The agony of the sick-room, prolonged through many weeks, was shared by the heart of England. Mr. Gladstone himself complained not. He said he had enjoyed so many thousand hours without pain that he was willing to accept this suffering from the hands of Providence. With all the depth of his religious emotion, and with the glow of his earnest faith, he walked bravely on into the valley of the shadow, and it was light everywhere about him. The old hymns which had so often been sung on Sunday nights in Hawarden Castle, were sung to him now. Little Dorothy Drew, the ever-loved grandchild, added her pathetic wail that her grandfather did not know her any more. Rev. Stephen Gladstone, son of the passing statesman, read the Litany to him day after day, and as the accents of his voice, as he read, died away from the attention of the dying man, he feebly murmured, "Amen!" No word he could have pronounced would have conveyed the full meaning and character of Gladstone's career more truly. His whole life had been an amen to all the divine impulses and hopes embodied in the cross of Jesus Christ.

The next morning all the world knew that William Ewart Gladstone had terminated his career, and from almost every nation under heaven came words of condolence and prayer. The Prince of Wales and his Royal Mother joined with the collier and cabdriver in the common grief. It is certain that the world felt that a mighty oak had fallen, and the forest looked strange without this colossal central figure.

It was the plain intention of Mr. Gladstone that his body should be buried in Hawarden churchyard, where the body of his wife might also lie. From the time when Sir Stephen Glynne placed his daughter's hand in that of Gladstone, up to the moment of the latter's passing away from earth, when she sat kissing the hand which had never been lifted in an unworthy cause, he had hoped, and she had hoped that no event would ever separate them, not even death itself. But England thought that Westminster Abbey should be honored with the remains of England's greatest Commoner, and, after preparation had been made by which the body of Mrs. Gladstone might in time rest beside that of her husband, it was announced that the interment would be in West· minster Abbey.

As the day of the funeral approached, London was most desirous of paying every tribute to the departed statesman. The Queen requested that all public celebrations of her seventy-ninth birthday be omitted, and there were no public demonstrations on the event, for the body of the great man lay in state, and invitations to Cabinet dinners and receptions were recalled.

Mr. Gladstone died at five o'clock on Thursday morning, May 19th, and on the next Tuesday, the body lay in the library at Hawarden Castle as beautiful and stately in death as in life.

> "Dead he lay among his books.
> The peace of God was in his looks."

On the white silk couch the great statesman appeared sleeping, as if he were taking a rest before addressing a great audience upon some academic occasion. There lay the body in evening dress, and over him hung the crimson silk robes of a doctor of civil law. By his side was the Oxford cap. The whole scene seemed to indicate that at any moment the man who was resting there on his side, would move the loosely interlocked fingers lying upon his bosom, then he would rise, and, with that youth which death had brought back to the expressive and noble face, he would again thrill the audience waiting yonder for his words of inspiration and wisdom.

Meantime the House of Commons, on May 19, was crowded in every part, and Mr. A. J. Balfour, the first Lord of the Treasury and leader in the House of Commons, who had come to the House seriously suffering from impaired health, arose, giving evidence in every attitude and in every tone of his voice, that he shared the public grief. The heads of all present were uncovered and Mr. Balfour proposed the address to the Queen.

Sir William Vernon Harcourt, on the part of the Liberals, offered but a word, but it was sincere and sympathetic, and the House adjourned.

The next day the Parliament of England forgot whether Gladstone had been counted a Conservative or a Liberal. This unparalleled career shone so radiantly before those who had been his antagonists or his allies that rarely, if ever, did friend and foe unite so heartily in generous words of appreciation, as upon this occasion. Lord Salisbury, perhaps the ablest man whom Gladstone ever met in debate, a man who perfectly shared Gladstone's passion for scholarship and his enthusiastic devotion to the Church, pointed to Gladstone's career as that of a great Christian statesman. Mr. Arthur Balfour, who rose above the weakness of body from which he was evidently suffering, uttered a most just and eloquent eulogy, while John Dillon, carrying in his trembling voice the tears of Ireland, gave Ireland's best and truest friend cordial words of praise that will always be repeated; and Sir William Vernon Harcourt, who had labored with Gladstone, for the most part, in perfect harmony, through the long trials of Liberalism in the last quarter of a century, enshrined the mighty dead in words as white and beautiful as was the life of his departed friend. Mr. Joseph Chamberlain also honored himself in offering memorable words of discriminating praise.

The mortal part of the generous neighbor and kind friend, followed by the family, was borne by loving villagers and lifelong servants past the nooks of Hawarden Park most often visited by the laborious statesman, and, having been placed in the village church, it received tenderest honor from the vast crowd of friends assembled there.

Every effort was made to avoid the gathering of crowds upon the streets of London, and on Thursday morning at two o'clock the catafalque was placed in Westminster Hall. Canon Wilberforce conducted an appropriate service. At each corner of the catafalque candles were lighted, and, in recognition that a chivalric crusader of Jesus Christ had come and passed that way, a large Armenian cross shone at the head. Daylight revealed thousands waiting in the street, anxious to view the remains. Dukes and peers jostled against costermongers and street cleaners; duchesses and wives of cabinet ministers vied with sewing women and shop girls to pay honor to a man of universal interests. Two thousand policemen were guiding the throng at three o'clock Thursday afternoon and seventy-five thousand people had then passed the coffin. Not alone was Sir William Vernon Harcourt unable to control his emotions as the calm face was seen and a celestial light radiated from the loved features. Hundreds were thrilled, as once by their music so now by the silence of those finely molded lips. He had found Life in death.

Without military pomp and pageantry, this least spectacular ceremonial in England's history went on. It was the funeral of the truest Commoner. Not so many human beings had crowded into the space about the Hall, even on the occasion of the Queen's Diamond Jubilee. As Gladstone's whispered request had made it, it was "very simple;" as his character and career had made it also, it was very sublime. The Prince of Wales and the Duke of York were among the pall-bearers, but a quarter of a million of people thronged about to carry Gladstone in their hearts forever. Here and there flamed a bit of color or gleamed a strip of gold, but more impressive than heralds, bishops, princes, privy councilors, laced diplomats and the richly attired Speaker of the House of Commons bearing the mace on his shoulder, was the hushed and mournful throng who beheld the family, the Hawarden villagers and servants following the oaken coffin into the Valhalla of England. The great Abbey quivered with the grandly solemn music. Handel and Schubert, and Beethoven, Toplady, Watts, Newman and David the psalmist, had loaned their genius to the hour, and Canning and Pitt, Browning and Tennyson gave Gladstone august companionship. The future King of England extended his hand in sympathy to the widow who looked long and tenderly into the grave and then glanced upward to heaven. The dirge trembled into a whisper and the ceremony was done.

As the latest echo of his favorite hymn, "Praise to the Holiest," resounding yet from the great choir of one hundred voices, was lost in the sorrowful tones of "The Dead March in Saul," which wept themselves away amidst the arches of the majestic Abbey, old and life-long friends lingered, unwilling to quit the solemn scene. Around them were memorials of those whom they, with Gladstone, had honored in life, and with these they were prone to remain. Upon their faces "the light that never was on sea or land" played fitfully through tears. Was Gladstone understood? They, at least, understood him, for to them, it was more clear than ever that he came into this world of ours, not the rondured and polished pearl his earlier friends exhibited with acclaim, but rather entered he, at birth, an acorn of true Anglo-Saxon genesis, a veritable forest-monarch as yet enfolded and soon to unfold, a great tree whose multiform development was destined to have nothing of the hard and hopeless consistency of even the brightest of lifeless jewels, but rather that deeper and more vital consistency with its past which a wide-limbed and constantly growing king of the woods has with the brown nut rotting at the root of the many-branched oak. None who first entered into the secret of his genius had expected otherwise. An acorn, indeed, was this, of God's own creation and planting. To attain himself, as feebly foreseen, there must needs be unwelcome disturbances, tragic breakings of the bepraised and glossy shell by unpleasant urgings of something within, spring-time pangs and innumerable out-reachings.

If Sir John Gladstone's son, William Ewart, had been only a perfectly sphered ivory or beryl ball of conservatism, brilliant and sufficiently pure, the gift of heaven might have been kept securely and comprehensively enough in a golden box, but no hope would have gone out in any proposed planting of such an unresponsive thing in our world's rich soil. But unfortunately for Toryism, and fortunately for Liberalism, he was a vital seed, not a cold gem, and, granted sun and rainfall, he could not and he did not remain ever an understandable, manageable, erubescent and dead item of human life's equation, but he was, instead, an ever wondrous, and perhaps to the dull-eyed, a too eager and elusive reality into whose career the life and hope of this planet ran for succor, and from whose being and action there went forth a revealment of God in the form of humanity. Three score and ten years had passed since Tennyson and he talked of the future they dreamed for Arthur Henry Hallam. Fifty years ago, death silenced Hallam and each of those years

had given Gladstone an opportunity to embody in himself the prophecy
made of the other:

> "A life with civic action warm,
> A soul on highest mission sent,
> A potent voice of Parliament,
> A pillar steadfast in the storm."

These words of Tennyson came to many a heart on that May day
when the silent crowd vanished from the Abbey. Yonder, by the side
of Robert Browning and in front of the Chaucer monument lay the poet
who wrote the prefatory sonnet for Gladstone's heart-searching appeal
for Montenegro; now and hither had been borne the remains of the
statesman to be buried next to the dust of William Pitt and close to the
bust of Lord Beaconsfield, which would still be the finest memorial
of Gladstone's most brilliant rival, had it not been that Gladstone himself made by his speech on the death of Beaconsfield, as Sir Stafford
Northcote said: "A more enduring monument than could be carved out
of stone."

It was not in keeping with the hour to compare the values of the
public services of poet and statesman. Gladstone had already awarded
the palm to Tennyson in lustrous and stately phrase, for he was sufficiently poetic to perceive that the poet is the true prophet of civilization.
On the other hand, Tennyson himself spoke of Gladstone as the loftiest
of English statesmen. The very method which Gladstone had often
adopted and for the adoption of which he was most often and bitterly
reproached—that of the Steersman, who seeking to reach a given point
and finding two channels possible, one with a cataract ahead, the other
more circuitous but with no fatal difficulty, chooses the bend as his
course—this, his friend, the singer urged upon him, for the reason that
Tennyson knew that a Gladstone, by endowment of genius, is account-
able, not for himself alone, but also and more especially for himself as
a leader and commander of men. Men said he yielded enough to his
theory of eloquence and the orator. He said: "It is an influence principally received from his audience (so to speak) in vapour, which he
pours back upon them in a flood. The sympathy and concurrence of
his time, is, with his own mind, joint parent of his work. He cannot

follow nor frame ideals; his choice is to be what his age will have him, what it requires in order to be moved by him or else not to be at all." But this must be balanced by the equally strong opinion of others that he was too attached to lofty ideals, and fought too far in front of his army. Bright called him a sunflower ever turning to the sun; but he was more, for he wooed all else sunward.

The question of questions to be asked concerning a man like Gladstone is not: Did he succeed in being popular? Did he reach the highest seat of power? Was he always of the opinion of his ancestors or of himself on some yesterday? It is this rather, granted that he had much to renounce and to forget and that therefore, he must have had to move out of one set of opinions and methods and to enter into another, did he grow, with that healthfulness of soul and that soundness of conscience, which, always, in the process of his development, kept him true to his own personality and to the integrity of the laws of human thought by which other equally true minds necessarily came into alliance with him? It is competent, in short, to ask how far did his transforming intelligence normally transform the nation he most influenced, toward permanent grandeur and good fame? The answers to these questions, it is believed, will be increasingly favorable to the name and to the honor of Gladstone. From first to last, by force of a lively intelligence, predestined to love and to seek increasing light and hope, he was in process of evolution. So also, but less swiftly, was England.

His inconsistencies are proof of the truth of Emerson's words: "Consistency is the hobgoblin of little minds." Times there were when any partial view could only say, as he was contemplated:

"Things are in process still; the segment ends are these
Within the plane upturned to-day. The perfect circles round but slow."

The verdict of all times, however, will be returned as the world, ever advancing toward the goal he dreamed of, perceives the whole range and the entire import of the influences he helped to create, to guard and to guide, and then with the names of Alfred and Hampden, William the Silent and Lincoln, will be found written the resplendent name of William Ewart Gladstone.